The Beast Cometh

Based on Historical Events

David Lee Corley

DEDICATION

Dedicated to all the men and women that fought and
sacrificed for their country.

Table of Contents

Quote.. 3

Prologue 4

A Debt Owed............................... 9

Black Virgin Mountain..................... 23

Resolution of 1975 36

The Test 50

The Bridge................................. 80

The Madness of War 106

Half Breeds 148

Convoy of Tears.......................... 188

Desperate Days 232

Showdown 270

Mayhem 300

Escape.................................... 313

The Journey North........................ 353

Epilogue 376

The Four Operations...................... 382

Letter to Reader 398

Author's Biography *400*

Quote

"Nothing is more precious than independence and liberty."

\- Ho Chi Minh

Prologue

Paris, France – June 15, 1921

Paris was a city of contrasts, where the glitter and glamour of the post-war era coexisted with the deep scars left by the devastation of World War I. The streets were filled with a mix of old-world elegance and modern energy, as the city struggled to rebuild and reinvent itself in the aftermath of the conflict.

Politically, France was in a state of flux. The war had shattered the old order, and new ideas and movements were emerging to take its place. The Russian Revolution of 1917 had sent shockwaves throughout Europe, and in France, the Communist Party was gaining strength, particularly among the working class and intellectuals.

At the same time, the country was grappling with the economic and social consequences of the war. Inflation was high, and many veterans struggled to find work and rebuild their lives. The government, led by the conservative bloc national, was focused on maintaining order and stability, often at the expense of social and political reforms.

In the cafes and salons of Paris, artists, writers, and intellectuals debated the future of France and the world. The city was a hub of cultural and artistic experimentation, with new movements like Dadaism and Surrealism emerging to challenge traditional forms of expression.

But beneath the surface, tensions were simmering. The French Empire, which stretched across Africa and Asia, was facing growing resistance from colonial subjects seeking independence and self-determination. In Paris, anti-colonial activists were beginning to organize and agitate for the liberation of their homelands.

As the summer of 1921 dawned, Paris was a city on the brink of change, poised between the old world and the new. The seeds of future conflicts and revolutions were being sown, even as the city struggled to heal the wounds of the past and build a brighter future.

Ho washed the last dish and stacked it on top of the others. The kitchen at the Cafe Richelieu sur Seine had closed for the night. He untied his apron, hung it on a peg, and walked out into the dark Paris streets. The air smelled of beef bourguignon and red wine drifting from the cafes and restaurants lining the narrow cobblestone road.

Ho turned up the collar of his worn wool coat as a chill ran through him, a coldness that had nothing to do with the night air. His thoughts were far from this place, from the City of Light with its grand boulevards and iconic landmarks. Instead, his mind was consumed with his people back in Vietnam, the country he had left behind but could never forget.

For centuries, the Vietnamese had suffered under the yoke of foreign powers. First, it was the Chinese, whose thousand-year rule had left an indelible mark on Vietnam's culture and society. Then came the French, who had slowly tightened their grip on the country since the mid-19th century, turning it into a colony they called Indochina. When would Vietnam be free? When would its people control their own destiny, free from the shackles of foreign domination?

Walking along the banks of the Seine, memories of Ho's childhood flooded his mind. He remembered working in the rice fields as a boy, his back bent under the scorching sun, his hands callused from the hard labor. He remembered the heavy taxes his father paid to the French, the constant struggle to make ends meet, to put food on the table for their family. The land should belong to those who worked it, not to foreign masters an ocean away who cared nothing for the Vietnamese people and their suffering.

He walked across the Seine, its dark waters flowing silently beneath the bridge that spanned its width. In the distance, the towers of Notre Dame rose into the night sky, timeless and solid, a testament to the enduring power of faith and human ingenuity. But empires rose and fell, even ones that seemed eternal. Nothing lasted forever, except the dreams in men's hearts. And Ho's dream, the dream that consumed him, was of a Vietnam for the Vietnamese, an independent nation that controlled its own destiny.

It would not be easy. The French would not give up their colony without a fight. Blood would water the fields before Vietnam was free. But Ho was prepared to do whatever it took, to sacrifice everything, even his own life, for the cause of Vietnamese independence. Vietnam was worth dying for, he believed with every fiber of his being.

As he reached the opposite bank and turned on the path that paralleled the river, Ho let his mind wander, trying to imagine what a free Vietnam would look like.

He pictured a country where the people were the masters of their own fate, where they could live with dignity and pride, free from the yoke of foreign oppression. He saw a Vietnam where every child had the chance to go to school, where every family had enough to eat, where the land belonged to those who worked it.

But to achieve this dream, Ho knew that the Vietnamese people would need to be united, to stand together against the French colonialists. They would need a leader, someone who could rally them, inspire them, guide them to victory. And in that moment, walking along the Seine in the heart of Paris, Ho knew that he was that leader.

He had been traveling the world for years now, using aliases to avoid detection by the French authorities who saw him as a troublemaker, a threat to their colonial order. In Paris, he went by the name Nguyen Ai Quoc, just one of the many identities he had assumed in his travels. Even Ho Chi Minh was not his real name. But no matter what name he used, his true identity remained the same: a Vietnamese patriot, a man who would stop at nothing to see his country free.

Ho's thoughts turned to the future, to the long struggle ahead. He knew that the road to Vietnamese independence would be long and difficult, that there would be setbacks and defeats along the way. But he also knew that the Vietnamese people were strong, that they had endured centuries of foreign domination and emerged unbroken.

And he knew that he was not alone in this fight. Around the world, other colonized peoples were rising up, demanding their freedom, their right to self-determination. In Russia, the Bolsheviks had overthrown the tsar and established a workers' state. In China, the revolutionaries were battling the warlords and foreign imperialists. The tide of history was turning and Vietnam would be part of this great global struggle for liberation.

But for Ho, the fight for Vietnamese independence was not about ideology or political philosophy. It was not about communism or capitalism, Marxism or nationalism. It was about something much simpler, much more fundamental: the right of the Vietnamese people to be free, to determine their own destiny. Ho's thoughts were not consumed with abstract ideas or theoretical debates. They were focused on the practical realities of his people's lives, on finding a way to lift them out of poverty and oppression, to give them a better future.

As he walked through the Paris night, Ho made a silent vow to himself and to his people. He would devote his life to the struggle for Vietnamese independence, no matter the cost. He would do whatever it took—organize, agitate, fight—to see his country free. And he would never rest until that dream became a reality, until the Vietnamese people were the masters of their own land and their own fate.

The Seine flowed on, timeless and indifferent, as it had for centuries. The city slept, unaware of the momentous thoughts taking shape in the mind of the young Vietnamese dishwasher walking its streets. One day the world would know his name. One day Vietnam would be free. And the great irony was that even though his ambitious dream would eventually come true, Ho Chi Minh would never see that day…

A Debt Owed

US Embassy - Saigon, South Vietnam

The US Embassy in Saigon stood as a bastion of American power and prestige, a gleaming modern building in the heart of the city. But as the North Vietnamese forces drew closer and the South Vietnamese government teetered on the brink of collapse, the embassy took on a different character, becoming a focal point of fear, desperation, and chaos.

Inside the embassy, the staff worked around the clock, trying to keep pace with the rapidly deteriorating situation. Diplomats and intelligence officers hustled through the hallways, their faces drawn and their eyes haunted by the knowledge of what was coming. They were the ones who had to deal with the unraveling of American policy, the ones who had to face the hard truths that Washington seemed determined to ignore.

In the consular section, Vietnamese employees and their families crowded the waiting rooms, desperate for visas, for any chance to escape the coming storm. Many had worked for the Americans for years, and now they found themselves begging for a seat on one of the few remaining flights out of the country. The

American staff did their best to help, but they were overwhelmed by the sheer numbers, and by the weight of their own emotions.

The CIA station was a hive of activity, with officers working to gather last-minute intelligence and to coordinate with the South Vietnamese forces they had spent so long trying to support. But even the most optimistic among them knew that it was a losing battle. The North Vietnamese were too strong, too determined, and the South Vietnamese government was crumbling from within.

In the ambassador's office, Graham Martin sat at his desk, a man increasingly isolated from the reality unfolding around him. He clung to the belief that the situation could still be salvaged, that with enough American aid and support, the South Vietnamese could hold out. He dismissed the warnings of his own staff, the urgent cables from Washington, the pleas of the Vietnamese allies who knew they were doomed. For Martin, admitting defeat was not an option.

But outside the embassy walls, the city was descending into panic. Rumors flew of impending attacks, of communist infiltrators, of a government that had already abandoned its people. Thousands fled their homes, seeking safety wherever they could find it. Many looked to the Americans for help, seeing the embassy as their last hope.

As the crowds grew larger and more desperate, the embassy's Marine guards struggled to maintain order. They watched with growing unease as the city they had come to know so well unhinged before their eyes. They knew that they might soon be called upon to make hard choices, to decide who would be saved and who would be left behind.

Inside the embassy, the American staff watched the chaos with a mixture of dread and sorrow. They had invested so much in this place, in these people. They had believed in the cause, in the idea that they were making a difference, that they were stopping the Communist revolution from engulfing the world. Now, as the end drew near, they were forced to confront the harsh reality of their own limitations.

Some wept openly, overcome by the enormity of what was happening. Others retreated into a kind of numb professionalism, focusing on the tasks at hand as a way to keep the despair at bay. They all knew that they were witnessing the end of an era, the collapse of a dream that had sustained them for so long.

And yet, even in the midst of this chaos, there were moments of grace and courage. Vietnamese employees who refused to abandon their American friends. American officers who risked their own lives to help their Vietnamese counterparts escape. Small acts of kindness and solidarity in the face of overwhelming odds.

As the embassy staff looked out over the city they had called home, they knew that they were witnessing a turning point in history. The Vietnam War, which had defined a generation of Americans and Vietnamese alike, was coming to a bitter and bloody end. And they, the men and women who had fought so long to hold back the tide, were now swept up in its final, inexorable rush.

In the end, the US Embassy in Saigon would become an iconic symbol of American failure and defeat, a place where the limits of power and the costs of hubris were laid bare for all to see. But for those who were there, who lived through those final desperate days, it would always be something more: a testament to the enduring strength of the human spirit, even in the face of unimaginable loss and grief.

Coyle and Granier sat across from Polgar in the cramped CIA station chief's office. The room was thick with cigarette smoke and tension. Coyle leaned forward, his elbows on his knees.

"Chief, we have a moral obligation to help these people. They risked their lives for us. We can't abandon them now."

Polgar sighed and rubbed his forehead. He looked tired, the lines on his face deeper than usual. "I understand your position. But we have orders from the ambassador. We're not to interfere with the refugees. Our job is to arm the South Vietnamese to keep fighting."

Granier shook his head. "That's a death sentence and you know it. Without proper air and artillery support, the militias can't stop the North. Not anymore. These people will die if we don't get them out."

Polgar leaned back in his chair. "You think I don't know that? But my hands are tied. Martin is calling the shots."

"Then we go over his head. Appeal to Washington. These are our allies, our friends. We owe them," said Coyle.

Granier nodded. "We wouldn't have lasted a year here without their help. The intelligence they provided, the operations they ran. We'd have been blind and deaf."

Polgar held up a hand. "I don't disagree. But the harsh reality is that we're pulling out. The war is over for us. There's only so much we can do."

"Bullshit. We have planes. Helicopters. Ships off the coast. We could evacuate thousands if we had the will."

"We're not talking about faceless crowds," said Coyle. "These are individuals. Men and women with families. People we've worked with for years. We can't just cut them loose."

"You're preaching to the choir," said Polgar. "But policy is being made at a level way above my pay grade. The ambassador is trying to downplay the situation, to avoid panic. Evacuating our Vietnamese allies would send the wrong message."

"So, we sacrifice them for political optics?" said Coyle.

"I don't like it any more than you do. But those are our orders. I expect you to follow them."

Granier shook his head. "Following orders is one thing. Standing by while people we know are slaughtered is another."

Polgar fixed him with a hard stare. "I'm not telling you again. Stay away from the refugees. Focus on arming the militias. That's the best we can do for our allies now."

"It's not enough. It'll never be enough. We'll have blood on our hands if we don't act," said Coyle.

Polgar stood, signaling the end of the meeting. "Then I suggest you take it up with Ambassador Martin."

"Wait," said Granier. "What about President Thieu?"

"I doubt he'll be much help. He's drinking the same Kool-Aid as Martin. They both believe the South can survive if it stands strong. South Vietnamese intelligence is vastly underestimating the North Vietnamese forces crossing the border."

"Why?"

"No idea, except they don't want to upset the boss."

"So, they lie to him."

"There is so much chaos out there it would hard to call it lying. In the past few months, the North Vietnamese have built up their air defenses along the border making it impossible for the South to fly reconnaissance missions without taking heavy losses. Our side is blind. We have no idea what's out there."

"What about American surveillance flights?"

"The Pentagon is reluctant to continue surveillance. The Soviets have armed the North with the new surface-to-air missiles that can reach our aircraft."

"So, we really are blind?"

"Yeah. Not an ideal situation," said Polgar as he walked to the door and held it open. "Now if you will excuse me, my plate is kinda full at the moment."

"So, that's it. We're just going to abandon our allies and let them be slaughtered?" said Granier.

"I'm sorry I don't have answers for you. I just have orders. And I expect you to obey them. Is that clear?"

Coyle and Granier exchanged a glance. They knew Polgar was in a tough spot.

Granier stood. "We understand, Chief."

"Do you? I won't be able to protect you if you go rogue again."

Coyle nodded. "We understand. But these people trusted us. We owe them our best effort."

"That doesn't sound like you're stepping in line with the program," said Polgar.

"We owe you a lot, Chief. You saved our asses bailing us out of prison," said Granier.

"You're damned right I did. A little loyalty would be appreciated at this point."

"We'll give you all we can."

"Why does that not sound reassuring?" said Polgar.

"We'll let you get back to work. Thanks for the time, Chief." said Coyle as he and Granier moved passed Polgar.

As they left Polgar's office, Coyle and Granier knew they were facing an uphill battle. Ambassador Martin was determined to downplay the crisis, to pretend everything was under control. And President Thieu was already making plans to save himself and his inner circle. The fate of the ordinary Vietnamese people didn't seem to factor into their calculations.

But for Coyle and Granier, it was the only thing that mattered. These were people they had fought beside, laughed with, mourned with. People who had risked everything to help the American and South Vietnamese cause. Leaving them to face the communists' wrath alone was unthinkable.

As they walked out into the Saigon heat, they knew they would have to act fast and decisively. Identify those most at risk and pull together a plan to get them out. It wouldn't be easy. They would be defying orders, putting their own careers on the line. But it was a small price to pay compared to the lives at stake.

Coyle and Granier knew they were embarking on their most important mission yet. Not for country or politics, but for friendship, loyalty, and the unshakable belief that America should never abandon those who had stood by her.

Bien Hoa Airbase, South Vietnam

Coyle and Granier walked into the empty hangar, the silence broken only by the distant sounds of the airbase. The space felt cavernous without the hulking presence of the Spectre gunship, a stark reminder of the losses they had suffered.

Granier turned to Coyle, his voice echoing slightly. "Any word on a replacement for the Spectre?"

Coyle shook his head, "I tried. Brass isn't keen on sending another one. Not with the way things are going. They're afraid it could fall into the enemy's hands and that they'd turn it over to the Soviets."

Granier nodded, unsurprised. He walked over to where the surviving Ghost Warriors were gathered, men still bearing the scars of their last mission. Some were bandaged, others leaned heavily on crutches. But they all had the same look in their eyes, a mixture of weariness and determination.

Coyle joined him, his gaze traveling over the assembled men. "You all know the situation. The North is closing in. Our allies, the ones who fought beside us, and their families are facing the worst. They need our help to get out."

Granier stepped forward. "We can't leave them behind. Not after everything. But we're not going to order anyone to do this. This isn't what you signed up for. We will be on the defensive side of things and there is far more risk involved. It's your choice. You've all given more than enough already. Nobody should be criticized for not joining us."

The men exchanged glances. Many had families of their own, loved ones they desperately wanted to protect. Going back into the fray meant risking everything, and there were no guarantees of coming back.

But these were no ordinary men. They had trained together, fought together, bled together. The bonds forged in battle were not easily broken.

One of the men, a grizzled sergeant with a heavily bandaged arm, spoke up. "I've got a wife and kid back home. Haven't seen them in two years. But these folks... they trusted us. They put their necks on the line for us. I can't just turn my back on them now."

Slowly, others began to nod. A young corporal, barely out of his teens, stood shakily on his crutches. "I'm in. These people, they're like family. You don't leave family behind."

One by one, the Ghost Warriors stepped forward, volunteering for what they knew could be their final mission. The pain of their wounds, the yearning for home and safety, was eclipsed by the knowledge that they were needed, that there was still one last duty to fulfill.

Coyle and Granier watched, humbled by the courage and loyalty of these men. They knew the risks, the sacrifices they were asking for. But they also knew that there was no other choice, not for men like these.

As the last man stepped forward, Coyle nodded solemnly. "All right. Let's get to work."

The Ghost Warriors dispersed, readying themselves for the task ahead. The hangar was no longer empty; it was filled with purpose, with the unbreakable spirit of men who had seen the worst of war and yet still chose to do what was right.

"We'll get them out. Whatever it takes," said Granier.

Coyle met his gaze, "Damned right we will. We owe them that much."

In that quiet moment in an abandoned hangar, a

handful of battered and weary men made the choice to risk everything once more, not for glory or country, but for the simple, unshakeable belief that no one should be left behind. It was a heavy burden, but one they bore willingly, knowing that in the end, it was the only path their honor would allow.

Set up on a wooden crate in a corner of the hangar, Coyle and Granier pored over the map of Vietnam. The red arrows representing the North Vietnamese forces that seemed to be advancing from all sides, a relentless tide threatening to engulf the country.

"We have to prioritize the border regions," Coyle said, his finger tracing the lines of the map. "The Central Highlands, the Montagnard villages. They'll be the first hit."

Granier nodded, "The NVA has always hated the tribes. They'll show no mercy."

The indigenous tribes of Vietnam, collectively known as the Montagnard, had been staunch allies of the Americans. Their fierce warriors had fought alongside U.S. Special Forces, their knowledge of the treacherous jungle terrain invaluable. But now, with the American withdrawal, they were vulnerable, exposed to the full wrath of the North Vietnamese.

Coyle tapped a series of points on the map. "We'll need to set up extraction points here, here, and here. Get as many out as we can before the hammer falls."

It was a daunting task. The border regions were vast, rugged, and remote. Getting assets in place, coordinating evacuations, it would stretch their resources to the limit. But they had no choice.

Granier traced his finger along the Laotian border. "The Hmong too. They've been fighting the communists for years. They'll be high on the NVA's list."

The Hmong, an ethnic group from the mountains of Laos, had been recruited by the CIA to fight a secret war against the communists. They had paid a heavy price for their loyalty, suffering devastating losses. Now, with the American pullout, they faced annihilation.

Coyle sighed, "We'll do what we can. But we have to be realistic. We can't save everyone."

It was a bitter truth, one that left a taste of ash in their mouths. They had fought alongside these people, had promised them support and protection. Now, they were forced to choose, to weigh one life against another in a grim calculus of survival.

Granier eyes hard, "We save as many as we can. And we make sure the world knows what happens to the ones we can't."

"Karen can help with that," said Coyle.

It was a small thing, a promise of witness, of remembrance. But in the face of the looming tragedy, it was all they had to offer.

They turned back to the map, to the hard choices and desperate plans. They would do their duty, would honor their commitments as best they could. But they knew, in the depths of their hearts, that it would never be enough, that the stain of America's abandonment would never fully wash away.

As they worked, the memory of the fallen seemed to hover at the edges of the room, the weight of their sacrifice bearing down. Coyle and Granier carried that weight, that burden of remembrance and obligation. And they would carry it into the battles to come, into the fire and the fury of a war that refused to end, even in its final, bitter days.

Coyle led Granier into a vast, dimly lit hangar, their footsteps echoing off the concrete floor. The air was thick with the scent of oil, metal, and the faint, lingering odor of aviation fuel. In the center of the space, illuminated by shafts of sunlight filtering through the high windows, sat an old aircraft, its once-gleaming silver skin now dulled by time and neglect.

"There she is," Coyle said, his voice tinged with a mixture of reverence and sadness. "A C-119 Boxcar. She's seen better days, but she's still got some life in her."

Granier walked around the aircraft, taking in the sight of the twin boom tail, the large cargo doors, and the empty mounting points where the miniguns had once been. The plane had a storied history, a veteran of countless missions over the jungles of Vietnam. But now, it sat abandoned, stripped of its weapons, a relic of a war that was rapidly approaching its end.

"The ARVN took the guns for perimeter defense," Coyle explained, running a hand along the fuselage. "But the airframe is still sound. With a little work, she could fly again."

Granier nodded, his mind already racing with possibilities. "You're thinking of using it for evacuations. From the remote areas."

"Exactly. She's not fast, but she's sturdy. She can handle rough airstrips, carry a decent load."

"Do you remember how to fly this beast?"

"Sure. It's like riding a bike. You never forget."

It was a daring plan, a last-ditch effort to save as many lives as possible. But it was also a daunting challenge. The plane would need repairs, maintenance, a crew that knew how to fly her. And they would be venturing into some of the most dangerous territory in Vietnam, into the path of the advancing North Vietnamese forces and well-positioned anti-aircraft emplacements.

Granier walked up the cargo ramp, into the cavernous interior of the plane. The space was bare, the walls still bearing the scars and stains of its former life. But he could see the potential, could envision it filled with desperate refugees, with the wounded and the terrified, all seeking a final chance at escape.

"We'll need a crew," he said, his voice echoing in the emptiness. "People we can trust."

Coyle nodded, "I've got some ideas. Guys who are ready to ride the tiger, one last time."

They stood in silence for a long moment, the weight of the task settling on their shoulders. More work. Always more work… and danger. They knew the risks they would be facing. But they also knew that they had no choice, that to do anything less would be a betrayal of everything they believed in.

"Alright. Let's do it," said Granier.

And so, in the dusty confines of that abandoned hangar, Coyle, Granier, and the Ghost Warriors set about their task, breathing new life into the old warbird, preparing it for one final mission of mercy. It was a desperate gamble, a race against time and the tide of war. But for these men, bound by honor and duty, it was the only path forward, the only way to keep faith with those they had sworn to protect.

As they worked, the old plane seemed to come alive around them, its engines stirring to life, its wings trembling with the promise of flight. And in that moment, amidst the chaos and the sorrow of a war in its final days, there was a flicker of hope, a glimmer of light in the gathering darkness.

Black Virgin Mountain

Bien Hoa Air Base, South Vietnam

Inside the hangar with the newly rebuilt C-119, the Ghost Warriors huddled around a map of the Cambodian border area 60 Northwest of Saigon near the city of Tay Ninh. Granier tapped the map, his voice tight with urgency. "I know we all wanted more time to prepare, but I think we've got our first customers. After several months of fighting off the NVA, ARVN forces are pulling out of the outpost at Nui Ba Den. There's a Hmong village nearby. They'll be slaughtered by the NVA crossing from Cambodia into South Vietnam unless we rescue them."

Coyle nodded, his mind already racing. "We'll need to coordinate this carefully. Scott, your choppers will have to do the pickup. The village is too remote for the Boxcar to land."

Scott Dickson, the gunship helicopter pilot and team leader, leaned in. "We'll get it done. But we'll need a place to bring them. Somewhere safe."

Coyle pointed to a spot on the map. "There's an old airfield here, not far from the village. I'll take the

Boxcar, set up a temporary base. You bring the refugees to us, and we'll fly them out to Bien Hoa. My guess is that we'll need to make several trips depending on the number of passengers."

"My team will provide ground security for the helicopters as they load the villagers," said Granier.

"My Huey gunship will fly overwatch," said Scott.

"Alright. There is no time to waste. Let's get it done," said Coyle ending the mission briefing.

The plan set, the Ghost Warriors sprang into action. Scott and his helicopter crews raced to their birds, prepping for the mission ahead. Granier and his team checked their weapons and climbed into the two Chinook helicopters. Scott flew the Huey gunship.

Coyle and his team boarded the Boxcar, and attempted to start the first engine. It sputtered but didn't engage. "Come on now. This is no time to be finicky," said Coyle to the aircraft.

He tried again and the first engine started kicking out a plume of black smoke. The second engine started without hesitation. He taxied the aircraft from the hangar onto the runway. The old plane shuddering as it lifted into the sky. Moments later, the helicopters lifted off.

As Coyle approached the abandoned airfield, the sound of distant battle echoed across the landscape. The NVA offensive was in full swing, and time was running out for the Hmong villagers.

Scott's voice crackled over the radio, tense and focused. "We're over the village now. NVA troops are everywhere. It's a madhouse down there."

Coyle gripped the radio, his voice steady. "Do what you can, Scott. We're waiting for you."

Above the village, Scott's helicopters darted and weaved, braving a hail of anti-aircraft fire as the two Chinooks descended into a clearing. The Hmong ran from their homes, clutching children and meager possessions, desperate for rescue.

Scott and his gunship crew flew overhead strafing the enemy troops with the door gunner's minigun. Everything was happening fast. Experience and training took over.

Scott spotted an RPG gunner near the tree line taking aim. Without hesitation, he swung his gunship around and opened fire with the four wing guns. The enemy gunner was hit and killed just as he fired the RPG. The grenade whizzed upward toward the Huey. Scott reacted on instinct banking the aircraft hard to the right. The grenade streaked under the belly of the Huey missing by less than two feet. The grenade exploded on landing in a rice field. With little time to consider the past, Scott hunted for their next target, an enemy machine gun set up on the edge of the village. Using his rockets, he fired. Exploding near the machine gun, the enemy heavy weapons team was killed, and the machine gun destroyed by shrapnel.

As the Chinooks descended into the clearing, the air was filled with the deafening roar of rotor blades and the sharp crack of gunfire. NVA troops swarmed the perimeter, their AK-47s chattering as they advanced on the desperate villagers, killing anyone in sight. The Hmong men fought back but were outgunned and outnumbered. Dozens fell dead and wounded.

As the first Chinook touched down, Granier leaped from the lead chopper, his sniper rifle clutched tight to his chest. He hit the ground running, scanning the chaos for targets. Beside him, the other Ghost Warriors fanned out, forming a defensive perimeter around the landing zone, opening fire on the NVA entering the village.

Granier sprinted to a low stone wall at the edge of the village, dropping into a crouch behind it. He brought his rifle to his shoulder, peering through the scope at the advancing enemy.

They were close now, too close. He could see their eyes and angry faces as they charged forward. Calming himself amid the chaos, Granier drew a deep breath, let it out slowly. Time seemed to slow, the world narrowing to the crosshairs of his scope.

He squeezed the trigger, the rifle bucking against his shoulder. Downrange, an NVA soldier tumbled to the ground, his chest a bloody ruin. Granier worked the bolt, chambering another round, seeking a new target.

They came on, wave after wave, heedless of their fallen comrades. Granier met them with lead, each shot precise, each one a killing blow. The Ghost Warriors fought beside him, their weapons cracking, holding the line against the enemy advance.

In the village behind them, the surviving Hmong raced for the waiting choppers, clutching children and meager possessions. They clambered aboard, eyes wide with fear, as the pilots revved their engines, ready for takeoff.

Granier knew they were running out of time. The NVA were closing in, their numbers seemingly endless. His finger aching from the trigger, his shoulder bruised from the recoil.

But he did not falter. He could not. These people were depending on him, on the Ghost Warriors. They were the only thing standing between the Hmong and certain slaughter.

Granier fought on, dropping NVA soldiers like cordwood, each shot a small victory, each one buying precious seconds for the refugees. He didn't think or feel, he performed.

Bullets pinged off the Chinooks' fuselage, rockets streaked past overhead. But the Ghost Warriors held their ground, determined to save as many as they could.

And then, suddenly, it was over. The first chopper lifted off, its cabin packed with terrified Hmong. The Ghost Warriors fell back, leaping aboard the final bird as it clawed for the sky.

Granier collapsed against the cabin wall, his rifle falling from nerveless fingers. He was spent, physically and emotionally, the adrenaline draining away like water from a shattered vase.

But as he looked out at the village receding below, at the columns of smoke rising from the jungle, the bodies of the Hmong warriors, women, and children strewn across the ground. A painful sight. They had saved who they could, but it wasn't enough. They had to do better. Response time was critical. They needed more firepower.

The villagers in the Chinook looked at their saviors with tearful gratitude, even though many of their fellow tribesmen and women had been left behind. They were safe because of these men. It was a small thing, in the grand scheme of the war. But for Granier, for the Ghost Warriors, it was everything. It was the reason they fought, the reason they endured the horrors and the hardships.

Because in the end, this was what it was all about. Not the politics, not the glory, but the simple act of helping those in need, of standing up for what was right.

Waiting in the cockpit of the C-119, Coyle watched as the choppers approached. The refugees stumbled out, dazed and terrified, but alive. Granier and the Ghost Warrior directed them aboard the Boxcar, his team working to secure them for the flight to safety.

As the last refugee boarded, the sound of approaching tanks filled the air. The NVA were closing in, determined to cut off their escape. Cannons roared, shells rained down, explosions chewed up the runway.

With only moments between death and survival, Coyle gunned the engines as he released the brake. The old plane roared down the runway, bullets pinging off its metal hide. It lifted into the sky, leaving the chaos of the battle behind.

It was a small victory, a glimmer of hope in a war that seemed increasingly hopeless. But for these refugees, it meant everything. It meant life instead of certain death.

And in the end, that was what mattered most. That was the true measure of a soldier, of a hero. Not the battles won or lost, but the lives saved, the hope preserved in the face of overwhelming odds.

Saigon, South Vietnam

Ambassador Graham Martin sat at his desk, his face flushed with anger as he shuffled through a stack of papers. The room was dimly lit, the heavy curtains drawn against the glare of the Saigon sun.

A sharp knock at the door drew Martin's attention. "Come in," he said, his voice thick with irritation.

The door swung open, revealing the figure of CIA

Station Chief Polgar. Polgar walked in, his expression guarded as he took in the ambassador's agitated state.

"You wanted to see me, Mr. Ambassador?" Polgar asked, his tone carefully neutral.

Martin slammed the papers down on his desk, fixing Polgar with a fierce glare. "What the hell is going on out there, Polgar? I've got reports coming in that Americans helped Hmong refugees escape an NVA assault on their village. Care to explain?"

Polgar's face remained impassive, but a flicker of something - defiance, perhaps - flashed in his eyes. "I'm not sure what you're referring to, Mr. Ambassador. My men are under strict orders not to interfere in refugee operations."

Martin let out a mirthless laugh, shaking his head in disbelief. "Don't play games with me, Polgar. I know your boys were involved. What were you thinking? We're trying to get the South Vietnamese to stand on their own feet, to fight their own battles. They're not going to do that if they think we'll swoop in and save them every time things get tough."

Polgar stepped forward, his posture straight and unyielding. "With all due respect, Mr. Ambassador, these are people's lives we're talking about. The Hmong have been loyal allies, and we owe them our protection."

Martin's face reddened further, his eyes narrowing in anger. "Protection? Is that what you call it? Undermining the very government we're trying to support? Sending a message that they don't need to fight, because Uncle Sam will always be there to bail them out?"

Polgar's anger rose to the surface. "And what message do we send if we abandon them? That

America's word means nothing? That we'll use them and then discard them when they're no longer convenient?"

The room fell silent, the two men staring each other down across the expanse of Martin's desk. Finally, Martin spoke, his voice low and controlled. "I understand your position, Tom. I really do. But we have to think of the bigger picture here. We're trying to give South Vietnam a fighting chance, to help them stand on their own against the communists. We can't do that if we're constantly holding their hand."

Polgar shook his head, "With all due respect, Mr. Ambassador, I don't think they stand a chance either way. The NVA is too strong, too determined. And the South Vietnamese government is too corrupt, too divided. We're just delaying the inevitable."

Martin's eyes flashed with anger, his fist clenching on the desk. "That's not your call to make. Our job is to support the South Vietnamese, to give them every opportunity to defend themselves. And that means not undermining President Thieu's orders to his people."

Polgar stood his ground, his expression unyielding. "What about our commitment to the people who have fought and died alongside us? Do we just abandon them, leave them to the mercy of the NVA? They and their families will be slaughtered."

Martin sighed, leaning back in his chair. The anger seemed to drain out of him, replaced by a bone-deep weariness. "I don't have all the answers, Tom. I wish I did. But I know that we can't keep fighting this war for them. They have to stand on their own, for better or worse."

Polgar nodded, a grudging respect in his eyes. "I understand, Ambassador. But I can't promise that my boys will stand by and watch innocent people be slaughtered. Not if there's something they can do to stop it."

Martin met his gaze, a hint of understanding softening his features. "I know, Tom. And I respect that, even if I can't condone it. Just... be careful out there. We're walking a damned thin line."

Polgar nodded, a faint smile playing at his lips. "Aren't we always, Mr. Ambassador? Aren't we always?"

And with that, he turned and walked out of the office, leaving Martin alone with his thoughts and the impossible decisions that lay ahead.

It was a scene that would play out again and again in the coming weeks and months, as the war ground on and the fate of South Vietnam teetered on the brink. And through it all, the men tasked with shaping that fate would struggle and clash, each driven by their own convictions.

But in the end, they knew, it would be the Vietnamese people who would bear the brunt of those choices. And that knowledge weighed heavily, a burden they would carry long after the guns fell silent and the smoke cleared from the sky.

Bien Hoa Air Base, South Vietnam

Coyle and Granier stood and watched as the Hmong villagers huddled together in a corner of the hangar. "Now, that we saved them, what are we gonna do with them?" said Coyle.

"Some sort of refugee camp, I suppose," said Granier, miffed.

"It better be a really big refugee camp. By the looks

of things, I think we have our work cut out for us."

"We'll figure it out. At least nobody's shooting at them at the moment."

"Good point. Listen, I hate to do this, but I need to check on something. I'll be back tomorrow evening at the latest."

"Okay. But what if we get another situation while you're gone?"

"My aircrew is more than capable. They can fly her in my absence."

"Alright. Does this have anything to do with McGoon's whore and her daughter?"

"Yes. And they have names – Nguyet and Tuyet."

"Which is which?"

"Does it matter?"

"I assume by your tone that you don't want me to call her a whore anymore."

"Nguyet is the mother and Tuyet is the daughter. And yes, calling Nguyet a whore is no longer acceptable."

"Roger that."

Coyle moved off to find another aircraft heading for Hue leaving Granier to deal with Hmong villagers.

Hue, South Vietnam

Coyle stepped out of the taxi, the hot Hue sun beating down on his neck as he surveyed the small house he had rented for Nguyet and Tuyet. It had been a year since he had last seen them, a year filled with the chaos and turmoil of the war. But now, with the NVA advancing and the country teetering on the brink of collapse, he knew he had to check on them, to make plans for their safety.

He walked up to the front door and raised his hand to knock. Before he could make contact, however, the door swung open, revealing the beaming face of Tuyet, a large girl, half Vietnamese and half American, the spitting image of his deceased best friend McGoon.

"Tom!" she exclaimed, her English heavily accented but filled with joy. "You here!"

Before Coyle could respond, Tuyet threw her massive arms around him, enveloping him in a hug that nearly knocked the wind out of him. He laughed, returning the embrace with equal fervor, marveling at how much she had grown in the past year.

"Surprise," he said, grinning down at her. "I wanted to see you."

Tuyet grabbed his hand, pulling him into the house with excitement. "Mẹ!" she called out. "Tom here!"

As they entered the living room, Coyle stopped short, his eyes widening in surprise. There, sitting on the couch next to Nguyet, was a man in an ARVN captain's uniform. The man looked up as they entered, his expression curious.

Nguyet rose to her feet, a tentative smile on her face. "Tom," she said, her English halting. "Good see you."

Coyle swallowed, his mouth suddenly dry. He had never really thought about Nguyet dating, had never considered the possibility that she might move on from McGoon with her life. But seeing her there, with another man, he felt a sudden pang of something he couldn't quite identify.

"Nguyet," he said, nodding in greeting. He turned to the ARVN captain, forcing a smile. "Hello. I'm Tom Coyle."

The captain stood, extending his hand. "Captain

Tran," he said, his English fluent and confident. "Pleased to meet you. Nguyet has mentioned you before."

Coyle shook his hand, trying to ignore the awkwardness that hung in the air. "I hope you've been well," he said to Nguyet, struggling to find the right words.

Nguyet nodded, her smile strained. "We... okay," she said, her English faltering.

Captain Tran stepped in, his tone friendly. "Nguyet and Tuyet have been navigating some challenges," he explained. "I've been trying to assist where I can."

Coyle nodded, a tight feeling in his chest. He was grateful for the captain's help, but couldn't shake the sense of unease at seeing him there, in the home he had provided for Nguyet and Tuyet.

Tuyet, seemingly oblivious to the tension, tugged on Coyle's arm. "Come, Tom," she said, her English excited. "I show my room!"

Coyle allowed himself to be led away, relieved to escape the uncomfortable situation. As he followed Tuyet down the hallway, however, he couldn't shake the feeling that everything had changed, that the simple, uncomplicated relationship he had enjoyed with Nguyet and Tuyet had been irrevocably altered.

He had come here to ensure their safety, to offer them a way out of the country if necessary. But now, seeing Nguyet with another man, he realized that he had no claim on her, no right to interfere in her life.

And yet, as he listened to Tuyet's excited chatter, her English broken but enthusiastic, he knew that he couldn't just walk away, couldn't leave them to face the uncertain future alone. He had made a promise to McGoon, long ago, to protect them, to be there for them when they needed him.

And he intended to keep that promise, no matter what it cost him, no matter how uncomfortable or awkward it might be. Because in the end, that was what mattered most - the bonds of friendship, of loyalty, of love that tied them together, even in the darkest of times.

Even if those bonds had to be redefined, even if the future held more uncertainty than ever before. He would be there for them, in whatever way they needed him to be.

Resolution of 1975

Hanoi, North Vietnam

The room was thick with the gray haze of cigarette smoke, curling lazily in the dim light. The air was heavy, oppressive, decisions to be made hanging like a palpable presence. Around the large wooden table, the generals and political leaders of North Vietnam sat, their faces serious, their eyes sharp with the knowledge of what was at stake.

It was the end of October 1974, and the North Vietnamese Politburo had gathered to decide on their strategy for 1975 and 1976. The war had reached its final stage, and the leadership knew that the decisions made in this room would shape the future of their nation.

At the head of the table, First Party Secretary Le Duan stood, his posture erect, his gaze sweeping the room. He began to speak, outlining the key points of what would become known as the Resolution of 1975.

"Comrades," he said. "The time has come for us to seize the initiative, to strike the decisive blow against the imperialists and their puppets in the South. In 1975, our army must consolidate its gains, eliminate the enemy's border outposts, and secure our logistical corridor. We will continue to build up our forces in the south, preparing for the final general offensive in 1976."

The men around the table nodded, some scribbling notes, others simply listening intently. They knew the importance of this moment, the gravity of the decisions being made.

Le Duan continued, his voice rising with passion. "We have fought long and hard for this moment, comrades. We have endured countless hardships, made immeasurable sacrifices. But now, victory is within our grasp. The Americans have left our shores. They are tired, their resolve weakening. They will not have the stomach for further fighting. We do not believe they will return, no matter the outcome of the war. And the ARVN, for all their bluster, are a hollow force, their leaders looking after their own interest counting their gold. Disillusioned and demoralized, their forces are ready to collapse under the weight of our onslaught."

There were murmurs of agreement around the table, heads nodding in assent. But there were also looks of concern, of uncertainty.

One general, his face lined with the scars of battle, spoke up. "Comrade Secretary, what if the Americans do intervene? What if they escalate the bombing, send in more troops? We must be prepared for all eventualities."

Le Duan's eyes flashed, "We are prepared, comrade. We have built up our air defenses, strengthened our supply lines. And we have the will of the people on our side. The Americans cannot match our resolve, our willingness to endure any hardship for the sake of our cause."

The room fell silent, the weight of Le Duan's words sinking in. They knew he was right, that the tide of history was turning in their favor.

A few weeks later, the PAVN field commanders and their political officers were summoned to Hanoi once again to assess the new strategy. The initial consensus was that an attack in the Central Highlands would have the greatest chance of success. But then, Lieutenant General Tran Van Tra, COSVN's military commander, challenged this notion.

Tra's staff had already drawn up a plan for a direct attack against Saigon. Tra proposed that his forces launch a "test" attack in Phuoc Long Province near the Cambodian border, to gauge the ARVN's will to fight and the likelihood of U.S. intervention. It was a bold move, offering the potential for great gain at relatively low risk.

Le Duan and the politburo members considered Tra's proposal. The room was silent as everyone awaited their decision.

"Comrade Tra," Le Duan said, his voice measured, "your plan is bold, perhaps even reckless. But it also shows great initiative, great daring. These are the qualities we need in this final stage of the war."

He paused, his gaze sweeping the room, making eye contact with each man in turn. "I approve of your plan, comrade. But I must warn you - failure is not an option. You must be sure of victory, no matter the cost."

Tra nodded, "I understand, Comrade Secretary. We will not fail. The ARVN will crumble before us, and Saigon will fall."

The meeting stretched on, the details of the plan being hammered out, contingencies discussed and debated. The smoke grew thicker, the air more stifling, but the men in the room barely noticed. They were focused on the task at hand, on the great undertaking that lay before them.

As the hours passed, a sense of excitement, of anticipation, began to build. They could feel it, the electric charge in the air, the sense that they were on the cusp of something momentous. The final offensive was taking shape, the pieces falling into place.

And yet, beneath the excitement, there was also a sense of solemnity, of the heavy responsibility they bore. They knew that the decisions made in this room would send hundreds of thousands of young men and women into battle, that many would not return. They knew that the road ahead would be hard, that victory would come at a terrible price.

But they also knew that it was a price worth paying, that the cause they fought for was just and right. They were fighting for the freedom of their people, for the right to determine their own destiny. And they would not rest until that fight was won.

As the meeting finally drew to a close, the men rose from their seats, shaking hands and clapping each other on the back. There was a sense of camaraderie, of shared purpose, that transcended rank and position. They were all in this together, all united in the great struggle that lay ahead.

Le Duan stood at the head of the table, his face lit with a fierce, determined smile. "Comrades," he said, his voice ringing out in the smoky air, "the die is cast. Let us go forward together, with courage and resolve, until victory is ours."

And with those words, the meeting was over. The generals and political leaders filed out of the room, ready to put the plan into action, ready to lead their people to the final, decisive victory.

Outside, the city of Hanoi bustled with life, the people going about their daily business, unaware of the momentous decisions that had been made, of the great events that were about to unfold. But soon, very soon, the whole country would be caught up in the maelstrom of war, in the final, fateful struggle for the soul of Vietnam.

And at the center of it all, the men of the Politburo stood, ready to see their great work through to the end. The Resolution of 1975 had been revised and passed, the course of history fixed. There would be no turning back now, no retreat, no surrender. The final victory was within their grasp, and they would not let it slip away.

Central Highlands, South Vietnam

Karen Dickson stood at the edge of the road, her camera held up to her eye as she focused on the scene before her. The sun beat down mercilessly from a cloudless sky, the heat shimmering off the asphalt in waves. But Karen barely noticed the temperature, her attention wholly absorbed by the human drama unfolding in front of her lens.

The road was a river of humanity, a seething mass of refugees flowing southward, away from the advancing NVA forces. They came on foot, on bicycles, in overloaded cars and trucks, a desperate tide of people fleeing the only homes they had ever known.

Karen's finger clicked on the shutter, capturing image after image. An old woman, her face lined with grief and exhaustion, struggling to keep pace with the crowd. A young mother, a baby clutched to her breast, tears streaming down her cheeks as she stumbled forward. A farmer, his water buffalo laden with all his worldly possessions, his eyes hollow with the knowledge of all he had lost and an uncertain future.

Each face told a story, each image a window into the human cost of the war. Karen felt a lump rising in her throat, a sense of overwhelming empathy threatening to engulf her. But she pushed it down, forcing herself to focus on her job, on the task of bearing witness to this moment in history.

As she worked, the sound of distant gunfire echoed across the landscape, a grim reminder of the danger that lurked just beyond the horizon. The refugees flinched at each report, their faces tightening with fear and desperation.

Karen moved through the crowd, her camera a constant companion. She captured images of families huddled together, of children crying for food and water, of the elderly and infirm struggling to keep up. Each picture was a homage of the unbreakable bonds of love and loyalty that held these people together in the face of unimaginable adversity.

As the day wore on, the flow of refugees began to slow, the crowd thinning out as people sought shelter from the relentless sun. Karen lowered her camera, her arms aching from the weight of her equipment and the emotional toll of her work.

She looked out over the sea of faces, the endless procession of lives uprooted and torn asunder by the tides of war. And in that moment, she felt a sense of overwhelming sadness that threatened to consume her.

But she also felt a flicker of hope. These people had lost everything, had seen their world shattered into a million pieces. And yet, they kept going, kept putting one foot in front of the other, driven by the unquenchable desire to survive, to build a better future for themselves and their children.

Karen raised her camera once more, capturing one final image. A young girl, no more than ten years old, walking hand in hand with her grandfather. The girl's face was streaked with dust and sweat, but her eyes shone with a stubborn refusal to give in to despair.

As Karen packed up her equipment and prepared to move on, she knew that she would carry that image with her, a beacon of hope in a world too often shrouded in darkness.

Saigon, South Vietnam

President Nguyen Van Thieu sat behind his ornate desk in the grand presidential palace, his face a mask of frustration and anger. The room was opulent, with high ceilings, intricate moldings, and plush carpets, but the atmosphere was far from comfortable. Tension hung in the air like a heavy fog, threatening to suffocate those present.

Across from Thieu sat U.S. Ambassador Graham Martin, his expression equally frustrated. The two men had been locked in a heated discussion for the better part of an hour, their voices rising and falling with the intensity of their emotions.

"The North Vietnamese have crossed the border and taken over the city of Tay Ninh," Thieu said, his voice tight with barely contained rage. "It is a clear violation of the Paris Peace Accords. President Nixon promised to bring back the American bombers if the NVA attacked in South Vietnam. It is now time for

America to keep its promise to us."

Martin sighed, leaning back in his chair. The difficult truths he had to convey, seemed to press down on him.

"Mr. President," he began, his tone measured but firm, "I'm afraid the situation has changed. Nixon is no longer president, and President Ford, while he supports South Vietnam's efforts to fight communism, is not obliged to honor any promise made by his predecessor. The political landscape in the U.S. has shifted, and there is little appetite for further military involvement in Vietnam."

Thieu's eyes flashed with anger, his fist clenching on the desk. "So, you abandon us now, after all we have sacrificed? After all the blood we have shed in the name of your fight against communism?"

"Our fight against communism."

"We could have negotiated with the North, but you and your president stood in the way. You bought our loyalty with your aid. Now, we have little to show for it and we must face the North alone."

Martin held up a hand, trying to placate the agitated president. "Please understand, Mr. President, that thanks to American aid, South Vietnam has one of the largest and best-supplied militaries in the world. You outnumber the North Vietnamese forces nearly four to one and have superior weapons. It is time for the South Vietnamese military to stand on its own."

Thieu let out a bitter laugh, shaking his head in disbelief. "You speak of our military strength, but do you know the truth, Ambassador? Only sixty-five percent of ARVN troops are physically reporting for duty every day. The rest are paying off their commanders to count them present. Our army is a hollow shell, riddled with corruption and incompetence."

Martin's eyes widened in shock, "That's... that's outrageous! How could such a thing be allowed to happen?"

"Your CIA and military advisors have known this for many years. Your feint of anger is a hollow lie."

"I will not sit here and be accused of lying, Mr. President."

"Very well. We will call it miscommunication if it pleases you."

"None of this pleases me, Mr. President. I am a strong advocate of South Vietnam. I want nothing but the best for your country, but you must take responsibility for the corruption in your military. You are the commander and chief."

Thieu spread his hands, a gesture of helplessness. "Corruption is part of the reality we face, Ambassador. And it is why we need more military assistance, more financial aid. Without it, we cannot hope to stand against the communists."

Martin's face hardened, his tone becoming more formal. "I'm sorry, Mr. President, but that is simply not possible. The Case-Church Amendment has tied our hands. While President Ford supports South Vietnam in the struggle against communism, even current levels of support are being scrutinized by Congress. We cannot increase aid, no matter how much we might wish to."

The room fell silent, the weight of Martin's words hanging in the air. Thieu's face was a mask of despair, his shoulders slumping as if under a great burden.

"Then what are we to do, Mr. Ambassador?" he asked, his voice barely above a whisper. "How are we to face the coming storm?"

"With honor and valor, Mr. President. Your country needs you more than ever."

"I doubt honor or valor will stop the North Vietnamese."

Martin leaned forward, his expression softening. "Mr. President, I can offer you and your family asylum in the United States, or one of its allies, should the worst come to pass. You would be safe, able to live out your days in peace and comfort."

Thieu's head snapped up, his eyes blazing with a fierce pride. "And abandon my people? Let it be known that I fled like a coward while they faced the enemy alone? No, Ambassador, I cannot accept such an offer. I will stand with my country, no matter the cost."

Martin nodded, a mixture of respect and sadness on his face. He understood Thieu's position, even as he feared for what it might mean.

The two men sat in silence, the grandeur of the room seeming to mock the gravity of their situation. Outside, the city of Saigon bustled with life, the people going about their daily business, unaware of the dark clouds gathering on the horizon.

But in this room, in this moment, the future seemed all too clear. The North Vietnamese were coming, their forces growing stronger by the day. And the U.S., once the bulwark against communist aggression, was pulling back, leaving South Vietnam to face its fate alone.

Thieu rose from his desk, "I will fight, Mr. Ambassador. I will lead my people as best I can, for as long as I can. We may be abandoned, but we are not defeated. Not yet."

Martin stood as well, offering his hand to the

president. "I understand, Mr. President. And know that, whatever happens, you have the respect and admiration of President Ford and the American people. We will do what we can, even if it is not as much as we wish."

The two men shook hands, a gesture of solidarity in the face of the coming storm. And then Martin was gone, leaving Thieu alone in the grand palace.

He turned to the window, looking out over the city he loved, the city he had sworn to defend. In the distance, the sound of gunfire could be heard, a reminder of the battles to come.

But Thieu would not yield, would not surrender. He would fight to the last, for the sake of his people, for the sake of his country. Even if it meant facing the end alone.

January 1, 1975 - Phnom Penh, Cambodia

As the first day of 1975 dawned over Cambodia, the Khmer Rouge forces began their final push towards the capital city of Phnom Penh. For months, they had been tightening their grip on the countryside, seizing control of key strategic positions and cutting off the city's supply lines. Now, with the government forces weakened and demoralized, the time had come for the final assault.

In the rural villages and rice paddies beyond the city limits, the Khmer Rouge fighters gathered in their thousands, their red and white checkered krama scarves fluttering in the early morning breeze. Among them was Sothea, a young man from Battambang province who had joined the revolution three years ago, driven by a deep-seated anger at the corruption and injustice of the Lon Nol regime.

Lon Nol was a Cambodian general and politician who served as the Prime Minister of Cambodia then as the self-proclaimed President of the Khmer Republic. He came to power in a coup that ousted Prince Norodom Sihanouk and aligned Cambodia with the United States, but his regime was plagued by corruption and political repression.

Sothea checked his AK-47 and adjusted his ammunition belt. He could feel the excitement and anticipation building. This was the moment he had been waiting for, the chance to strike a blow against the enemies of the people and build a new, better world.

Around him, his comrades were making their own preparations, sharpening their knives and cleaning their rifles. They had all suffered under the Lon Nol government, had seen their families and communities torn apart by war and oppression. And now, with the Vietnamese communists on the verge of victory in their own struggle, the Khmer Rouge knew that their time had come.

As the sun rose higher in the sky, the order came down from the Khmer Rouge leadership: the attack on Phnom Penh was to begin. With a roar of engines and a clatter of treads, the rebel tanks and artillery pieces began to move forward, their sights set on the distant skyline of the capital.

In Phnom Penh itself, the first signs of the impending attack were met with a mixture of fear and disbelief. For months, the government had been assuring the people that the city was safe, that the Khmer Rouge were nothing more than a ragtag band of guerrillas who posed no real threat to the capital.

But as the sound of gunfire and explosions drew

closer, as the first shells began to fall on the outskirts of the city, the illusion of safety was shattered. Panic and chaos ensued as thousands of civilians fled their homes, seeking shelter in government buildings and foreign embassies.

At the presidential palace, Lon Nol and his advisors watched the unfolding crisis with a sense of growing despair. They had long known that the Khmer Rouge was a force to be reckoned with, but they had hoped for more time to prepare, to shore up their capital's defenses and rally their allies.

Now, with the enemy at the gates and their own forces in disarray, they could only watch and wait, their fate hanging in the balance. Some talked of trying to negotiate a peaceful surrender, but Lon Nol himself was adamant that they would fight to the end, determined to go down in a blaze of glory rather than submit to the communists.

As the day wore on and the fighting intensified, the people of Phnom Penh huddled in their makeshift shelters, praying for deliverance and fearing the worst. Many had heard the stories of the Khmer Rouge's brutality, of the forced marches and labor camps that awaited those who fell into their hands.

And yet, even in the midst of the chaos and the violence, there were moments of humanity and compassion. Sothea watched as one of his fellow fighters stopped to help an elderly woman who had been wounded in the crossfire, carefully bandaging her injuries and giving her a drink of water from his canteen.

For Sothea, it was a reminder of what they were fighting for - not just the overthrow of the Lon Nol regime, but the creation of a new society based on equality and justice for all. It was a dream that had sustained him through the long years of struggle, and one that he knew he would die for if necessary.

As night fell over Phnom Penh and the first day of the Khmer Rouge's final offensive came to an end, the outcome of the battle was still far from certain. The government forces had put up a stubborn resistance, and the rebel advance had been slowed by the need to clear the city street by street, building by building.

But for Sothea and his comrades, there was no turning back. They had set their sights on the capital, and they would not rest until it was theirs. The road ahead would be long and the sacrifices many. But in the end, they knew that victory would be worth any price.

And so, as the smoke and dust of battle settled over the embattled city, the Khmer Rouge pressed on. For them, the fall of Phnom Penh was not just a military objective, but a historic necessity - the first step on the road to a new and better world.

The Test

Staging Camp, Cambodian Border

Lieutenant General Tran Van Tra stood before his three divisional commanders. Tra's eyes swept over the men, taking in their expressions of anticipation and resolve.

"Comrades," he began, "the time has come for us to strike a decisive blow against the enemy. Our forces are poised to cross the Cambodian border and begin the offensive that will test the ARVN's ability to fight and the Americans' resolve to come to their aid."

He paused, letting his words sink in. The commanders leaned forward, their attention rapt.

"As you know, the district of Phuoc Long is our target," Tra continued, his finger tracing the lines of the map spread before them. "It is a vital link in the enemy's defensive chain, a key to the protection of Saigon and the southern provinces. If we can break their hold there, we will open the door to victory."

One of the commanders, a battle-hardened veteran with a scar running down his cheek, spoke up. "Has the intel changed since their last report? What forces will we face, comrade? What resistance can we expect?"

Tra's eyes glinted with a fierce light. "The ARVN regular units in Phuoc Long are well-entrenched and determined. They have disrupted our supply lines along Route 14 for too long. But they are spread thin, their resources stretched to the breaking point. They will not be able to withstand the full might of our assault."

He gestured to the map, his hand sweeping across the military zones surrounding Phuoc Long. "In the first phase of our operation, we will capture these key areas - Bu Dang, Bu Na, Bo Duc, Duc Phong, Don Luan, and the firebases around Ba Ra mountain. We will cut off their reinforcements, isolate their positions, and crush their resistance."

The commanders nodded in agreement. They knew the stakes, knew the price that would be paid in blood and sacrifice. But they also knew the importance of their mission, the critical role they would play in the final victory. And finally, they knew the consequences if they failed.

Tra's voice rose, filling the room with its intensity. "And then, comrades, we will launch our frontal assault on Phuoc Long itself. We will smash through their defenses, overrun their positions, and plant our flag on the heights of Ba Ra mountain. We will show the world the strength and determination of our people's army, the inevitability of our triumph."

The room erupted in a chorus of shouts and cheers, the commanders caught up in the fervor of the moment. Tra basked in the energy and passion of his men.

But then, he raised a hand for silence, his expression growing serious once more. "But let us not underestimate our enemy," he cautioned, his voice low and measured. "The ARVN forces in Phuoc Long are well-trained and well-equipped. They will fight with the desperation of cornered rats, knowing that their survival and the survival of their country depends upon their actions and courage. And the Americans, for all their talk of withdrawal and disengagement, may yet find the stomach for one last fight. Their bombers are still just a few hours away should they decide to use them."

The commanders sobered. Tra's eyes swept the room once more, taking in the determined faces of his men. "We will prevail," he said, his voice ringing with conviction. "We will break the back of the ARVN, shatter the myth of American invincibility, and open the way for the final liberation of our homeland. This is our destiny, comrades, and we will seize it with both hands."

The commanders rose to their feet, their fists clenched in salute. "For the revolution!" they shouted, their voices echoing off the walls of the room. "For the people of Vietnam!"

Tra returned their salute, his own fist raised high. "For the revolution," he repeated with an intense growl. "And for the certain victory that awaits us on the other side of the border."

And with those words, the test offensive had begun, and the fate of a nation hung in the balance. The road ahead would be long and hard, filled with sacrifice and suffering. But for the men in that room, for the fourteen thousand soldiers who would follow them into battle, there was no turning back, no surrender, no retreat.

They would fight to the last, for the sake of their cause, for the dream of a Vietnam united and free. And in the end, they knew, history would be their judge, and their deeds would echo through the ages.

The North Vietnamese forces massed along the Cambodian border were a sight to behold, a vast and formidable array of men and machines poised to unleash devastation upon the province of Phuoc Long. At the heart of this juggernaut were the battle-hardened divisions of the 4th Corps and the elite units of the B2 Front Command, a fearsome combination of skill and firepower.

The 7th Infantry Division, with its renowned 165th, 141st, and 209th Regiments, formed the backbone of the assault force. These men were veterans of countless battles, their skills honed to a razor's edge through years of relentless combat. Alongside them stood the 9th Infantry Division, its 1st and 2nd Regiments equally seasoned and ready for the fight ahead.

But it was the presence of the B2 Front Command that truly set this force apart. The 3rd Infantry Division, with its 201st and 271st Regiments, was known throughout the North Vietnamese Army as a unit of exceptional skill and courage, capable of breaking through even the strongest enemy defenses. The 429th Sapper Regiment, masters of stealth and infiltration, would lead the way, neutralizing key targets and sowing chaos in the enemy's ranks. And the 16th Infantry Regiment, hand-picked for this critical mission, would serve as the hammer blow, smashing through any resistance with overwhelming force and firepower.

Supporting this formidable assembly of infantry and sappers were the unsung heroes of the 25th Engineer Group, the 210th Logistical Group, and the

235th Logistical Group. These men would build the bridges, clear the roads, and ensure that the advancing troops had everything they needed to maintain their relentless momentum.

But perhaps the most impressive aspect of this force was the sheer scale of its anti-aircraft defenses. The NVA had learned hard lessons in previous battles, and they were determined not to let the South Vietnamese Air Force, or, God forbid, the American Air Force should they arrive, turn the tide against them. A staggering array of guns, missiles, and radar systems had been deployed along the border, creating an impenetrable umbrella of protection for the advancing troops.

The 37mm and 57mm anti-aircraft guns, deadly accurate and highly mobile, could engage targets at ranges of up to 4,000 meters. The larger 85mm and 100mm guns, their barrels bristling with menace, could reach even higher, plucking enemy aircraft from the sky with ease. And the SA-7 surface-to-air missiles, a new addition to the NVA's arsenal, promised to be a game-changer, capable of knocking down even the most advanced enemy fighters and bombers.

Overseeing this vast network of air defenses were the specialists of the radar units, their eyes and ears constantly scanning the skies for any hint of threat. They would direct the guns and missiles with uncanny precision, ensuring that no South Vietnamese aircraft could penetrate the protective bubble surrounding the NVA troops.

As the final preparations were made and the order to advance was given, a sense of invincibility rippled through the ranks of the North Vietnamese forces. They knew that they were part of something historic, a turning point in the long and bloody struggle for their homeland's freedom. And with their overwhelming numbers, their unshakeable resolve, and their impenetrable shield of anti-aircraft fire, they felt certain that victory was within their grasp.

The province of Phuoc Long, with its strategic importance and its symbolic value, would be the first domino to fall. And after that, the NVA knew, there would be no stopping them. The South, with its corrupt and demoralized army, its fickle American allies, and its crumbling political structure, would soon be swept away in a tidal wave of revolutionary fervor.

With a roar of engines and a clatter of treads, the North Vietnamese juggernaut began its inexorable advance across the border, ready to make history and claim its place in the annals of Vietnam's long and tragic struggle for liberation.

Private Chau crouched in the dense underbrush, his AK-47 clutched tightly to his chest. Around him, the soldiers of the 7th Infantry Division waited in tense silence, their faces painted with streaks of mud and camouflage.

Chau had been with the NVA for two years, ever since he had turned eighteen and been conscripted into the army. He had grown up in a small village near Hanoi, the son of rice farmers who had struggled to make ends meet under the yoke of French colonialism.

For Chau, joining the army had been a way to escape the grinding poverty of his childhood, to make a difference in the world and fight for the liberation of his people. He had been filled with a sense of purpose and idealism, a belief that he was part of something greater than himself.

But now, as he prepared to cross the border into South Vietnam and attack his fellow Vietnamese, Chau couldn't shake the feeling that had settled in his stomach. He had been taught to see the South Vietnamese as puppets of the Americans, as traitors to the cause of national liberation. But he knew that many of them were just like him - poor farmers and workers who had been caught up in a war they didn't understand.

Chau thought of his own family, his parents and siblings who were still living in the North. He wondered what they would think of him now, as he prepared to kill his own people in the name of the revolution. Would they be proud of him, or would they see him as just another cog in the communist machine of war?

Next to Chau, his squad leader, Sergeant Tran, was giving final instructions to the men. Tran was a hardened veteran, a man who had seen more than his share of combat. He spoke in a low, almost bored tone, as if he had given this speech a hundred times before.

"Remember, comrades, our objective is to break through the enemy's defenses and secure the key positions along Route 14. The 9th Infantry Division will be supporting us on the left flank, while the B2 Front Command units will be pushing forward on the right. Our air defenses will keep the skies clear, so all you need to worry about is the enemy in front of you."

Tran paused, his eyes scanning the faces of the men in front of him. "I know that some of you may have doubts about our mission, about fighting against our own people. But remember, the South Vietnamese are not our true brothers and sisters. They have been corrupted by the imperialist aggressors. It is our duty to liberate them, to bring them back into the fold of the true Vietnam."

Chau nodded along with the other soldiers, but he couldn't shake the doubts that had taken root in his mind. He had seen the propaganda posters and heard the speeches, but he had also heard whispers of the reality on the other side of the border. The South Vietnamese were not all corrupt puppets, but rather ordinary people caught in the middle of a war they hadn't asked for.

As the order came to move out, Chau took a deep breath and steeled himself for the battle ahead. He knew that he had no choice but to follow orders, to do his duty as a soldier of the NVA. But as he advanced toward the border into South Vietnam, he couldn't help but wonder if there was another way, a path that didn't involve killing his own people.

The jungle closed in around them, the sounds of artillery and gunfire growing louder with each passing step. Chau gripped his rifle tighter, his hands wet with sweat. He knew that he was just one small part of a much larger machine, the wheel of history that was turning inexorably towards its final destination.

And as he advanced towards the enemy lines, Chau whispered a silent prayer to whatever gods might be listening, asking for the strength to do what needed to be done, and for the wisdom to know what was right in a world turned upside down by war.

Phuoc Long, South Vietnam

ARVN Captain Tran Giang Quang of the 362nd Security Battalion" stood at the edge of his fortified position, his eyes scanning the dense jungle that stretched out before him. The air was thick with a moving mist, and the only sound was the occasional rustling of leaves in the warm breeze.

Quang had been tasked with guarding the main roads from Vinh Thuan to Bu Dang, a crucial responsibility in the defense of Phuoc Long. He knew that his battalion was just one piece of a larger puzzle, with other units spread out across the region to protect vital routes and key positions.

The 341st and 352nd Security Battalions were dug in at Don Luan, while the 363rd held the line at Bu Na. The 340th Security Battalion served as a reserve force, ready to reinforce any position that came under heavy attack. And at the heart of Phuoc Long District, an artillery battalion stood ready, their 150mm and 155mm guns prepared to rain down fire on the enemy.

But despite the bravery and determination of the ARVN forces, Quang couldn't shake the feeling of unease that had settled in his gut. Intelligence reports had confirmed what many had long suspected: the North Vietnamese Army and Viet Cong were massing on the other side of the Cambodian border, poised to strike at any moment.

Quang had seen the satellite imagery himself, the endless columns of tanks and trucks, the masses of infantry and artillery. The enemy had committed the feared 7th and 9th Infantry Divisions to the assault, along with the elite units of the B2 Front Command. The 3rd Infantry Division, the 429th Sapper Regiment, the 16th Infantry Regiment - these were names that struck terror into the hearts of even the most seasoned ARVN soldiers.

And then there were the anti-aircraft defenses, a vast network of guns and missiles that seemed to stretch across the entire border region. They formed an impenetrable umbrella that would make it all but impossible for the South Vietnamese Air Force to provide support to his ground troops.

Quang knew that his men were vastly outnumbered and outgunned. The ARVN forces in Phuoc Long were dug in and fortified, but they were spread thin, tasked with defending a vast area against an enemy that seemed to have an endless supply of men and materiel.

As he looked out across the jungle, Quang couldn't help but feel a sense of inevitability. The North Vietnamese had been planning this assault for months, and they had chosen their moment carefully. The American forces had long since withdrawn, and the South Vietnamese government was in disarray, racked by corruption and infighting.

Quang thought of his family, his wife and young son, who were waiting for him back in Saigon. He had joined the army to protect them, to ensure that they could grow up in a country free from the tyranny of communism. But now, as he stood on the frontlines of what he knew would be a devastating battle, he couldn't help but wonder if he had made the right choice.

The radio on Quang's hip crackled to life, snapping him out of his reverie. It was the voice of his commanding officer, Lieutenant General Du Quoc Dong, the man tasked with the overall defense of Phuoc Long.

"All units, this is Lieutenant General Dong. Intelligence reports confirm that the enemy is preparing to launch their assault. We expect the first wave to hit our positions within the next twenty-four hours. I know that many of you are feeling the weight of the task before us, but I want you to know that your bravery and sacrifice will not be forgotten. The fate of our country rests on your shoulders, and I have every confidence that you will rise to the challenge. Remember your training, trust in your fellow soldiers, and fight with the knowledge that the hopes and dreams of the South Vietnamese people are with you. Together, we will hold the line against the communist aggressors and secure a brighter future for our nation. May God watch over us all."

As the transmission ended, Quang felt a flicker of hope in his heart. The odds were stacked against them, but he knew that he was part of something larger than himself, something worth fighting for. And with that thought, he shouldered his rifle and returned to his position, ready to face whatever the enemy had in store.

Sky above the battlefield…

VPAF Captain Nguyen Thanh Phuoc sat in the cockpit of his Cessna A-37 Dragonfly, his hands gripping the control stick tightly as he flew low over the dense jungle canopy. Beside him, his co-pilot and weapons officer, Lieutenant Tran Duc Huy, scanned the horizon for signs of the enemy.

The two men were part of a hunter-killer team, tasked with softening up the South Vietnamese defenses in preparation for the ground assault that was about to begin. Phuoc had been flying the Dragonfly for over a year, ever since the NVA had captured a handful of the planes during the disastrous South Vietnamese offensive into Laos.

As they approached the target area, Phuoc could see

the outlines of the South Vietnamese trenches and bunkers, dug into the hillsides and surrounded by thick tangles of barbed wire. He knew that the enemy soldiers were waiting for them, their fingers on the triggers of their anti-aircraft guns.

"Huy, arm the rockets and prepare to engage," Phuoc said, his voice calm and focused over the roar of the engines.

"Roger that, Captain," Huy replied, flipping switches and checking his instruments. "Rockets armed and ready."

Phuoc nodded, his eyes scanning the terrain ahead. He knew that they had to be precise in their attack, hitting the enemy positions without wasting ammunition or exposing themselves to unnecessary risk.

As they closed in on the target, Phuoc could see the muzzle flashes of the enemy guns, the tracer rounds streaking up towards them like angry hornets. He jinked the plane to the left, then back to the right, trying to throw off their aim.

"They're holding their fire," Huy said, his voice tight with tension. "Probably trying to conserve ammo for the ground assault."

Phuoc nodded, "Their mistake," he said, as he lined up the first rocket pod and squeezed the trigger.

The rockets streaked away from the Dragonfly, leaving trails of smoke in their wake as they arced towards the enemy trenches. Phuoc watched as they impacted, sending up geysers of dirt and debris, the shockwaves rippling through the air.

"Good hits," Huy said, as he checked the damage through his targeting scope. "Multiple enemy positions destroyed."

Phuoc didn't have time to celebrate, as he was already lining up for another pass. The enemy guns were starting to find their range now, the tracers getting closer with each burst.

"Watch that flak on the left," Huy warned, as a particularly heavy barrage streaked past their wingtip.

Phuoc pushed the stick forward, sending the Dragonfly into a steep dive. He could feel the G-forces pushing him back into his seat, the blood rushing to his head as he leveled out just above the treetops.

"Guns, guns, guns," he called out, as he triggered the nose-mounted minigun. The weapon roared to life, spitting out a stream of 7.62mm rounds that chewed through the enemy positions like a hot knife through butter.

As they pulled up and away from the target, Phuoc could see the other Dragonfly in their team, piloted by his wingman, Lieutenant Nguyen Van Thang. Thang was already lining up for his own attack run, his rockets and guns ready to add to the destruction.

"Good shooting, Thang," Phuoc said over the radio, as he watched his wingman's rockets impact the enemy trenches.

"Same to you, Captain," Thang replied, his voice filled with adrenaline and excitement. "Let's give these bastards a taste of what's coming their way."

For the next several minutes, the two Dragonflies worked together seamlessly, their rockets and guns tearing through the South Vietnamese defenses like a scythe through wheat. Phuoc could see the enemy soldiers scattering, their resolve crumbling in the face of the relentless onslaught.

As they made their final pass over the target area, Phuoc looked down at the smoking ruins of the enemy trenches, the bodies of the fallen littering the ground like broken dolls. He felt a twinge of regret, knowing that many of these men were just like him – young and scared.

But he also knew that this was the price of victory, the cost of liberating his country from the grip of foreign imperialism and puppet rulers. And as he banked the Dragonfly back towards his base in Cambodia, the adrenaline still pumping through his veins, he felt a fierce surge of pride.

They had struck the first blow, softened up the enemy for the ground assault that was about to begin. And with the full might of the NVA and the Viet Cong behind them, Phuoc knew that it was only a matter of time before the South Vietnamese defenses crumbled completely, and the real battle for the future of Vietnam could begin.

Phuoc Long, South Vietnam

Captain Quang lay in the bottom of the trench, his ears ringing from the deafening roar of the Dragonflies' rockets and guns. Around him, the air was thick with the acrid smell of smoke and cordite, the dust from the explosions still settling over the shattered landscape.

Slowly, painfully, Quang pushed himself up to his knees, his head pounding from the concussive force of the blasts. He looked around, taking in the scene of devastation that surrounded him.

The trench was a mess of twisted metal and shattered concrete, the sandbags and timbers that had once provided cover now little more than smoking ruins. And everywhere, there were bodies - the still, silent forms of his men, the soldiers he had trained and fought alongside for months.

Quang felt a surge of grief and anger rise up in his throat, threatening to choke him. These were more than just his men - they were his brothers-in-arms. Men he had laughed with, shared meals with, confided in during the long, lonely nights on the front lines.

He crawled over to the nearest body, a young private named Nguyen. Nguyen had only been with the unit for a few weeks, a fresh-faced recruit straight out of basic training. Quang had taken him under his wing, tried to teach him the ropes and keep him safe.

Now, Nguyen lay still and silent, his eyes staring sightlessly up at the sky. Quang reached out and gently closed them, his own vision blurring with tears.

"I'm sorry," he whispered, his voice choked with emotion. "I'm so sorry."

Around him, the other survivors were starting to stir, their groans and cries of pain filling the air. Quang forced himself to his feet, knowing that he had to take charge, to be the leader his men needed now more than ever. The enemy was coming.

He made his way down the trench, checking on the wounded and offering what comfort he could. Some were beyond help, their injuries too severe to survive. Others were more fortunate, their wounds painful but not life-threatening.

As he worked, Quang couldn't help but feel a sense of despair. They had been hit hard, their defenses crushed by the relentless assault from the air. And he knew that this was only the beginning - the NVA ground forces would be coming soon, pressing their advantage and driving towards the heart of Phuoc Long.

"Captain!" a voice called out, snapping Quang out

of his thoughts. He turned to see one of his sergeants, a grizzled veteran named Tran, limping towards him, his face streaked with blood and dirt.

"What is it, Sergeant?" Quang asked, trying to keep his voice steady.

"The radio, sir," Tran replied, holding out a battered field telephone. "It's Lieutenant General Dong. He wants to speak with you."

Quang took the phone, his heart sinking. He knew what was coming - the order to retreat, to fall back to the next defensive line. It was the right call, the only way to save what was left of his men. But it still felt like a defeat, a betrayal of all those who had fallen.

"Captain Quang," Dong's voice crackled over the line, the static making his words almost unintelligible. "The situation is critical. The enemy is pressing their attack all along the front. We cannot hold them here. You are to withdraw your men to the next defensive position, regroup and await further orders."

"Yes, sir," Quang replied, his voice hollow. "Understood."

He handed the phone back to Tran. They would have to move fast, before the enemy could cut them off completely. And they would have to leave the dead behind, their bodies abandoned to the mercy of the jungle and the scavengers.

It was a bitter pill to swallow, but one that Quang knew he had no choice but to accept. The lives of his remaining men were his responsibility now, and he would do whatever it took to keep them safe.

As he gave the order to withdraw, Quang took one last look around the shattered trench, his heart heavy with the loss and the sacrifice.

He knew that he had to keep going, to honor the

memory of those who had fallen by continuing the fight. And so, with a final salute to the dead, Captain Quang turned and led his men out of the trench, back towards the uncertain future that awaited them all.

The sound of distant explosions and gunfire shattered the eerie calm that had settled over the outskirts of Phuoc Long. The NVA forces, led by the battle-hardened soldiers of the 7th Infantry Division, surged forward with a relentless tenacity, their ranks swelling with the addition of the 9th Infantry Division and the elite troops of the B2 Front Command.

Among the advancing NVA soldiers was Private Hai, the young man from a small village near Hanoi. Hai had joined the army with a sense of duty and purpose, determined to fight for the liberation of his country from the yoke of foreign imperialism. But now, as he charged forward alongside his comrades, the reality of war crashed over him like a tidal wave, threatening to sweep him away in its terrible current.

Beside Hai, his squad leader, Sergeant Tran, barked orders and encouragement, his voice cutting through the din of battle like a knife. Tran was a seasoned veteran that knew that the key to victory lay in pressing the attack, in keeping the pressure on the enemy until they broke.

On the other side of the battlefield, Captain Quang watched with growing dread as the NVA forces massed on the horizon. He had known that this day would come, had spent countless hours preparing his men for the inevitable assault. But now, as the enemy surged forward with a ferocity that took his breath away, he couldn't shake the feeling that they were hopelessly outmatched.

Quang's men were dug in and fortified in their new position, but they were spread thin, trying to cover too much ground with too few troops. And as the NVA forces split into multiple columns, attacking from different directions, he knew that they would be hard-pressed to hold the line.

As the battle raged on, the ARVN troops fought, their weapons blazing as they poured fire into the advancing NVA ranks. But for every enemy soldier that fell, two more seemed to take their place, an endless tide of flesh and steel that threatened to overwhelm the South Vietnamese defenses.

In the midst of the chaos, Lieutenant Nguyen Van Thao of the 362nd Security Battalion found himself in the thick of the fighting, his rifle bucking in his hands as he fired round after round into the enemy ranks. Beside him, his fellow soldiers fell one by one, their bodies torn and bloodied by the relentless barrage of NVA fire.

As the enemy pressed forward, Thao knew that they were running out of time, that they would soon be forced to fall back towards the city center. But even as he gave the order to retreat, he couldn't shake the feeling of despair that threatened to overwhelm him, the sense that they were fighting a losing battle against an enemy that would stop at nothing to achieve victory.

For Private Hai and Sergeant Tran, the battle was a blur of smoke and fire, a relentless push forward that seemed to consume every ounce of their strength and courage. They watched as their comrades fell around them, their bodies shattered by the ARVN defenses.

But still, they pressed on, driven by a sense of duty and purpose that transcended the horror of the battlefield.

As the sun began to sink towards the horizon, the NVA forces finally broke through the ARVN lines, surging forward into the outskirts of Phuoc Long itself. The South Vietnamese troops, battered and bloodied, fell back towards the city center, their ranks thinning with every passing moment.

For Captain Quang and his men, it was a bitter pill to swallow, a stark reminder of the desperate situation they now faced. They had fought bravely, had given everything they had to hold back the enemy tide. But in the end, it had not been enough, and now they found themselves in a fight for their very survival, a battle that would determine the fate of Phuoc Long and the country they had sworn to defend.

As the NVA forces consolidated their gains and prepared for the final push into the city, the stage was set for a clash that would echo through the ages, a battle that would test the courage and resolve of every man and woman caught in its terrible embrace. And for those who fought and died on that blood-soaked field, there was no greater honor, no higher calling, than to give their lives in defense of their homeland and their way of life.

Bien Hoa Air Base, South Vietnam

Granier was hunched over a map of the Phuoc Long province when the door to the command center burst open. Coyle marched in.

"We have another situation," Coyle said. "The NVA have crossed the border. They're hitting Phuoc Long with everything they've got. Three divisions. In all, fourteen thousand men and that's not counting the VC units joining them once they entered South Vietnam."

"Jesus," said Granier. He had known this day was coming, had seen the signs and warnings for weeks now. But somehow, hearing it out loud made it all too real.

"What's the status of our forces in the area?" he asked.

Coyle shook his head, "Not good. The ARVN units are putting up a fight, but they're outgunned and outnumbered. It's only a matter of time before the defenses collapse completely."

Granier nodded as he processed the information. "Van, our CIA translator," he said, his voice barely above a whisper. "…and his family. They're still in Phuoc Long, aren't they?"

Coyle's face darkened, "Yeah, they are. And if the VC find out they've been helping us, they're as good as dead. The same is true with the teachers, plantation owners, government officials, judges, police, journalists, intellectuals, Catholic priests, and anyone accused of collaborating with the ARVN or the Americans, including doctors and nurses. They're all targets of the Viet Cong."

Granier felt a wave of guilt wash over him. These were people they had worked with, relied on, promised to protect. And now, they were in mortal danger, caught in the crosshairs of a war that had already claimed too many innocent lives. "We have to get them out," he said. "We can't just leave them there to die."

Coyle nodded, "I know. I'm taking the C-119 and the Chinooks straight into Phuoc Long airfield. We'll extract as many of them as we can, bring them back to safety."

"Flying straight into Phuoc Long could get hairy if they shell the runway."

"Yeah. But there is no other airfield nearby. It'll take too long to shuttle the refugees using the Chinooks."

Granier felt a surge of admiration for his friend, mixed with a twinge of fear for his safety. Flying into a hot LZ was always a risky proposition, even for a pilot as skilled as Coyle. But he knew that there was no other choice, no other way to save the lives of those who had risked everything to help them. "I'm coming with you," he said, his voice brooking no argument. "I'll take a team to rescue our translator and his family."

As they made their way out of the command center, Granier could feel the adrenaline starting to pump through his veins, the familiar rush of excitement and fear that always came before a mission. He knew that what they were about to do was risky, that there were no guarantees of success or survival.

But he also knew that it was the right thing to do, the only thing that mattered in that moment. These were their allies, their friends, and they had made a promise to stand by them.

The Ghost Warriors grabbed their weapons and piled into the Chinooks and C-119. As Granier climbed into the cockpit of the C-119 beside Coyle, he felt a sense of purpose drowning out the fear and uncertainty. Granier knew that he would rather die trying than live with the knowledge that he had turned his back on those who needed him most.

A few minutes later, the aircraft lifted into the sky and headed toward the Cambodian border and Phuoc Long.

TWILIGHT OF WAR

Phuoc Long, South Vietnam

As the battle for Phuoc Long raged on, ARVN Captain Quang found himself in the thick of the fighting. His 362nd Security Battalion had been tasked with holding the main roads from Vinh Thuan to Bu Dang, a critical responsibility in the defense of the district.

Quang crouched behind a battered concrete wall, his rifle clutched tightly to his chest as he surveyed the chaos unfolding before him. The sound of gunfire and explosions filled the air, the acrid smell of smoke and cordite burning his nostrils.

Across the battlefield, NVA Private Hai advanced with his squad, the 7th Infantry Division pressing forward relentlessly. Hai's heart pounded in his chest as he moved through the shattered landscape, his eyes scanning the ruins for any sign of the enemy.

Suddenly, a burst of gunfire erupted from a nearby building, the bullets kicking up dirt and debris around Hai's feet. He dove for cover, his breath coming in ragged gasps as he huddled behind a pile of rubble.

From his vantage point, Captain Quang saw the NVA soldiers scattering, seeking shelter from the withering fire of his men. He shouted orders, directing his troops to concentrate their fire on the enemy positions.

Private Hai risked a glance over the top of his cover, his eyes widening as he saw an ARVN soldier aiming his rifle directly at him. In that moment, time seemed to slow, the world narrowing to the space between the two men.

Hai raised his own weapon, his finger tightening on the trigger. But before he could fire, a sudden explosion rocked the ground beneath him, sending him sprawling to the dirt.

Captain Quang saw the NVA soldier fall, saw the opportunity to press the advantage. With a yell, he ordered his men forward, urging them to close the distance and engage the enemy at close quarters.

As the ARVN soldiers surged forward, Private Hai struggled to his feet, his head ringing from the concussion of the blast. He looked up to see the enemy advancing, their bayonets fixed.

In that moment, Hai knew that he was fighting not just for his own life, but for the future of his country. He gripped his rifle tighter, steeling himself for the clash to come.

The two sides met in a brutal melee, rifle butts and bayonets flashing in the sun as they fought hand-to-hand. Captain Quang found himself face to face with a young NVA soldier, their eyes locking for a brief moment before they lunged at each other, weapons forgotten in the primal struggle for survival.

Through the din of battle, Quang could hear the distant sound of helicopters, the thump of their rotors drawing closer with each passing second. He knew that they were coming to evacuate the civilians, to save as many lives as they could in the face of overwhelming odds.

But for now, his focus was on the enemy in front of him, on the struggle for control of the shattered ruins of Phuoc Long. And as he fought, he sent up a silent prayer for the lives of the civilians caught in the crossfire, for the men under his command, and for the fate of his beloved country.

Phuoc Long Airfield, South Vietnam

The C-119 shuddered as another explosion rocked the earth below, sending a ball of fire into the air, the shockwave buffeting the aircraft like a leaf in a hurricane. In the cockpit, Coyle gripped the controls with white-knuckled intensity, his eyes scanning the chaos of the Phuoc Long airfield as he lined up for approach.

Beside him, Granier sat in the navigator's seat. He knew that there was nothing he could do to help, that the fate of the mission and the lives of those on the ground rested squarely on Coyle's shoulders.

"One mile out," Coyle said, his voice tense but focused over the roar of the engines. "Runway looks like hell."

Granier nodded, his eyes fixed on the scene unfolding before them. In the distance, he could see the muzzle flashes of the NVA artillery, the shells arcing through the sky like deadly fireworks, exploding across the runway and ripping corrugated metal building apart like cardboard.

As Coyle guided the C-119 toward the ravaged Phuoc Long airfield, the true extent of the devastation became apparent. The runway and surrounding areas were littered with the twisted, burning wrecks of both civilian and military aircraft, evidence of the relentless NVA artillery bombardment.

Off to one side of the runway, the shattered remains of a South Vietnamese Air Force C-47 transport plane lay crumpled and smoldering. Its once-proud fuselage was now riddled with jagged holes, the metal torn and blackened by the force of the explosions. One wing had been completely sheared off, the ragged edges still glowing with the heat of the fires that had consumed it.

Nearby, the wreckage of a civilian Cessna 172 Skyhawk bore mute witness to the indiscriminate nature of the shelling. The small, single-engine plane had been caught on the ground when the attack began, its pilot and passengers unable to escape in time. Now, it lay on its side, the cockpit a twisted mass of metal and glass, the once-white fuselage stained with soot and blood.

Across the tarmac, the burned-out husk of an American-made Bell UH-1 Huey helicopter sat forlornly, its rotors bent and warped by the heat of the flames. The Huey had been a workhorse of the South Vietnamese Army, ferrying troops and supplies to the front lines of the conflict. But now, it was just another casualty of the war, its crew either dead or fled in the face of the overwhelming onslaught.

Everywhere Coyle looked, the story was the same. Planes and helicopters, both military and civilian, reduced to piles of rubble and ash by the relentless pounding of the NVA guns. It was a scene of utter devastation, a stark reminder of the terrible toll that the war had taken on the people and machines of Vietnam.

The Chinooks, their rotors still spinning defiantly, sat untouched on the far side of the runway, their crews working frantically to load desperate refugees aboard. "The Chinooks are already on the ground," Granier said. "But they're sitting ducks out there. We need to get in and out fast."

Coyle grunted in acknowledgment, his hands flying over the controls as he made minute adjustments to their course. He was a master of his craft, a pilot who could coax impossible feats out of even the most unwieldy of aircraft.

As the C-119 approached the war-torn airfield of Phuoc Long, the runway stretched out before Coyle, a patchwork of jagged concrete and gaping craters. Coyle knew that landing on such a surface would be a challenge, even for a pilot of his skill and experience. The C-119 was a large, unwieldy aircraft, not designed for the kind of precision maneuvering that this situation required. "Hold on," he said, his voice barely audible over the din. "This is going to be rough."

As the plane descended towards the runway, Coyle could see the extent of the damage up close. The concrete surface pitted with holes and debris. Smoke rose from the smoldering wrecks of destroyed aircraft, and the air was thick with the acrid stench of burning fuel and rubber.

Coyle eyes scanned the runway for the best path forward. He knew that he would have to dodge the worst of the craters, threading the needle between the jagged edges of broken concrete and the twisted metal of wrecked vehicles.

With a deft touch on the controls, Coyle brought the C-119 down towards the runway, the landing gear extended and ready. The plane shuddered as it touched down on the broken concrete, the wheels bouncing and skidding on the uneven surface.

Coyle fought to keep the aircraft steady, his arms straining against the controls as he worked to maintain his heading. The C-119 veered to the left, then to the right, as he swerved to avoid a particularly large crater that loomed ahead.

For a moment, it seemed as if the plane might lose control, might careen off the runway and into the smoldering wreckage that lined the edges. But Coyle held firm as he coaxed the aircraft back on course.

The C-119 shuddered and bounced, the fuselage groaning under the strain of the rough landing. But Coyle kept his focus, his eyes locked on the end of the runway that was rapidly approaching.

The plane roared down the last few hundred feet of shattered concrete, dodging the final few craters and obstacles with a sudden, jarring swerve. And then, with a shuddering jolt, the C-119 rolled to a stop, its engines whining as Coyle eased back on the throttle.

For a moment, there was silence in the cockpit, broken only by the sound of Coyle's ragged breathing and the distant crackle of gunfire. The Ghost Warriors sat stunned, their faces pale and their hands shaking with the adrenaline of the landing.

Coyle leaned back in his seat, his hands trembling slightly as he released his grip on the controls. He knew that they had been lucky, that the landing could easily have ended in disaster. But he also knew that luck was a fickle thing in war, and not to be discounted.

There was no time to celebrate, no time to rest. The refugees were still waiting, the Chinooks still vulnerable to the relentless artillery fire.

Explosions blossomed all around them, the shockwaves slamming into the aircraft like a prizefighter's blows. Granier could feel the heat of the flames, could smell the acrid tang of burning fuel. "Grab your gear and let's get going," said Granier to his team.

Thirty seconds later, they were on the ground and advancing toward the city, their weapons sweeping the surrounding area.

Coyle and his aircrew helped refugees aboard the C-119. He knew they couldn't take everyone, there were too many, and he needed to leave room for Granier and his team plus the translator and his family. It was a hard choice deciding who boarded the aircraft.

Route 14, South Vietnam

As the sound of gunfire and explosions drew ever closer, Thi Pham clutched her young daughter close to her chest, her heart pounding with fear and desperation. Around her, a sea of humanity surged down Route 14, a ragtag collection of refugees fleeing the carnage that had engulfed their homes and villages.

Thi had seen the terror firsthand, had watched as the North Vietnamese troops swept through the countryside like a plague, leaving nothing but death and destruction in their wake. She had grabbed her daughter and what few possessions she could carry, and joined the desperate throng of refugees seeking safety and protection.

Now, as she stumbled down the dusty road, her feet blistered and bleeding, Thi found herself swept along by the current of bodies. Ahead, she could see a column of ARVN troops marching towards Phuoc Long, their faces unsure.

For a moment, Thi felt a flicker of hope. Surely these soldiers, with their guns and tanks, would be able to protect them, to stem the tide of the North Vietnamese advance. She pushed forward, her daughter whimpering softly in her arms, desperate to reach the safety of the military convoy.

But as she drew closer, Thi realized that something was wrong. The soldiers looked haggard and worn, their uniforms tattered and stained with blood. Many were limping or leaning on their comrades for support, their eyes haunted by the horrors they had witnessed.

Suddenly, the air was rent by a deafening explosion, and the world around Thi erupted into chaos. Artillery shells rained down on the road, shattering bodies and sending shrapnel flying in all directions.

Thi felt a searing pain in her back and legs, and she stumbled forward, her vision blurring with tears. Around her, the refugees were screaming and crying, their bodies torn and bloodied by the relentless barrage.

Through the haze of pain and confusion, Thi saw the ARVN soldiers struggling to take cover, their ranks thinned by the deadly artillery fire. Some were trying to help the wounded refugees, while others simply huddled in terror, their weapons forgotten in the face of the onslaught.

And then, in a moment of stark clarity, Thi realized the terrible truth. The refugees, in their desperate quest for safety, had unwittingly become human shields for the ARVN troops. Their bodies, shattered and broken, had absorbed the worst of the shrapnel and debris, protecting the soldiers from the full force of the artillery barrage.

Thi clutched her daughter tighter, her mind reeling with the horror of it all. She had come seeking protection, had believed that the soldiers would be their salvation. But instead, she and her fellow refugees had become nothing more than expendable assets, their lives sacrificed on the altar of a war.

Through the smoke and the chaos, Thi could see the North Vietnamese troops advancing in the distance, their guns blazing as they pushed forward towards the shattered remnants of the ARVN column. She knew that they would show no mercy, that they would slaughter the wounded and the helpless without a second thought.

And so, with a final burst of strength, Thi staggered to her feet, her daughter clinging to her neck with a fierce grip. She pushed forward, past the broken bodies of her fellow refugees, past the shell-shocked ARVN soldiers who had failed to protect them.

She didn't know where she was going, or what lay ahead. All she knew was that she had to keep moving, had to find some way, any way, to keep her daughter safe. It was a slim hope, a fragile thing, but it was all she had left in a world gone mad with violence and despair.

And as the battle raged on around her, Thi stumbled forward into the unknown, a refugee seeking shelter in a land torn asunder by the forces of history and the folly of men.

The Bridge

Phuoc Long, South Vietnam

As Granier and his team moved through the war-ravaged streets of Phuoc Long, the sound of gunfire and explosions echoed all around them, a constant reminder of the chaos and destruction that had engulfed the city. The once-bustling neighborhoods and markets were now a warped maze of rubble and debris, the buildings pockmarked with bullet holes and scorch marks.

Granier led the way, his rifle held at the ready as he picked his way through the shattered remains of homes and shops. Behind him, the rest of the team followed in a tight, staggered formation, their eyes scanning the shadows for any signs of danger.

As they pushed deeper into the city, the sounds of battle grew louder and more intense. To their left, a fierce firefight raged between a group of NVA soldiers and a squad of ARVN troops, the two sides trading bursts of automatic weapons fire and the occasional grenade.

Granier signaled for his team to take cover, and they ducked into the shell of a ruined building, pressing themselves against the crumbling walls as the bullets whizzed overhead. For a moment, they watched the battle unfold, the NVA soldiers advancing while the ARVN troops fought to hold their ground using whatever they could as cover.

But as much as Granier felt the urge to join the fight, to lend his team's firepower to the beleaguered South Vietnamese soldiers, he knew that it was not their mission. They were here for one purpose and one purpose only - to find the translator and his family and bring them to safety.

With a nod to his team, Granier motioned for them to move out, and they slipped away from the firefight, sticking to the shadows and the side streets as they made their way towards the translator's neighborhood.

As they walked, they passed scenes of unimaginable devastation - homes reduced to piles of rubble, streets littered with the bodies of civilians and animals caught in the crossfire, the air thick with the stench of death and decay. It was a hellish reveal of the brutal realities of war.

But still, they pushed on, their focus unwavering. They had a job to do, a promise to keep, and they would not be deterred by the chaos and the carnage that surrounded them.

Finally, after what seemed like an eternity of navigating the war-torn streets, they reached the translator's neighborhood. The houses here were still standing, but they bore the scars of the fighting that had swept through the area - shattered windows, bullet-riddled walls, doors splintered and hanging off their hinges.

Granier motioned for his team to fan out, to search the houses one by one until they found their objective.

They moved quickly and efficiently, their weapons at the ready, their senses on high alert.

But as they searched, a growing sense of unease settled over them. The houses were empty, the streets deserted. There was no sign of the translator or his family, no indication that anyone had been here for days.

And then, as they rounded a corner and entered a small courtyard, they saw it - a sight that stopped them cold in their tracks, a horror that would stay with them for the rest of their lives.

There, hanging from a makeshift gallows, was the body of the translator, his lifeless eyes staring sightlessly at the sky. And on the ground beneath him, sprawled in a pool of their own blood, were the bodies of his wife and children, their faces frozen in expressions of terror and agony.

For a moment, Granier and his team could only stare in shock, their minds reeling from the brutality of what they were seeing. And then, as the reality of their failure sank in, a wave of grief and searing pain that cut to the very core of their being.

They had come too late, had failed in their mission to save the very people they had sworn to protect. And now, as they stood in the shadow of that terrible sight, they knew that they would carry the weight of that failure with them forever, a burden that would never truly be lifted.

And so, with heavy hearts they turned away from the courtyard and the terrible sight that awaited them there. They had other lives to save, other promises to keep in this war-torn land.

The bridge…

As Granier and his team made their way back to the airfield through the battle-scarred streets of Phuoc Long, the sound of gunfire and explosions grew louder with each passing step. They had seen the horrors of what the NVA and Viet Cong were capable of, had witnessed the brutal execution of the translator and his family. And now, as they pushed towards the airfield and the promise of escape, they knew that every second counted.

As they rounded a corner, they came upon a scene of utter chaos. Civilians were running for their lives, their faces filled with terror as they fled across a narrow bridge that spanned a rushing river. NVA troops were closing in, their weapons blazing as they sought to cut off the escape route.

Mortar and artillery rounds exploded all around, the shockwaves slamming into the bridge and sending bodies flying into the churning waters below. Women screamed, children cried, and the air was filled with the stench of blood and smoke.

Without hesitation, Granier and his team sprang into action. They took up positions on the near side of the bridge, their weapons at the ready as they sought to buy time for the civilians to make their escape. Johnson and Nguyen laid down a withering barrage of covering fire, while Chen and Granier used their sniper rifles to pick off the enemy soldiers one by one with deadly precision.

But even as they fought, Granier could see that it wasn't going to be enough. The NVA were too many, their numbers seeming to grow with every passing moment. And the civilians, many of them elderly or carrying young children, were moving too slowly, their progress hampered by fear. It was only a matter of minutes before the NVA would outrun those that had already escaped across the bridge.

In that moment, Granier knew what he had to do. He turned to his engineer, a young man named Tran, and gave him a curt nod.

"Rig the bridge," he said, his voice tight with urgency. "We need to blow it before the NVA can cross."

Tran didn't hesitate. He pulled a satchel of explosives from his pack and set to work, his hands moving with practiced efficiency as he climbed under the bridge and wired the charges to the support struts. It was a delicate operation, one that required precision and skill. But Tran was one of the best.

As Tran worked, Granier and the others continued to hold off the enemy, their barrels of their weapons growing hot as they fired round after round into the advancing horde. But even as they fought, Granier could feel a sense of dread growing in the pit of his stomach.

Civilians were still running across the bridge, their faces contorted with fear and desperation. And as he looked out over the chaos, Granier saw a young woman, her leg twisted and bloody, dragging herself towards safety. She was so close, just a few feet from the end of the bridge. But then, out of nowhere, a group of NVA soldiers appeared, their hands reaching out to grab her and drag her back.

In that moment, Granier knew that he was out of time. He had to make a choice, one that would haunt him for the rest of his days. On one side of the bridge were the civilians who had already made it across, their lives hanging in the balance. On the other were those who were still trying to escape, their only hope of survival the narrow span of metal and concrete that stretched out before them.

Granier closed his eyes as he made his decision. Then, with a heavy heart, he gave the order. "Blow it," he said, his voice barely a whisper.

Tran didn't hesitate. He triggered the detonator, and the world erupted in a flash of light and sound. The bridge buckled and twisted, the metal shrieking as it tore itself apart. And then, with a roar that seemed to shake the very foundations of the earth, it collapsed into the river below, taking with it the lives of those who had been too slow, too weak, too unlucky to make it across.

Through the smoke and the dust, Granier could see the young woman, her eyes wide with terror as she was dragged back by the NVA soldiers. And then, in a moment that would stay with him forever, she was gone, swallowed up by the churning waters and the rubble of the shattered bridge.

As the dust settled over the jagged remains of the bridge, Granier stood motionless, his rifle hanging limply at his side. Around him, the cries of the wounded and the dying filled the air, a terrible symphony of human suffering that echoed in his ears like a twisted lullaby.

For a long moment, Granier couldn't move, couldn't breathe. His mind reeled with the enormity of what had just happened, with the terrible knowledge that he had been responsible for the deaths of so many innocent people.

He had always prided himself on his detachment, on his ability to compartmentalize the violence and the bloodshed that were an integral part of his job. As a sniper, he had taken countless lives without hesitation, had pulled the trigger with a steady hand and a clear eye, secure in the knowledge that he was doing what needed to be done.

But now, as he stood amidst the carnage and the chaos, something deep inside him began to crack and splinter. The walls he had so carefully constructed around his emotions, the barriers he had erected to keep the horror at bay, came crashing down with a force that left him reeling.

He saw the faces of the people he had killed, the men and women whose lives he had ended with a single, well-placed shot. He heard their screams, saw the blood and the brains and the shattered bones, and felt a wave of revulsion and self-loathing wash over him like a tidal wave.

And then, in a moment of terrible clarity, he saw the face of the young girl, the one he had watched disappear beneath the churning waters of the river. Her eyes, wide with terror and incomprehension, seemed to bore into his very soul, accusing him, condemning him for his actions.

Granier felt his knees buckle, and he sank to the ground, his rifle clattering to the dirt beside him. He buried his face in his hands, his shoulders shaking with silent sobs as the weight of his sins came crashing down upon him.

For so long, he had convinced himself that he was doing the right thing, that his actions were justified by the larger cause he served. But now, in the face of so much senseless death and destruction, those justifications rang hollow and empty.

He had become a monster, a soulless killing machine who had lost touch with his own humanity.

And in that moment, as he knelt amidst the rubble and the ruin, Granier knew that he could never go back to the way things had been before.

Something had broken inside him, some fundamental part of his being that could never be repaired. The cold-blooded sniper was gone, replaced by a man who was raw and bleeding, torn apart by the realization of his own complicity in the horrors of war.

And yet, even as he grappled with the weight of his own guilt and shame, Granier knew that he could not simply walk away, could not abandon the mission that had brought him to this place. He had a job to do, a duty to fulfill, and he would see it through to the end, no matter the cost to his own soul.

But as he rose to his feet and picked up his rifle, Granier knew that he would never be the same again. The bridge had been more than just a physical structure - it had been a symbol of his own disconnection from the human cost of his actions. And now that it lay shattered and broken, so too did the facade of detachment and indifference that he had so carefully cultivated over the years.

In the days and weeks to come, Granier would struggle to come to terms with his new reality, to find some way to reconcile the man he had been with the man he had become. It would be a long and painful journey, one that would test him in ways he had never been tested before.

But for now, as he turned his back on the smoking ruins of the bridge and the terrible knowledge of what he had done, Granier knew only one thing for certain - that he would never again be able to look at the world through the cold, unfeeling eyes of a sniper. He had been forever changed, and there could be no going back.

The airfield…

As Granier and his team approached the airfield, the roar of the C-119's engines filled the air, a welcome sound after the chaos and carnage of the city streets. They had made it back, battered and bloodied but alive, their mission complete even as the weight of what they had seen and done hung heavy.

Coyle was waiting for them as they climbed aboard the aircraft, his face filled with concern and anticipation. He had heard the explosions, had seen the smoke rising from the direction of the city, and he knew that something had gone terribly wrong.

As Granier stepped into the cargo hold, Coyle grabbed him by the shoulders, his eyes searching his friend's face for answers.

"Where are they?" he asked, "The translator and his family. Where are they?"

For a moment, Granier couldn't speak. The words stuck in his throat, the images of what he had seen flashing through his mind like a nightmare on repeat. He could still see the translator's body, swinging gently in the breeze, could still hear the screams of the civilians as they fled across the bridge.

Finally, he forced himself to meet Coyle's gaze, his eyes haunted and filled with pain.

"They're dead," he said, his voice barely a whisper. "The NVA got to them before we could. They executed the translator, shot his family. We were too late."

Coyle's face went slack with shock, his grip on Granier's shoulders loosening as the weight of the news sank in. For a moment, he couldn't speak, couldn't move, his mind reeling with the horror of what he had just heard.

Behind them, Johnson and Nguyen climbed into the cargo hold, their faces ashen. Chen followed close behind, his eyes downcast and his shoulders slumped with exhaustion and grief.

Coyle looked at them each in turn, his eyes searching their faces for some sign of hope, some glimmer of good news amidst the darkness. But there was none to be found, only the awful, unspoken truth of what they had witnessed.

Finally, he turned back to Granier, his voice thick with emotion. "What happened out there?" he asked, almost pleading. "What went wrong?"

"Everything," he said, his voice raw and broken. "Everything went wrong. The NVA were everywhere, the civilians were caught in the crossfire. We tried to save as many as we could, but it wasn't enough. It was never going to be enough."

He told Coyle about the bridge, about the impossible choice he had been forced to make. About the young woman, dragging herself to safety only to be pulled back by the enemy, about the explosives that had torn the bridge apart and sealed the fate of those still trying to cross.

Around them, the rest of the team stood in silence, their heads bowed and their hearts heavy with the weight of what they had seen and done. They had completed their mission, had saved as many lives as they could. But the cost had been high, the toll on their souls immeasurable.

As the C-119 lifted off from the shattered runway of

Phuoc Long airfield, Granier and his team knew that they would carry the scars of this day with them forever. The faces of the dead, the screams of the dying, the impossible choices that they had been forced to make in the name of duty and honor.

Saigon, South Vietnam

In the halls of power in Saigon, the mood was one of growing unease. As reports from the front lines at Phuoc Long filtered in, painting an increasingly dark picture of the ARVN's chances against the North Vietnamese onslaught, the South Vietnamese leadership found themselves absorbed by a sense of impending doom.

In the grand presidential palace, President Thieu sat hunched over his desk as he pored over the latest intelligence reports. The news was dire - the NVA had committed three full divisions to the battle, along with a fearsome array of armor and artillery. Against such overwhelming firepower, the ARVN forces were struggling to hold their ground.

Thieu's advisors clustered around him. They urged him to act, to release the reserves and send reinforcements to bolster the flagging South Vietnamese defense. But Thieu hesitated, his mind torn between the need to save his men and the fear of the political consequences that such a move might bring. Even now, there were those generals that questioned Thieu's decisions and his ability to lead in these perilous times. Thieu know that South Vietnam could not withstand another coup and survive.

In the Joint General Staff headquarters, the

atmosphere was no less tense. General Vien, the Chief of the Joint General Staff, leaned over a map of the Phuoc Long region, his fingers tracing the lines of the NVA advance. He had warned Thieu of the danger, had pleaded with him to approve the deployment of additional troops. But the president had been noncommittal, his indecision a source of growing frustration for the military leadership.

As the hours ticked by and the situation at Phuoc Long grew ever more desperate, Vien's patience finally snapped. He picked up the phone and dialed the presidential palace, his voice tense with barely controlled anger as he demanded to speak with Thieu himself.

The conversation was brief and terse, with Vien laying out the stakes in no uncertain terms. By letting the North Vietnamese attack one city at a time and refusing to reinforce the ARVN troops in place, Thieu was handing the North guaranteed victories, allowing them to consolidate their forces and surround the ARVN with no chance of repercussions. If Thieu did not act, if he did not release the reserves and send reinforcements, then Phuoc Long would fall, and with it, perhaps the entire III Corps region.

For a long moment, there was silence on the other end of the line. Then, finally, Thieu spoke, his voice heavy with resignation. He would not release the reserves, would not send additional troops. The risk was too great, the potential for political fallout too high. South Vietnam's soldiers must be reserved for the defense of the major cities of Hue, Da Nang, Saigon, and the Mekong Delta, South Vietnam's rice bowl.

Vien slammed the phone down in disgust, his face

flushed with anger and frustration. He knew that Thieu's decision had just sealed the fate of the men fighting and dying at Phuoc Long, had condemned them to a battle that they could not hope to win.

But even as he grappled with the weight of that realization, Vien knew that he could not let his own despair show. He was an officer, a leader of men, and he had a duty to those under his command. And so, with a heavy heart, he turned back to the map as he sought some way, any way, to snatch victory from the jaws of defeat.

In the streets of Saigon, the mood was one of growing anxiety and fear. Rumors of the battle at Phuoc Long had begun to spread, and with them, a sense of impending doom. Phuoc Long was less than sixty miles from Saigon. The people of the city went about their daily lives with a sense of forced normalcy, but beneath the surface, tension simmered like a pot about to boil over.

At the U.S. Embassy, Ambassador Graham Martin watched the unfolding events with a sense of growing dread. He had long been an advocate of the American commitment to South Vietnam, had believed in the cause with a fervor that bordered on the messianic. But now, as the reports from Phuoc Long painted an increasingly bleak picture, he found himself confronted with the harsh reality of the war's endgame.

Martin knew that the fall of Phuoc Long would be a turning point, a signal to the world that the South Vietnamese government was crumbling from within. And he knew, too, that the United States could not hope to prop it up forever, that sooner or later, the American people were already tired of the endless bloodshed and were demanding an end to the conflict.

As he sat in his office Martin could not help but feel a sense of deep, abiding sadness. For all the sacrifices that had been made, for all the lives that had been lost, it seemed that the war in Vietnam was destined to end in tragedy and defeat.

And yet, even in that moment of despair, Martin clung to a flicker of hope, a belief that somehow, against all odds, the South Vietnamese people might yet find their courage and find a way to prevail. It was a slim hope, a fragile thing, but it was all he had left to cling to in the face of the gathering darkness.

And so, as the battle for Phuoc Long raged on and the fate of a nation was fading, the people of Saigon and the leaders tasked with defending them grappled with the bitter realities of a war that had already claimed too many lives, and whose final chapter was yet to be written. They faced the future with a mixture of fear and anxiety.

Phuoc Long, South Vietnam

As the battle of Phuoc Long reached its bloody climax, Private Chau of the PAVN 141st Regiment found himself in the heart of the chaos, his rifle clutched tightly as he advanced through the shattered streets of the town. The operation had been far from the assured victory his superiors had promised. And even the NVA were now winning, the ARVN had fought like tigers and many of his brothers had fallen.

Around him, his comrades surged forward, their faces twisted with the fierce determination of men who had given everything for the cause. They had endured hardships that most could scarcely imagine, had fought and bled and died for the dream of a united Vietnam, free from the yoke of foreign domination.

Chau had seen the tide of the war turn in their favor with each passing day. And now, as they stormed the last remaining strongholds of the ARVN defenders, he felt a sense of exhilaration and pride that engulfed him.

But even in the midst of the triumph, Chau could not shake the sense of unease that gnawed at his gut. He had seen too much death, had watched too many of his friends fall in the relentless pursuit of victory. And he knew, deep down, that the cost of this war would be paid for in generations to come.

As he rounded a corner, Chau came face to face with an ARVN soldier, his eyes wide with fear and desperation. For a moment, the two men stared at each other, their weapons raised and ready, both armed with bayonets. But then, in a moment of startling clarity, Chau saw the humanity in his enemy's eyes, saw the same hopes and fears and dreams that he himself harbored.

He hesitated, his finger hovering over the trigger of his rifle. And in that moment of hesitation, the ARVN soldier made his move, lunging forward with a desperate cry.

Chau reacted on instinct, his training taking over as he sidestepped the attack and brought his rifle to bear. A single shot rang out, and the ARVN soldier crumpled to the ground, his life snuffed out.

But even as Chau stared down at the quivering body of his dying enemy, he felt a sense of profound sadness. This was not the glorious victory he had imagined, not the noble sacrifice in the name of a greater cause. It was a tragedy, a waste of life that could never be undone.

Even in the midst of his despair, Chau knew that he had no choice but to press on, to see the battle through to its bitter end. He owed it to his comrades, to the memory of all those who had fallen in the long and bloody struggle for Vietnam's freedom.

As he stepped over the body of the fallen ARVN soldier and pushed deeper into the heart of Phuoc Long, Chau could not shake the sense that the world had shifted beneath his feet, that the very fabric of his reality had been torn asunder by the brutality and the horror of the war.

He thought of his family back home, of his mother and father and siblings who had sacrificed so much to support him in his struggle. He thought of the life he had left behind, of the simple joys and pleasures that had once seemed so important, but now felt like a distant memory, a half-forgotten dream.

And he knew, with a certainty that chilled him to his very core, that nothing would ever be the same again. The world had changed, and he had changed with it, forever altered by the crucible of war and the weight of all that he had seen and done. And so, with a heavy heart and a spirit that refused to be broken, Private Chau pressed on.

As the battle for Phuoc Long reached its devastating conclusion, the once vibrant town lay in ruins, a shell of its former self. The streets were littered with rubble and the bodies of the fallen, proof of the savage fighting that had raged for days on end.

For the soldiers of the North Vietnamese Army, the victory was hard-won but decisive. They had thrown everything they had into the battle, pouring in reinforcements and pounding the South Vietnamese defenses with a relentless barrage of artillery and tank fire. The 141st and 201st Regiments had spearheaded the assault, their troops battling house to house, street by street, until the last pockets of resistance were finally crushed.

But even as they savored their triumph, the North Vietnamese knew that the cost had been high. Many of their comrades had fallen in the fierce fighting, their blood staining the earth alongside that of their enemies. The scars of the battle would linger long after the guns had fallen silent.

For the South Vietnamese troops tasked with defending Phuoc Long, the battle had been a nightmare from the start. They had fought with skill and courage, but they were simply outmatched by the overwhelming firepower and numbers of the North Vietnamese forces.

Desperate attempts to reinforce the beleaguered garrison had met with disaster. Helicopters carrying troops from the 8/5th Infantry Division had been driven back by withering anti-aircraft fire, while resupply drops had gone awry, their precious cargo falling into enemy hands. The final bid to turn the tide, a daring insertion of the elite 81st Ranger Battalion, had ended in catastrophe, with entire companies annihilated by the North Vietnamese guns.

As the defenses crumbled and the enemy closed in, the South Vietnamese had fought on making the North Vietnamese pay for every inch of ground they took. But in the end, it wasn't enough. The town center and market, the last bastions of resistance, had been overrun in a final, bloody assault. Only a handful of defenders managed to escape the carnage, slipping away into the jungle under cover of darkness.

The fall of Phuoc Long sent shockwaves throughout South Vietnam. For the battered survivors of the ARVN, it was a bitter blow, a sign that their sacrifices and suffering had been in vain. They had given everything they had, but it had not been enough to stem the communist tide. Many began to despair, sensing that the end was now only a matter of time.

For the ordinary people of South Vietnam, the battle was a terrifying harbinger of what was to come. They had seen the might of the North Vietnamese war machine firsthand, had witnessed its terrible power and implacable resolve. Deep down, many knew that their government and armed forces could not hope to hold out forever against such an adversary.

Amidst the fear and despair, there were still those who clung to hope, however faint. They looked to their American allies for aid and comfort, praying that the world's greatest superpower would not abandon them in their hour of need. Some even dared to dream of a miraculous turnaround, of a reversal of fortune that would snatch victory from the jaws of defeat.

Such hopes would prove to be in vain. The fall of Phuoc Long marked the beginning of the end for South Vietnam, a final, inexorable slide towards collapse and defeat. The once bright future that so many had fought and died for grew dimmer by the day, as the shadow of communist domination loomed ever larger on the horizon.

The battle of Phuoc Long may have been lost, but the struggle for the soul of Vietnam would go on. In the end, it was this spirit, this unbreakable will, that would endure long after the last battle had been fought, the last shot fired.

Saigon, South Vietnam

President Thieu sat behind his ornate desk, his face a mask of barely contained fury as he stared down at the head of South Vietnamese intelligence, Colonel Tran Duc Lan. The room was heavy with Thieu's anger and disappointment.

"Colonel Lan," Thieu began, his voice deceptively calm, "I have just received reports from the front lines that paint a very different picture than the one you have been presenting to me. The North Vietnamese forces are not only stronger and more numerous than we anticipated, but they are also better equipped and more determined. Their morale soars while ours plummets."

Lan shifted uncomfortably in his seat, his face pale. "Mr. President," he began, his voice unsteady, "I can assure you that our intelligence has been thorough and accurate. We have been monitoring the enemy's movements closely and—"

But Thieu cut him off with a sharp wave of his hand, his eyes flashing with anger. "Spare me your assurances, Colonel," he snapped, his voice rising in volume. "The facts on the ground speak for themselves. We have underestimated the enemy, and now our troops are paying the price for your incompetence in blood."

He leaned forward, his gaze boring into Lan's face. "I have lost confidence in your ability to provide me with reliable intelligence," he said coldly. "From now on, I will be taking a more direct role in military operations. I will no longer rely on your reports or those of the CIA."

Lan's face drained of color, his mouth opening and closing soundlessly as he struggled to find words. "But

Mr. President," he managed at last, "I have been working closely with our American allies to gather the most up-to-date information. Surely you don't mean to disregard their input as well?"

Thieu's lips curled into a sneer, his voice dripping with contempt. "The Americans?" he scoffed. "They have their own agenda, their own interests. They will tell us what they think we want to hear, not what we need to know."

He rose from his desk, "No, Colonel Lan," he said firmly. "From this moment forward, I will trust only my own instincts and the reports of my field commanders. We cannot afford any more mistakes, any more miscalculations."

Lan rose shakily to his feet, his head bowed in defeat. "I understand, Mr. President," he said. "I will... I will do whatever you ask of me."

Thieu nodded curtly, his eyes still hard and unyielding. "See that you do, Colonel," he said coldly. "The fate of our nation hangs by a thread. We cannot afford to fail."

With that, he turned and strode from the room, leaving Lan alone with his thoughts and his shame. The intelligence chief slumped back into his chair, his head in his hands as the weight of his failure crashed down upon him.

He had let his president down, had failed in his most sacred duty. And now, with Thieu taking direct control of the military, the future of South Vietnam was more uncertain than ever.

In the end, that was all that mattered - the survival of his nation, the protection of his people. And he would do whatever it took to ensure that South Vietnam emerged victorious from this long and bitter struggle.

Washington DC, United States of America

In the hallowed halls of the United States Congress, a fierce debate raged over the fate of South Vietnam. President Gerald Ford had come before the legislative body, pleading for additional aid to bolster the beleaguered nation in its fight against the communist North. But even as he spoke, it was clear that his words were falling on deaf ears.

In the House of Representatives, the mood was one of skepticism and outright hostility. Many of the members had been elected on a platform of ending American involvement in Vietnam, and they saw Ford's request as a betrayal of that promise. They spoke passionately of the need to bring the troops home, to stop pouring American blood and treasure into a conflict that seemed to have no end.

Representative Elizabeth Holtzman, a young Democrat from New York, stood to deliver a scathing rebuke of the president's position. "How many more lives must be lost, how many more billions of dollars must be squandered, before we admit that this war is unwinnable?" she asked, her voice ringing out over the chamber. "The American people have spoken, Mr. President. They want an end to this madness, not another blank check for a corrupt and incompetent regime."

Holtzman's words were met with a chorus of cheers and applause from her fellow Democrats, while the Republicans sat in stony silence. They knew that the tide of public opinion had turned against the war, and that to support the president's request would be political suicide.

In the senate, the debate was no less heated. Senator George McGovern, the Democratic nominee for president in 1972 and a long-time critic of the war, took to the floor to denounce Ford's request. "This is not our fight," he declared, his voice heavy with emotion. "The Vietnamese people must determine their own destiny, without American interference. We have done enough damage, caused enough suffering. It is time for us to leave, to let the chips fall where they may."

But even as McGovern spoke, there were those who argued for a different course. Senator John Tower, a Republican from Texas, stood to defend the president's position. "We cannot abandon our allies in their hour of need," he insisted, his voice rough with conviction. "To do so would be a betrayal of everything we stand for as a nation. We must stand with South Vietnam, must give them the tools they need to defend themselves against communist aggression."

Tower's words were met with scattered applause from his fellow Republicans, but it was clear that they were in the minority. The mood in the Senate was one of disillusionment and war-weariness, a sense that the time had come to cut their losses and move on.

In the end, the vote was not even close. Both the house and the senate resoundingly rejected Ford's request for additional aid, delivering a stinging rebuke to the president and his policy. The message was clear: the American people had had enough of the war in Vietnam, and they would no longer support any effort to prolong the conflict.

As the final votes were tallied, a sense of resignation settled over the Capitol. For better or worse, the

United States had abandoned its ally, had left South Vietnam to fend for itself against the might of the communist North. Some saw it as a betrayal, a shameful abdication of American responsibility. Others saw it as a long-overdue recognition of reality, a necessary first step on the road to healing the wounds of a nation torn apart by war.

But for the people of South Vietnam, the message was all too clear. They were on their own now, left to face the onslaught of the communist forces without the support of their once-powerful ally. The future looked bleak, the path ahead filled with uncertainty and danger.

In the White House, President Ford sat in his office, his head in his hands as he contemplated the meaning of the vote. He had staked his presidency on the idea that America could not abandon its allies, that it had a moral obligation to stand with those who shared its values. But now, that vision lay in tatters, shattered by the cold reality of a nation tired of war and sacrifice.

As he looked out the window at the sun setting over the nation's capital, Ford knew that the decision had been made by its citizens and their representatives. America would leave Vietnam to its fate, would turn its back on the people it had once pledged to defend. It was a bitter pill to swallow, a painful acknowledgment of the limits of American power and will.

But even in that moment of defeat, Ford knew that the struggle was not over, that the fight for freedom and democracy would go on, in Vietnam and around the world. America might have lost this battle, but the war for the soul of a nation, for the future of a people, was far from over.

TWILIGHT OF WAR

Hanoi, North Vietnam

In the halls of the Politburo in Hanoi, an atmosphere of electric excitement filled the air. The stunning victory at Phuoc Long had sent shockwaves throughout the Communist leadership, igniting a newfound sense of confidence and ambition.

As the members of the Twenty-third Plenum gathered to discuss the implications of the battle, all eyes were on one man: Lieutenant General Tran Van Tra. The mastermind behind the daring Phuoc Long offensive, Tra had emerged as the North's newest hero, a symbol of the bold new direction the war was taking.

With a steely gaze and a voice filled with conviction, Tra addressed the assembled leaders. "Comrades, the fall of Phuoc Long has proven what we have long suspected - that the Americans have lost the will to fight, and that the ARVN is a paper tiger, ready to crumble at the first sign of our might."

A murmur of agreement rippled through the room, as the Politburo members nodded in assent. They had seen the reports, had studied the intelligence - the weakness of the South's defenses had been laid bare, and the opportunity for a decisive blow was now at hand.

But Tra was not content to rest on his laurels. With a sweeping gesture, he pointed to a map of South Vietnam, his finger coming to rest on the town of Duc Lap. "This should be our next target," he declared, his voice ringing with authority. "A border outpost in the heart of enemy territory - if we can take it, we will have a foothold for even greater victories to come."

Some of the Politburo members exchanged skeptical glances - Duc Lap was a daring target, and the risks were high. But Tra pressed on, his eyes blazing with a fierce determination. "We have a chance here, comrades, to seize the initiative and change the course of the war. We must not let it slip through our fingers."

As the debate raged on, one voice rose above the rest - that of Le Duc Tho, the wily strategist and confidant of General Secretary Le Duan. "I agree with Comrade Tra," he said, his words cutting through the din like a knife. "But why stop at Duc Lap? Why not aim even higher - at Buon Ma Thuot itself, the capital of the province?"

A hush fell over the room as the implications of Tho's words sank in. To attack Buon Ma Thuot would be a gamble of the highest order, a risk that could make or break the entire Communist cause. Le Duan, ever the cautious leader, hesitated.

But as he looked around the room, at the faces of his comrades filled with a newfound sense of purpose and resolve, he knew that the time for caution had passed. "Comrade Tho is right," he said at last, his voice ringing with a quiet authority. "We have a strategic advantage now that we have never had before. We must seize it with both hands."

With those words, the decision was made. General Dung, the North's most brilliant military mind, was ordered south to take command of the new offensive - Campaign 275, a name that would soon become synonymous with the turning of the tide in Vietnam.

As the meeting adjourned and the Politburo members filed out, a sense of history in the making hung heavy in the air. They had set their course, had chosen to embark on a path from which there could be no turning back.

In the streets of Hanoi, the news of the Politburo's

decision spread like wildfire. For the people of the North, who had endured so much hardship and sacrifice in the long years of war, it was a moment of great hope and anticipation. They could sense that the end was near, that the final victory was within their grasp.

And as the orders went out to the waiting armies, as the tanks and artillery pieces began to rumble south towards the border, a new chapter in the long and tragic history of Vietnam began to unfold.

The Americans had abandoned their allies, had lost the will to fight - and now, with the boldness and daring of leaders like Tra and Tho, with the courage and determination of the Vietnamese people, the North would seize the moment and the victory that had so long eluded them. The fate of a nation and a people would be decided, once and for all.

The Madness of War

Bien Hoa Air Base, South Vietnam

As the C-119 touched down on the tarmac at Bien Hoa Air Base, Coyle could sense that something was off with Granier. The normally unflappable sniper had been unusually quiet during the flight back, his gaze distant.

As they disembarked from the plane and made their way towards the hangar, Coyle watched his friend closely, noting the stiffness in his gait and the shadows in his eyes. It was clear that the events of the past few days had taken a toll on Granier, that the weight of what he had seen and done was hanging heavy on his shoulders.

But Coyle knew better than to push. Granier was a private man, a soldier who kept his own counsel and dealt with his demons in his own way. And so, as they entered the hangar and began the process of debriefing and resupply, Coyle gave his friend the space he needed, the time to process and come to terms with all that had happened.

Hours later, as the sun began to dip towards the horizon and the base settled into the uneasy quiet of the evening, Coyle found Granier sitting alone on a crate at the edge of the tarmac. The sniper was staring off into the distance, his rifle cradled loosely in his hands, his face a mask of inner turmoil.

Coyle approached slowly, his boots crunching on the gravel underfoot. "Hey, Granier, you okay?" he asked softly, his voice tinged with concern.

For a moment, Granier didn't respond, didn't even seem to register Coyle's presence. But then, with a visible effort, he shook himself out of his trance, his eyes focusing on his friend's face.

"Oh, yeah. I'm fine," he said, his voice flat and unconvincing.

Coyle frowned. "You don't look fine," he said gently, taking a seat beside his friend on the crate." What's going on?"

"It's none of your business, Coyle. I'll handle it myself."

"Right. Of course. I shouldn't pry."

"Then don't."

"Okay, but if you need to talk… I'm here."

"You're always here, Coyle. Maybe that's the problem."

"Got it," said Coyle getting up to leave. "I'll leave you alone."

"I know you're just trying to help, but there's really nothing you can do," said Granier softening. "Just tired, you know? It's been a long few days."

"Yeah. Some sack time would probably do us all a world of good."

Granier sighed, his shoulders slumping as if under

a great weight. "I don't know what's happening. This isn't like me," he said at last, his voice barely above a whisper. "It's just... it's all hitting me now, you know? The things we saw out there, the things we did..."

He trailed off, his eyes distant and haunted. Coyle nodded slowly, his own memories of the battle still fresh and raw. "I know," he said softly. "It's never easy, seeing the things we see, doing the things we have to do."

Granier shook his head, "It's more than that," he said, his voice tight and strained. "I've done things, Coyle. Things I never thought I'd do, things I never wanted to do. And now... now I don't know how to live with myself. Knowing what I'm capable of."

"Hey," Coyle said, his voice firm but gentle. "You did what you had to do out there, Granier. You saved lives; you protected the innocent. That's what matters."

But Granier just shook his head, his eyes filling with a deep, abiding pain. "Did I?" he asked. "Or did I just add to the body count, just contribute to the endless cycle of violence and death?"

Coyle sighed, understanding all too well the weight of the questions that plagued his friend. "I don't have all the answers, Granier. I'm pretty messed up myself." he said at last. "But I do know this - you're a good man. And whatever you did out there, you did it for the right reasons. That counts for something."

Granier was silent for a long moment, his gaze fixed on the distant horizon. Then, slowly, he nodded, a flicker of something like hope in his eyes. "Yeah," he said softly. "Yeah, I guess it does."

They sat like that for a while, two warriors bound by the weight of their shared experience, by the unbreakable bonds of brotherhood forged in the heat of battle.

That was the code of the soldier, the sacred trust that bound them one to the other. And in a world torn asunder by violence and chaos, it was all they had left to cling to, the only thing that made sense in the madness of war.

Granier sat at chow, his plate untouched. Coyle sat across from him and stabbed a roasted potato off of Granier's plate hoping for reaction. There was none. Then...

"It's not working," said Granier as if he had come to a conclusion after a deep think.

"What's not working?" said Coyle.

"What we're doing. We can't reach the refugees in time once an NVA assault on a city starts. They must have some list with addresses or maybe there are informants helping them."

"Maybe they have kill teams that move behind the front lines."

"Maybe... or maybe we're just too slow."

"So, what do you propose?"

"We need more intelligence, and we need to buy more time. We need to slow them down until we can reach our people."

"Sabotage?"

"Yeah, plus hit and run."

"Hit and run isn't going to slow down a division."

"Depends on who ya hit."

"I suppose that's true."

"We don't need to buy much time. Maybe an hour or two."

"We should put together a couple of teams. One for hit and run, and one for sabotage."

"Yeah. And maybe a third team for rescue. We send them in at first sign of an upcoming assault. We get ahead of the curve."

"That could work," said Granier feeling a bit more satisfied now that they were doing something about the situation.

"As far as more intelligence I'm not sure how effective it will be."

"What do you mean?"

"Beyond the occasional flyby, the US Air Force has ceased most of their reconnaissance flights since the Soviets outfitted the North Vietnamese with their new SAM2 missiles."

"What about South Vietnamese reconnaissance?"

"President Thieu has given up on his intelligence units. He thinks they're unreliable."

"That doesn't mean that they are unreliable."

"No, it doesn't, but it does mean Thieu is unwilling to commit resources to the intelligence group. He figures he's better off with reports from his field commanders."

"That's absurd."

"It's a strange strategy. I'll grant you that. Regardless, there's little chance we are going to get anything useful out of the South."

"The Americans still have satellites, don't they?"

"Yeah, but they're in the process of retasking them to other regions where they can be more productive."

"More productive?! No wonder we're losing the damned war," said Granier, then turned as if he had an idea… "What about creating our own reconnaissance flights?"

"It's a big country, Granier. We don't have the manpower or the aircraft."

"Okay, I can see that, but what if we could narrow it down to say a few miles and a narrow window of time?"

"Well, my aircrew and I could handle that. But we'd need some smaller planes. The Boxcar is just a big target waiting to have holes punched in it."

"Can we get smaller planes?"

"It'll take some doing… but yeah, we could get 'em. It's still a risky proposition."

"I wouldn't ask if I didn't think we really needed it."

"I know you wouldn't. Let me see what I can do."

"Thanks, Coyle."

"Those potatoes are pretty good."

Granier looked down at his plate reminded that he hadn't eaten all day. He dug in.

Command Post, South Vietnam

In a dimly lit command tent, two North Vietnamese generals, Lieutenant General Hoang Minh Thao and Major General Nguyen Huu An, huddled over a map of the Central Highlands, their eyes focused on the strategic city of Ban Me Thuot. They were discussing the upcoming offensive, weighing the options before them. The politburo was in the mood to takes calculated risks to quickly advance the revolution and they expected their field commanders to do the same.

General Thao, the commander of the Central Highlands Front, spoke first,. "Comrade, we have two paths before us. The first, a direct strike at the heart of the enemy, Ban Me Thuot itself. Swift, decisive, and with minimal damage to the city and its people."

General An, his subordinate, nodded thoughtfully. "It would catch the ARVN off guard, giving them little time to respond. But what of their outlying defenses at Pleiku and Tom Kum? They could still pose a threat to our flanks."

Thao acknowledged the concern with a tilt of his head. "True, but if we move quickly enough, secure the key highways, we can isolate the city and prevent reinforcements from reaching them. It's a gamble, but one that could pay off handsomely."

An traced his finger along the map, following the routes of Highways 14, 19, and 21. "And if we fail to secure the highways in time? The ARVN could mobilize up to a dozen regiments, armored brigades, artillery, and air support. It would be a costly fight."

"Which brings us to our second option," Thao said, his eyes flickering to the outlying ARVN installations marked on the map. "We destroy their outer defenses first, methodically, one by one. It would take longer, but it would ensure a more secure approach to Ban Me Thuot."

An considered this, "It would also give us time to assess their strength, adjust our strategies accordingly. But the longer we take, the more time the ARVN has to prepare, and the greater the risk of American intervention."

Thao's face darkened at the mention of the Americans. "Yes, their Seventh Fleet off our coast looms large. But our intelligence suggests they are unlikely to commit ground forces, at least not in significant numbers, but they might send in the aircraft. It's a factor we cannot ignore."

The two generals fell silent for a moment, each weighing the risks and rewards of the two strategies. Finally, Thao spoke, "We will proceed with the second option. Destroy the outlying defenses, but be prepared to switch to a direct assault if the opportunity presents itself. We must be flexible, adaptable, ready to seize the initiative at a moment's notice."

An nodded his assent, his eyes gleaming with a fierce resolve. "Understood, comrade. Our forces will be ready, poised to strike like a snake in the grass."

Thao was pleased with his subordinate's enthusiasm. "Good. But remember, comrade, our ultimate goal is not just the capture of Ban Me Thuot, but the liberation of our people, the unification of our homeland. Let that be the fire that drives our forces, the purpose that guides our every action."

An snapped to attention, his fist clenched in a salute. "For the revolution, comrade. For the people of Vietnam."

Thao returned the salute, his own fist raised in solidarity. "For the revolution, comrade. And for the certain victory that awaits us."

As the two generals bent once more over the map, their minds refocused on the details of the coming offensive. Ban Me Thuot would fall, and with it, the dreams of the American imperialists and their puppet regime in the South. And from the ashes of that victory, a new Vietnam would rise, united and free at last.

Cambodian Border

The night was dark and moonless as the North Vietnamese Army forces silently made their way through the rugged mountain pass that straddled the border between Cambodia and South Vietnam. The only sounds were the occasional crunch of boots on gravel and the muffled clanking of weapons and gear.

At the head of the infantry column, Major Nguyen Van Tho, a veteran of many campaigns, led his men. They had been preparing for this moment for months, training and equipping themselves for the decisive battle that lay ahead.

As they emerged from the pass, the sprawling hills of the Central Highlands stretched out before them, the distant lights of Ban Me Thuot twinkling on the horizon. Tho raised a clenched fist, and the column came to a halt, the soldiers fanning out to take up positions among the rocks and scrub brush.

In the eerie stillness of the night, Tho gathered his platoon leaders around him, their faces illuminated by the soft glow of a single flashlight. "Comrades," he began, his voice low and intense, "the time has come to strike a decisive blow against the enemy. The game has changed. The puppet regime in Saigon is crumbling, and the Americans have all but abandoned their allies. Ban Me Thuot is ripe for the taking."

He unfolded a worn map, tracing his finger along the contours of the terrain. "We will approach the city from multiple directions, using the hills and valleys to mask our movements. Our spies have provided us with detailed information on the enemy's defenses, and we will exploit their weaknesses without mercy."

The platoon leaders nodded, their eyes gleaming

with anticipation. They had waited long years for this moment, had sacrificed and suffered for the chance to strike a final blow against the hated enemy.

As the first hints of dawn began to lighten the eastern sky, the NVA forces moved out, spreading across the hills like a deadly virus.

In the distance, the people of Ban Me Thuot began to stir, unaware of the danger that lurked just beyond their doorsteps. For them, it was just another day in a city that had known too many days of war and suffering.

But for Major Tho and his men, it was the beginning of a new chapter in their struggle for liberation and unification. They were the vanguard of a new Vietnam, a nation that would rise from the ashes of war to take its rightful place in the world.

As the sun crept over the horizon, painting the hills in shades of gold and crimson, the NVA soldiers looked to the city with eyes filled with a fierce, unwavering resolve. They were ready for battle, prepared to sacrifice everything for the cause that had sustained them through the long years of hardship and struggle. With their preparations completed, they began their advance toward the distant city.

Command Tent, Cambodian Border

In a command tent situated in the rugged hills bordering South Vietnam, Lieutenant General Thao pored over a map. The reports from the field had been streaming in all morning, painting a picture of a city being surrounded with his troops advancing on multiple sides.

Thao's subordinate, Major General An, entered the tent, his face flushed with excitement. "Comrade General," he said, snapping off a crisp salute, "I have just received word from our forward units. The infantry has secured the key positions in the hills and valleys around the city. As far as we can tell, the enemy is unaware of our presence."

A rare smile flickered across Thao's face, but it was gone as quickly as it had appeared. "Excellent work, Comrade An," he said, his voice filled with a quiet intensity. "But we cannot afford to rest on our laurels. The enemy is still dangerous, and they will fight desperately to hold onto their last stronghold in the highlands."

He turned back to the map, his finger tracing the contours of the terrain. "It is time to bring up the artillery and armor," he said, his eyes narrowing. "We must pound the city into submission, break the will of the defenders before we move in for the final assault."

An nodded in agreement, "I will give the order immediately, Comrade General," he said. "Our gunners and tank crews are ready and eager to join the fight."

Thao looked up, fixing An with a piercing gaze. "Remind the field commanders of the importance of their task," he said. "The fate of this campaign, perhaps even the fate of our nation, rests on their shoulders. They must be precise, ruthless, and above all, relentless."

An saluted once more, his back ramrod straight. "They will not fail us, Comrade General," he said with conviction. "They know what is at stake, and they will give everything to ensure our victory."

As An strode from the tent, barking orders to his

subordinates, Thao turned back to the map. He knew that the coming days would be crucial, that the battle for Ban Me Thuot would be a turning point in the long and bitter struggle for Vietnam's future.

But he also knew that his men were ready, that they had been preparing for this moment for years. They were the most dedicated and fearless soldiers in the North Vietnamese Army.

Thao felt a surge of pride and confidence. The enemy was strong, but his men were stronger. They had the will, the courage, and the determination to see this fight through to the end.

Duc Co, South Vietnam

As the first light of dawn crept over the horizon, Captain Nguyen Van Bao of the North Vietnamese Army's 320th Division looked out over the rugged terrain of the Central Highlands. For months, he and his men had been preparing for this moment, stockpiling weapons and supplies, gathering intelligence on the enemy's defenses, and rehearsing their battle plans.

Now, as the distant sound of artillery fire echoed through the hills, Bao knew that the time had come. The offensive that would finally break the back of the South Vietnamese army and open the way to Saigon had begun.

Bao's unit had been tasked with attacking the ARVN base at Duc Co, a key outpost near the border with Cambodia. It was a daunting challenge, but one that Bao and his men were more than ready to meet.

As they moved through the dense jungle, Bao's thoughts turned to his family back home in the North.

He had not seen them in years, had missed the birth of his daughter and the growth of his young son. But he knew that their sacrifice was not in vain, that he was fighting for a better future for all of Vietnam.

Lieutenant Tran Van Hien of the ARVN's 23rd Division stood atop the fortified walls of the Duc Co base, his eyes scanning the dense jungle that stretched out before him. For weeks, he and his men had been on high alert, knowing that the North Vietnamese Army was on the move and that an attack could come at any moment.

Hien had grown up in a small village not far from Duc Co, had joined the ARVN to defend his homeland and his way of life. He believed in the cause of the South, in the dream of a Vietnam free from the yoke of communism.

But now, as he looked out over the rugged terrain of the Central Highlands, he could feel a sense of unease growing. The NVA was out there somewhere, amassing its forces, preparing to strike.

Suddenly, the stillness of the morning was shattered by the roar of artillery. Hien dove for cover. Shells rained down on the base, exploding with a deafening thunder that shook the earth and sent geysers of dirt and debris flying high into the air.

In the distance, Hien could see the enemy infantry rising up and running toward the combat base like banshees.

With the first round of shells expended, Hien rushed to his position, shouting orders to his men as they scrambled to respond to the attack. The NVA was hitting them with everything they had, wave after wave of infantry supported by tanks and heavy weapons.

The fighting was brutal and intense, with Hien and his men holding their ground against impossible odds. They fought with a desperate courage, knowing that they were the only thing standing between the enemy and the people they had sworn to protect.

But the NVA's numbers and firepower were too great. Slowly, inexorably, they began to gain ground, pushing the ARVN defenders back foot by bloody foot.

Hien saw many of his friends and comrades fall in those terrible hours, their bodies torn apart by bullets and shrapnel. He himself was wounded, a piece of metal lodging in his thigh and sending waves of agony coursing through his body.

But he refused to give up, refused to let the pain and the fear overcome him. He rallied his men, urged them on with shouts of encouragement and defiance.

In the end, though, it was not enough. The NVA broke through the ARVN's defenses, surging into the base with a savage intensity. Hien and his surviving men were forced to retreat, fighting a desperate rearguard action as they fell back towards the city of Pleiku.

As he limped through the jungle, his wound throbbing with every step, Hien felt a sense of despair. He had failed in his duty, had let down the people who were counting on him. But what could he and his men have done differently?

Even in that moment of darkness, he knew that he could not give up. He thought of his family, of the people of his village, of all those who were depending on him to keep them safe.

He knew that he and his comrades had no choice but to keep fighting, to hold the line against the enemy for as long as they could. They were the soldiers of the South, the defenders of a dream that refused to die.

As the sounds of battle faded into the distance, Hien looked back at the smoking ruins of the Duc Co base. It was a bitter defeat, a blow that would be felt throughout the region. What's done is done. There was nothing he or his men could do. Duc Co was gone.

With an unshakable resolve, Lieutenant Hien turned his face towards the future, ready to meet whatever challenges lay ahead.

The attack on Duc Co was fierce and brutal, with Thao's men facing determined resistance from the ARVN defenders. But the NVA's superior numbers and firepower soon began to tell, and slowly but surely, they gained ground.

As the base fell, Thao felt a surge of pride and elation. But there was no time to celebrate. The offensive was just beginning, and there were many more battles to be fought.

The NVA's 968th Division, supported by the 271st Regiment and the 202nd Tank Brigade, attacked Pleiku from the north and west, while the 10th Division simultaneously assaulted the city from the east. The fighting was intense and brutal, with the NVA using a combination of infantry assaults, artillery bombardments, and armored thrusts to break through the ARVN's defenses.

Despite fierce resistance from the South Vietnamese forces, the NVA managed to seize control of several key positions in and around Pleiku, including the city's airfield and several important road junctions. This effectively cut off the ARVN's supply lines and made it difficult for them to bring in reinforcements or evacuate their wounded.

With Pleiku and several other key outposts in the region now under their control, the NVA was able to concentrate its forces for the main assault on Ban Me Thuot. The capture of these outlying positions had not only weakened the ARVN's overall defensive posture in the Central Highlands but had also allowed the NVA to stockpile weapons, ammunition, and other supplies closer to their ultimate objective.

Thus, by the time the NVA launched its attack on Ban Me Thuot itself, it was able to bring to bear a formidable array of troops, tanks, and artillery, all of which had been carefully positioned and supplied thanks to the earlier successful assaults on Pleiku and the surrounding outposts.

The fall of these key positions in the lead-up to the battle of Ban Me Thuot was a testament to the NVA's careful planning, coordination, and execution of its offensive operations. It also underscored the rapidly deteriorating position of the South Vietnamese forces in the face of the NVA's relentless and determined onslaught.

As the NVA tightened its grip on the Central Highlands, Thao and his unit were ordered to join the main assault on Ban Me Thuot. It was the key to the entire region, the prize that would open the way to Saigon and the final victory.

Ban Me Thuot, South Vietnam

The Pilatus PC-6 Porter soared over the lush Vietnamese landscape, its single turboprop engine humming steadily. At the controls, Coyle scanned the ground below, his eyes searching for any sign of NVA activity. Beside him, Karen readied her camera, the long lens poised to capture the critical reconnaissance photos.

It had been a hard-fought battle to convince Coyle to let her join him on this mission. As an Associated Press photographer, she was determined to document the truth of the war, to show the world the reality on the ground. But as her father, Coyle's instinct was to protect her, to keep her far from the dangers of the front lines.

In the end, Karen's determination had won out. She was her father's daughter, after all - stubborn, fearless, and committed to making a difference.

As they flew over the outskirts of Ban Me Thuot, Coyle's eyes narrowed. There, snaking along the roads and trails, was a massive column of NVA soldiers and vehicles, kicking up dust as they advanced towards the city.

"Karen, two o'clock," Coyle called out, banking the plane to give her a better view. "Looks like a whole damned division down there."

Karen leaned forward, her camera clicking rapidly as she captured frame after frame of the enemy force. "They're moving fast," she observed, "The ARVN won't stand a chance if they hit the city in full force."

The intelligence they had gathered was critical, but it also painted an ugly picture. The NVA offensive was larger and more advanced than anyone had anticipated. Ban Me Thuot, and everyone in it, was in grave danger.

Suddenly, a harsh pinging sound filled the cockpit, followed by the unmistakable rattle of anti-aircraft fire. Tracer rounds streaked past the wings, glowing like angry hornets in the bright sunlight.

"Hang on!" Coyle yelled, wrenching the controls

hard to the left. The Porter responded instantly, banking sharply as Coyle jinked and weaved, trying to throw off the aim of the NVA gunners below.

Karen braced herself against the door, her knuckles white as she gripped her camera. Despite the danger, she kept shooting, determined to document every moment of the harrowing experience.

The plane shuddered as a round found its mark, tearing through the thin metal skin of the fuselage. Coyle fought to keep the aircraft level as warning lights flashed on the control panel.

"We can't stay up here," he shouted over the din of the engine and the rushing wind. "We've got to get this intel back to base."

With a final, stomach-churning twist, Coyle pointed the nose of the Porter towards friendly territory, pushing the throttle to the wall. The plane leaped forward, its engine straining as it clawed for altitude and speed.

Behind them, the NVA guns continued to fire, their tracers arcing through the sky in a futile attempt to bring down the fleeing aircraft. But Coyle's skill and the Porter's agility won out, and soon they were out of range, the enemy fire fading into the distance.

As the adrenaline began to fade, Coyle glanced over at Karen with a mix of pride and concern. "You okay?" he asked, his voice gruff with emotion.

Karen nodded, a shaky smile spreading across her face. "Never better," she replied, holding up her camera. "And I got the shots. The people in the South need to see this, Dad. They need to know what's coming."

Coyle nodded. The intelligence they had gathered was invaluable, but it was only the beginning. With the

NVA closing in, time was running out for Ban Me Thuot and all those caught in the crosshairs of the advancing enemy.

As he turned the plane towards base, Coyle was already racing ahead, formulating plans and strategies. There was an orphanage in the city, filled with innocent children, many of them the sons and daughters of American servicemen. They would need to be evacuated, and quickly, before the NVA's iron grip closed around the city.

And as the Pilatus PC-6 Porter soared through the endless blue of the Vietnamese sky, Coyle knew that he and his men would stop at nothing to save those children, to give them a chance at a future beyond the war.

Command Post, South Vietnam

The commanding general's face darkened as he listened to the report from his forward observers. The small reconnaissance plane that had buzzed overhead just hours before had changed everything. The enemy now knew they were coming, and the carefully planned element of surprise was gone.

Thao slammed his fist on the map table, his eyes blazing with anger. "The Americans and their puppets think they can stop us with their spy planes and their technology," he growled, his voice filled with contempt. "But they underestimate the will of our people, the strength of our cause."

He turned to Major General Nguyen Huu An, who stood nearby, awaiting orders. "Comrade An," Thao said, his voice sharp and urgent, "we must accelerate our plans. The enemy knows we are coming, but they do not know our true strength. We will hit them hard and fast, from all sides, before they have a chance to reinforce their defenses."

An nodded, "I will relay the orders immediately, Comrade General," he said, "All units will close in on the city with maximum speed and force, stealth be damned. We will overwhelm them with our numbers and our firepower."

Thao nodded, his eyes scanning the map once more. "We must seize the key positions quickly," he said, his finger stabbing at the various objectives marked on the map. "The airfield, the government buildings, the main roads in and out of the city. We will cut off their escape and their reinforcements, and then we will crush them without mercy."

Thao felt a surge of adrenaline coursing through his veins. The American plane had thrown a wrench into their plans, but it had also presented an opportunity. The enemy would be confused, disorganized, scrambling to react to the sudden change in the situation.

And in that chaos, the North Vietnamese Army would strike like a thunderbolt, a force of nature that could not be stopped or contained. They would pour into the city from all directions, their tanks and artillery leading the way, their infantry swarming over the defenses like a tidal wave.

In the hills and valleys around Ban Me Thuot, the NVA units began to move, abandoning their carefully concealed positions and surging forward with a renewed sense of urgency. The sound of engines and marching feet filled the air, a symphony of war that grew louder and more intense with each passing moment.

And at the head of the column, Lieutenant General Thao and Major General An rode in their command vehicles. They knew that victory was within their grasp, that the long years of struggle and sacrifice were finally coming to a head.

Ban Me Thuot Command Post, South Vietnam

Colonel Tran Minh Quang, the ARVN commander at Ban Me Thuot, sat at his desk, his eyes fixed on the array of photographs scattered before him. The images had arrived just minutes ago, delivered in an unmarked package by a breathless runner from the intelligence section.

At first, Quang had been puzzled by the contents of the package, wondering why someone had sent him a collection of landscape photos. But as he looked closer, his heart sank with a cold, sickening feeling of dread. He hoped it was some sort of trick, a trap laid by the enemy's counterintelligence unit. But he quickly realized that the photos were the real deal and he needed to pay close attention.

There, in stark black and white, was the unmistakable evidence of a massive North Vietnamese Army force, snaking its way through the hills and valleys around Ban Me Thuot. Tanks, artillery, infantry - all moving with a terrible sense of purpose towards the city he had sworn to defend.

Quang's hands began to tremble as he shuffled through the photographs, each one painting a more dire picture than the last. He had known that the enemy was planning an offensive, had heard the rumors and the intelligence reports. But nothing could have prepared him for the scale of the force that was now bearing down on his position.

A knock at the door startled him from his reverie, and he looked up to see his staff officers filing into the room. They had heard about the package, had seen the concerned expressions on the faces of the intelligence officers who had delivered it.

For a moment, Quang struggled to find the words, his mouth dry and his throat tight. He could see the fear and the uncertainty in the eyes of his men, could feel the weight of their expectations and their trust.

Finally, he cleared his throat and stood, his voice steady and calm despite the turmoil raging inside. "Gentlemen," he said, "we have received clear evidence of a massive enemy force approaching our position. The photographs in front of me show a level of strength and coordination that we have not seen before."

He paused, letting his words sink in, watching as the faces of his officers paled and their jaws tightened. "I will not lie to you," he continued. "The situation is challenging. We are outnumbered and outgunned, and the enemy has the momentum. But we are soldiers of the Republic of Vietnam, and we will not yield, not without a fight."

Quang's eyes met the gaze of each of his officers in turn. "We have a duty to the people of this city, to the men and women and children who are counting on us to keep them safe. And we will not fail them, not as long as there is breath in our bodies and strength in our arms."

He reached out and picked up one of the photographs, holding it aloft like a talisman. "This is our enemy," he said. "This is the face of the force that seeks to destroy us and everything we hold dear. But we will not be intimidated, and we will not be defeated. We will fight with every ounce of courage and skill we possess, and we will make them pay for every inch of ground they try to take."

As he looked around the room, Quang could see the fear and the uncertainty in the eyes of his men slowly giving way to resolve. They knew the odds they were facing, knew the price they might have to pay. But they also knew that they had a duty, a sacred trust to defend their homeland and their people.

And as they filed out of the room, their backs straight and their eyes filled with a fierce determination, Colonel Quang felt a surge of pride and hope. The battle ahead would be the greatest test of his life, a crucible of fire and blood that would forge the destiny of his nation.

Bien Hoa Air Base, South Vietnam

Coyle and Granier huddled over the map of Ban Me Thuot, their faces revealing their concern. The latest intelligence report lay on the table before them, its contents both startling and urgent. Karen's photos helped fill in the picture of what the ARVN were up against, and what they were up against. "So, we send Scott and the helicopters to rescue the survivors of Pleiku and Tom Kum. We use the C-119 and the Ghost Warrior for the rescue missions around Ban Me Thuot."

"Feels like we're stretched thin," said Granier.

"We are. Not only do we need to get our informant and his family out, we need to rescue a bunch of American-Vietnamese orphans just outside the southeastern side of the city," said Coyle.

"American-Vietnamese children... They'll be no mercy for them when the NVA rolls through," said Granier. "Maybe we could get a message to the nuns that run the orphanage and have them meet us at the airport with the children."

"Maybe. But there's a lot that can go wrong between the orphanage and the airport, especially with the NVA closing in."

"Alright, we take a couple of trucks and go fetch them. That way we're in control of the situation."

"Control? Seriously, do you know nothing about children?"

"I know a little."

"Well, I know this is not going to be a cakewalk," said Coyle tracing a finger along the map. "We need to get them out, and fast, before the NVA overrun the airport and cutoff our exit plan."

"I say we break the team up. We send Chang and Tran to slow down the NVA, buy us some time."

"Agreed. What do you have in mind?"

Granier pointed to a mountainous area to the west of the city. The NVA armor will need to go through this pass to get to the city. Tran might be able to rig an avalanche, trap some of their armor vehicles. They'll want to dig out their armor before advancing."

"Good. What about Chang?"

"He'll take out the field commanders in the lead units. He knows what to do. I trained him myself."

"And what about our informant and his family?"

"I'll send a small team to get them out and meet us at the airport."

"And the rest of the team goes with us?"

"Why are you going? You should stay with the plane."

"Because I know more about kids than you."

"Everyone knows more about kids than I do. There're fathers in the team. They'll know what to do."

"Yeah, but you don't always listen. I'll be there to make sure you do. Besides, my aircrew will watch over the Boxcar."

"I guess that's fair."

They spent the next hour poring over the map, discussing strategies and contingencies. They knew they would need to buy time, to keep the NVA at bay long enough to evacuate the children.

The plan began to take shape. Chang and his spotter would be the eyes, picking off high-value targets. Tran and his team would be the roadblock, forcing the NVA to detour. A small team would rescue the informant and his family. And Coyle and Granier would lead the main force to the orphanage, to evacuate the children and nuns.

"It's a gamble," Granier said quietly, voicing the apprehension that hung between them.

Coyle met his gaze, a silent understanding passing between them. They had seen too much death, too much destruction. If they could save these children, give them a chance at a life beyond the war, it would all be worth it. "Let's get the team moving," said Coyle.

Ban Me Thuot, South Vietnam

As dawn broke over the Central Highlands, the distant rumble of artillery shattered the morning stillness. The North Vietnamese Army had begun its inexorable advance on Ban Me Thuot, the strategic heart of the region.

The citizens of Ban Me Thuot awoke to a sense of

unease that hung heavy in the air. The distant sound of artillery seemed closer now, more urgent and more threatening.

In the streets, the normal bustle of daily life was replaced by a tense, watchful silence. Shopkeepers hurried to shutter their stores, while families gathered their most precious belongings and prepared to flee. The city had seen war before, but never like this, never with such a sense of impending doom.

At the ARVN headquarters, Colonel Tran Minh Quang and his staff worked feverishly to shore up their defenses. Reports flooded in from the front lines, each one painting a picture of a city under siege. The North Vietnamese Army was approaching from all sides, their tanks and artillery pounding the outer defenses with a relentless fury.

Quang dispatched his reserves to the most threatened sectors, hoping to buy time for the civilians to evacuate. He knew that every minute counted, that every life saved was a victory against the enemy.

But even as his men fought with a desperate courage, Quang could feel the tide turning against them. The NVA was too strong, too well-equipped and too determined. They surged forward like a tidal wave, their numbers seeming to grow with every passing moment.

In the streets, panic began to set in as the reality of the situation became clear. Families clutched each other in terror as the sounds of battle grew closer, the earth shaking beneath their feet with each explosion. Some tried to flee, piling into cars and trucks and motorcycles, only to find the roads choked with debris and the wreckage of burning vehicles.

Others sought shelter where they could, huddling in basements and bunkers, praying for a miracle that seemed increasingly unlikely. The city's hospitals and clinics were soon overwhelmed, the wounded and the dying spilling out into the streets in a grey demonstration of the savagery of the fighting.

In a command tent on the outskirts of the city, General Nguyen Huu An pored over a map updating the positions of friendly and enemy units. The red arrows representing his divisions snaked towards Ban Me Thuot from all directions, a constricting noose around the throat of the enemy.

"The 320th and 10th Divisions will strike from the north and west," he said, his voice crisp and assured. "The 968th will come in from the east, cutting off Highway 14. We will isolate the city, crush their defenses, and liberate the people."

Beside him, Lieutenant Colonel Tran Ngoc Hue nodded in agreement, his eyes gleaming with the fervor of revolutionary zeal. "The Americans have abandoned their lackeys," he said, his tone laced with contempt. "They have no stomach for this fight. Ban Me Thuot will soon be ours and then Saigon will follow. It will be good when the war finally ends with victory."

"While I appreciate your confidence, Colonel, remember… we still have a battle to fight… and win."

"Of course, I only met that destiny is clearly on our side."

"Let's hope so."

On the front lines, Private Chau crouched in a hastily dug foxhole, his AK-47 clutched tightly to his chest.

The distant crack of small arms fire set his nerves on edge, but he steeled himself, remembering the words of his political officer.

"We fight for the liberation of our people," the officer had said, his voice ringing with conviction. "We fight to reunite our homeland under the glorious banner of socialism. Let no man falter, let no man doubt the righteousness of our cause."

Chau whispered a prayer to his ancestors, his fingers tightening around the worn photograph of his family back in the north. He would fight with honor, with courage, and if necessary, he would die for the revolution.

Across the lines, in the besieged city, Major Tran Huu Duc of the ARVN paced anxiously in his command post. The reports from his forward observers painted a bleak picture - the NVA was coming in force, their numbers and firepower far exceeding his own. "We must hold the line," he barked into the radio, his voice hoarse with desperation. "Call in air support, artillery, everything we have. We cannot let Ban Me Thuot fall."

But even as he spoke, Duc knew that it was a losing battle. The Americans had withdrawn their support, and his men were tired, demoralized, and woefully undersupplied. The logistics unit was rationing ammunition – eighty-seven bullets per soldier per day. It was only a matter of time before the city fell.

In a small house on the outskirts of Ban Me Thuot, Nguyen Thi Hoa huddled with her children, her eyes wide with fear. The sound of gunfire and explosions drew ever closer, and she could hear the distant shouts of the NVA soldiers as they advanced.

"Mother, I'm scared," whimpered her youngest daughter, burying her face in Hoa's shoulder.

Hoa stroked the girl's hair, her own heart racing with terror. "Hush, my child," she whispered, her voice trembling. "We must be brave. Our ancestors will watch over us."

But even as she spoke the words, Hoa couldn't help but wonder if their ancestors had abandoned them, if the gods had turned their backs on the suffering of the innocent.

Having advanced into the outskirts of the city, Private Chau crouched behind the shattered remains of a concrete wall. The acrid smell of smoke and cordite filled his nostrils, and the deafening roar of gunfire and explosions assaulted his ears.

Beside him, his comrades from the 320th Division lay in wait, their faces smeared with dirt and sweat, their eyes filled with the intensity of battle. They had been fighting for hours, pushing the ARVN forces back inch by bloody inch, but the enemy was stubborn, clinging to their positions in desperation.

Chau risked a glance over the top of the wall, his eyes scanning the pockmarked landscape for any sign of movement. Suddenly, a burst of machine gun fire ripped through the air, the bullets whizzing past his head like angry wasps. He ducked back down, his heart hammering against his ribs.

"Grenades!" yelled Tran his squad leader. "On my mark!"

Chau reached for the grenades clipped to his belt, his fingers trembling with a mixture of fear and adrenaline. He pulled the pins, feeling the cold metal of the spoons biting into his palms.

"Now!" roared Tran, and Chau surged to his feet, hurling the grenades over the wall with all his might. The explosions just a few yards away shook the earth, sending geysers of dirt and debris into the air.

"Charge!" bellowed Tran. Chau leaped over the wall, his AK-47 spraying fire as he ran. All around him, his comrades surged forward, their bayonets fixed, their faces twisted with the fury of battle.

The ARVN soldiers fell back, their lines broken by the ferocity of the NVA assault. Chau saw one enemy soldier fall, his chest torn open by a burst of automatic fire. Another threw down his rifle and raised his hands in surrender, his face white with terror.

But there was no time for mercy, no time for hesitation. Chau shot the enemy, shouldered and pressed forward, his boots pounding against the blood-soaked earth, his heart filled with a savage joy. This was what he had trained for, what he had dreamed of since he was a boy listening to the stories of the revolution.

Suddenly, a searing pain ripped through his shoulder, and Chau stumbled, his vision blurring. He looked down to see blood spreading across the front of his uniform, a dark, glistening stain.

But even as he fell to his knees, even as the world began to spin and darken around him, Chau refused to yield. With a final, defiant roar, he raised his rifle and fired, the bullets tearing through the smoke and the chaos, seeking out the enemy.

And then he was falling, the sky tilting crazily above him, the sounds of battle fading into a distant roar. As he hit the ground, Chau's last thought was of his family, of the small farm in the north where he had played as a child, of the dream of a Vietnam united and free.

He had given his life for that dream, had spilled his

blood on the soil of his homeland. And as the darkness claimed him, Private Nguyen Van Chau knew that his sacrifice had not been in vain. Even in death, his spirit would live on, a shining beacon of hope and courage in the long, bitter struggle for Vietnam's future.

As the battle raged on, the streets of Ban Me Thuot became a hellish landscape of fire and blood. NVA tanks rumbled through the rubble-strewn streets, their cannons belching smoke and flame, their machine guns chewing through belts of ammunition. ARVN soldiers fought desperately from hastily erected barricades, their faces revealing their impending defeat. It was clear as day, outgunned and outmanned, they would lose.

And caught in the middle, the civilians of Ban Me Thuot cowered in their homes, praying for deliverance from the storm of violence that had engulfed their once-peaceful city.

In his command tent, General An watched the reports from the front with a growing sense of triumph. The enemy was crumbling, their defenses shattered, their will to fight broken. "You were right, Colonel, Ban Me Thuot will soon be ours," he declared, his voice ringing with the certainty of victory.

But even as he spoke, An knew that the battle for Ban Me Thuot was only the beginning. There were other cities to liberate, other enemies to vanquish. And yet, as he looked out over the map, at the red arrows that symbolized the unstoppable advance of the People's Army, An couldn't help but feel a surge of pride and purpose. They were writing history, forging a new Vietnam in the crucible of war.

At the ARVN headquarters, Colonel Quang and his staff fought on, directing the battle. They knew that they were the last line of defense, the only thing standing between the people of Ban Me Thuot and the horrors of a North Vietnamese occupation.

But as the day wore on, the situation grew increasingly desperate. The NVA had broken through the outer defenses and was now fighting in the streets, their tanks and infantry moving from block to block with a methodical, ruthless efficiency. The ARVN forces dwindling, the areas they controlled shrinking.

Quang ordered his men to fall back to the city center, hoping to make a last stand in the heart of Ban Me Thuot. They took up positions in government buildings and key intersections, determined to hold out as long as they could.

But it was a losing battle, and everyone knew it. The NVA was too strong, too relentless. They surged forward like a force of nature, their numbers seemingly endless, their resolve unbreakable.

Ban Me Thuot Airport

The Ban Me Thuot airport was a scene of chaos and desperation as the ARVN forces fought to hold back the relentless advance of the North Vietnamese Army assaulting the perimeter. When the airport was finally under NVA control, the ARVN would be unable to reinforce or resupply by air. They would have little choice but to surrender. The sound of artillery and mortar fire filled the air, the ground shaking with each explosion.

Amidst the din of battle, a lone C-119 transport

plane appeared on the horizon, flying low and fast towards the besieged airfield. At the controls, Coyle gripped the yoke tightly, his eyes scanning the ground for enemy activity.

Behind him in the cargo hold, Granier and the rest of the Ghost Warriors sat in tense silence, their weapons checked and at the ready. They knew that the mission ahead would be a race against time to save the lives of innocent children caught in the crosshairs of war.

Mortar rounds exploded across the tarmac. A shell hit a hangar. Drums of oil and fuel ignited, exploding. The hangar burst into flames. Aircraft burned. Buildings crumbled.

Coyle keyed the mic, "Delta five niner inbound. Taking heavy fire. Over."

No response. More explosions rocked the airport.

Coyle pushed the throttles forward. The engines roared. The C-119 picked up speed. He had to get his aircraft on the ground before the NVA anti-aircraft weapons opened fire.

An artillery round hit the tower. It collapsed in a heap of twisted metal.

Coyle gripped the yoke. Tracer rounds zipped past the cockpit. Red and green streaks. The ARVN were putting up a hell of a fight, but so were the NVA.

A rocket slammed into the runway. Leaving a crater the size of a truck. Coyle pulled back on the stick. The C-119 pitched up.

Moments later, the main gear touched down. Coyle stood on the brakes. He reversed pitch on the props. The plane slowed.

Another explosion. Too close.

Coyle turned off the runway. He steered for a patch

of grass away from the battle. As the plane rolled to a stop, the Ghost Warriors wasted no time and leaped to the ground. "Good hunting," said Granier as Chang and Tran's teams split off from the main group and headed toward their assignments. Sgt. Forest headed up a small third team that would rescue the informant and his family.

Coyle, Granier, and the rest of the team searched the airport for vehicles that could transport the orphans. Granier found an old bus used to shuttle passengers from the terminal and the planes on the tarmac. Hotwiring the bus, he drove it over to the C-119 and climbed out. "How about this?" he said.

"I don't know. We don't what shape the road is in leading the orphanage," said Coyle.

"We'll it ain't like we've got a lot of choice."

"I suppose you're right. We'll make it work."

The team climbed in with Granier behind the wheel and Coyle acting as navigator. The bus sped out the main gate.

Coyle navigated through the war-torn streets of Ban Me Thuot. Granier gripped the steering wheel of the bus. He swerved around debris and abandoned vehicles many of them burning or smoldering.

Gunfire erupted from a side street. Bullets pinged off the bus. The Ghost Warriors returned fire from the windows.

Granier glanced at Coyle, "Which way?"

Coyle scanned the road ahead. The NVA were everywhere. Trying to block their path. He spotted an alley to the right.

"There. Take that alley."

Granier turned the wheel hard. The bus careened into the narrow passage. Scraping against the walls on both sides.

An NVA soldier appeared at the end of the alley. He raised his rifle.

One of the Ghost Warriors popped up through the bus's roof hatch and fired his weapon. The soldier fell.

The bus burst out of the alley. Onto a main street. More NVA troops opened fire from the buildings lining the road.

Granier floored it. Weaving and dodging.

"RPG!" Coyle yelled.

A rocket streaked across the hood of the bus and slammed into a storefront. The explosion rocked the bus. Showering it with glass and debris.

Granier fought for control. Trying to keep the vehicle moving forward.

Coyle looked for another route. There. That bridge.

Granier saw it. A small stone bridge over a canal. He spun the wheel. The bus lurched toward it. Engines straining.

They reached the other side. Speeding past startled civilians huddled in doorways.

As they made their way through the city, the fighting intensified. NVA troops seemed to be around every corner.

The Ghost Warriors kept up a steady barrage. Laying down suppressing fire, driving the enemy back.

Coyle kept one eye on the road. The other on his map. Trying to find a clear path to the orphanage. It wasn't going to be easy. But they had to get those kids out. Before the city fell.

As they raced through the streets of Ban Me Thuot, the signs of battle were everywhere. Buildings lay in ruins, their walls pockmarked with bullet holes and scorch marks. Civilians ran for cover, their faces filled with fear and desperation.

As the bus turned onto the main road leading to the orphanage, Coyle's eyes widened in alarm. In the distance, he could see the smoke and dust of a large NVA force moving towards the airport, their tanks and artillery creating a rolling thunder that shook the earth.

"They're going to cut us off," he said, his voice tight with urgency. "If they take the airport, we'll have no way out."

Granier floored the accelerator, the bus's engine roaring as they hurtled towards the orphanage. The Ghost Warriors braced themselves against the jolting and bouncing of the vehicle.

Outskirts of Ban Me Thuot...

Chang lay prone on the rocky outcropping, his eyes glued to the scope of his sniper rifle. Beside him, his spotter, Binh, scanned the terrain below through a pair of high-powered binoculars, his breathing slow and steady.

The sun beat down mercilessly from a cloudless sky, the heat shimmering off the asphalt road in waves. But Chang barely noticed the discomfort, his focus entirely on the task at hand.

They had been watching the NVA advance, tracking the movements of the enemy forces as they made their way towards Ban Me Thuot. They had seen the tanks and the armored vehicles, the endless columns of infantry marching beneath the red and gold banners of the People's Army.

But they had also seen something else, something that had made Chang's heart race with anticipation. The NVA commanders, the men who held the fate of the enemy advance in their hands, were moving among the troops, their presence marked by the distinctive insignia on their uniforms and the deference shown to them by their subordinates.

It was a rare opportunity, a chance to strike a blow against the enemy leadership that could throw their entire offensive into disarray. And Chang was determined not to let it slip through his fingers.

"Three hundred meters, two o'clock," Binh whispered, his voice barely audible over the distant rumble of engines. "Two officers, looks like a major and a captain."

Chang adjusted his scope, the crosshairs settling on the chest of the major. He could see the man's face clearly now, the hard lines of his features, his cap shielding his eyes from the sun.

For a moment, Chang hesitated, his finger resting lightly on the trigger. To take a life, even the life of an enemy, was no small thing. It was a burden that would weigh on his soul for the rest of his days.

But then he thought of the people of Ban Me Thuot, of the innocent civilians caught in the crossfire of this brutal war. He thought of the children, the mothers and fathers, the old and the infirm, all those who would suffer and die if the NVA advance was not stopped.

And with that thought, his hesitation vanished, replaced by a cold, unflinching resolve.

He took a deep breath, letting it out slowly, his heartbeat slowing to a steady rhythm. The world around him seemed to fall away, his entire being focused on the tiny circle of the scope, the slight pressure of his finger on the trigger.

"Windage, half value, left," Binh murmured, his voice calm and even. "Fire when ready."

Chang made the adjustment, the crosshairs settling once more on the major's chest. He could see the rise and fall of the man's breathing, could almost feel the thrum of his heartbeat through the scope.

And then, with a final, gentle squeeze of the trigger, he fired.

The rifle bucked against his shoulder, the sharp crack of the shot echoing off the rocks. Through the scope, Chang saw the major stagger, his hand clutching at his chest, his eyes wide with shock and pain.

A heartbeat later, the man crumpled to the ground, his blood staining the dry earth beneath him.

"Hit," Binh confirmed, his voice filled with a grim satisfaction. "Target down."

Chang was already adjusting his aim, the crosshairs settling on the captain who stood frozen in shock beside the fallen major. The man had barely begun to react, his hand fumbling for his sidearm, when Chang's second shot caught him in the throat, the high-powered round tearing through flesh and bone in a spray of crimson.

"Two for two," Binh said, a note of admiration in his voice. "Nice shooting."

Chang allowed himself a small, tight smile, the adrenaline still coursing through his veins. It was a small victory, a tiny piece of a much larger puzzle. But every little bit counted, every delay and disruption to the enemy advance bought precious time for the defenders of Ban Me Thuot and the orphans the team was rescuing.

For the next hour, they continued their work, picking off enemy officers and key personnel with ruthless efficiency. Each shot was carefully calculated, each kill a blow against the NVA's ability to coordinate and control their forces.

By the time the sun began to dip towards the horizon, the enemy advance had begun to falter, their formations becoming ragged and disorganized as they struggled to adapt to the loss of their leadership.

It was a temporary reprieve, a fleeting moment of hope in a war that often seemed hopeless. But for Chang and Binh, it was enough.

As they packed up their gear and prepared to make their way back to the airport, Chang couldn't help but feel a sense of pride in what they had accomplished. They were the silent killers, the unseen guardians who struck fear into the hearts of the enemy and gave hope to those who fought beside them.

Mountain Pass Near Ban Me Thuot…

Tran crouched on the rugged mountainside, his eyes narrowed against the glare of the sun as he surveyed the winding road below. Beside him, his two assistants, Linh and Huy, worked with quiet efficiency, carefully placing the charges of C4 explosive at key points along the rocky slope.

The air was thick with the smell of dust and diesel fumes, the distant rumble of engines growing louder with each passing minute. Tran knew that the enemy column was approaching, a formidable array of tanks and armored vehicles that could spell doom for the defenders of Ban Me Thuot.

But he also knew that this mountain pass was the key to their plan, the one place where they could strike a decisive blow against the invading forces. With the charges in place and the detonator in hand, they could unleash a devastating avalanche that would bury the enemy vehicles and block the road, buying precious time for the city's defenders.

"How much longer?" Tran asked, his voice tense with anticipation.

Linh, a wiry man with a perpetual squint, looked up from his work, wiping the sweat from his brow with the back of his hand. "Almost done, sir. Just a few more charges to place."

Tran nodded, his gaze returning to the road below. In the distance, he could see the first hints of the approaching column, the glint of metal in the sun, the plume of dust rising from the wheels of the heavy vehicles.

"Work faster," he urged, his tone insistent. "They'll be in range soon."

Huy, a broad-shouldered man with a scar running down the side of his face, grunted in acknowledgment, his hands moving with practiced speed as he molded the charges into place.

The minutes ticked by with agonizing slowness, each second feeling like an eternity as the enemy column drew closer. Tran could feel the sweat trickling down his back, the pounding of his heart in his ears.

And then, just as the first tank rounded the bend in the road, Linh straightened up with a triumphant grin. "All set, sir."

Tran allowed himself a small smile, the first real expression of emotion he had shown all day. "Good work, both of you. Now, take cover behind those rocks and wait for my signal."

The two men nodded, scurrying back from the edge of the cliff and crouching behind a jagged outcropping of stone. Tran took a final, steadying breath, his finger hovering over the detonator.

Below, the lead tank rumbled closer, its massive treads churning up the dirt and gravel of the road. Tran could see the soldiers walking beside the vehicle, their weapons at the ready.

He waited until the tank was almost directly beneath him. And then, with a final, decisive movement, he pressed down on the detonator.

The mountainside erupted in a deafening explosion, a searing flash of light and heat that seemed to engulf the world. Tran felt the shockwave slam into him like a physical blow, the force of the blast throwing him back against the rocks.

For a moment, he lay stunned, his ears ringing, his vision blurred. But then, slowly, painfully, he pushed himself up on his elbows, blinking away the dust and the debris.

The scene below was one of utter devastation. The road was buried beneath a massive pile of rubble, the jagged rocks and boulders forming an impassable barrier. The lead tank lay on its side, its armor crumpled and twisted, smoke pouring from its ruined engine.

Further back, other vehicles had been caught in the avalanche, their hulls crushed and mangled by the weight of the falling boulders. Tran could hear the screams of the wounded, the frantic shouts of the survivors as they struggled to free themselves from the wreckage.

"We did it," Linh whispered, his voice filled with awe.

Huy clapped him on the shoulder, a fierce grin splitting his scarred face. "Damned right we did. Those bastards won't be going anywhere anytime soon."

Tran pushed himself to his feet, his body aching from the force of the explosion. He knew that this was only a temporary victory, that the enemy would find a way around the blockage eventually.

But for now, they had bought the defenders of Ban Me Thuot some precious time, had given them a fighting chance to regroup and prepare for the battles to come.

Half Breeds

Sisters of the Sacred Heart Orphanage, South Vietnam

As the bus sped away from the embattled city of Ban Me Thuot, Coyle couldn't help but feel a sense of relief mixed with apprehension. The countryside stretched out before them, a patchwork of lush green rice paddies and dense forests of towering bamboo. The road wound its way through the rural landscape, the bus bouncing and jostling as it navigated the uneven terrain. Inside the bus, the Ghost Warriors sat in tense silence, their weapons at the ready, their eyes scanning the treeline searching for the enemy.

As they drove deeper into the countryside, the signs of war began to fade away, replaced by the gentle rustling of the wind through the bamboo leaves and the chirping of exotic birds. The sun cast a golden glow over the landscape, the rice paddies shimmering in the fading light. Coyle marveled at the beauty of the scene before him, finding it hard to believe that such a peaceful place could exist amidst the chaos and violence.

The bus approached the Sisters of the Sacred Heart Orphanage. Coyle couldn't help but feel a sense of unease. Originally built by the French, the orphanage was nestled in a serene bamboo forest near a tranquil lake, far from the chaos and destruction of the city.

As the bus pulled to a stop and the Ghost Warriors quickly took up defensive positions around the perimeter, Coyle and Granier couldn't help but admire the grand French colonial mansion that had been repurposed to serve as a home for the orphaned children. The building, formerly a plantation house, stood proudly amidst the lush tropical landscape.

The house had once belonged to Madame Rousseau, a wealthy French widow who had made her fortune in the thriving rubber industry. Upon her passing, she had bequeathed the property to the Catholic Church, with the express wish that it be used to provide shelter and care for the orphans of Vietnam.

The church had embraced Madame Rousseau's vision, transforming the plantation house into a sanctuary for children who had lost their families to the ravages of war and poverty. The nuns had worked tirelessly to create a nurturing environment, adapting the spacious rooms and sprawling grounds to meet the needs of the growing number of children under their care.

The main house, with its high ceilings and elegant French architecture, had been converted into dormitories, classrooms, and a refectory. The grand salon, once the site of lavish parties and social gatherings, now served as a library and study area, its floor-to-ceiling bookshelves filled with tomes on various subjects, providing the older children with a wealth of knowledge and inspiration.

The former plantation grounds had been transformed into gardens and play areas, where the children could run, laugh, and enjoy the simple pleasures of childhood. The old stables had been converted into a small chapel, its wooden pews and simple altar a place of solace and prayer for the nuns and the children alike.

Despite the many changes the property had undergone, the essence of its French colonial heritage remained intact. The yellow walls and green shutters, though weathered by time and the harsh tropical climate, still exuded a sense of elegance and refinement. The wrought-iron balconies and the intricate tile work on the floors and walls served as reminders of the house's storied past.

The children were playing in the yard, their laughter and chatter filling the air. The nuns went about their daily tasks, seemingly unperturbed by the distant sound of artillery and gunfire.

As they approached, a tall, elderly nun – the Mother Superior – stepped forward to meet them. She had a serene smile on her face, her eyes filled with a deep, unwavering faith.

"Welcome, gentlemen," she said, her voice soft and calm. "What brings you to our humble orphanage?"

Coyle spoke urgently. "Mother Superior, I'm afraid we have bad news. Ban Me Thuot is on the verge of being overrun by the North Vietnamese Army. When that happens, they will undoubtedly come here to harm the American-Vietnamese children under your care."

The Mother Superior's smile didn't falter. She clasped her hands in front of her and spoke with a gentle conviction. "My dear, we appreciate your concern, but we have nothing to fear. God will watch over us and protect these innocent children."

Coyle exchanged a glance with Granier, who looked equally troubled by the nun's response. He tried again, his voice more insistent. "Mother Superior, with all due respect, the NVA will show no mercy. They will see these children as the enemy, and they will not hesitate to kill them. We must evacuate the orphanage immediately."

The elderly nun shook her head, her eyes filled with compassion. "I understand your fear, but we cannot abandon our faith. These children are in God's hands, and He will not forsake them."

Granier stepped forward, his voice low and urgent. "Ma'am, we don't have much time. The NVA could be here at any moment. We have a plane ready to take you and the children to safety. Please, let us help you."

For a moment, the Mother Superior's calm facade wavered. She looked at the children playing in the yard, their innocent laughter a stark contrast to the distant sounds of war. Then, she turned back to Coyle and Granier, her resolve unwavering.

"I'm sorry, gentlemen, but we will not leave. This is our home, and these children are our family. We will trust in God's plan, no matter what may come."

Coyle felt a growing sense of frustration and desperation. They had risked their lives to come here, to save these children from a terrible fate, and now they were being met with a wall of blind faith. He knew they couldn't force the nuns to leave, but he also knew that he couldn't leave these children to face the NVA alone.

He turned to Granier, his voice low and determined. "We need to come up with a plan."

Granier nodded, his jaw set with resolve. "Agreed. We'll do whatever it takes to keep the children safe, even if we have to stay here and fight."

As the distant sound of artillery grew louder, Coyle knew that time was running out. They had to act fast, or the orphanage would become just another casualty of this brutal war.

"You must leave before the communists arrive," said the Mother Superior. "If they find you here, they will assume that we are collaborators."

"She's got a point," said Granier.

"So, we leave them unprotected. We both know how that will go."

"Another good point. But I think we need to deal with reality. Even if we stay, it won't take the NVA long to overrun us. We are vastly outnumbered and outgunned."

The tranquil surroundings of the Sisters of the Sacred Heart Orphanage shattered as the distant thunder of artillery fire grew louder with each passing moment. Shells exploded in the nearby jungle, sending shockwaves through the ground and causing the children to cry out in fear, their tiny hands clutching at the habits of the nuns who tried to comfort them.

"Get the children inside, sisters," shouted the Mother Superior.

The nuns rushed the children into the main building. Just as the last of the children and nuns were about to step inside, a deafening explosion rocked the compound. The bus they had arrived in erupted in a ball of flames, the force of the blast sending shards of metal and debris flying through the air. More shells rained down, exploding, some shattering the perimeter wall, others demolishing the converted chapel. The children screamed, tears flowed.

As the smoke cleared, the Mother Superior confronted Coyle and Granier, her voice trembling with emotion. "You brought this upon us!" she accused, her finger pointing at them in condemnation. "The NVA would never have come here if it weren't for your presence. You have put us all in danger!"

Coyle, his voice firm but understanding, tried to reason with her. "Mother Superior, please listen to me. The NVA were always going to come, with or without us. They see these children as a threat, and they won't stop until they've eliminated them. We're here to help, to get you and the children to safety."

Granier nodded in agreement, his eyes scanning the treeline as another explosion shook the ground nearby. "The NVA are closing in, and we need to act quickly before it's too late."

The Mother Superior's resolve began to waver as the reality of the situation sank in. She looked at the frightened faces of the children, their eyes wide with terror, and the fearful expressions of her fellow nuns. She realized that their lives were truly in danger, and that the men before her may be their only hope of survival.

"Perhaps you're right. For the children's safety, we should leave," she conceded, her voice heavy with resignation. "But we cannot leave any of the children behind. We must take all of them with us, not just the American-Vietnamese ones. They are all God's children, and we will not abandon them."

Coyle and Granier exchanged a glance, knowing that this would complicate their mission, but they nodded in agreement. "We'll make it work," Coyle assured her. But we're gonna need another mode of transportation."

The Mother Superior's face suddenly lit up with a realization. "There's a banana plantation not far from here," she said, her voice urgent. "The owner, Mr. Nguyen, is a kind man. He may have trucks we can use to transport the children and the nuns. It's our best chance."

Granier turned to Coyle, "It's worth a shot."

"Great. But we've got a bigger problem."

"What's that?"

"We can't fit everyone on the plane."

"What do you mean? The children are small. We can cramp them in there."

"I wish that were true, but I've been doing this a long time and I'm telling you, not everyone is going to fit."

"So, what do we do?"

"I don't know. Maybe we can drive them out of the area."

"Sure as shooting, the NVA are going to have roadblocks on all the main roads."

"We could take back roads."

"The main roads are in bad shape, I can't imagine what the back roads look like."

"We'll figure something out. Let's get moving and get those trucks."

Coyle and Granier moved swiftly through the dense bamboo forest, their boots crunching against the fallen leaves and twigs that littered the ground. The towering stalks of bamboo swayed gently in the breeze, their leaves rustling like whispers in the air, their great stalk hitting each other with loud Thwacks.

As they approached Mr. Nguyen's banana plantation, their heard voices shouting in Vietnamese.

The distant sound of crackling flames and the acrid smell of smoke drifted through the forest, growing stronger with each step they took. Coyle and Granier exchanged a worried glance, their hands instinctively tightening around their weapons.

Breaking through the final line of bamboo, they stumbled upon a scene of utter devastation. The plantation's warehouse, once a hub of activity and storage for the banana harvest, was engulfed in flames. The wooden structure crackled and groaned as the fire consumed it, sending plumes of thick, black smoke billowing into the sky.

The manor house, a once-stately building that served as the residence for Mr. Nguyen and his family, was also ablaze. The flames licked at the walls and roof, shattering windows and reducing the structure to a smoldering ruin. The sight of the destruction sent a chill down Coyle and Granier's spines. The NVA had already confiscated all the vehicles at the plantation and were driving them away.

As they scanned the area, their eyes fell upon a horrifying sight. In the center of the plantation grounds, Mr. Nguyen, the owner of the plantation, was being strung up by a group of NVA soldiers. The elderly man, his face bruised and bloodied, struggled against his captors as they secured a rope around his neck. The soldiers, their faces hardened with hatred, showed no mercy as they prepared to execute the helpless plantation owner.

Coyle and Granier, their instincts kicking in, quickly retreated back into the cover of the bamboo forest. They knew that any attempt to intervene would only result in their own capture or death, and they had a greater mission to fulfill. The orphanage and the innocent children under the care of the Sisters of the Sacred Heart were now in grave danger, and time was running out.

As they made their way back through the forest, they considered the implications of what they had witnessed. The NVA had already struck at the plantation, confiscating the trucks and eliminating any potential means of escape for the orphanage.

"So, now what?" said Coyle.

"I don't see that we have much choice. We take them on foot through the jungle," said Granier.

"That's not going to work."

"Why not?"

"They're kids, Granier. They'll be lucky if they make it a mile. Besides, it'll be slow going and the NVA are sure to catch up with us."

"Okay, so what's your plan?"

"I don't have one, at least not yet."

"Well, you'd better come up with one real quick."

"I'm working on it. The lake… I wonder where it goes?"

Granier reaches into his shirt pocket and pulls out a folded map that he opens. "Nowhere by the looks of it."

Coyle takes a look and points to a narrow river, "This tributary, it goes right by the airport."

"That'd be upstream."

"So, we find a boat with a motor somewhere around the lake.

"That'll take time."

"It's better than trying to take the kids on foot."

"I agree, but we're gonna be cutting it real close."

"If the NVA come, we fight them off until we can load the kids on the boat and escape."

"It's a shaky plan, Coyle. But at least it's a plan that could work. Let's do it."

Coyle and Granier quickened their pace as they navigated the bamboo thickets. As they emerged from the forest and back onto the grounds of the Sisters of the Sacred Heart Orphanage, Coyle and Granier relayed the brutality of the enemy they had witnessed firsthand.

The nuns gasped in horror, their hands flying to their mouths as they learned of Mr. Nguyen's vicious execution at the hands of the NVA soldiers. The Mother Superior, her face pale and her eyes glistening with unshed tears, crossed herself and whispered a prayer for the plantation owner's soul. If she had doubts about the need to keep the children out of the hands of the communists, they were gone now. The thought of anything similar to what occurred to Mr. Nguyen and his family happening to the children made her nauseous.

Coyle pulled out Granier's worn map from his pocket and spread it out on a nearby table. The nuns and the other Ghost Warriors gathered around, their eyes scanning the paper for any glimmer of hope. Coyle's finger traced a thin blue line that snaked its way from the lake adjacent to the orphanage, winding through the jungle before emptying into a river that flowed directly in front of the airport runway. "If we can find a boat, we can transport the children directly to the airfield without having to go through the city and risk encountering the NVA," said Coyle.

The nuns exchanged concerned glances. "We don't have any boats large enough to carry all the children," one of them said, her voice trembling slightly.

"But there are boats with motors?"

"We have a small one that we use to cross the lake and go to market."

"Okay. That's a start. Does it run?"

"Yes."

"So, we build a few rafts and tow them with your boat."

"We can use the bamboo from the forest," said Granier. "It's strong and buoyant. We can lash them together and create enough rafts to hold the children, you nuns and our men."

Coyle nodded, "That could work. We'll need everyone's help to gather the bamboo and construct the raft as quickly as possible. We don't know how much time we have before the NVA arrive, but I don't imagine it will be long."

"We can split the team – half build the rafts and half keep guard."

The Mother Superior, her face set with resolve, turned to her fellow nuns. "Sisters, we must act swiftly. Gather the children and prepare them for the journey. We will trust in God's providence and the bravery of these men to see us through this trial."

Coyle and Granier, along with half of the Ghost Warriors, ventured back into the bamboo forest, their machetes slicing through the thick stalks with practiced precision. They worked tirelessly, felling the bamboo and dragging it back to the orphanage grounds, where they began the arduous task of constructing the rafts.

As the hours ticked by, the raft took shape. The children, their eyes wide with wonder, watched as the structures grew. When each raft was finished, it was dragged to the lake and launched to ensure it floated.

By nightfall, the rafts were nearly complete. Coyle and Granier, their faces streaked with sweat and their hands raw from their labors, heard a machine gun burst outside the perimeter wall of the orphanage.

"Shit, almost made it," said Granier turning to Coyle. "You finish the last raft. I'll join the security team and hold the NVA off."

Coyle nodded. More machine gun bursts as the Ghost Warriors returned fire. Then three mortar rounds exploded as Granier joined the team at the perimeter. "We're almost done with the rafts. We just need to hold them off for a few more minutes."

Granier lay prone behind a fallen tree, his sniper rifle nestled against his shoulder, eyes scanning the bamboo forest for the enemy. The chaos of battle swirled around him. Gunfire crackled. Mortar rounds exploded. Sending geysers of dirt and shrapnel into the air.

Through his scope he saw an NVA soldier firing his weapon. An easy shot.

Granier took aim and exhaled as he started to squeeze the trigger. Then froze.

The soldier's face blurred. Shifted. Became the face of the girl on the bridge. Her eyes wide with terror as the bridge exploded and she fell into the river. Pleading. His doing. He gave the order. He had killed her.

"Not now, dammit," he said to himself. This wasn't him. He didn't feel, not like the others. He was a emotionless killing machine. A sniper. He did what had to be done without regard to the consequences.

But the more he tried to squeeze the trigger, the worst things got. His fingers trembled. He didn't know how to stop them. His eyes widened as the image of the girl shifted to the translator hanging with his dead family below him. He was too late. His fault. His trembling fingers grew into his hands shaking uncontrollably. He couldn't stop it. Granier squeezed his eyes shut. Tried to block out the image. But it wouldn't go away.

A warrior near him looked over and saw him shaking. "What the hell, Granier?" he said.

Granier locked eyes with him as if pleading for help.

"Get in the fight, dammit!"

But he couldn't. The memory of the bridge crashed over him once again. The girl's face. But Granier couldn't respond. The girl's face filled his vision. Her blood on his hands.

Around him the battle raged on. His fellow Ghost Warriors firing. Yelling. But Granier couldn't move. Couldn't bring himself to raise his rifle. The faces of those he had killed came flooding back, overwhelming him.

An explosion nearby. Dirt showered over him. Still he lay there. Paralyzed by guilt and grief. He looked over at the soldier beside him. He was gone. Only a smoldering crater remained. The mortar shell has been a direct hit. His fault. Everything was his fault.

More explosions. Closer now. The NVA were advancing. Taking ground.

Granier knew he had to act. Had to fight. But the weight of his memories held him down. Crushed the air from his lungs.

Bullets whizzed overhead. Thudded into the wall surrounding the orphanage. Still Granier didn't move.

The battle was turning. The NVA pushing forward. But Granier was lost. Trapped in his own mind.

He heard the cries of the children. The shouts of the nuns. But they seemed distant. Unreal.

All he could see was the girl. All he could feel was

the guilt.

And so he lay there. As the battle raged on. As his fellow warriors fought and died.

Granier, the legendary sniper. Paralyzed by his own demons. Unable to do the one thing he had always done best.

Take the shot.

With the last raft finished, Coyle and his team drug it into the lake. As the nuns and children boarded the raft, the Mother Superior turned to Coyle, her eyes shining with gratitude. "May God bless you for your bravery and selflessness," she whispered, her voice filled with emotion.

"Get that boat's motor started and take up the slack," said Coyle stepping off the raft. "If I'm not back in five minutes, you go without me."

Vastly outnumbered by the NVA, the Ghost Warriors fought on, taking heavy casualties. Leaderless without Granier, they seemed to be faltering, their moves incoherent, their defense unorganized. But Granier, shaking on the ground was in no condition to lead. *We die here,* he thought. *Holy ground. Not so bad. It has been one helluva fight.*

Granier felt a hand grip his shoulder and flip him over. He looked up. It was Coyle standing above. The NVA were close, real close. Coyle grabbed Granier by the shirt and pulled him to his feet. Granier was wobbling, like a drunken fool. Coyle picked up his rifle and threw Granier's arm around his shoulder. He pulled Granier back into the orphanage.

"Fall back," shouted Coyle. The surviving Ghost Warriors grabbed their wounded and followed Coyle, fighting as they fell back into the orphanage.

The NVA pressed forward. Mortar shells rained down around the orphanage. Shaking the ground. Sending shrapnel flying. Coyle kept going, toward the lake where the rafts were waiting. The Ghost Warriors kept firing, keeping the NVA back.

Granier could see the children and the nuns frightened. He wanted to help, to reassure them, but he was voiceless, lost his own abyss. As they came to the lake's edge, Granier stumbled in the mud and fell. Coyle picked him up in a fireman's hold and stepped onto the last raft. He threw Granier down on the bamboo. "Everyone get down, as flat as you can," he shouted. "Get that boat moving!"

Mother Superior in the boat revved the motor and pulled up the slack in the tow rope. The Ghost Warriors piled on the raft almost capsizing it from too much weight, but it held. They laid flat, shouldering their rifles, returning fire as bullets zigged over their heads, some hitting the raft splintering the bamboo.

The rafts began to pull away from the shoreline, slowly, much too slowly. Mortar rounds whistled down and exploded in the lake sending showers of water down on the frightened children. Mother Superior had the motor at full throttle, but it wasn't enough for such a heavy load. Coyle grabbed a bamboo pole and plunged it into the water. He found bottom and pushed with everything he had. Several nuns jumped up and grabbed poles, helping Coyle to get the rafts moving. The bamboo convoy slowly gained speed.

A nun was hit, her body crumpled as she fell into the lake, dead. Hit in the head, there was no helping her.

Finally, the rafts were pulled out of range from the

NVA on shore. The firing ceased. The children, their faces streaked with tears, clung to the nuns, their tiny bodies trembling with fear and exhaustion.

The only sounds, the sputtering of the boat's motor, the cries of the children and the prayers of Mother Superior.

NVA Command Post

The NVA commander stood over the map, his eyes surveying the front lines of the battle for Bao Me Thuot. A knock at the door broke his concentration. "Enter," he said, his voice flat.

A young officer stepped into the room, his face tight with tension. He snapped a salute. "Comrade Commander, I bring news from the front."

The commander looked up. "Report."

"The children and the nuns from the orphanage... they have escaped. Our forces were unable to stop them."

For a moment, the commander was silent. His jaw tightened, the only sign of his displeasure. "How did this happen?"

"They had help, sir. American soldiers. They delayed our forces and bought time for the others to flee."

"I see."

He turned back to the map, his finger tracing a route. "Do you understand why those children are important, comrade?"

The officer shook his head. "No, sir."

The commander's voice was cold, matter-of-fact. "They are a symbol. A remnant of the American presence in our country. As long as they exist, they are a reminder of our subjugation. A stain on our honor. They must be wiped from the land. Purged, like a disease. It is a distasteful, but necessary task. When they are gone our victory here will be complete."

The soldier nodded, "I understand, sir."

The commander studied the map a moment longer. Then he looked up, his eyes hard. "They will be heading for the airport. It is the only way they can escape now."

He pointed to a spot on the map. "Set a trap here, where the river narrows. They will have to pass through. When they do, we will be waiting."

The officer saluted. "Yes, Comrade Commander. It will be done."

The commander dismissed him with a wave. As the door closed, he turned back to the map. They could run, these children. They could hide. But in the end, it would make no difference. He would find them. And he would end them.

It was only a matter of time.

Lake Ho Ea Cuor Kap

The sun hung low on the horizon, casting a warm glow over the tranquil lake. A gentle mist rose from the water's surface, curling and twisting in the cooling air. It drifted lazily across the lake, obscuring the far shore and cloaking the world in a soft, dreamlike haze.

Through the mist, a small boat emerged, its engine puttering softly, Mother Superior at the helm. It cut a slow, steady path through the still waters, leaving a widening wake behind it. Tethered to the boat were several rafts, lashed together with sturdy ropes. They bobbed gently on the water, their bamboo frames creaking softly with each gentle swell.

On the rafts huddled the children, their small forms wrapped in blankets to ward off the chill. They sat quietly, their eyes wide and watchful. Some clutched worn teddy bears or dolls, seeking comfort in their familiar softness. Others simply stared out at the misty lake, their young faces showing a mix of fear and wonder.

Among the children moved the nuns, their dark habits a stark contrast to the fading light. They tended to their young charges with gentle hands and soothing words, offering comfort and reassurance in the face of the unknown. Their faces were lined with worry, but also with a fierce fortitude. They had vowed to protect these children, and they would not waver in that duty.

At the front and back of the boat, the Ghost Warriors stood watch, their weapons at the ready. They were a battle-hardened lot, their faces scarred and their eyes haunted. This mission was different from what they were accustomed, unique in ways they did not fully understand.

The sniper rifle in his lap, Coyle sat next to Granier on the gently rocking raft, occasionally glancing over to check on his friend. The mist swirled around them, dampening their clothes and beading on their skin. Granier seemed lost, staring at the water seeping up between the bamboo poles lashed together. Coyle glanced down at the sniper rifle resting across his lap. Granier's rifle. The weapon was a part of him, an extension of his being. To see it discarded, abandoned... it was a troubling sign.

"You can have this back anytime you're ready," said Coyle motioning to the rifle.

Granier stayed silent and didn't reach for his

weapon.

"Hey," Coyle said softly. "You, okay?"

Granier didn't respond. He seemed lost in his own world, a world of dark memories and haunting regrets. A man broken.

Coyle hesitated, choosing his words carefully. He knew Granier's mind was a minefield, one wrong step could trigger an explosion of emotion. But he had to try. The team, the nuns, and the children needed the old Granier.

"I know it's hard," he said finally. "What we've seen, what we've done... it stays with you."

Granier's jaw tightened, but he remained silent.

Coyle pressed on, his voice gentle but firm. "But we can't get lost in it. We've got a job to do. These kids, these nuns... they're counting on us."

A muscle twitched in Granier's cheek. His eyes flickered, a brief spark of life in their haunted depths.

"I keep seeing her," he said, his voice barely a whisper. "The girl on the bridge. I can't... I can't shake it."

Coyle nodded, his own memories stirring. "That wasn't your fault. You did what you had to do."

Granier shook his head. "Did I? I wonder. I didn't even think. I just gave the order… like it was nothing. Another piece of the mission. Victory at all costs."

Coyle held out the rifle, offering it to his friend. "You're a good soldier, Granier. The best. Don't let one moment define you. There is no time for sorrow. We need you."

Granier stared at the weapon, his eyes tracing the familiar contours. But he didn't reach out.

"Okay," said Coyle. "I'll keep it until you're ready."

"And what if I'm never ready?"

Coyle placed a hand on Granier's shoulder, feeling the tension coiled beneath the surface. "That would be a shame. You're one of a kind."

Deep down, Granier knew Coyle was right. They sat in silence for a while, watching the mist swirl over the water. The raft rocked gently beneath them, a frail island of humanity in a sea of uncertainty.

Finally, Coyle stood up. "I'm gonna check on the kids. Make sure they're holding up okay."

Coyle moved off, leaving Granier to unravel his tangled thoughts.

As he sat in silence, Granier noticed a small half-Vietnamese, half-American boy, no older than seven, edging closer to him. The child's movements were furtive, and Granier's instincts kicked in. He tensed, his hand automatically reaching for his knife.

Suddenly, the boy's hand darted towards Granier's belt pouch. In a flash, Granier grabbed the child's wrist, his voice sharp and accusing. "What do you think you're doing? Trying to steal from me?"

The boy's eyes widened in fear, and he shook his head vigorously. Granier's grip tightened, suspicion coursing through him. In the midst of war, trust was a rare commodity.

But as he stared into the child's face, Granier paused. The boy's eyes held no malice, only a profound sadness that seemed to pierce through Granier's hardened exterior.

Slowly, he loosened his hold on the boy's wrist, his tone softening. "What's your name?"

The boy hesitated, glancing nervously at the other children huddled nearby. "Luc," he whispered, his voice barely audible over the lapping water.

A wave of shame washing over Granier for his

harsh reaction. This child had undoubtedly witnessed unspeakable horrors and lost everything he held dear. And here he was, treating the boy like a common thief.

"I didn't mean to frighten you. I thought... I thought you were trying to take something from me."

Luc shook his head, his small hand reaching out to touch the glinting metal object inside Granier's belt pouch. "I just wanted to see," he murmured, his fingers touching the object – a compass.

Granier's features softened, a smile tugging at his lips despite their dire circumstances. He removed the compass from the pouch and placed it in Luc's palm, watching as the boy's eyes sparkled with wonder.

"This is a compass," he explained gently. "It helps me find my way when I'm lost."

Luc nodded solemnly, his fingers tracing the compass's intricate design. For a fleeting moment, the war seemed to melt away, and a pure, unblemished connection formed between two souls adrift in the chaos.

"Your father… he was American?"

"Yes. A soldier like you."

"You knew him?"

"No. He died before I was born."

"Sorry. Who taught you English? You speak good for a boy."

"My mom. But she died too. A bomb. In the market."

"Oh. That's when you came to the orphanage?"

"I lived on the street for a while, until the sisters found me."

"You're lucky then."

"I am. Sometimes, we get candy."

"Well, that's important… candy."

"Yeah. Really important."

"Do you want me to show you how to use that… the compass?"

"Can you?"

"I think I can manage."

"Yes please."

Motioning for Luc to sit next to him, Granier patiently showed Luc how the compass worked. He was unthreatened by the boy. He wanted so little. Few expectations. It was all Granier could offer at the moment, but it seemed to be enough. Slowly, patiently, Luc helped bring Granier back into the world as they sat on a raft in the middle of a lake, the mist swirling around them, hiding them from evil.

As the boat and its precious cargo glided through the water, a hush fell over the lake. It was as if the world itself was holding its breath, waiting to see what would happen next. The only sounds were the soft lapping of the water against the rafts, the humming of the motor, and the muffled murmur of the children's voices.

Slowly, the inlet came into view, a narrow channel that wound its way through the reeds and cattails. The mist swirled and eddied around it, creating an eerie, otherworldly atmosphere. But to the children and their protectors, it represented hope, a path to safety and freedom.

Using poles, the Ghost Warriors guided the rafts into the inlet, their movements careful and precise. They knew that the slightest mistake could spell disaster, could alert the enemy to their presence. But they were determined to see this through, to deliver their precious cargo to the waiting plane and the promise of a better life. As the sun set, the mist closed around them, the boat and the rafts disappeared from view, swallowed up by the gathering darkness.

The lesson finished, Granier handed the compass back to Luc, the young boy's eyes wide with wonder as he cradled the instrument in his hands. The mist swirled around the raft like a gentle whisper.

"Thank you for showing me how it works," Luc said, his voice soft but earnest. "I want to learn everything I can."

"Curiosity is a good thing, especially for a young boy," said Granier.

"I want to be strong, like you."

Granier smiled sadly, his eyes haunted by memories of a life lived in the shadow of war. "Being a soldier isn't about strength, Luc. It's about duty. About doing what needs to be done, even when it's hard because you know it's right."

Luc nodded, his face grim with the weight of his own dark thoughts. "I want to be a soldier," he said, his voice trembling slightly. "I want to kill the men who killed my parents."

Granier's heart clenched at the boy's words. He recognized the pain, the anger, the thirst for vengeance. He had felt those same emotions himself, burning in his veins like poison.

"I understand," he said softly. "Believe me, I do. But killing... it changes you. It rots your soul from the inside out."

Luc looked up at him, "But they deserve it. They took everything from me."

"They do deserve it. But a soldier's job is to focus on completing the mission and protecting the innocent, to save lives. It's not about revenge."

Luc frowned, his young face clouded with

confusion. "But what about the bad guys? Don't they deserve to be punished for what they've done?"

Granier sighed, his heart heavy with the weight of his own experiences. "They do. But if we let ourselves be consumed by revenge, by hate... it'll eat us up inside. Until there's nothing left but the desire to hurt, to kill. That's not what being a soldier is about. It's about serving something greater than yourself. About protecting what's right, even when it means putting your own life on the line."

Luc nodded slowly, his eyes wide with a new understanding. "I think I get it. It's not about getting back at the bad guys. It's about doing what's right, no matter what."

"Exactly. And that's what I want for you, Luc. Not a life of hatred and revenge, but a life of purpose and meaning. A life where you can be proud of who you are and what you stand for. A life where you can feel happy."

Luc's lower lip trembled, a single tear tracing a path down his cheek. "I don't know how to do that. How to be happy again."

Granier's heart broke for the boy, for the childhood that had been stolen from him. "It's not easy," he admitted. "But you have to try. You have to find something to live for. Something that brings you joy, that makes you feel alive."

Luc wiped at his eyes, his gaze drifting out over the dark water. "I used to love to draw," he said softly. "Before... before everything changed."

"Then draw," said Granier. "Draw the world as you want it to be. Fill it with beauty and light."

"Will it make the pain go away?"

Granier shook his head. "No. The pain never goes

away, not all of it. But it gets easier to bear. And in time, you'll find that there's still beauty in the world. Still reasons to keep going."

Luc nodded, "Okay. I think I can do that."

Granier pulled the boy into a gentle embrace, his arms a shield against the darkness that threatened to engulf them all. "And remember, no matter what happens, you're not alone. You have people who care about you. Who will always be there for you."

As they sat there on the raft, the mist swirling around them like a protective cocoon, Granier felt a flicker of hope. Hope for Luc, for the children, for a future free from the shadow of war.

It was a fragile hope, as delicate as a candle flame in the wind. But it was enough. Enough to keep him going, to give him the strength to face tomorrow.

In the end, that was all any of them could do. To keep going, to keep fighting, to keep hoping. Until the day when peace finally came, and the wounds of the past could begin to heal.

As the raft drifted through the mist-shrouded river, the airport's faint silhouette emerged in the distance, the flood lights a beacon of hope amidst the darkness. The children huddled close to the nuns. The Ghost Warriors, their weapons at the ready, scanned the shoreline, their senses heightened by the eerie stillness that enveloped them.

Suddenly, the night erupted in a cacophony of gunfire and explosions. Mortar rounds rained down from the shore, sending geysers of water into the air. The NVA, hidden in the dense foliage, had launched a devastating surprise attack. Bullets whizzed past the raft, splintering the bamboo and sending the children screaming in terror, the nuns pushing them down to the bamboo deck.

The Ghost Warriors sprang into action and returned fire, their weapons blazing in the darkness. Granier, his eyes scanning the shoreline, saw the muzzle flashes of the enemy guns. In that moment, something shifted inside him. The haunting visions of the girl falling from the bridge, the weight of his past failures, began to dissolve. Instead, he turned and saw Luc, the other children, the nuns, and his fellow warriors – people who needed him, people he could still save.

Granier ran forward to find Coyle. Coyle was doing his best to return fire with Granier's sniper rifle. As Granier approached, he said, "My turn."

"By all means," said Coyle handing Granier his weapon and picking up a nearby M16.

Granier knelt on the bamboo raft and took aim, his hands steady and unwavering. He was back in control, ready to fight. He became a force of nature. Each bullet found its mark, claiming the lives of the NVA soldiers with ruthless efficiency.

The Ghost Warriors, emboldened by Granier's display of skill, fought with renewed intensity. They laid down a wall of suppressing fire, driving the NVA to cover.

Tragedy struck when a mortar round exploded near the boat, sending shrapnel tearing through the air. Mother Superior was hit in the neck, severing her carotid artery. Blood flowed. She fell to the deck, her habit stained with crimson. She reached for the boat's tiller arm and tried to keep it going straight. For a moment, she steadied the boat's direction and kept pulling the rafts. But her blood loss proved too great and her eyes rolled back as she fell unconscious, releasing boat's controls. The children and nuns watched in horror as her life slipped away.

Pilotless, the boat ran aground, jarring the rafts to a sudden stop. Jolted violently, a little girl rolled over the side of the raft and into the river. A nun jumped into the water to save the child from drifting away. As she grabbed the child and pulled her back to the safety of the raft, a shot rang out, hitting the nun in the back. A Ghost Warrior reached in the water to help her, but it was too late. She was gone under the black water. But the child was safe back on board the raft, a final act of sacrifice in a war that had already taken so much.

Stalled in the river, the rafts were vulnerable and exposed. An easy target. The NVA, sensing an opportunity, intensified their attack. Mortar rounds exploded all around, sending water and debris flying. The children screamed, their small hands clutching at the nuns' robes, seeking comfort and protection.

Coyle ran across the bamboo deck of the lead raft and leaped into the water beside the boat. He pushed the boat away from the shore and into the river, then climbed in. Bullets whizzed over his head. Pushing the body of the Mother Superior aside, he rotated the gear shifter to neutral, then fought to restart the outboard motor, pulling the starter rope. It didn't start. He didn't know a lot about outboard motors, but he did know about engines. He figured it was flooded with gasoline. He found a toolbox on the boat's deck beside the motor and pulled out a pair of pliers. He opened the motor's cover and used the pliers to remove a sparkplug. An enemy bullet hit the flywheel sending a flurry of sparks through the air, but leaving the thick piece of metal undamaged. He carefully dried the gasoline-soaked spark plug on his shirt and threaded it back into the motor, tightening it with the pliers. He gave the motor's starter rope a tug. Nothing. He tried two more times and nothing. He realized that the gasoline in the motor's carburetor had probably evaporated. He gently turned the throttle giving it a little gas, but careful not to flood it. He pulled the rope again. Nothing. Then again… and the motor chug, chug, chugged to life. He carefully reeved the engine to keep it from stalling. He was back in business.

Careful not to flood it gain, he backed off the throttle and engaged the gear to forward. Slowly increasing the throttle and steering the boat back into the middle of the river, he pulled the rafts once more, moving away from the NVA on shore. Granier and the Ghost Warriors continued to provide covering fire.

Seeing the rafts moving again toward the airport, the NVA, undeterred, ran along the shore, keeping pace with the rafts, stopping every couple of yards to fire their weapons.

As the battle raged on, the NVA collided with the ARVN troops defending the airport's perimeter. The two forces clashed in a brutal exchange of gunfire and explosions.

Granier and the Ghost Warriors seized the opportunity, flanking the NVA and attacking them from the side. The chaos of the battlefield worked in their favor, allowing the raft to finally reach the shore in front of the end of the airport's runway.

The nuns ushered the children off the rafts and onto solid ground. Granier and the Ghost Warrior ran to the ARVN perimeter and opened fire to hold back the NVA, buying time.

Coyle led the nuns and the children towards the waiting C-119. Coyle knew that the plane was not large enough to accommodate everyone – the nuns, the children, and the Ghost Warriors. He needed a solution, and he needed it fast.

He led the children and nuns to the back door of the C-119. The informant and his family were already seated inside, waiting. The children and nuns filed in and took seats on the aircraft's deck. The cargo hold quickly filled up. The thought of leaving the Ghost Warriors behind to face the enemy wrenched his gut. He looked around the airfield at the charred remains of the damaged aircraft. He spotted a C-47 with one of its engine covered in soot from a fire and its wing peppered with holes from anti-aircraft shrapnel.

Coyle turned to the crew chief and yelled, "I need a tow rope."

"What are we towing?"

"C-47."

"You know, they come with engines."

"Usually, yeah. Just get me the damned rope."

"Okay, I'm on it."

The chief nodded, jumped to the tarmac, and went in search of a tow rope. Coyle jumped down and ran to the damaged C-47 and climbed into the cockpit. There was blood all over the cockpit from where the shrapnel had shredded the aircraft's skin and broken through the side windows to pelt the aircrew. The bodies of the fallen were gone. He figured the pilot or the copilot must have survived and landed the plane. *Helluva thing,* he thought as he sat down in the pilot's seat. He prepped the plane and started the one good engine. It sputtered to life.

He reeved the engine and taxied the Gooney Bird to the start of the runway and turned it ready for takeoff.

Leaving the engine running, he left the aircraft and met the crew chief on the tarmac with a huge coil of rope on a pushcart.

"Are you sure this thing can even fly?"

"I've flown worst."

"Okay. You think the tow rope will hold?" said the crew chief.

"It better," said Coyle.

"How are we gonna attach it? There ain't no cleat on the belly."

"I don't know. Wing landing gear, I suppose."

"And what are you going to do when you land? It'll foul the landing gear on landing."

"You're assuming I get that far."

"I'm a positive person."

"See if you can rig some sort of knot to release the tow rope from the cockpit side window once I get airborne."

"You know that's a bit crazy."

"Yeah, I know. But it's all I can think of."

"Will do."

Coyle ran to the C-119 and told his copilot his plan. The copilot taxied the boxcar to the start of the runway and turned in front of the C-47. The crew chief rigged the tow rope to several cleats in the C-119s deck. The two aircraft were now connected, and both had their engines running, minus the burned engine on the C-47.

Coyle ran to Granier and the Ghost Warriors at the airport's perimeter. "Time to go," he said.

"We can't leave these guys," said Granier nodding toward the line of ARVN troops.

"Yes, we can, Granier. This is their fight. We gotta let them have it and get these children to safety. That's our mission."

Granier thought for a moment, then nodded in agreement, "You're right. Mission first."

Granier ran over to the ARVN commander and told him they were pulling out. He shook Granier's hand and thanked him for the help. Granier shouted to the Ghost Warriors, "We're moving out. On me."

Each Ghost Warrior emptied his rifle's clip into the enemy then pulled back joining Granier and Coyle back toward the waiting planes at the start of the runway.

Coyle and the Ghost Warriors sprinted across the tarmac, their boots pounding against the concrete as bullets whizzed past them. The roar of the C-119's engines filled the air, a deafening reminder of the urgency of their mission. Granier, his sniper rifle slung over his shoulder, led the way, his eyes scanning the edges of the runway for any sign of enemy movement.

As they reached the waiting C-47, Coyle leaped into the cockpit, his hands already racing over the controls. The Ghost Warriors piled into the fuselage, their weapons at the ready. The smell of blood and burnt metal hung heavy in the stale air.

Coyle glanced out the side window and saw the crew chief give a final thumbs up. The tow rope was secure, the knot on the tow rope rigged to release from the cockpit by a smaller rope. It was now or never.

"Hold on tight!" Coyle yelled over the roar of the engine. "This is gonna be a bit rough!"

He pushed the throttle forward, the C-47's lone engine sputtering, then roared. The plane lurched forward, straining against the weight of the tow rope. In the C-119, the copilot did the same, the two planes moving in unison down the runway, the tow rope still slack.

Bullets pinged off the fuselage, the NVA soldiers desperate to stop their escape. Granier and the Ghost Warriors returned fire out the side door, their weapons blazing, the muzzle flashes lighting up the darkened interior of the plane.

The C-47 shuddered and groaned, its damaged wing struggling to generate lift. Coyle hands wrapped around the yoke as he fought to keep the plane steady.

Coyle radioed his copilot and told him to take up the slack and pull the C-47 with the tow rope. The tow rope raised up off the tarmac and snapped tight like a piano wire. Moments later, the C-119 lifted off from the runway, then it wheels slammed down as the C-47 pulled it back down to earth. The copilot let the two planes gain more speed, then tried again, lifting the wheels of the C-119 of the runway. This time it stayed aloft.

"Close the damned door! It's dragging us down," yelled Coyle in the C-47's cockpit.

Inside the cargo hold, Granier grabbed the side door, slammed it shut and yelled back, "Damned side door shut!"

As the C-47 and C-119 raced down the runway, engines roaring, the NVA commander spotted the planes making their desperate bid for freedom. His eyes narrowed, as he barked an order to his mortar teams, his voice cutting through the chaos of the battle.

"Fire on those planes!" he shouted, his finger stabbing the air. "Don't let them take off!"

The mortar teams swung into action, their weapons trained on the vulnerable aircraft. Shells arced through the night sky, whistling as they hurtled towards their targets. The first rounds exploded near the runway, sending geysers of dirt and debris into the air.

Inside the C-47, Coyle gripped the yoke tighter as he fought to keep the plane steady from the impact of the mortar blasts. The Ghost Warriors, their weapons at the ready, braced themselves for impact. The children and nuns huddled together, their eyes wide with fear, their prayers a desperate whisper.

Suddenly, a mortar round struck the C-119's fuselage, the explosion ripping through the thin metal skin. Shrapnel peppered the interior, shredding seats and puncturing equipment. One of the aircrew, a young man named Nguyen, using his body as a human shield over a nun and several of the children, was hit by the deadly fragments.

Nguyen jerked as the shrapnel tore into his flesh, his blood splattering on the nun's face. The children screamed at the horrifying sight. He slumped to the floor, his life a final act of sacrifice in a war that had already claimed so much.

In the cockpit, the copilot fought to keep the plane in the air, the controls shuddering in his grasp. The C-119 groaned and shuddered from the damage. The tow rope, strained to its limit, threatened to snap at any moment.

More mortar rounds exploded around the planes, the concussive blasts rocking the aircraft. The damaged C-119, strained to pull its wounded comrade aloft. The copilot pushed the engines to their limit, the propellers clawing at the air. The end of the runway was coming up fast. They were out of the time.

Coyle could see they weren't going to make it. There was no reason to for both aircraft to crash. He reached over and pulled the small rope that was attached to the tow rope's knot on the front landing gear... and nothing happened.

Coyle tried again giving the rope a strong tug and still nothing happened. "Oh shit," said Coyle.

The only option was to fly. Coyle pushed the throttle to full and kept the plane as straight down the runway as it could, then just a few yards before reaching the end of the runway, he pulled back on the yoke with every ounce of strength he had left.

Against all odds, the C-47 lifted off the runway, the tow rope snapping taut as the two planes clawed their way into the sky. The mortar rounds fell away, their explosions fading into the distance as the aircraft gained altitude. Everyone cheered.

As the planes climbed higher into the night sky, the battle at the airport faded into memory, a nightmare left behind.

The C-47 and C-119 flew on, their engines a defiant roar against the darkness.

Bien Hoa Air Base, South Vietnam

As the C-47 and C-119 approached Bien Hoa air base, Coyle still had no solution for releasing the tow rope attached to the wing landing gear. The damaged plane had held together through the harrowing escape, the makeshift tow system a fragile lifeline between the two aircraft. Granier moved up beside him in the cockpit and said, "Nice flying, Coyle."

"You might wanna hold that thought," said Coyle.

"Why what's wrong?"

"I tried to release the tow rope before take-off and it didn't work."

"Well, I'm kinda glad you didn't."

"If we can't release it before we land, there's a good chance the landing gear will foul and we'll crash."

"Okay," said Granier looking out the side window. "I can climb out and cut it off."

"You know, I actually believe you'd try that… and promptly get yourself killed. We're moving at 150 miles per hour. The wind would sweep you off like a bug on a windshield."

"Bullshit. I can hang on."

"Fine, but there's a couple of things I'd like to try before you commit suicide, if you don't mind?"

"Nobody's stopping you."

Coyle radioed his copilot in the C-119 and ordered him to release the tow rope from his end.

The crew chief unsheathed his Kbar and cut the tow rope free from the cleats inside the C-119. The severed rope wiggled out the back door like a snake and fell, disappearing.

In the C-47 cockpit, Coyle felt a lurch as the heavy tow rope fell beneath his aircraft, still tied to the front landing gear and caused more drag that the one engine aircraft didn't need. The rope flailed underneath the belly of the fuselage.

"Now what?" said Granier.

"We give it a minute to loosen the knot," said Coyle.

"Will that work?"

"It could."

"You don't sound very sure."

"I'm not. But when Chuck Yeager's engine failed on a test flight and his aircraft went in a flat spin, he just started to try stuff to restart the engine – one thing at a time as he spun toward the ground."

"So, what happened?"

"He finally restarted the engine and became a legend."

"And you hope that's gonna happen here?"

"It could."

"Again, I'm not feeling your confidence."

"Yeah, well… confidence doesn't have a lot to do with knot tying. Here goes nothing."

Coyle pulled the smaller rope tied to the knot on the landing gear and… nothing happened. He yanked it hard several times and still nothing.

"Dammit. I really thought that was gonna work," said Coyle.

"Okay, you had your shot. Now it's my turn," said Granier. "What's best way to get out there?"

"There ain't no good way to get out there during flight, Granier. You're gonna die."

"Let's just say I'm feeling lucky. Are you gonna help me or not?"

Coyle considers for a moment, then… "The door in the cargo hold. You might be able to grab the tow rope and pull yourself to the landing gear. But I still say it's a long shot. And even if you do, I don't know how you're gonna climb back in the aircraft. It's a one-way trip."

"But if I cut the rope from the landing gear, you can land, right?"

"Yeah, I'll be able to land her."

"Okay. Don't worry about me. I'll figure something out. You just land the plane."

"Alright. This is the stupidest thing you've ever done."

"I don't know. I've done some really stupid things in my life."

"You might wanna strip down to your skivvies. Less drag."

"That's probably a good idea."

Granier stripped down and pulled out his knife

from the sheath on his web gear belt.

"The door is not meant to open during flight, so it's gonna be a bear to open in the wind."

"Another fun fact."

As Granier prepared to exit the cockpit, Coyle turned to him and said, "It's been good knowing you, Granier."

"I feel the same, Coyle," said Granier, then disappeared through the cockpit door.

Granier and two of the Ghost Warriors unlocked and pushed the cargo hold door open against the 150 mile per hour wind. One of the Ghost Warriors jammed a knife next to the door's hinges to keep it open.

"Grab my feet," said Granier. They grabbed his ankles as he put the knife between his teeth and crawled out the bottom of the doorway. The wind stung his bare skin. As he lowered himself down under the plane's belly, he could see the thick tow rope flailing back and forth in the wind. He reached out to grab it, but it was too thick to get a good grip and it jerked out of his hands. He removed the knife from his teeth and waited until the tow rope moved close enough, then stabbed it at a forward angle. The knife held. He twisted his legs loose from the grip of the two Ghost Warriors. His body slid beneath the belly, only the knife in the tow rope keeping him from being swept away by the wind. He flailed back and forth with the tow rope. Wrapping his legs and one arm around the rope to hold himself, he pulled himself forward, then yanked the knife clear of the rope for a moment before planting it once again in the strands of the rope. He pulled himself forward inch by inch until he reached the landing gear below the burned engine. He crawled up, wedging himself between the vertical strut and the angled drag brace on the back of the wheel assembly. Steadying himself, he used the knife to cut the rope free from the landing gear. Severed, it fell away. But in doing so, he had sealed his fate. There was no way back into the C-47. He would have to ride out the landing wedge in the landing gear. He wedged his knife between two steel rods giving himself something to hang onto when the wheel touched down on the concrete. There was nothing left to do but wait as the aircraft descended toward the runway.

Inside the cockpit, Coyle felt the heavy tow rope away. The plane was more manageable. "Well done, Granier," he said to himself.

The C-119 landed first and taxied off the runway with no issues. The C-47 was next.

Coyle could see if Granier was still alive and holding on outside the aircraft, but he knew from experience that Granier was hard to kill, so there was a fair chance he was still alive. Coyle was determined to give Granier every chance of surviving the landing wherever he was. As he approached the runway, he lowered the airspeed to stall speed – sixty-seven miles per hour, the minimum airspeed that allowed him to control the aircraft.

Granier watched as the tire beneath him descended to the runway, then touched down with a loud screech. Jolted violently, he hung on for dear life. He wasn't strong enough and lost his grip. He was rocked out of his cradle and fell to the concrete. He hit hard with a grunt and rolled wrapping his arms around his head for protection. The tail wheel missed him by only a foot. The concrete bit into his skin like a cheese grater as the plane rolled clear of his battered body. There was no way to slow himself. He just spun keeping his arms and legs together as best he could until it was finally over.

Coyle slowed the aircraft at the end of the runway and spun it around so he could see back out the windshield. In the distance, he saw Granier's body, motionless on the runway. He felt his lungs catch like he had forgotten how to breath. Then, Granier rolled over on his stomach and climbed to his knees. He was naked, his skivvies had been stripped off by the concrete. His skin was covered in bloody scratches, but he was alive and on his feet walking slowly toward the end of the runway.

Coyle taxied toward him, then pulled the plane on the grass along the apron. Coyle and the Ghost Warriors piled out and ran toward Granier cheering him. Coyle was the last to reach him and said, "That is not a pretty sight."

"Damn, and I so wanted to look nice for you," said Granier with a slight grin.

"You look like you could use a drink."

"Maybe after the hospital."

"Good plan. That was one helluva thing you did, Granier… and really stupid. But thanks."

"Don't mention it, just get me a couple of aspirin."

"That I can do."

It would be another unbelievable story about the man everyone called "Granier." Most would call it an exaggeration at best and an out and out lie at worst. But there was little doubt Rene Granier was a legend.

Ban Me Thuot, South Vietnam

As night fell, the city was in flames, the streets echoing with the screams of the wounded and the dying.

Colonel Quang and the ARVN troops fought on, their ammunition running low, their ranks thinning with every passing hour.

And in the end, it was not enough. The NVA broke through their final defenses, surging into the heart of the city like a tidal wave. Quang and his men fought to the last, their sacrifice was accepted by fate as they were killed by the communists overrunning their position.

As the flag of the North Vietnamese Army was raised over the smoldering ruins of Ban Me Thuot, as the sounds of battle faded into an eerie, haunted silence, it was clear that a great tragedy had taken place. A city had fallen, a people had been brought to their knees, and the course of history had been forever changed.

In the days and weeks that followed, the people of Ban Me Thuot would struggle to come to terms with the enormity of what had happened. They would mourn their dead, rebuild their shattered lives, and try to find a way forward in a world turned upside down.

But they would never forget the courage of those who had fought and died to defend their city, their homes, and their way of life. And they would carry the memory of that day with them forever, a scar upon the soul of a nation that would never fully heal.

Convoy of Tears

Saigon, South Vietnam

President Nguyen Van Thieu stared at the map in dismay. Another red pin had been added, marking the fall of Ban Me Thuot, a crucial regional capital in the Central Highlands. Despite the ARVN's best efforts, they had failed to hold the city against the relentless North Vietnamese assault.

Thieu turned to his assembled advisors: Prime Minister Tran Thien Khiem, Chief of the ARVN General Staff General Cao Van Vien, and Lieutenant General Dang Van Quang. "The loss of Ban Me Thuot makes it clear," he said gravely. "We cannot stop the NVA in the Central Highlands. They are too strong, and we are spread too thin."

General Vien nodded solemnly. "Mr. President, since we cannot hold the highlands, what do you propose?"

Thieu traced his finger along the map, down to the

southern tip of the country. "We must consolidate our forces to protect Saigon and the Mekong Delta. That is where our people and resources are concentrated. It is the heart of South Vietnam. We will withdraw all of our forces in the Northern Provinces immediately."

Prime Minister Khiem frowned. "But Mr. President, what of our people in the North Provinces? Without our military's protection they will be defenseless. Are we to abandon them entirely?"

Thieu sighed heavily. "This is no longer about we want and don't want. We have no choice. We cannot defend every inch of our territory. As I have said before, we must lighten the top and heavy the bottom. The survival of our nation depends on it."

"Our people will see our withdrawal from the Northern Provinces as a betrayal. That we are forsaking them, leaving them in the hands of the communists."

"If you have a better idea, Mr. Prime Minister, I wish to hear it."

Khiem said nothing.

"I didn't think so. These are the toughest of decisions that we as leaders must make for the sake of our country – who to save and who not to save. While we take no pleasure in it, we must do our duty."

"They will be slaughtered by the communists," said General Vien.

"That is why we must do this now while our people still have time to head south and save themselves," said Thieu.

"This is capitulation, Mr. President. Something you swore you would never do."

"This is necessity, General Vien. And I swore to defend my country no matter the cost. If we choose to defend the entire country, we will lose. If we reinforce the key provinces and let the others go, we can always reclaim them when our forces are stronger and more prepared."

"You still believe the Americans will recognize their mistake and come to our rescue?"

"What choice do they have? Let Southeast Asia fall to the communists? Their entire western coastline would be under threat. It's just a matter of time before they accept the reality of the situation and return to Vietnam to bolster their defensive position. We must hang on until that happens."

Lieutenant General Quang leaned forward. "Mr. President, if we are to withdraw our forces from Kon Tum and Pleiku, we must decide on a route. Highway 19 is too exposed, too vulnerable. The NVA will surely cut off our men before they reach the coast."

General Vien leaned forward with concern. "Mr. President," he said, "I too must caution against moving our forces down Highway 19. We cannot forget the lessons of the past."

Thieu looked up from the map, "What do you mean, General?"

Vien took a deep breath. "In 1954, during the Battle of Mang Yang Pass, the French Group Mobile 100 attempted to move their forces along that same route. It was a disaster."

He paused, the weight of history heavy in his words. "The Viet Minh ambushed them, using the terrain to their advantage. The French were trapped, their convoy stretched out for miles. They were sitting ducks."

Vien's voice grew quieter, almost reverent. "The French lost over 2,000 men in that battle. Their vehicles were destroyed, their supplies captured. It was a turning point in the war."

Thieu nodded slowly, "I remember. It was a brutal loss."

Vien pressed on, "We cannot risk the same fate, Mr. President. Highway 19 is too vulnerable to be used. If we send our forces down that route, we could be setting them up for slaughter."

Thieu was silent for a long moment, his eyes distant as he considered Vien's words. Finally, he spoke. "What do you suggest, General?"

Vien pointed to the map, his finger tracing an alternate path. "We should consider using Route 7 instead. It's in poorer condition, but that could work to our advantage. The North Vietnamese may not expect us to take that road."

"Route 7 is nothing more than a trade road that hasn't been properly maintained since the war started," said Quang.

"That is why the NVA commanders will never suspect we would use that route. The poor condition of the road will work to our advantage, catching the North Vietnamese off guard," said Vien. "I admit, it is a gamble. But it is a risk we must take if our troops are to survive."

Thieu studied the map. The dangers were enormous, no matter which path they chose. But the specter of Mang Yang Pass loomed large in his mind, a dark reminder of the price of miscalculation.

"Very well," he said at last, "We will use Route 7. But we must move quickly and carefully. The lives of our men, and the fate of our nation, depend on it."

Vien nodded, his face set with determination. "Yes, Mr. President. I will make the necessary arrangements."

As the meeting adjourned and his advisors filed out, Thieu remained at the table, his gaze fixed on the map. The fate of South Vietnam hung in the balance, and he could only pray that this desperate gamble would pay off. The alternative was too terrible to contemplate.

Central Highlands, South Vietnam

In the aftermath of President Thieu's order to withdraw from the Central Highlands, a great exodus began, a tragic procession of humanity stretching hundreds of miles across the war-torn landscape of South Vietnam. Soldiers and civilians alike took to the roads, fleeing the advancing North Vietnamese Army in a desperate bid for survival.

The once-bustling cities of Pleiku and Kon Tum lay in ruins, their streets littered with the debris of war. Homes and businesses had been reduced to rubble, their walls pockmarked by bullets and shrapnel from artillery shells. Smoke hung heavy in the air, a pall of destruction that seemed to reach to the very heavens.

On the roads, a great tide of humanity flowed, a river of the displaced and the desperate. ARVN soldiers, their uniforms tattered and stained, marched alongside civilians, their weapons slung over weary shoulders. Families trudged along, their meager possessions bundled on their backs or piled high on overloaded vehicles, pushcarts, and motorbikes. The elderly and the infirm struggled to keep pace, their faces filled with the lines of exhaustion and fear.

The convoy was a seemingly endless procession of misery and despair. Abandoned vehicles littered the roadside, their engines silent and their tires flat. The corpses of those who had fallen along the way lay where they had died, a harsh reminder of the toll the war had taken.

As the days passed, the conditions grew ever more dire. Food and water were scarce, and the heat of the Vietnamese sun beat down mercilessly upon the refugees. Children cried out in hunger and thirst, their voices rising above the constant rumble of engines and the clatter of boots on pavement.

And yet, even in the midst of such suffering, there were moments of grace, of human resilience in the face of unimaginable hardship. Soldiers shared what little food they had with civilians, their shared humanity transcending the divisions of war. Strangers helped one another, carrying the weak and the wounded, offering comfort to those who had lost everything.

But the specter of death was never far away. The North Vietnamese Army pursued the convoy relentlessly, their artillery and rockets raining down upon the fleeing masses. The road behind was littered with the wreckage of vehicles and the bodies of the fallen, a trail of destruction that seemed to have no end.

The caravan pressed on, driven by the desperate hope that somewhere, somehow, there would be safety, that there would be a future beyond the horror of war. What choice did they have? They clung to one another, to their faith, to the stubborn belief that they would endure, that they would survive.

Some went toward Da Nang, others to Hue, and still others all the way to Saigon where the president and the generals lived. Surely, the Army would protect Saigon no matter the risk.

Pleiku, South Vietnam

Corporal Nguyen Van Tuong felt the weight of his rifle against his back as he urged the civilians forward, his voice nearly drowned out by the cacophony of engines, shouts, and cries that filled the air. The road out of Pleiku was a river of humanity, a chaotic mix of soldiers and civilians all desperate to escape the advancing North Vietnamese Army. Tuong's unit had been ordered to withdraw, to pull back to the relative safety of the Mekong Delta to defend Saigon. But everywhere he looked, he saw the faces of his people - men, women, and children - all terrified and pleading for help.

"Keep moving!" Tuong shouted, his throat raw from hours of repeating the same command. "We have to get farther south before the NVA cuts us off!"

The road was a mess of vehicles and people, with cars, trucks, and buses jostling for space amid a sea of bicycles and motorbikes. The traffic snarl was so bad that many had resorted to walking, carrying their meager possessions on their backs or balanced precariously atop their heads. The air was thick with dust and exhaust fumes, making it hard to breathe.

Beside Tuong, Private Tran Duc Huy was helping an elderly woman who had collapsed under the weight of her belongings. Her eyes dulled by the horrors she had witnessed. Huy gently lifted her bag onto his own shoulders and took her arm, guiding her back into the stream of refugees.

Tuong felt a surge of pride at his comrade's compassion. The ARVN might be retreating, but they were still South Vietnamese, still bound by a deep sense of duty to protect their people. It was a bond that ran thicker than blood, a shared understanding of the sacrifices they were all making.

Suddenly, the high-pitched whistle of incoming artillery filled the air, growing louder with each passing second. Tuong's eyes widened in horror as he realized the shells were headed straight for the crowded road.

"Get down! Lay on the ground as low as you can!" he screamed, his voice cracking with urgency. He dove to the ground, grabbing a small child and pulling her close as he rolled into the shallow ditch beside the road.

The world exploded in a deafening roar of fire and metal. The ground shook with the force of the impact, and the air was filled with the acrid smell of smoke and burnt flesh. Shrapnel whizzed overhead, slicing through the air like a swarm of hornets. Around him, people were screaming, their cries of pain and panic mixing with the ringing in his ears.

After several minutes of terror, as the smoke began to clear, Tuong staggered to his feet, still clutching the child. She was crying, her small body shaking with sobs, but she seemed miraculously unhurt. He set her down gently and looked around, his heart sinking at the scene of devastation.

The road was a nightmare of carnage, with bodies strewn everywhere amid the twisted metal of destroyed vehicles. Some lay still, their eyes staring blankly at the sky. Others writhed in agony, their clothes soaked with blood. The elderly woman Huy had been helping lay motionless, her bag still clutched in her lifeless hand. Huy himself was slumped against the shattered trunk of a tree, his chest torn open by a jagged piece of shrapnel. Dead.

Tuong felt bile rise in his throat, but he swallowed it back down. There was no time for grief, no time for shock. The NVA would be upon them soon, and they had to keep moving.

"On your feet!" he yelled to the survivors, his voice rough with emotion. "We have to go, now! Leave the dead, carry the wounded if you can. But we have to move!"

Slowly, painfully, the refugees began to stir. Mothers carried wailing children, their faces streaked with tears and dust. The injured leaned on the shoulders of the strong, their faces pale with pain and shock. Tuong took up a position at the rear of the column, his rifle at the ready, determined to defend his people to the last.

As they limped on towards Saigon, Tuong couldn't shake the image of Huy's lifeless body from his mind. His friend, his brother-in-arms, cut down in an instant by the merciless machinery of war. How many more would they lose before this nightmare was over? How many more innocent lives would be shattered, how many families torn apart?

In spite of it all, he kept walking, his boots crunching on the debris-strewn road. For now, all he could do was keep putting one foot in front of the other. Keep leading his people to safety, even as the road behind them ran red with blood and echoed with the cries of the dying.

In the distance, the mountains loomed, a promise of shelter, of respite. But Tuong knew it was only a brief reprieve. The war would find them again, as it always did. All they could do was keep moving, keep fighting, keep holding on to the hope that one day, peace would come.

Until then, the road stretched on, an endless ribbon of suffering and sorrow. And Tuong would walk it, step by bloody step, until his last breath left his body.

For his country, for his people, for the memory of those like Huy, who had given everything in the name of freedom.

Ban Me Thuot, South Vietnam

The road out of Ban Me Thuot was a scene of pure chaos. Thousands of civilians, desperate to escape the advancing North Vietnamese Army, clogged Route 7 with every manner of vehicle and conveyance. Cars, trucks, buses, motorcycles, and even bicycles jostled for space on the narrow, potholed road, their progress slowed to a crawl by the sheer mass of refugees.

Nguyen Thi Hoa clutched her infant daughter to her chest as she fought her way through the crowd. Her husband, Tran, pushed their heavily laden bicycle, their meager possessions balanced precariously on the back. Around them, the air was filled with the sound of engines, shouting, and the cries of frightened children.

"Keep moving," Tran urged, his voice barely audible above the din. "We have to get as far south as possible."

Hoa nodded, too terrified to speak. She had seen what the communists did to those who opposed them. The executions, the forced labor camps, the "re-education" centers. She would rather die than let her daughter fall into their hands.

As they inched forward, Hoa saw a group of ARVN soldiers manning a checkpoint up ahead. They were waving people through, their faces showing their exhaustion. Suddenly, the sound of gunfire erupted from somewhere behind them. Screams filled the air as panic swept through the crowd.

"The NVA! They're coming!" someone shouted.

The crowd surged forward, desperate to reach the safety of the checkpoint. In the chaos, Hoa lost sight of Tran. She was swept along by the tide of bodies, her daughter wailing in fear.

"Tran!" she screamed. "Tran, where are you?"

But her husband was nowhere to be seen. Hoa fought back tears as she struggled to keep her footing. She had to be strong, for her daughter's sake.

As she neared the checkpoint, Hoa saw a group of ARVN soldiers trying to maintain order. They were shouting instructions, directing people to keep moving. But it was no use. The road was simply too congested, the people too panicked.

Suddenly, Hoa heard the roar of engines overhead. She looked up to see helicopters flying low over the road, their rotors whipping the air into a frenzy. For a moment, she felt a surge of hope. Surely the airmen would help them, would save them from the communists.

But the helicopters flew on, disappearing into the distance. Hoa felt her heart sink. They were on their own, with nothing but the long, difficult road ahead. She adjusted her grip on her daughter and kept pushing forward, praying that somewhere at the end of this nightmare, there would be safety and a chance for a new life.

Scott Dickson guided the Huey helicopter low over the chaos of Route 7, his eyes scanning the scene below. Beside him, his sister Karen leaned out of the open door, her camera clicking rapidly as she captured image after haunting image of the desperate exodus.

"My God," she murmured, her voice almost lost

over the roar of the rotors. "It's a disaster."

Scott nodded, his hands steady on the controls. "President Thieu's withdrawal order has turned into a nightmare. These people have nowhere to go, no one to protect them."

Karen turned to him, "Scott, I need to get down there. I can't tell this story from the air. I need to be on the ground, with those people."

"That's crazy, Karen. It's too dangerous. The NVA could be anywhere. And the crowd... it's a powder keg waiting to explode."

But Karen was insistent. " Someone has to show the world what's happening. This is what I do, Scott. But I can't do that from up here."

She placed a hand on his arm, her voice softening. "Please, Scott. I need you to trust me on this."

Scott hesitated, torn between his duty as a soldier and his love for his sister. He knew the risks, knew the danger she would be putting herself in. But he also knew the strength of her conviction, the fire that drove her to tell the stories that needed to be told.

With a heavy sigh, he nodded. "Alright. I'll find a place to set down. But at the first sign of trouble, you get out of there. Alright?"

Karen nodded, but she knew it was a lie. She knew that once she left the helicopter, there would be no way to contact Scott, no way to be saved if things got rough. She was in the duration.

As Scott brought the Huey in low, searching for a clear spot to land, Karen's gaze was drawn back to the scene below. She saw a young mother clutching an infant to her chest, her face etched with the same fear and desperation that seemed to permeate the entire crowd.

For a moment, the woman looked up, her eyes locking with Karen's. In that instant, a connection was forged, a silent understanding of the shared human experience that transcended language and culture.

Then the moment was gone, and the woman disappeared back into the sea of humanity, just another face in the crowd.

As Scott set the Huey down in a small clearing beside the road, Karen gathered her gear with a mixture of excitement and trepidation. She knew that this was where she needed to be, on the front lines of history, bearing witness to the human cost of war. With a final nod to her brother, Karen jumped out of the helicopter and into the maelstrom of Route 7.

Karen stepped into the churning sea of people, her camera held tightly to her chest. The noise was deafening - the roar of engines, the shouts of soldiers, the cries of children. The air was thick with dust and exhaust fumes, making it hard to breathe.

She pushed her way through the crowd, her eyes searching for the stories that needed to be told. She snapped photos families huddled together, their meager possessions bundled on their backs. She photographed the elderly and the infirm, struggling to keep up with the relentless pace of the convoy. And she took photos of the soldiers, their faces etched with the strain of the long march and the weight of their duty to protect their fellow countrymen.

As she walked, Karen felt the gnawing ache of hunger in her own belly, a reminder of how long it had been since she had last eaten. But she pushed the feeling aside, knowing that her discomfort was nothing compared to the suffering of those around her.

Suddenly, a voice rang out above the din, harsh and

angry. "You! American woman! What are you doing here?"

Karen turned to see an ARVN soldier striding towards her, his face contorted with rage. He was young, no more than a boy really, but his eyes were haunted by the horrors he had seen.

"I'm a photojournalist," Karen said, keeping her voice calm and steady. "I'm here to document what's happening, to tell the world the truth."

The soldier laughed, a harsh, bitter sound. "The truth? What truth? That we are abandoning our people, leaving them to the mercy of the communists?"

He stepped closer, his hand tightening on his rifle. "You have no right to be here, American. You have no right to judge us."

Karen met his gaze unflinchingly, her camera held up like a shield. "I'm not here to judge," she said. "I'm here to bear witness."

With a click of the shutter, she captured the soldier's image - his anger, his pain, his desperation. For a moment, he seemed to deflate, the fight going out of him. Then he turned and stalked away, his shoulders hunched against the weight of his own helplessness.

Karen watched him go, knowing there would be more moments like this, more stories that needed to be told. The world had turned away from Vietnam wanting to forget it. She couldn't let that happen.

And so, she walked on, deeper into the heart of the convoy, her camera at the ready. She would not abandon these people. How could she and remain human?

As the miles passed beneath her feet, Karen felt herself becoming part of the exodus, part of the great human tide that flowed towards an uncertain future.

She shared in their hunger, their thirst, their fear. She listened to their stories, captured their faces, bore witness to their struggle.

And through it all, she held on to the hope that someday, when the war was over and the world had moved on, these images would endure - a testament to the resilience of the human spirit in the face of unimaginable hardship.

For now, though, all she could do was keep walking, keep documenting, keep telling the stories that needed to be told. One step at a time, one image at a time, she would make sure that the world did not forget the people of the convoy, the people of Vietnam.

As the convoy wound its way through the Central Highlands, Karen couldn't shake the eerie feeling that had settled over her. The once-vibrant cities and villages that dotted the landscape were now ghost towns, their streets empty and their homes abandoned, their businesses ransacked.

Dak Lak, once a bustling university town, lay silent and still, its buildings scarred by the ravages of war. The market stalls that had once been filled with the colorful wares of local artisans now stood vacant, their contents scattered and broken on the ground. The laughter of children, the chatter of families, the hum of daily life - all had been replaced by an oppressive silence that seemed to press down upon the very earth.

Karen wandered through the empty streets, her camera at the ready, capturing the haunting images of a world that had been left behind. Bullet holes pockmarked the walls of homes and businesses, their jagged edges a stark reminder of the violence that had torn through these communities. Doors hung off their hinges, windows gaped like sightless eyes, and the wind whistled through the deserted alleyways like a mournful cry.

In the village of Khanh Xuan, Karen came across a small schoolhouse, its brightly painted walls now faded and peeling. The desks inside were overturned, the blackboard cracked and dusty. A child's drawing fluttered in the breeze, a poignant reminder of the young lives that had been uprooted by the war.

As she explored further, Karen discovered a makeshift shrine, its altar laden with offerings of fruit and incense. Photographs of the missing and the dead were pinned to the walls, their faces staring out at her with silent accusation. How many families had been torn apart by this conflict? How many lives had been lost, how many dreams shattered?

The silence of these abandoned places was a heavy weight upon Karen's soul, a reminder of the incalculable human toll of the war. Each empty house, each deserted street, represented a life that had been forever changed, a future that had been stolen away.

A single flower bloomed in the rubble of a bombed-out building, a defiant splash of color amidst the gray. A faded poster clung to a wall, proclaiming the unbreakable spirit of the nation.

Karen made her way back to the convoy, her soul was weighed down by what she had seen. The haunting silence of the abandoned cities and villages was a witness to the enduring impact of the war, a reminder of the countless lives that had been forever altered by the conflict.

As Karen made her way through the chaos of the convoy, she heard a commotion up ahead. Pushing her way through the crowd, she stumbled upon a scene that made her blood run cold.

A group of ARVN soldiers, their faces twisted with fear and desperation, were ransacking a civilian truck, tearing through the meager possessions of the refugees who had been riding in it. An elderly woman lay on the ground nearby, her face bloodied and her arm twisted at an unnatural angle.

"Please," she begged, her voice weak and trembling. "Please, don't take our food. My grandchildren, they haven't eaten in days."

But the soldiers ignored her pleas, their eyes wild with the madness of survival. They shoved past the woman, grabbing sacks of rice and cans of fish, stuffing them into their own packs.

Karen raised her camera, her hands shaking with anger and disbelief. The click of the shutter rang out like a gunshot, and one of the soldiers whirled around, his rifle pointed directly at her.

"Don't move," he snarled, his finger tightening on the trigger. "Give me the camera."

Karen hesitated. She knew that the images she had captured were important, that they needed to be seen by the world. But she also knew that her life hung in the balance.

Slowly, she lowered the camera, her eyes never leaving the soldier's face. "Take it," she said, her voice barely above a whisper. "Just let me help her."

For a moment, the soldier seemed to waver, his eyes flicking to the elderly woman on the ground. Then, with a grunt of disgust, he snatched the camera from Karen's hands and turned back to his comrades.

Karen still had her camera bag with a half dozen finished rolls of film. In it, evidence enough to show the world the desperate situation faced by the South Vietnamese, of the human cost of this terrible war. The camera was replaceable, the film wasn't.

Karen rushed to the woman's side, cradling her head in her lap. "I'm so sorry," she murmured, tears streaming down her cheeks. "I'm so sorry this is happening."

The woman looked up at her, her eyes filled with a profound sadness. "You have nothing to apologize for," she said softly. "You are not the one who has abandoned us."

As Karen helped the woman to her feet, she caught a glimpse of the soldiers disappearing into the crowd, their stolen goods clutched tightly to their chests. The breakdown of discipline, the abandonment of their duty to protect the civilians in their charge, was a stark reminder of how far things had fallen, of how desperate the situation had become.

As the convoy stretched endlessly along the road, Karen heard a woman's cries rising above the din. Pushing her way through the sea of refugees, she found a young woman lying on the ground, her face contorted in pain. Refugees and soldiers walked around her, nobody helping the desperate woman. Seeing the woman was in the final days of her pregnancy, Karen knelt beside her.

"Please, help me," the woman gasped, clutching at her swollen belly. "My baby, it's coming."

Karen took her hand in her own. "I'm here," she said. "I'm going to help you. What's your name?"

"Linh," the woman panted, her eyes filled with fear. "I'm Linh."

"Where is your baby's father, Linh?"

"No father. I alone."

"Okay. That's okay. I'm with you."

As the contractions intensified, Karen held Linh's

hand tightly, offering words of encouragement. "You're doing great, Linh. Just keep breathing, and focus on my voice."

Linh nodded, her face contorted with pain. "I'm scared," she whispered, her voice barely audible above the chaos of the convoy.

Karen smiled reassuringly, even as her own heart raced with fear. "I know, but you're strong. You can do this. Tell me, do you want a boy or a girl?"

Linh managed a weak smile. "A girl," she said, her voice wistful. "I've always wanted a daughter."

"And what will you name her?" Karen asked, trying to keep Linh's mind off the pain.

"Mai," Linh replied, her eyes distant. "It mean 'apricot blossom.'"

Just then, Karen heard the sound of engines revving, and she looked up to see the convoy beginning to move forward. A surge of panic shot through her as she realized they were being left behind.

Karen looked around frantically, searching for anyone who might be able to assist. But the soldiers and civilians around them were too caught up in their own struggles, too desperate to escape the advancing enemy.

"Wait!" she cried out, waving frantically. "Please, wait! We need help!"

But her pleas were drowned out by the roar of the engines, and the convoy disappeared into the distance, leaving Karen and Linh alone on the side of the road.

"Okay, Linh," Karen said, trying to keep her voice calm and steady. "We're going to do this together. I need you to take deep breaths and push when I tell you to, alright?"

Linh nodded, gritting her teeth as another

contraction rippled through her body. Karen positioned herself at the woman's feet. She had never delivered a baby before, had never even seen it done. But she knew that she had to try, that she couldn't let this woman and her child become just another casualty of the war.

For precious minutes, they labored together, Linh pushing with all her strength while Karen coached and encouraged her. The sun beat down upon them, and the sounds of the convoy faded into the background as they focused on the task at hand.

Karen's heart sank as she realized the gravity of their situation. The North Vietnamese Army was close, and without the protection of the convoy, they were in serious danger.

She looked down at Linh, who was panting and straining with the effort of labor. Karen wondered if the mother would survive without a doctor or midwife. She thought about what would happen if she, an American, were captured by the NVA. It was a gruesome thought. Karen knew she had a choice to make. She could try to catch up with the convoy, leaving Linh to fend for herself, or she could stay and help her through the birth, knowing that they might not survive the approaching enemy.

In that moment, Karen made her decision. She would not abandon Linh, not when she needed her most. She would stay, and face whatever came, together.

"Linh," she said softly, squeezing the woman's hand. "I'm here with you. I'm not going anywhere."

Linh's eyes filled with tears of gratitude, even as another contraction ripped through her body. "Thank you," she whispered, her voice ragged with pain.

As the sound of gunfire grew closer, Karen focused all her attention on Linh, coaching her through the final stages of labor. "Push, Linh!" she urged, her voice firm and steady. "Your baby is almost here. Just a little more."

With a final, guttural cry, Linh delivered her daughter into the world. Karen quickly wrapped the tiny, squalling infant in an extra t-shirt from her camera bag, her hands shaking as she tied off the umbilical cord.

"You did it, Linh," she said, her voice choked with emotion. "Your little Mai is here, and she's perfect."

Linh's face was a mixture of exhaustion and joy as she cradled her newborn daughter to her chest. For a moment, the world around them seemed to fade away, and there was only the miracle of new life, pure and untainted by the horrors of war.

But the moment was short-lived. The sound of approaching footsteps and shouted commands in Vietnamese jolted Karen back to reality. The NVA soldiers were almost upon them.

"Linh, I'm sorry to do this, but we have to go," she said urgently, helping the woman to her feet. "Can you walk?"

Linh nodded, her face pale but determined. "For Mai," she said softly, "I do anything."

Together, they stumbled forward, the baby nestled close to Linh's heart. Karen's eyes scanned the horizon for any sign of shelter or safety. She knew that their chances of survival were slim, but she refused to give up hope.

As they disappeared into the jungle, the sound of gunfire echoing behind them, Karen knew that whatever lay ahead, she would face it with courage and resolve. For in that moment, she had found a purpose greater than herself, a reason to keep fighting, even in the face of impossible odds. And though the future was uncertain, she knew that she would never forget the precious gift of life that had been entrusted to her care, or the brave woman who had brought it into the world against all odds.

Karen cradled the tiny baby in her arms as Linh lay on the ground beside her, her face pale and her breathing shallow. They had managed to find a small clearing just off the road, hidden from view by a dense thicket of trees and undergrowth.

"Linh, you need to rest," Karen said softly, her voice laced with concern. "You've lost a lot of blood."

Linh shook her head weakly, a small smile playing at the corners of her lips. "I need to feed Mai," she whispered, reaching for her daughter. "She needs her mother's milk."

Karen hesitated, knowing that Linh was in no condition to nurse. But the look of determination in the woman's eyes was unmistakable, and Karen couldn't bring herself to refuse.

Gently, she placed the baby in Linh's arms, watching as the woman brought the tiny mouth to her breast. Mai latched on eagerly, her small hands kneading at her mother's skin.

For a moment, everything seemed to fade away - the war, the fear, the exhaustion. There was only the bond between mother and child, a connection that transcended all else.

But as the minutes ticked by, Karen noticed a change in Linh's demeanor. Her eyes began to drift closed, her head lolling to the side. The hand that had been supporting Mai's head slipped away, and the baby began to fuss.

"Linh?" Karen said urgently, shaking the woman's shoulder. "Linh, wake up!"

But Linh didn't respond. Her breathing had grown shallow and labored, and her skin was cold to the touch.

Panic rising in her throat, Karen looked around desperately for help. But there was no one, only the forest and the distant sound of gunfire.

"Help!" she screamed, her voice raw with desperation. "Please, someone help us!"

But her cries were met with silence. She was alone, with a newborn baby and a dying woman, in the middle of a war zone.

Tears streaming down her face, Karen gathered Mai into her arms, rocking her gently as she sobbed. She knew that Linh was slipping away, that there was nothing she could do to save her.

"I'm so sorry, Linh," she whispered, her voice choked with grief. "I'm sorry I couldn't do more. I'm sorry I couldn't save you."

Linh's eyes fluttered open, and she looked up at Karen with a weak smile. "Don't be sorry," she murmured, her voice barely audible. "You gave Mai a chance at life."

She reached out a trembling hand, brushing her fingers against her daughter's cheek. "Promise me," she whispered, her eyes fierce with determination. "Promise me you'll take care of her. Promise me you'll keep her safe."

Karen nodded, her vision blurred with tears. "I promise," she said, her voice breaking. "I'll protect her with my life."

Linh's eyes drifted closed, and her hand fell away. For a moment, Karen thought she had fallen asleep. But then she realized that the woman's chest was no longer rising and falling, that the life had gone out of her.

A sob tore from Karen's throat as she hugged Mai close, the baby's cries mingling with her own. She knew that she couldn't stay here, that she had to keep moving, for the sake of the child in her arms.

With a heavy heart, she laid Linh's body down on the ground, crossing her arms over her chest. She whispered a silent prayer, asking for the woman's soul to find peace, for her spirit to watch over her daughter.

Then, with Mai nestled close to her heart, Karen set out once again, following the road that would lead her back to the convoy. She didn't know what lay ahead, or how she would keep her promise to Linh. But she knew that she had to try, that she had to find a way to give this child the life that her mother had dreamed of.

As Karen walked along the road, little Mai's cries grew louder and more insistent. The baby was hungry, and Karen knew that she needed milk soon, or she wouldn't survive.

But in the chaos of the convoy, with people pressed together in a desperate bid for survival, there was no milk to be found. Karen had no way to feed the newborn in her arms.

Desperation rising, Karen scanned the crowd, searching for anyone who might be able to help. And then, she saw her - a young mother, sitting by the side of the road, nursing a toddler at her breast.

Without hesitation, Karen pushed her way through the throng of people, clutching Mai close to her chest.

When she reached the woman, she knelt beside her, her eyes pleading.

"Please," she said, her voice raw with emotion. "This baby, she needs milk. She's starving. Can you help us?"

The woman looked up at Karen, her eyes wary. She took in the American woman's disheveled appearance, the desperation in her face.

"I have barely enough for my own child," she said, her voice hard. "Why should I give it to you?"

Karen's heart sank, but she refused to give up. Reaching into her pocket, she pulled out a handful of American dollars - the last of her money.

"I can pay you in American dollars," she said, holding out the bills. "Just let her nurse, just for a little while."

The woman's eyes widened at the sight of the money. In a country ravaged by war and poverty, American dollars were a rare and precious commodity.

"Two dollars," she said, her voice firm. "For two dollars, I'll let her nurse."

Karen didn't hesitate, "Yes. Two dollars." She counted out the bills and pressed them into the woman's hand, her own shaking with relief.

Gently, the woman took Mai from Karen's arms and brought her to her breast. The baby latched on eagerly, her tiny mouth working furiously as she drank.

As Karen watched, tears of gratitude streamed down her face. She knew that this woman's milk would give Mai the strength she needed to survive, at least for a little while longer.

"Thank you," she whispered, her voice choked with emotion. "Thank you so much."

The woman nodded, her eyes softening as she

looked down at the nursing baby. For a few precious minutes, the two women sat together, the sound of Mai's contented suckling filling the air between them. It was a moment of respite, a brief oasis from the madness.

But all too soon, it was over. The woman gently detached Mai from her breast and handed her back to Karen, a small smile playing at the corners of her lips.

"She strong," she said, nodding at the baby. "She'll make it through this."

Karen hugged Mai close, her heart swelling with love. She would do whatever it took to keep this child safe, to give her the life that Linh had dreamed of. And with the kindness of a stranger and the strength of her love, she knew that anything was possible.

As the sun dipped below the horizon, casting long shadows across the road, Karen found a quiet spot to rest for the night. She was exhausted, her body aching from the miles she had walked and the weight of the baby in her arms.

Beside her, the young mother who had nursed Mai earlier in the day sat cross-legged on the ground, her own child sleeping soundly in her lap. Karen approached her cautiously, Mai cradled close to her chest.

"I'm sorry to bother you again," she said softly, her voice tinged with embarrassment. "But Mai needs to nurse, and I don't have any other way to feed her. I can pay you, like before."

The woman looked up at Karen. "Of course," she said, reaching out her arms for the baby. "I'm happy to help."

Karen handed Mai over gratefully, watching as the woman settled the baby at her breast. Mai latched on eagerly, her tiny hands kneading at the woman's skin as she drank.

As before, Karen counted out two American dollars and pressed them into the woman's hand. "Thank you," she whispered, her voice thick with emotion. "I don't know what we would do without you."

The woman smiled, her eyes crinkling at the corners. "You're a good woman," she said, nodding at Karen. "Your baby is lucky to have you."

Karen felt tears prick at the corners of her eyes. She thought of Linh, of the sacrifice she had made to bring Mai into the world. "I'm trying," she said softly, her voice barely audible above the chirping of the crickets. "I promised her mother I would keep her safe."

The woman nodded. "Then that is what you will do," she said simply. "You will keep her safe, and you will give her a good life. That is all any mother can ask for."

For a long moment, the two women sat in silence, the only sound the gentle suckling of the baby at the woman's breast. Then, Mai pulled away, her tiny mouth stretching in a yawn.

The woman handed her back to Karen, a smile playing at the corners of her lips. "She's finished," she said softly. "You should both get some rest now."

Karen nodded, cradling Mai close to her chest. She settled back against a tree, the rough bark pressing into her skin through the thin fabric of her shirt.

As the night deepened around them, Karen looked down at the baby in her arms, marveling at the perfect curve of her cheek, the delicate flutter of her eyelashes. "Hello, little one," she whispered, her voice soft with wonder. "I'm your Aunt Karen. I know I'm not your real mom, but I'm going to take care of you now."

Mai stirred in her sleep, her tiny hand curling around Karen's finger. Karen felt a surge of love so powerful it took her breath away. In that moment, she knew that she would do anything for this child, that she would move mountains to keep her safe and happy.

"I love you, Mai," she whispered, pressing a gentle kiss to the baby's forehead. "I promise I'll always be here for you, no matter what."

As the stars twinkled overhead and the sounds of the jungle filled the air, Karen held Mai close, marveling at the miracle of new life in the midst of so much death and destruction. She knew that she had found a purpose greater than herself, a reason to keep fighting, even in the darkest of times.

With a soft sigh, Karen closed her eyes, letting the rhythm of Mai's breathing lull her into a peaceful sleep. And as she drifted off, she dreamed of a world where children could grow up without fear, where mothers didn't have to say goodbye too soon, and where love and hope could triumph over even the deepest of sorrows.

As dawn broke over the horizon, Karen woke to the sound of a distant helicopter. At first, she thought she was dreaming, her mind still foggy with sleep. But as the sound grew louder, she realized it was real.

Karen scrambled to her feet, Mai clutched tightly to her chest. She scanned the sky frantically, searching for the source of the noise.

And then she saw it - a lone helicopter, flying low over the treetops. It was a military chopper, its rotors slicing through the air with a deafening roar.

Karen's heart leaped with hope. She knew that helicopter, knew the pilot who flew it. It was her brother, Scott.

But even as joy surged through her, Karen realized the problem. The convoy was on the move again, a long line of vehicles and people stretching out along the road. And she was just one person, one tiny speck in a sea of humanity. How would Scott ever find her?

Desperately, she rummaged through her bag and pulled out a bright red baseball hat. She climbed to the top of a nearby abandoned vehicle, waving the hat frantically in the air, hoping to catch Scott's attention. But as the helicopter flew closer, it didn't slow down. Karen's heart sank. Scott hadn't seen her signal, and the chopper continued on its path towards the enemy forces chasing the convoy.

Karen watched helplessly as Scott's helicopter engaged the enemy, launching a fierce air assault in an attempt to slow their advance. The sound of gunfire and explosions filled the air, and Karen held her breath, praying that her brother would make it out alive.

Moments later, the helicopter emerged from the fray, smoke trailing from its fuselage. Karen could see that it had been hit, but somehow, Scott had managed to keep it in the air. He flew low over the convoy once more, searching desperately for any sign of his sister.

Karen knew she had to act fast. She dug through her camera bag and found a lens filter, no bigger than the palm of her hand. She held it up to the sun, angling it just right, and a bright beam of reflected light shot out towards the helicopter.

In the cockpit, Scott's co-pilot squinted against the sudden glare. "There!" he shouted, pointing towards the source of the light. "I think that's her!"

Scott knew only Karen would think to use a camera lens filter to catch his attention. He quickly maneuvered the helicopter towards the ground, finding a small, open field nearby to set down.

As the helicopter touched down, hundreds of desperate refugees began to swarm towards it, hoping for a chance at rescue. The door gunner had no choice but to fire warning shots into the air, driving the mob back.

Karen fought her way through the crowd, Mai clutched tightly to her chest. She could see Scott jumping out of the helicopter, running towards her with a look of relief.

"Karen!" he shouted, his voice barely audible over the roar of the helicopter blades. "Thank God you're alive!"

Karen fell into her brother's arms, tears streaming down her face. "I knew you'd find me," she sobbed, holding him tight. "I knew you'd come for us."

"Us?" said Scott looking down at the newborn in her arms.

"This is Mia. I'll explain later."

"Let's get you out of here," he said, leading Karen and Mai back towards the helicopter.

As Scott led Karen and Mai towards the helicopter, Karen suddenly stopped in her tracks. "Wait," she said, her voice filled with urgency. "We can't leave them behind."

Scott followed his sister's gaze to where the nursing mother and her toddler stood, watching the scene with a mixture of fear and desperation. He knew that the damaged helicopter was already overloaded, that taking on more passengers would be a risk.

But as he looked into Karen's pleading eyes, he knew he couldn't refuse her. "Okay," he said, nodding his head. "We'll take them with us."

Karen rushed over to the woman, grabbing her

hand and pulling her towards the helicopter. "Come with us," she urged. "We'll keep you safe."

The woman hesitated for a moment, looking down at her toddler with tears in her eyes. But as the sound of gunfire echoed in the distance, she knew she had no choice. She scooped up her child and followed Karen towards the waiting chopper.

Scott helped the woman and her toddler into the helicopter, then turned to assist Karen and Mai. As he lifted the tiny baby into the cabin, he couldn't help but marvel at the strength and resilience of his sister.

"You're amazing, you know that?" he said, his voice filled with pride and admiration. "I don't know how you do it."

Karen smiled through her tears, holding Mai close to her chest. "I had a good teacher," she said, thinking of her mother and the lessons she had taught them about courage and compassion.

As the helicopter lifted off, Karen looked down at the sea of refugees below, her heart aching for all those they had left behind. She knew that their fight was far from over, that there were still so many more who needed help.

But for now, she had to focus on the precious cargo in her arms. She had to keep Mai safe, and give her the chance at a better life that her mother had dreamed of.

As they flew over the war-torn landscape, Karen made a silent promise to herself and to Mai. She would never stop fighting for what was right, never stop working to build a world where children could grow up in peace and safety.

Saigon, South Vietnam

Karen sat in the editor's office, in the middle of a heated argument. Mai squirmed in her arms, blissfully unaware of the tension that filled the room.

"Karen," her editor said, his voice firm but not unkind. "I know you care deeply for Mai, but you have to think about what's best for her in the long run."

Karen felt tears prickling at the corners of her eyes. "I am thinking about what's best for her," she said, her voice trembling. "I'm the only family she has left. I can't just abandon her."

The editor leaned forward, his eyes filled with a mix of sympathy and concern. "Karen, you're not abandoning her. You're giving her a chance at a better life, with a family who can provide her with everything she needs."

Karen shook her head stubbornly. "I can provide for her. I can be the mother she needs."

"Can you really?" the editor asked gently. "Karen, you're a photojournalist and a damned good one. Your job takes you to dangerous places, keeps you away from home for weeks or even months at a time. Is that the kind of life you want for Mai?"

Karen felt a sob rising in her throat. Deep down, she knew he was right. Her job was demanding, unpredictable. She couldn't give Mai the stability and security she needed.

"I know this is hard," he said softly. "But you have to think about Mai's future. She deserves a chance to grow up in a safe, loving home, with parents who can give her their undivided attention."

Karen looked down at Mai, at the perfect curve of her cheek and the tiny fist curled around her finger. She thought about all the hopes and dreams she had for this child, all the love she wanted to give her.

But she also thought about the reality of her life, about the dangers and uncertainties that came with being a journalist in a war-torn country. She couldn't subject Mai to that, couldn't risk her safety and well-being for the sake of her own selfish desires.

After considering for a long moment, Karen nodded. "You're right," she whispered, her voice choked with emotion. "I have to do what's best for Mai."

The editor smiled sadly. "I know it's not easy, Karen. But you're doing the right thing. Mai will always be a part of your life, even if you're not the one raising her."

Karen hugged Mai close, breathing in the sweet scent of her skin. She knew that saying goodbye would be the hardest thing she had ever done, but she also knew that it was the only way to give Mai the life she deserved.

Karen sat in the rocking chair in the living room of her small apartment, Mai cradled in her arms as the soft glow of the lamp cast a warm light over the room. Outside, the bustling sounds of Saigon had faded into a distant hum, the city settling into the quiet of the night.

Mai cooed softly, her tiny hands reaching up to touch Karen's face. Karen smiled down at her, memorizing every detail of her features - the curve of her cheek, the straight tuffs of her black hair, the trusting innocence in her eyes.

"I love you, little one," Karen whispered, her voice thick with emotion. "I will always love you, no matter where life takes us."

She rocked gently back and forth, humming a

lullaby she remembered from her own childhood. Mai's eyelids began to droop, her breathing slowing as she drifted off to sleep.

Karen knew that this was their last night together, that in the morning she would have to say goodbye to the child who had stolen her heart. The thought filled her with a deep ache, a sense of loss that threatened to overwhelm her.

But even in the midst of her grief, Karen knew that Mai would be going to a good home, to a family who would love her and cherish her as their own. And she knew that the bond they had forged would never truly be broken. As the night wore on, Karen held Mai close, savoring every moment of their time together.

Even in the depths of her sorrow, Karen knew that she was giving Mai the greatest gift of all - a chance at a better life, a future filled with love and hope and possibility.

The next day, Karen stood outside the orphanage, staring into space, tears rolling down her face, her arms empty. Mai was gone. She had done the right thing and it hurt like hell. At least Mia had a chance at a happy life. But Karen felt her life was hollow, her purpose gone.

After a long, lonely moment, Karen walked down the building's stairs and turned down the sidewalk. She felt her strength sapped, even walking was a chore. But she knew, she had to get on with herlife, get on with her job. Somehow, she had to find meaning again.

Karen walked into the camera shop, the bell above the door jingling softly as she entered. The familiar scent of new electronics and polished glass filled her nostrils, but today, even the prospect of a new camera couldn't lift her spirits.

The shop owner, an elderly man with kind eyes and a warm smile, greeted her from behind the counter. "Good morning, miss," he said, his voice gentle. "How can I help you today?"

Karen forced a smile, trying to push away the thoughts of Mai that haunted her. "I'm looking for a new camera," she said, her voice sounding hollow even to her own ears. "Mine was stolen recently."

The owner nodded sympathetically. "I'm sorry to hear that," he said, reaching beneath the counter and pulling out a sleek, black camera. "This is the latest model from Canon. It has a high-resolution sensor, advanced autofocus, and excellent low-light performance."

He began to explain the various features of the camera, pointing out the different buttons and dials. But Karen found herself only half-listening, her mind drifting back to the tiny weight of Mai in her arms.

She picked up the camera, running her fingers over the smooth metal casing. It felt heavy in her hands, a reminder of the weight of her responsibilities, the burden of the choices she had made.

The owner continued to talk, his voice fading into a distant buzz as Karen stared down at the camera. She thought of all the photos she had taken in Vietnam, the captured moments of joy and sorrow, hope and despair. She imagined of how Mai would have looked through the lens, her eyes wide with wonder and curiosity. She remembered that she didn't even have a photo of the child. Pain struck here like a bolt of lightning. Fierce. Too much to bear. She took a deep breath, trying to steady herself, but the ache in her chest only seemed to grow.

Suddenly, the owner's voice cut through her trance.

"So, what do you think?" he asked, his eyes searching her face. "Is this the one you want?"

Karen blinked, startled out of her thoughts. She looked down at the camera in her hands, feeling a sudden rush of emptiness, of loss. "I've changed my mind," she said.

Karen burst through the doors of the orphanage, her heart pounding in her chest as she strode up to the front desk. The receptionist looked up, startled by the sudden intrusion.

"I want my baby back. I want Mia," Karen said, her voice tight with barely controlled anger. "Now."

The receptionist hesitated for a moment, taken aback by Karen's intensity. But something in Karen's eyes must have convinced her of the urgency of the situation, because she quickly picked up the phone and dialed the manager's office.

A minute later, the manager appeared, a middle-aged woman with a kind but tired face. "Can I help you?" she asked, her voice wary.

"I want my baby back," Karen said, her words coming out in a rush. "I made a mistake. I never should have left her here."

The manager's expression softened slightly, but she shook her head. "I'm sorry, but we have to follow procedure," she said gently. "If you want to adopt the child, you'll need to fill out the proper paperwork and go through the necessary channels."

Karen felt a surge of fury rising in her chest. "I don't want to adopt her," she snapped, her voice rising with each word. "She's already mine. I'm her mother."

The manager sighed, rubbing her temples with her fingertips. "I understand your feelings," she said, her voice firm but not unkind. "But the fact is, you signed the papers relinquishing your parental rights. Legally, the child is now a ward of the state."

Karen slammed her hand down on the desk, making the receptionist jump. "I don't care about legalities," she said, her voice shaking with rage. "I care about my daughter. And I'm not leaving here without her."

Karen pulled a folded carbon copy of the document she had signed and said, "This is what I signed." She ripped the copy into pieces. "Rip up your original and give me my daughter back. It'll be like it never happened."

"I can't do that," said the manager.

"Yes, you can. This is Vietnam. Things like that are done all the time."

"Not here they are not. We follow the rules."

"Do you even know what's happening out there, beyond this city? The country is falling apart. In a few weeks, the communists are going to overrun Saigon. Your precious paperwork will mean nothing. I'm just asking you to let me save this one child. I can keep her safe."

"I'm sorry. I can't…"

Without waiting for the rest of the manager's response, Karen pushed past her and stormed down the hallway, her eyes scanning the rooms for any sign of Mai. She could hear the manager calling after her, but she ignored her, focused solely on finding her child.

Finally, she spotted her, lying in a crib in a room with several other infants. Karen's heart leaped into her throat as she rushed over and scooped Mai up into her arms, holding her close and breathing in the sweet scent of her skin.

"I'm here, Mia," she whispered, tears streaming down her face. "I'm so sorry. I never should have left you."

The manager appeared in the doorway, her face a mix of frustration and sympathy. "You can't just take her," she said, her voice strained. "There are procedures that need to be followed, paperwork that needs to be filed."

Karen turned to face her, Mai clutched tightly to her chest. "I don't care about your procedures or your paperwork," she said, her voice low and fierce. "I care about my daughter. And I'm not letting her go again."

For a long moment, the two women stared each other down, the tension in the room palpable. And then, something in the manager's expression shifted. She sighed, her shoulders slumping in resignation.

"Fine," she said, her voice tired. "I'll rip up the admittance paperwork. But you need to understand the consequences of this decision. You'll be solely responsible for this child, for her care and well-being. Whatever your reasons for giving her to us will still be there."

Karen nodded, her eyes never leaving Mai's face. "I understand," she said softly. "And I'm ready for that responsibility. I'm ready to be her mother, in every sense of the word."

The manager nodded, a small smile tugging at the corners of her mouth. "Then go," she said, gesturing towards the door. "Take your daughter and give her the life she deserves."

With a final, grateful nod, Karen turned and walked out of the orphanage, Mai cradled safely in her arms.

She knew that she had made the right choice, that Mai was meant to be a part of her life, now and forever.

Over the next few days, Karen faced a barrage of well-meaning but misguided advice from her colleagues and friends. They all seemed to think that she had lost her mind, that the stress of the war had finally gotten to her.

But Karen refused to budge. She knew in her heart that she was making the right decision, and she wasn't going to let anyone talk her out of it.

One evening, as Karen was feeding Mai in her small apartment, there was a knock at the door. When she opened it, she was surprised to see her father standing in the hallway, a grin on his face.

"Dad," Karen said, her voice filled with surprise. "What are you doing here?"

"Is that her?" said Coyle, his eyes falling on the baby in Karen's arms. "Scott told me what happened," he said gently. "And I couldn't wait any longer. I had to meet my granddaughter."

Karen felt tears prick at the corners of her eyes. She had always had a complicated relationship with her father, but in that moment, she was grateful for his presence. "This is Mia."

"Good name. Fits her. Can I hold her?"

"She just ate. I haven't burped her yet."

"I think I can handle it," said Coyle scooping Mia in his arms as he pushed his way past Karen and sat down in the living room. As she watched Coyle rock Mai gently in his arms, Karen felt a sense of peace wash over her.

She picked up her new camera, framed the perfect

picture, and snapped two photos of grandpa and his granddaughter. It was a perfect moment, then Mia threw up her milk all over Coyle's shirt.

"Mia?!" said Karen. "He's your grandpa."

"It's okay," said Coyle. "I needed to be christened. Do you have a towel or something?"

"Yes, of course," said Karen as she retrieved a clean dipper and dabbed her father's shirt. Coyle kept holding Mia like he had no intention of ever letting her go.

"So, what's the plan?" said Coyle.

"I don't have one… yet."

"Karen, we're in a war and the communists are coming. I would think a plan should be a priority."

"I know, Dad. It's just that so much has happened. My mind is mush."

"You and Mia need to leave Vietnam, now, before things get really bad."

"I need to be here to document what happens."

"No, you don't. You need to watch after your child. Being a parent is the most important thing you can do."

"Like you're the expert?"

"Yeah. I wasn't there for you and Scott when you were growing up. I didn't even know you existed. But now, it's my biggest regret."

"I know. And I'm gonna be there for Mia no matter what happens."

"Karen, you think you control everything, but you don't. Nobody knows what's going to happen when the communists arrive, but I'm pretty sure it's not going to be good… or safe."

Even though Karen had known she needed to make this decision, she was torn. "I can't just leave."

"Yes, you can and that is exactly what you should

do."

"What kind of example would I be setting for Mia if I just leave at the first sign of trouble?"

"The first sign of trouble? Where have you been the last few months?"

"You know what I mean."

"Yeah, I know what you mean and I am telling you, you and Mia need to leave. It's going to get bloody and it's no place for a baby. Look what happened to her mother. Mia doesn't deserve for that to happen twice in her lifetime."

"I know that. But how can I just leave these people?"

"You and Mia get on a plane and go. That's it. There is no other good choice. It's time to leave. It's time to go home."

"Home? This is her home."

"Not anymore. Home is wherever her family is and you're her family."

"I guess I know that you're right. I've been in denial thinking I can do everything. I'm so damned tired."

"Babies will do that."

"Where should I go?"

"Your mom hasn't seen her granddaughter yet."

"That's true. What about you and Scott?"

"We'll be along. We just need to wrap things up here."

"Jesus, I can't believe I'm going to leave Vietnam."

"Believe it. It's what's best for Mia. And make sure you give me a copy of those photos you just took before you leave. Something to remember her by."

"And what about me?"

"You? I could never forget you. It's not possible."

Karen's eyes teared up. She hugged Coyle and Mia.

"I guess it's time for a new adventure, little one. Does that sound good?"

Mia gurgled, then threw up again on Coyle's shirt.

Saigon Airport, South Vietnam

The Saigon airport was beyond packed with people lucky enough to get a visa and an airline ticket. Nobody wanted to wait to see the outcome of the final days of the war.

Karen stood at the gate, Mai cradled in her arms, as she watched the TWA jet taxi up to the jetway. The bustling chaos of the airport seemed to fade into the background as she turned to face her father and brother, a bittersweet smile on her face.

Scott stepped forward, his eyes misty as he looked down at his niece. "You sure about this, Karen?" he asked softly, his voice gruff with emotion. "It's a big decision, raising a child on your own."

Karen nodded, her gaze never leaving Mai's face. "I've never been more sure of anything in my life," she said, her voice steady. "Mai is my daughter, in every way that matters. And I'm going to give her the best life I possibly can."

Coyle reached out and squeezed his Karen's shoulder, a proud smile on his face. "You're going to be an amazing mom," he said, his voice thick. "And Mai is lucky to have you."

Karen felt tears prickling at the corners of her eyes as she looked up at her brother. "I couldn't have done this without you," she said softly. "Without either of you. Your support has meant everything to me."

Coyle cleared his throat, blinking back his own tears. "You just promise me one thing," he said, his voice stern. "You show that little girl my photo every day, so she doesn't forget me."

"Mine too," said Scott.

Karen laughed, a watery sound that was half-sob, half-joy. "I promise," she said, hugging Mai close. "And you promise to come visit us as soon as you get back."

"We promise," said Coyle and Scott in unison.

The boarding call echoed over the loudspeaker, and Karen knew it was time to go. She took a deep breath, steeling herself for the journey ahead.

"I love you both," she said, her voice wavering slightly. "More than you'll ever know."

Scott and Coyle both stepped forward, wrapping Karen and Mai in a tight embrace. For a long moment, they stood there, holding each other close, a family united by love and the unbreakable bonds of shared experience.

Finally, Karen pulled away, wiping the tears from her cheeks. "We'll call as soon as we land," she said, her voice steady once more. "And we'll see you soon."

With a final, loving glance at her father and brother, Karen turned and walked towards the jetway, Mai nestled safely in her arms. As she stepped onto the plane, she felt a sense of peace that she was exactly where she was meant to be.

She settled into her seat, Mai cooing softly in her lap. Karen looked out the window, watching as the plane lifted off the runway and into the clear blue sky.

As the plane soared over the lush green landscape of Vietnam, Karen leaned down and pressed a gentle kiss to Mai's forehead, whispering a promise into her soft skin. "It's just you and me now, little one," she said "And I'm going to give you the world."

Mai cooed in response, her tiny hand curling around Karen's finger. And as the plane carried them towards a new life and a new beginning, Karen knew that she had everything she needed, right there in her arms.

Desperate Days

Da Nang, South Vietnam

Da Nang sat on the coast of the South China Sea. American Marines landed there first in 1965. The city had a deep water port. It was an important place for ships to dock and unload men and supplies. The airport was crucial too. Many of the bombers that flew raids over North Vietnam took off from Da Nang. The long runways could handle big planes like B-52s.

Da Nang was the second largest city in South Vietnam. Only Saigon was bigger. The government center was there. So was the headquarters of I Corps. The Marines and the Army had bases around the city. They built them to withstand attacks. But no one thought Da Nang would fall.

In the past the North Vietnamese attacked remote outposts and bases in the mountains to the west. Places near the Ho Chi Minh Trail. Da Nang was different. It was on the coast far from the border. It had a large defending force. There were big guns and tanks. The South Vietnamese First Division was there. It had a reputation as one of the best units in the ARVN. The 3rd Division was there too along with the South Vietnamese Marines and regional forces.

The monsoon season was ending. The roads were dry. Good for tanks and trucks. The North Vietnamese Army was coming. The CIA knew an attack would happen soon. They didn't know where or when. The ARVN generals in Da Nang were confident they could defend the city. They had plans for a counterattack to push the NVA back into the mountains. No one was sure if the ARVN could do it. Da Nang was about to be tested.

Scott Dickson was the leader of a helicopter squadron based out of Da Nang. It was a new assignment. He was on loan from the CIA to the South Vietnamese Air Force. He was one of the best helicopter pilots in the agency. The CIA had trained Scott to fly secret missions all over Southeast Asia. He had flown in Laos and Cambodia. He had even gone into North Vietnam a few times. He was a man that knew how to get out of trouble as fast as he could get in it.

The South Vietnamese needed experienced leaders like Scott. Many of their senior officers had been killed or wounded in the fighting. Others had deserted or fled the country. The ARVN was desperately short of men who could lead troops in battle.

Scott's job was to help the South Vietnamese defend Da Nang. He would fly reconnaissance missions to find the NVA forces. Then he would report what he saw to the ARVN commanders. They would use the information to plan their defense.

But Scott was more than just a pilot. He was also a leader. He knew how to motivate men and keep them focused on the mission. Scott worked closely with the ARVN officers. He helped them plan operations and gave them advice on tactics. He didn't push. He knew better than that. Face was a big deal in Vietnam and the fastest way to demoralize a trooper was to make them lose face. It was also a good way to get a sock full of coins slammed in your nose while sleeping. Scott liked his nose and avoid insulting the Vietnamese under his command

The South Vietnamese soldiers respected Scott. They knew he was a skilled pilot and a brave man. They also knew that he cared about them. Scott did everything he could to keep his men safe in the air. The ARVN trusted him with their lives.

Scott was a natural pilot. He could fly any helicopter in the squadron. He knew the quirks of each aircraft. How to coax a little more power out of the engines. How to find the right approach when landing in a tight spot.

Scott handpicked his aircrew. Each man was an expert in his position. The copilot was a young man named Nguyen. He was the son of an ARVN colonel. Nguyen wanted to fly from the first time he saw a helicopter. He was good at it too. The crew chief was an older man called Tran. He had been with the squadron for ten years. Tran could fix any problem with the aircraft. He kept them flying no matter what.

The door gunners were Hao and Minh. They were cousins from the Mekong Delta. Both were strong and fearless. They could shoot the eyes out of a rat at a hundred meters with their M60 machine guns. The crew had been together for a year before Scott took over as commander. They trusted each other with their lives.

Scott and his men flew reconnaissance missions over the advancing NVA forces. The heavy air defenses made it dangerous. SA-2 missiles could hit an aircraft from thirty miles away. Each missile battery had a radar vehicle. It tracked the aircraft. Then it guided the missile to the target. The missiles flew three times the speed of sound. A helicopter had no chance to outrun them, but an experienced pilot like Scott could use the hills as cover and jink his way out of a missile attack. He had done it several times over his career. Even so, he kept a deep respect for the Soviet-made missiles and avoided them whenever possible.

Anti-aircraft guns were deadly too. The NVA had radar guided 57mm and 37mm guns. They put up walls of flak that could shred an aircraft. The door gunners fired at the gun crews. But it was hard to hit them. The enemy's guns were usually dug in and camouflaged.

Scott had to fly low and fast. He used the terrain to hide from the radar. Mountains and valleys were good for that. He popped up quick to look then dove down before the missiles could track him. It was dangerous work. But it was the only way to see what the NVA was doing. The ARVN relied on Scott and his squadron. They were the eyes of the army.

The North Vietnamese Army was building up its forces around Da Nang. They had moved the 2nd Corps into position. The 304th and 324th Divisions were the main assault units. They had T-54 and T-55 tanks. Armored personnel carriers too. The tanks had 100mm guns. They could punch through any defenses the ARVN put up.

The NVA had massed artillery west of the city. 130mm guns and 152mm howitzers. They could hit any target in Da Nang. The big guns were dug in and camouflaged. Hard for aircraft to spot and destroy.

Antiaircraft missiles and guns protected the artillery. SA-2 missile batteries were set up in the hills. They could shoot down any plane that came near the NVA artillery batteries. 37mm and 57mm anti-aircraft guns were scattered around the batteries. They put up a wall of flak that few aircraft could fly through.

The 2nd Corps had moved into the base areas. They were close. Dong Ha-Ai Tu to the north. Khe Sanh-Ba Long to the west. A Luoi-Nam Dong in the south. The 304th Division and the 324th Division were in Nong Son and Thuong Duc. They were ready to attack Da Nang from the west.

On paper the numbers favored the ARVN: 138,000 troops against 75,000 NVA; 513 tanks and armored vehicles against sixty. More artillery and aircraft too. But numbers didn't tell the whole story.

The NVA had momentum. They had won every battle during the campaign so far. Their men had high morale. They were ready to fight and die for their cause. The ARVN was tired and demoralized. They had lost so many men. The Americans had gone home. Many of the ARVN soldiers just wanted the war to be over. They knew they were on the losing side.

ARVN General Truong had to hold Da Nang. His men were spread out. The 3rd Division was in the city. The Rangers were on the perimeter. The tanks and armored vehicles were scattered. They would have to move fast to meet the NVA attack wherever it happened.

NVA field commander Colonel Hoang Dan was ready. He had planned the assault carefully. His men would hit hard and fast. They would punch through the ARVN defenses and take the city, then the all-important air base and deep-water port. The NVA had done it before. They could do it again. Da Nang would fall like all the other cities. It was just a matter of time.

Flying another recon mission in his Huey gunship, Scott was the first to see the beginning of the communist assault as NVA forces moved toward Da Nang and its defensive perimeter. He and his crew were flying near An Lo Bridge on Highway 1, north of Hue, when it suddenly blew up, it's steel trestle crashing into the gorge below. Scott immediately radioed in his observation. Everyone suspected the An Lo Bridge would be one of the NVA's first targets. It separated Da Nang from Hue and its destruction would greatly delay any reinforcements from either city trying to support the other. Scott knew where to head next. He banked his Huey and headed north to Hai Van Pass.

The Hai Van was a long mountain pass on National Route 1 in South Vietnam, a key transport road. It traversed a spur of the larger Annamite Range that juts into the South China Sea on the border of Da Nang and Hue, near Bạch Ma National Park. Its name, translated as "ocean cloud pass" refers to the mists that rise from the sea, reducing visibility.

As promised, Scott couldn't see down through the heavy mist, but he suspected what was happening. He just had to confirm it. He carefully lowered the Huey into the mist forming miniature tornados with the chopper's blades. As he descended, he saw what he was looking for – an ARVN supply column. Moments later, the ARVN trucks and armored cars were under attack from a well-hidden NVA ambush. Scott fired his rockets at the NVA positions, but they made little difference. Although the desperate ARVN troops fought back, the convoy was quickly overrun, and its cargo destroyed. In less than an hour, Da Nang was cut off and would have to survive on what it had stored in the city. The siege had begun.

When Scott and his crew returned to Phu Bai Airbase it was a living hell. The airbase was under attack. Artillery shells rained down from the surrounding hills. The NVA had moved up 130mm guns during the night. They had dug them in deep. Camouflaged them with nets and branches.

Scott brought the helicopter down fast. The landing skids hit the tarmac hard. He kept the rotors turning. He knew the Huey was a tempting target and his time on the ground would be limited. The door gunners jumped out and crouched low. They scanned the hills for any sign of the enemy. Nothing. They jumped back in the Huey.

The first shells had hit the runway. They blasted craters in the concrete. Red-hot shrapnel flew everywhere. It ripped through the thin metal walls of the hangars. Fuel drums exploded in bright fireballs.

Scott yelled into the intercom. Told Nguyen to keep the engines running. They might have to take off fast. Tran worked the radio. He called the tower for instructions. No one answered. The tower had taken a direct hit. It was just a pile of rubble now.

Hao and Minh fired their M60s at the hills. They couldn't see the enemy guns. But they raked the treeline anyway laying down a withering suppressing fire, hoping to hit something, making the NVA gunners keep their heads down.

The base was in chaos. Soldiers ran in every direction. Some tried to find cover. Others just stood in shock. They couldn't believe what was happening. A shell hit a barracks. It collapsed like a house of cards. Men screamed inside.

In the distance, Scott saw a group of ARVN officers. They were huddled behind a sandbagged bunker. He told Nguyen to take off and land near them. The helicopter took off, then flared and settled onto the grass. Scott jumped out and ran to the officers.

One of them was a colonel. He had a radio in his hand. The colonel was shouting orders into it. Trying to organize a defense. But it was too late. The NVA had the high ground. They could shoot down on the base at will.

Scott told the colonel they had to evacuate. Get as many men out as possible. The colonel nodded. He knew Scott was right. They couldn't hold the base. It was time to go.

Scott ran back to the helicopter. Shells were falling all around him. He zigzagged and kept his head low. A near miss knocked him down. Dirt and rocks pelted his back. But he got up and kept going.

He climbed into the cockpit. Told Nguyen to get ready to take off. Tran was on the radio again. Calling for any other helicopters in the area. They would need all the help they could get to evacuate the base.

The door gunners kept firing as the helicopter lifted off. They laid down a wall of lead. Tried to suppress the enemy guns. But it was a losing battle. The NVA had too many guns and their anti-aircraft weapons were a constant threat to allied aircraft. And they had the advantage of height.

Scott flew low and fast. He hugged the ground. Used the terrain to mask his movement. They had to get out of range of the artillery. Find someplace safe to land and regroup. But nowhere was safe anymore. The NVA was coming. And they wouldn't stop until they had taken everything.

Scott knew he had to find a way to fight back, or all would be lost. He just didn't know how... yet. Then, it hit him...

Scott landed the Huey behind a blast wall. The crew jumped out and ran to the supply shed. Tran and Nguyen rolled out five barrels of avgas. They hoisted them into the passenger compartment and lashed them down with cargo straps.

Hao and Minh taped white phosphorus grenades to the barrels. The grenades would ignite the barrels on impact and set off the avgas. Scott checked each barrel. Made sure the grenades were secure. He didn't want them coming loose in flight.

They climbed back into the Huey. Scott lifted off and turned toward the hills. He kept the chopper low, skimming the treetops. The door gunners scanned for targets. Nguyen spotted the gun flashes on the crest. He pointed them out to Scott.

Scott circled wide and came in behind the hill. He didn't want to fly straight at the guns. That would make them an easy target. He approached from the side, using the terrain to mask the Huey's signature.

Hao and Minh unstrapped the first barrel. They rolled it to the open cargo door. Minh pulled the pin on the smoke grenade. White phosphorus poured out licking at the barrel.

Flying over the NVA position, Scott gave the signal and they pushed it out. The barrel tumbled end over end and crashed into the gun pit. The grenade sprayed burning phosphorus over the gun crew. The avgas ignited a second later. A huge fireball erupted from the pit killing everyone in the pit.

Scott dipped the nose and flew along the crest. Hao and Minh kicked out the next barrel. It hit the second gun pit dead center. The explosion blew the gun off its mount. It flipped into the air and came down on the gun crew.

The door gunners whooped and high-fived. They were enjoying this. Scott brought the chopper around for another pass. The third barrel took out the ammo dump. Rockets and shells cooked off in massive secondary explosions.

Scott saw an antiaircraft gun swivel to track them. He jinked hard right as it fired. Tracers streaked past the tail boom. Too close. He flew back down the hill. Hao and Minh unstrapped the fourth barrel.

The gun fired again. Bullets punched holes in the fuselage. Scott felt the Huey shudder. He struggled with the controls. Hydraulic fluid sprayed the windshield. A line had been hit.

Nguyen yelled that they were losing pressure. Scott knew they had to get out of range fast. He flew low down the valley, using the ground to shield them. The door gunners kicked out the fourth barrel. It exploded in the jungle behind them. The fifth barrel was still strapped into the cargo area.

Black smoke poured from the engine cowling. Scott felt the rotors lose power. He aimed for a clearing near the river. The Huey was going down. He auto-rotated to lose altitude. The skids hit hard and the chopper bounced. It slid into the trees and came to rest on its side. Everyone turned to stare at the fifth barrel bomb hanging by the straps. If it blew up, they would all be incinerated in an instant. It didn't

Scott shook his head to clear it. His crew was already piling out. They took up defensive positions around the wreck.

Scott grabbed the radio and called Phu Bai. Told them their location and situation. The ARVN Colonel acknowledged. He would send a rescue team. ETA thirty minutes. Scott and his men would have to hold out until then.

In the distance, they heard the rumble of approaching tanks. The NVA wasn't going to give them a chance to catch their breath. Scott checked his rifle and made sure a round was chambered. It was going to be a long thirty minutes.

Scott deployed his crew in a perimeter around the downed Huey. Hao and Minh set up their M60 machine guns to cover the likely approaches. Carrying their M16s over their shoulders, Tran and Nguyen grabbed extra ammo, Claymore mines, and grenades from the cargo compartment. They distributed them to the others.

Scott climbed a nearby hill to get a better view. He scanned the valley through his binoculars. A cloud of dust rose in the distance. He focused on it and saw the telltale signs of armored vehicles. NVA tanks, probably PT-76s or T-55s.

He counted at least six of them, accompanied by infantry in trucks. They were moving fast, kicking up a plume of dirt behind them. Scott estimated they would reach the crash site in ten minutes.

He scrambled back down to his men and briefed them on the situation. They had to hold out until the ARVN rescue team arrived. Scott picked a spot where the valley narrowed. It was a natural choke point. The NVA would have to pass through it to reach them.

Hao and Minh set up the M60s to cover the choke point. They piled rocks and dirt to create firing positions, then placed a Claymore mine in front of each position.

Scott positioned himself behind a fallen log. He had a clear view of the valley. The rumble of the tanks grew louder. He could feel the ground vibrate beneath him. The NVA was closing in.

Twenty yards in front of the firing positions, Tran and Nguyen rolled the last barrel bomb into the middle of the most likely avenue of approach. Using shovels from the Huey, they dug a shallow hole like gophers, dirt flying. They rolled the barrel bomb into the hole. They could hear the tanks approaching and knew they would appear at any moment. They placed a double bundle of grenades next to the barrel and rigged the safety pins with wire which Tran strung back to Scott. They covered the barrel with leaves and branches. It wasn't a great camouflage job, but it was all they had time for. As the first tank, a PT-76 Soviet-made light amphibious tank appeared, they scrambled back to the firing positions and readied their weapons.

The tank's turret swiveled as it scanned for targets. Scott and the aircrew kept their heads low and out of sight. They needed the tank to come closer for the barrel bomb to be effective. Behind the tank was a platoon of infantry holding back, letting the tank clear the way before advancing. The tank rolled forward on its treads. It was too far to one side and not going to roll over the barrel bomb. There was nothing Scott or his crew could do about, except hope.

When the tank reached the side of the hidden barrel bomb, Scott yanked the wires attached to the safety pins. He saw one of the grenades' spoons flip into the air. He hoped it would be enough. It was. The grenade exploded and a second later the barrel bomb exploded in a huge ball of flame. It was a powerful eruption and while it didn't destroy the tank or its crew, it did tip the tank on its side. The bottom of the tank was engulfed in flames from the bomb, heating the crew compartment like a skillet.

Scott sprinted from his position and ran to the tank's turret just as the hatch opened. The commander popped his head out. Scott pulled the pin on a grenade and threw it like a baseball, hitting the commander in the head and knocking him unconscious. A moment later, the grenade exploded decapitating the commander.

Coughing and stumbling, the tank's crew pushed their commander's headless body out the hatchway. The infantry was already moving up to protect the crew and opened fire at Scott. With bullets pitting the ground beside him, Scott pulled the pin on his last grenade and pitched it through the turret opening. Scott scrambled to his feet and ran back to his team's firing positions twenty yards away.

The grenade exploded killing the crew and igniting the ammunition inside the tank. A jet of flame shot out of the turret opening. Avoiding the flames, the infantry climbed the surrounding hillside and descended on the aircrew's firing positions.

As Scott jumped over the rocks and dirt mound, Hao and Minh opened up with the M60s. The heavy bullets stitched across the hillside and into the infantry. NVA soldiers fell, their bodies riddled with holes. The others scrambled for cover wherever they could find it. Scott reached for the claymore's detonator. He waited.

While Hao and Minh were reloading the NVA pushed forward in a terrible charge. Scott waited until the were within ten feet before clicking the detonator three times. The Claymores exploded in front of the firing positions sending hundreds of steel balls through the air and shredding the NVA infantry. A dozen fell dead. The survivors pulled back and hid behind the burning tank.

More tanks emerged from the dust. They fired their main guns and machine guns at the downed Huey crew. Shells whistled overhead and exploded in the trees. Bullets cracked past Scott's ears and chewed up the ground around him.

He returned fire with his rifle. Aimed for the vision slots and commander's hatches. He saw a head pop up in a turret and put a round through it. The man slumped over the gun, blood streaming down the tank's sides.

Emboldened by the tanks arrival, the infantry surged forward once again. Tran and Nguyen lobbed grenades at the oncoming soldiers. The explosions sent bodies flying. Dirt and smoke obscured the battlefield. Scott heard screams and groans over the gunfire. The NVA was taking casualties but they kept coming.

Seeing that their position was about to be overrun, Scott ordered his men to retreat back to the Huey. Using the downed aircraft for cover, Scott and his crew resumed firing at the advancing infantry. They were running low on ammunition and were out of grenades.

A shell hit the Huey and it exploded in a ball of flame. Burning debris rained down around them. Scott felt the heat wash over him. Their cover was gone. They were exposed now.

Scott made a decision. They couldn't stay there and survive. They had to fall back to a new position. He signaled to his men and they started to withdraw, leapfrogging back by pairs. Hao and Minh laid down covering fire as Tran and Nguyen moved. Then they switched. Laying down suppressing fire, Scott was the last to go.

Bullets kicked up dirt at Scott's feet as he ran. He zigzagged and kept his head low. An explosion from an enemy mortar round knocked him off his feet. He rolled and came up in a crouch. A tank was bearing down on him, its gun traversing to aim at him.

Scott froze. He knew he couldn't outrun a tank round. He braced for the end, firing his last magazine into the oncoming infantry. As his rifle clicked empty, he heard the whoosh of rockets and the tank exploded. Flaming debris kicked up all around.

Huey gunships roared overhead, machine guns blazing, rockets streaking toward the tanks below. The NVA soldiers scattered as rockets and grenades rained down. The ARVN had arrived, just in the nick of time. A Huey set down in a clearing. Scott and his crew scrambled to reach it. They climbed in and the chopper took off. They were safe… for the moment.

Scott and his aircrew landed onto the tarmac at Da Nang Airbase. The scene that greeted them was one of controlled chaos. Soldiers and civilians rushed about, loading equipment and supplies onto waiting aircraft.

There was a sense of urgency in the air, a palpable feeling that time was running out.

As they climbed out of the helicopter, a harried-looking officer ran up to them. "Are you Scott Dickson?" he asked, his voice tight with stress.

Scott nodded. "That's me. What's going on here?"

The officer shook his head. "President Thieu has ordered a full retreat. All forces in the Central Highlands and northern coastal cities are to pull back to Saigon immediately."

Scott's eyes widened. "A full retreat? But what about the civilians? The refugees?"

"We're doing what we can," the officer said. "But our priority is to get the troops out. We've lost a lot of aircrews in the last few days. That's why I'm here. We need every able pilot and crew member we can get."

He pointed to a large Chinook helicopter sitting on the far side of the airfield. "That's your ride. We need you to ferry troops across the gorge. The bridge was destroyed, and it's the only way out."

Scott looked at his crew. They were exhausted, their faces streaked with grime and sweat. But he knew they would do what was needed. They always did.

"All right," he said. "Let's get to it."

They sprinted across the tarmac, ducking instinctively as artillery shells whistled overhead. The NVA was getting closer. They could all feel it. Soon the base would be surrounded.

They clambered into the Chinook, Scott and Nguyen taking the controls while Tran and the door gunners strapped themselves in the back. The helicopter was already packed with soldiers, their faces tense and frightened.

Scott ran through the pre-flight checks with

practiced speed. The rotors began to whir, slowly at first, then faster. The Chinook lifted off the ground with a lurch, the soldiers in the back clutching their weapons tightly.

They flew low and fast, skimming the treetops to avoid enemy fire. The gorge came into view, a gaping chasm that split the earth. The destroyed An Lo Bridge was a twisted ruin, its broken spans hanging precariously.

Scott brought the Chinook down on the far side of the gorge. The soldiers leaped out, quickly forming a perimeter. Scott could see the fear and confusion in their eyes.

He lifted off again, the Chinook straining with the effort. They flew back to Da Nang, where another group of soldiers was already waiting. They loaded up and flew back, again and again, ferrying as many as they could.

But time was running out. Reports crackled over the radio of NVA units closing in, cutting off escape routes. Scott pushed the Chinook to its limits, flying faster and lower each time.

As Scott brought the Chinook in for another landing at the airbase, he couldn't believe the scene unfolding before him. The once orderly airbase had descended into utter chaos. ARVN troops, gripped by panic and desperation, were abandoning their posts and equipment in a frenzied attempt to escape the advancing NVA.

Tanks careened across the tarmac, their drivers steering them haphazardly before leaping out and sprinting towards the waiting helicopters. The heavy vehicles rolled to a stop, engines idling, hatches flung open. It was a surreal sight, these powerful machines of war suddenly abandoned like discarded toys.

Everywhere Scott looked, it was the same. Trucks, armored cars, artillery pieces, all left where they stood as their crews scrambled to find a spot on any aircraft that would take them. Heavy mortars and rocket launchers lay on their sides, ammunition scattered about like forgotten playthings.

In the distance, Scott could even see fixed-wing aircraft, once the pride of the ARVN air force, sitting deserted on the runway. Their pilots had simply walked away, leaving these sophisticated machines to whoever would claim them.

It was a staggering waste, a hemorrhaging of military assets that would take years to replace, if ever. Millions upon millions of dollars worth of equipment, just abandoned in the face of the enemy. Scott felt a surge of anger and frustration at the sight.

But he also understood the fear that drove these men. They had fought long and hard, had seen their comrades fall and their country crumble. And now, with the end so clearly in sight, the urge to survive, to escape, was overpowering.

As he set the Chinook down, soldiers swarmed towards it like ants, clambering over each other to get inside. They carried only what they could hold, leaving behind everything else. Rifles, packs, even boots were discarded as they sought to lighten their load.

Scott's crew worked feverishly to get as many aboard as possible, pushing and shoving to make room. They were crammed in, sitting on each other's laps, crowding into every available space. The smell of sweat and fear was overpowering in the confined space.

As they lifted off, Scott could see the NVA troops

on the perimeter, moving in to claim their prize. They would find an airbase filled with equipment, a treasure trove of military hardware. It was a bitter pill to swallow.

But there was no time for recrimination or regret. They had to keep moving, keep flying, keep pulling out as many as they could. The fall of Da Nang was inevitable now, but every soldier they saved was a small victory against the tide of defeat and the defense of Saigon.

Scott guided the overloaded Chinook into the sky, the rotors straining with the weight. Behind them, the airbase receded, a scene of chaos and abandonment. He could see the NVA crashing through the main gate, charging across the runway. It was done. The Phu Bai Airbase had been overrun as was the city of Da Nang. Millions of refugees now fleeing for their lives in unorganized caravans heading south. Saigon was their only hope for safety.

On the final run, as they approached the gorge, Nguyen suddenly shouted a warning. "Rocket! Two o'clock high!"

Scott saw it, a smoking trail arcing towards them. He wrenched the controls, the Chinook banking hard. The rocket passed so close he could see the heat wave from its exhaust as it flew past his windshield.

The door gunners opened fire, raking the jungle with bullets. Scott saw muzzle flashes below, enemy soldiers taking aim. He jinked and weaved, avoiding their fire.

They reached the gorge and set down hard on the opposite side. The soldiers piled out, some helping wounded comrades. "Now, where do we go?" said Nguyen.

"South like everyone else," said Scott.

"All the way to Saigon?"

"Yeah. Why not? I have a feeling our ferrying service isn't over."

"We're gonna need more fuel."

"Right. One problem at a time. We need to load up the wounded, especially those that cannot walk."

His crew went to work triaging the wounded, loading those unable to walk or badly wounded. The helicopter was filling up fast. The need was beyond its capacity.

An explosion rocked the earth nearby. NVA artillery, zeroing in. ARVN troops scattered looking for cover.

Scott revved the engine and lifted off, the rotors straining. Another explosion, closer this time.

As the Chinook ascended into the smoke-filled sky, Scott felt a surge of relief, mixed with guilt. How many had they left behind? But there was no time for such thoughts. There was nothing he could do about it now. Wasted energy.

Scott looked at his crew. They were haggard, pushed to the brink of endurance. But they were alive, and they were together. In this war, that was the most important thing of all.

Hue, South Vietnam

Coyle guided the Pilatus Porter over the patchwork of rice paddies and villages that surrounded Hue. The scene below was eerily familiar, a grim echo of the past. He had flown this same route years ago, during the Tet Offensive, when the city had been a battleground between the NVA and the American and South

Vietnamese forces.

Now, as then, he was here for Nguyet, McGoon's whore, and her daughter Tuyet. Though Nguyet had long since moved on, finding love with an ARVN captain, Coyle still felt a deep sense of responsibility for their safety. He couldn't just leave them to the mercies of the advancing NVA. Tuyet was obviously of mixed race as she towered over the other children her age. If the Viet Cong suspected her of having an American father, she would be killed on the spot and Nguyet with her.

As the long-nosed aircraft approached the city, Coyle could see the signs of the impending battle. NVA forces were taking up positions on the outskirts, digging trenches and setting up artillery. The ARVN troops were hunkered down in their own fortifications, determined to make a stand.

Coyle knew it was only a matter of time before the fighting started in earnest. While the ARVN had the advantage in number of troops, tanks, and artillery, the NVA had the momentum and high morale. Coyle knew they wouldn't stop until they had taken Hue. He had to get Nguyet and Tuyet out before it was too late.

With the area crawling with NVA, Coyle brought the Porter down in a steep approach, the small airfield appearing at the last moment.

As he touched down and rolled to a stop, Coyle could hear the distant thunder of artillery. The NVA was starting its bombardment, softening up the ARVN positions. He had to move fast. He leaped out of the plane and set out toward the city.

Coyle moved through the streets of Hue, his senses on high alert as the city crumbled around him. The sound of NVA artillery was a constant backdrop, the shells exploding with terrifying regularity, shrapnel pinging on buildings and walls. The ground shook with each impact, showering the streets with rubble and debris.

As he navigated the maze of alleys and boulevards, Coyle witnessed scenes of utter desperation. Wrapped in saffron robes, Monks huddled around their masters, forming human shields to protect the elderly from the falling shells. Their chants and prayers were drowned out by the relentless bombardment, but still they held fast, their faith unyielding in the face of destruction.

Shopkeepers worked frantically to board up their windows and chain their doors shut. They knew that the artillery was just the beginning, that the real horror would come when the NVA troops entered the city. They sought to protect what little they had left, their livelihoods and memories secured behind flimsy barricades.

Civilians ran past Coyle, their faces full of terror. They carried whatever they could grab, their belongings hastily stuffed into bags and baskets. Some stumbled and fell, tripping over the debris that littered the streets. Others simply kept running, their eyes fixed on some distant point of safety. In reality… there was none.

The streets were choked with abandoned vehicles, their owners long since fled. Cars and trucks sat empty at gas stations, their fuel tanks drained dry. The underground reservoirs had been emptied days ago, the precious gasoline hoarded by the military or sold on the black market.

Coyle pressed on, his destination clear in his mind. He had to reach Nguyet and Tuyet, had to get them out of the city before it was too late. He had made a promise to his dead friend McGoon, and he intended to keep it. His only problem was that he was lost.

As he turned a corner, he saw a group of ARVN soldiers huddled behind a barricade. They were young, their faces smeared with dirt and sweat. They clutched their rifles with shaking hands, their eyes.

Coyle approached them cautiously, his hands held out to show that he was unarmed. "I'm looking for Nguyen Thi Street," he said in Vietnamese. "Do you know where it is? The street signs are down."

One of the soldiers nodded, pointing down a narrow alley. "Two blocks that way," he said. "But you'd better hurry. The NVA are getting closer."

Coyle thanked him and set off at a run. The alley was dark and narrow, the buildings on either side leaning in as if to crush him. He could hear the sound of fighting in the distance, the rattle of small arms fire and the thump of grenades.

As he emerged from the alley, he saw Nguyet's house. Its walls pockmarked with bullet holes. The front garden had a large artillery crater that had unearthed Nguyet's carefully planted flowers. The windows were shattered, the front door hanging off its hinges.

Coyle's heart sank as he approached the house. Had he come too late? Were Nguyet and Tuyet already gone, or worse?

Another artillery shell exploded nearby. Then he heard a voice from inside the house, a voice he recognized. It was Tuyet, crying out in fear.

Coyle burst through the door, his eyes scanning the room. Nguyet was huddled in a corner, her arms wrapped around Tuyet. They looked up at him with a mixture of relief and terror.

"Tom," Nguyet said, her voice shaking. "You came."

Coyle nodded, reaching out to help them to their feet. "We have to go," he said urgently. "The NVA are almost here. Where is your captain?"

"He is fighting with his men."

"Leave him a note. Tell him we're going to Saigon. He can contact me through the US Embassy."

"Okay. I do."

They gathered what little they could carry and set off through the streets. Coyle led the way, his senses on high alert. They dodged fallen power lines and piles of rubble. Nguyet and Tuyet jumped with each explosion.

At the rate the NVA were closing on the city, Coyle knew the odds were slim that they had no captured and confiscated his aircraft. Getting to the Porter would be difficult if not impossible. Still, he had to try. Flying to Saigon would be much safer than traveling on the roads. Desperate people did desperate things when survival was at stake. Not to mention, there was always a chance the Viet Cong could attack any refugee caravan.

As Coyle, Nguyet, and Tuyet made their way through the war-torn streets of Hue, they turned a corner and found themselves face to face with a surreal scene. In the middle of the chaos and destruction, a small group of musicians sat on the steps of a partially collapsed building, playing their instruments with a haunting intensity.

The group consisted of an old man playing a traditional Vietnamese dan bau (monochord), a young woman with a dan tranh (sixteen-string zither), and a middle-aged man with a sao (bamboo flute). Their music was a strange and beautiful contrast to the sounds of war that surrounded them.

Coyle, Nguyet, and Tuyet stood transfixed for a moment, unable to look away from the musicians. The old man looked up and met Coyle's gaze, his eyes filled with a deep sadness and understanding. He nodded slightly, as if acknowledging their shared humanity in the midst of the madness.

Suddenly, a shell exploded nearby, shaking the ground and showering them with debris. The musicians never missed a beat, their melody unbroken by the chaos. Coyle knew they had to keep moving, but he felt a strange reluctance to leave this moment behind.

As they started to walk away, the young woman with the dan tranh called out to them. "Wait," she said, her voice barely audible over the music. "Take this."

She held out a small, intricately carved wooden box. Coyle hesitated for a moment before reaching out to take it. As his fingers closed around the box, he felt a strange sensation, as if a tiny spark of electricity had passed between them.

"What is it?" he asked, his voice hushed.

The woman smiled enigmatically. "A reminder," she said. "Of what endures, even in the darkest of times."

With that, she turned back to her instrument, the music swelling once again. Coyle tucked the box into his pocket and moved off with Nguyet and Tuyet.

They pressed on through the streets, the music fading behind them. But Coyle could still feel the presence of the box in his pocket, a tiny beacon of hope in a world gone mad.

After an hour of walking through the decimated city, Coyle found a relatively secluded spot for them to rest and catch their breath. Nguyet and Tuyet sat down on a low stone wall, their faces drawn and exhausted. Coyle stood watch, his eyes scanning the surrounding area for any signs of danger. In his hand, his airmen pistol – a revolver. It would do little to protect them against a machine gun or mortar shell, but it made him feel better knowing there was at least something to protect Nguyet and her daughter.

As he stood there keeping watch, his hand drifted to his pocket, feeling the small wooden box the musician had given him. He pulled it out, turning it over in his hands. It was a beautiful thing, intricately carved with symbols and patterns he didn't recognize.

Curiosity got the better of him, and he gently lifted the lid. Inside, nestled on a bed of soft, red silk, was a small, perfect lotus flower, carved from a single piece of jade. It seemed to glow with an inner light, its petals so delicate and lifelike that Coyle almost believed it was real.

He picked it up, feeling the cool smoothness of the stone against his skin. It was such a simple thing and yet it moved him, a lump forming in his throat. He thought of the musicians, playing their hearts out amid the ruins of their city. He thought of Nguyet and Tuyet, who had lost everything but still clung to each other and to hope. And he thought of himself, a man who had seen so much war and destruction, but who still believed in the power of compassion and courage.

He carefully placed the jade lotus back in the box, then closed the lid, and slipped the box back in his pocket.

Then he turned back to Nguyet and Tuyet, who were watching him with curious eyes. He smiled at them, a smile that held sadness and purpose.

"Come on," he said, holding out his hand. "Let's keep going. We've got a plane to catch."

As they approached the outskirts of the city, Coyle saw a sight that made his blood run cold. NVA tanks were rolling down the main boulevard, their cannons swiveling back and forth. Infantry soldiers marched alongside them, their weapons at the ready. The ARVN were retreating, leaving the inhabitants of Hue defenseless against the communist onslaught.

Coyle knew they had only one chance. He led Nguyet and Tuyet into a narrow side street, praying that the tanks would pass them by.

For a moment, it seemed as if his prayers had been answered. The tanks rumbled past, the ground shaking beneath their treads. But then, one of the soldiers turned and saw them. He called out raising his rifle and taking aim.

"Run!" Coyle shouted, pushing Nguyet and Tuyet ahead of him.

They ran blindly, the sound of gunfire echoing behind them. Bullets whizzed past their heads, shattering windows and ricocheting off walls.

Miraculously, they made it, gasping for breath and trembling with exhaustion. Behind them, Hue burned, the flames of war consuming everything in their path.

Coyle looked at Nguyet and Tuyet. They were safe, but at what cost? Their home, their city, everything they had known was gone, lost to the relentless tide of war. But they were alive, and for now, that was enough.

As Coyle, Nguyet, and Tuyet approached the outer edge of the city, the fighting between the ARVN and NVA forces intensified. The once-quiet streets had become a hellish battlefield, echoing with the relentless sounds of gunfire and explosions.

The ARVN soldiers had taken up defensive positions in the shattered remnants of buildings, using the rubble as cover. They fired their M16 rifles and M60 machine guns at the advancing NVA troops, desperately trying to hold the line. Mortar shells fell and exploded randomly rocking the remains of the buildings causing the walls to collapse. The air was thick with the smell of cordite and the cries of the wounded.

The NVA, for their part, attacked with a ferocious determination. They surged forward in waves, heedless of their own casualties. Their AK-47 rifles chattered incessantly, the muzzle flashes lighting up the smoky haze that hung over the battlefield. Every now and then, the deeper boom of an RPG would resound, as the NVA troops tried to dislodge the ARVN from their positions.

In the distance, the heavy thud of artillery could be heard as the NVA pounded the city with shells. The ground shook with each impact, and plumes of smoke and dust rose into the air like macabre geysers. The ARVN responded with their own artillery, the counter-battery fire creating a deafening noise.

Amid the chaos, Coyle could see the ARVN soldiers fighting with desperation. They were outnumbered and outgunned, but they held their ground with a stubborn courage. He saw a young ARVN soldier, barely out of his teens, manning a machine gun nest. The boy's face was streaked with sweat and grime, but his eyes were clear and focused as he fired controlled burst after burst at the enemy.

Nearby, a group of ARVN Rangers were engaged in a fierce close-quarters battle with a squad of NVA infantry. The fighting was hand-to-hand, bayonets and rifle butts flashing in the murky light. The Rangers fought with a savage skill, but the NVA were relentless, pressing forward with a fanatical zeal.

Coyle knew they had to get through this maelstrom of violence if they were to reach the airfield. He scanned the battlefield, looking for a path, any path, that might offer a chance of escape. But everywhere he looked, the fighting was intense and unrelenting.

A sudden explosion nearby threw Coyle to the ground, showering him with dirt and debris. His ears rang and his vision blurred, but he forced himself back to his feet. Nguyet and Tuyet huddled behind him, their faces pale with fear.

Coyle knew he had to act fast. The ARVN lines were crumbling, the NVA pressing their advantage. If they didn't move now, they might never make it out of the city.

Out of options, Coyle gathered Nguyet and Tuyet close. He would find a way through this hell, even if he had to carve it out himself.

Taking a deep breath, Coyle plunged forward into the maelstrom, guiding Nguyet and Tuyet through the shattered streets. The battle raged around them.

Coyle spotted a narrow alley between two bombed-out buildings. It looked risky, but it might just lead away from the worst of the fighting.

Gathering his courage, Coyle sprinted from cover, running in a crouch to stay below the whizzing bullets. An explosion nearby threw him off balance, showering him with dirt and debris. Ears ringing, he rolled into the alleyway just as a mortar round detonated behind him.

Coughing from the dust, Coyle picked himself up and assessed the alley. It zigzagged between buildings, but seemed empty of soldiers for now. He moved cautiously forward, rifle at the ready. Nguyet and her daughter followed close behind.

The alley ended at a small courtyard. Coyle peered around the corner, his heart sinking at what he saw. A squad of NVA soldiers was setting up a machine gun nest directly in his path. Getting past them would be close to impossible. He motioned for Nguyet and Tuyet to remain quiet.

He was debating doubling back to find another route when he noticed a small side passage, barely wide enough for a man to pass through. It was choked with rubble and debris, but it seemed to lead in the general direction of the airfield.

Taking a deep breath, Coyle squeezed into the passage. He had to contort his body to fit through the narrow gaps, jagged stones and splintered wood tearing at his clothes and skin. The sounds of battle were muffled here, but still all too close for comfort.

The passage twisted and turned, and for a terrifying moment, Coyle feared it would dead-end, trapping him and the girls. But then he saw a glimmer of light ahead, and with a final push, he stumbled out into a deserted street.

He paused for a moment, gasping for air and trying to get his bearings. The airfield was close, he could make out the shape of the hangars in the distance. But the way was still treacherous, with pockets of fighting flaring up all around.

Coyle, Nguyet, and Tuyet set off at a run, darting from cover to cover. They avoided the main streets, sticking to alleys and side passages where they could. Twice they had to backtrack to avoid NVA patrols as they pressed themselves into the shadows, praying they hadn't been seen.

But through a combination of skill, instinct, and sheer luck, Coyle and the girls made it through and reached a grove of trees next to the airfield.

Constantly checking that nobody was watching them, Coyle moved silently through the shadows of the airfield, Nguyet and Tuyet following close behind. The Porter was just ahead. But as they approached, Coyle's heart sank. Two young Viet Cong soldiers, barely more than boys, stood guard over the area where the plane was parked, AK-47s held at the ready.

Coyle couldn't risk a firefight, not with Nguyet and Tuyet so close. He signaled for Nguyet and Tuyet to stay low and out of sight, then crept forward, using the scattered crates and barrels for cover.

As he drew near, Coyle saw his chance. One of the soldiers had his back turned, his attention focused on the distant sounds of battle. Moving with the speed and silence of a jungle cat, Coyle lunged forward and struck the soldier on the back of the head with the butt of his pistol. The boy crumpled to the ground. Coyle tried to catch him but was too late. The boy landed with a thud.

Coyle's luck didn't hold. The other soldier heard the scuffle and came running, his AK-47 raised and ready. Coyle had only a split second to react. He fired his pistol, aiming low. The bullet struck the young soldier in the leg, sending him tumbling to the ground, his rifle clattering away. He cried out in pain.

Coyle sprinted forward, kicking the fallen AK-47 out of reach. The young soldier groaned, clutching at his wounded leg. Blood seeped between his fingers, staining the concrete.

For a moment, Coyle hesitated. The boy was no threat now, and every instinct urged him to get to the plane, to get Nguyet and Tuyet to safety before more Viet Cong arrived. But he couldn't just leave the young soldier to bleed out on the tarmac.

Cursing under his breath, Coyle knelt beside the boy. He tore off his belt and wrapped it around the soldier's thigh, pulling it tight to stem the flow of blood. It was a rough tourniquet, but it would have to do.

"I'm sorry," Coyle muttered, meeting the young soldier's pain-filled eyes. "I didn't want this."

The distant shouts of more Viet Cong soldiers echoed across the airfield. Coyle knew they had only moments before they would be discovered. He signaled urgently to Nguyet and Tuyet, who sprinted from their hiding place and clambered into the Porter.

Coyle leaped into the pilot's seat, his hands flying over the controls. The engine coughed to life, the propeller spinning into a blur. Bullets pinged off the fuselage as the Viet Cong soldiers opened fire, alerted by the noise of the plane's engine starting.

Coyle pushed the throttle forward, and the Porter surged down the runway. More bullets whizzed past, some punching through the thin metal skin of the plane. Nguyet and Tuyet huddled in the back, their faces filled with terror.

And then they were airborne, the Porter climbing steeply into the smoke-filled sky. Coyle's thoughts were heavy. The image of the young soldier, his leg shattered by Coyle's bullet, weighed on his conscience. It had been necessary, he told himself. A matter of survival. But that didn't make it any easier to bear.

He glanced back at Nguyet and Tuyet, huddled together in the rear of the plane. They were safe, at least for now. That was what mattered. Coyle had made a promise, and he had kept it. Coyle turned the plane towards Saigon, towards salvation.

As the Porter flew low over the countryside, Coyle, Nguyet, and Tuyet witnessed the unfolding tragedy below. The once peaceful landscape of farms and rice fields had been transformed into a scene of desperate exodus and unrelenting destruction.

The roads and highways were choked with refugees, a winding river of humanity stretching as far as the eye could see. Thousands upon thousands of civilians trudged along the asphalt, their belongings bundled on their backs or piled high on overloaded carts and bicycles. The heat shimmered off the road, and the dust kicked up by countless feet hung in the air.

Among the civilians, Coyle could make out the scattered figures of ARVN soldiers. Some marched in ragged columns, their weapons slung over their shoulders, their faces filled with exhaustion and defeat. Others simply walked alone, having shed their weapons and blended into the civilian crowd, their will to fight finally broken.

In the distance, the horizon was lit by the flash of explosions and the billowing smoke of burning villages. The NVA artillery was relentless, pounding the countryside with a merciless intensity. Coyle could see whole hamlets being consumed by flames, the thatched roofs of huts igniting like kindling. The distant thunder of the bombardment rolled across the landscape, a ceaseless drumbeat of ruin.

Nguyet pressed her face to the window, tears streaming down her cheeks as she watched her homeland being devoured by the flames of war. Tuyet clung to her mother, her face buried in Nguyet's shoulder, her frame shaking with silent sobs.

Coyle felt a lump in his throat as he witnessed their grief. This was the human cost of the conflict, played out on a scale that defied comprehension. Each of those tiny figures below was a life, a story, a thread in the vast tapestry of suffering that the war had woven.

As they flew on, the scenes of devastation continued to unfold beneath them. Bridges lay shattered, their twisted remains jutting from the rivers like the bones of fallen giants. Refugees risking their way across the fast-flowing waters.

Fields that had once been lush with crops were now pockmarked with craters, the earth scorched and barren. Everywhere, the scars of war were carved into the very fabric of the land.

And yet, amid the chaos and the carnage, there were still flickers of hope. Coyle saw farmers stubbornly tending to their rice paddies, even as the shells fell around them. Villagers formed bucket brigades to put out the flames engulfing their huts. Children leading the family water buffalos away from danger. All demonstrations of the unquenchable will to survive.

US Embassy - Saigon, South Vietnam

Ambassador Martin sat behind his large mahogany desk in the U.S. Embassy, a scowl on his face as he listened to the CIA Station Chief's report. Polgar sat before him, a thick manila folder clasped in his hands.

"I'm afraid the news from Da Nang and Hue is what we expected, Ambassador," Polgar began, his voice steady despite the weight of his words. "Both cities have fallen to the North Vietnamese."

Martin leaned back in his chair, his eyes closing briefly as if to shut out the harsh reality. "How did it happen, Tom? I thought General Truong had assured us that at least Da Nang could be held."

Polgar opened the folder and pulled out a series of aerial reconnaissance photos marked with red arrows reflecting enemy troops movements. He laid them on the Ambassador's desk one by one.

"As you can see here, the NVA launched a multi-pronged assault on the city. They had at least three divisions, supported by tanks and heavy artillery. The ARVN forces put up a fierce fight, but they were simply overwhelmed."

He pointed to a particular photo, his finger tracing the lines of a shattered bridge. "The NVA blew this bridge early in the battle, cutting off the main route of retreat. That caused a panic among the civilian population."

Martin picked up the photo, his eyes scanning the image of the ruined structure. "And the ARVN? How did they respond?"

"Many fought bravely, Ambassador. But once the civilians began to flee, discipline broke down in some units. There were reports of soldiers abandoning their posts, even turning on each other in the scramble to get out."

The Ambassador set the photo down, his face pale. "And Hue?"

"A similar story, I'm afraid," Polgar continued. "The NVA hit the city from three sides. They had the high ground, and they used it to their full advantage. Artillery, rockets, even tanks. The ARVN held out for as long as they could, but in the end, they had to withdraw."

Ambassador Martin sat heavily in his chair as Polgar finished his report. The losses were staggering, the details painting a picture of a military and government in utter disarray.

"An entire army corps lost in Hue and Da Nang," said Polgar. "Over 120,000 men.

Martin responded, his voice weary. "I knew Thieu's retreat order was a mistake, but I never imagined a disaster on this scale."

"It was a rout, Ambassador. The PAVN pursued the retreating forces relentlessly. They didn't even leave troops to protect the territory they had won."

"They didn't need to, their enemy was on the run."

"Exactly. And when the ARVN took a stand, the were quickly wiped out. Phu Cat, Qui Nhon, Tuy Hoa - the 22nd Division was shattered trying to hold that line. Over 10,000 men, gone in a matter of days."

Martin shook his head. "And the chaos that followed... soldiers deserting, looting. Civilians caught in the crossfire. It's a humanitarian disaster."

"That's not the worst of it," Polgar said. "The equipment losses are catastrophic. Billions of dollars of material abandoned or captured - 129 aircraft, 179 tanks and armored vehicles, 327 artillery pieces, 184 transport vehicles and forty-seven naval craft. More than 10,000 tons of bombs, ammunition, grenades, food supplies, combat rations, and other materials were also captured. Most of it is irreplaceable. It's a logistical nightmare."

"The psychological impact of this will be severe," Martin said quietly. "Da Nang and Hue were symbols of our commitment, of the ARVN's ability to resist. I warned Thieu that his inconsistent orders were crippling the ARVN's ability to resist. First telling them to abandon Hue, then to hold it at all costs. Pulling the Airborne back to Saigon instead of reinforcing I Corps.

It's been one contradictory decision after another."

"And now he's arresting generals to prevent imaginary coups, dissolving the government in the middle of a crisis. The man is unraveling, and he's taking the country with him."

Martin stood and paced to the window, his gaze distant. "I fear it may be too late, Tom. Thieu's leadership has broken the ARVN's will to fight. Morale is shattered. And the PAVN senses weakness. They'll drive on Saigon with everything they have."

Polgar was quiet for a moment, then… "Ambassador, I must strongly recommend that we begin preparations for an evacuation. We have thousands of American citizens in Vietnam - diplomats, advisors, contractors, journalists. If the NVA offensive continues at this pace..."

Martin spun around, his eyes flashing. "Evacuate? And send what message to our allies, Tom? That we're abandoning them? That we have no faith in their ability to hold the line?"

Polgar met the ambassador's gaze unflinchingly. "With respect, sir, our first duty is to protect American lives. If the South Vietnamese see us making preparations, yes, it might damage morale. But if we wait too long, we risk being caught in a situation like Da Nang. Chaos. Panic. Lives needlessly lost."

The ambassador was silent for a long moment. Then he sighed, his shoulders slumping. "I hear you, Tom. But the president has been clear. We are to maintain a presence in Vietnam for as long as possible. To support our allies, to show that America keeps its commitments."

Martin stood abruptly and walked to the window. He stared out at the bustling streets of Saigon, as if trying to reassure himself that the city was still there, still functioning.

"I will not be the ambassador who presides over the fall of Saigon. We will hold the line. We must."

Polgar nodded slowly, understanding the difficult position the ambassador was in. "Of course, sir. I understand. But I must, for the record, state my strong disagreement with this course of action."

Turning to Polgar, Martin waved a hand, as if brushing the objection aside. "Noted, Tom. But the decision is made. We stay the course. No evacuations until I give the order."

He turned back to the window, his gaze distant. "God help us all if we're wrong."

Showdown

Saigon, South Vietnam

The atmosphere in the grand hall of the presidential palace was thick with tension. President Thieu sat at the head of a large conference table, his face drawn and haggard, as the leaders of South Vietnam's National Assembly gathered around him. Tran Van Lam, the President of the Senate, and Pham Van Ut, the Speaker of the House, both wore expressions of grave concern.

Lam was the first to speak, his voice filled with anger and frustration. "This is a disaster, Mr. President!" he exclaimed, slamming his fist on the table. "The ARVN is in shambles, the south is falling, and the enemy is at our doorstep. How did we come to this?"

Thieu remained calm, his voice even as he replied, "Senator Lam, I understand your frustration. And I admit we are facing a difficult crisis. But we must remain focused and united in this hour of need.

Ut interjected, "United? How can we be united

when our military is collapsing, our people are losing faith, and our allies are abandoning us? This is a failure of leadership, Mr. President. Your leadership."

Thieu bristled at the accusation, his voice rising slightly as he defended himself. "I have done everything in my power to defend this nation, Speaker Ut. I have made difficult decisions, yes, but always with the best interests of our people in mind."

Lam was not convinced. "The best interests of our people? Is that why the streets are filled with refugees, why our soldiers are deserting in droves, why the enemy is knocking at the gates of Saigon? No, Mr. President. This is a failure of your policies, your strategies, your leadership."

Thieu stood abruptly, his voice growing louder as he confronted the senator. "And what would you have me do, Senator? Surrender? Abandon our people to the communists? I will not betray the sacrifices of our soldiers, our allies, our fallen heroes."

Ut rose to meet Thieu's challenge, his own voice filled with passion. "And what of the sacrifices of our people, Mr. President? What of their suffering, their despair, their loss of faith in this government? We cannot continue on this path. We need change, and we need it now."

There was a long pause as Thieu considered his next words carefully. When he spoke again, his voice was calmer, but no less urgent. "I understand your concerns, gentlemen. Truly, I do. But we must think carefully before we act. A change of leadership now, in the midst of this crisis, could be disastrous. It could send a signal of weakness to our enemies, of disunity to our allies."

Lam shook his head in disagreement. "And what

signal do we send now, Mr. President? That you are willing to cling to power even as our nation burns?"

Thieu leaned forward, his eyes intense as he tried to convey the gravity of the situation. "Listen to me. We are at a critical juncture. The next few days, the next few hours, could determine the fate of our nation. If we falter now, if we show division or uncertainty, it could be the end of everything we have fought for."

He paused, looking around the room at the faces of the assembled leaders. "I know I have made mistakes. I know I have asked much of our people, of our military. But I ask you now, as leaders of this nation, to stand with me. To show our enemies, and our allies, that we are united, that we will not yield in the face of adversity." Thieu stood tall, his voice ringing with conviction. "I will not resign. Not now, not in this hour of need. I will lead this nation, I will fight for our people, until my last breath. And I ask you to stand with me, to fight with me, to show the world that the spirit of South Vietnam will not be broken."

A heavy silence filled the room as the leaders considered Thieu's words. Finally, Lam spoke, his voice reluctant but resolute. "Very well, Mr. President. We will stand with you, for now. But know this - the fate of our nation rests on your shoulders. If we fall, if Saigon falls, it will be on your head."

Thieu nodded solemnly, the weight of responsibility etched on his face. "I understand, Senator. And I accept that responsibility, with all my heart and all my soul."

Xuan Loc, South Vietnam

Granier lay prone on a hilltop overlooking a winding

jungle road. He peered through his binoculars, scanning the terrain below for any signs of movement. The air was thick with humidity and the distant echoes of artillery fire. Somewhere to the west, the battle for Xuan Loc was about to begin, the ARVN's last stand against the communist onslaught.

The CIA was doing everything in its power to help the ARVN defend what remained of South Vietnam and that included using Granier as a scout. He was the best they had to offer. Polgar knew he could trust the intel from Granier. It would be accurate and within political slant. The truth was hard to find in those troubled days where every politician and general was trying to save their ass. The strange thing was that everyone knew it was just a matter of time before Saigon fell and the war was over. But they needed time to move their gold and relatives to someplace safe out of Vietnam. The longer they stayed in power, the easier it was to make their arrangements.

The United States was the e-ticket for most South Vietnamese. But time was running out and airline seats were full. And then there was US Customs that would ask questions about large amounts of gold in luggage. It was best not to be too choosey when your life was on the line.

The ARVN already knew where the communists would attack as their opening stroke. It was nothing fancy. They would hit the city's lines of communications cutting off supplies and reinforcements. Highways, bridges, and outposts would be their first targets. The big question was what their next move would be.

Granier had been sent to scout the enemy's movements, to try to predict where they would strike next. His best guess was that after the initial assault on Xuan Loc, the communists would attempt a flanking move. What nobody knew on the ARVN headquarters was where that flanking move would occur and how strong the forces behind it. That was Granier's job.

Granier had sent separate recon teams to the east. His team was covering the southwest. Granier felt that Long Khanh would be the enemy's flanking move. In addition to being a flanking move on Xuan Loc, Long Khanh had the additional advantage of threatening Bien Hoa and could cause the ARVN to over reinforce the airbase rather than risk losing it. Granier wasn't sure it mattered. If they lost Xuan Loc there was an open pathway straight into Saigon. This battle would truly be the last great battle of the Vietnam War. Everyone was counting on it and were in the process of pushing all their chips onto the table. The only question was where to place them.

For days, Granier and his team had watched as the PAVN forces massed in the surrounding hills, their numbers growing with each passing hour. Now, it seemed, they were finally on the move.

As he watched, a column of NVA and VC soldiers emerged from the jungle below. They moved with a deliberate, almost casual pace, as if they had all the time in the world. Their uniforms were a mix of green and brown, blending perfectly with the surrounding foliage. Some wore the distinctive pith helmets of the NVA, while others sported the conical hats of the Viet Cong.

Granier counted at least a hundred men in the first group, with more emerging from the jungle behind them. They were armed, carrying AK-47s, RPGs, and light machine guns. Some pushed bicycles laden with supplies, while others led pack mules burdened with ammunition and mortar rounds.

As the column advanced, Granier marveled at their discipline and organization. These were not the ragtag guerillas of years past, but a well-oiled fighting machine, honed by years of combat and hardship. They moved with a sense of purpose, a determination born of the knowledge that victory was within their grasp. If only the ARVN could have such purpose. But that was just a dream at this point.

Granier's watched more and more enemy soldiers pour out of the jungle. There seemed to be no end to them, a vast human wave that would crash over the ARVN's defenses like a tsunami. He thought of the men of the 18th Division, dug in at Xuan Loc. They were brave soldiers, but they were outnumbered and outgunned. Against a force like this, what chance did they really have?

As the enemy column passed below his position, Granier saw something that made his blood run cold. Mixed in among the NVA regulars were soldiers wearing the uniforms of the ARVN. At first, he thought they must be prisoners, forced to carry supplies for their captors. But as he looked closer, he realized the truth was far worse.

These were ARVN deserters, men who had abandoned their posts and joined the enemy. Some looked haggard and gaunt, as if they had been on the run for weeks. Others seemed almost relieved, as if a great burden had been lifted from their shoulders. Granier felt a surge of anger and disgust at the sight of them. How could they turn their backs on their comrades, on their country?

But even as he watched, Granier knew that the deserters were only a symptom of a much deeper problem. The ARVN was coming apart at the seams, its morale shattered by years of corruption, incompetence, and defeat. The men had lost faith in their leaders, in their cause, in themselves. And now, with the enemy at the gates, that lack of faith was proving fatal.

Granier made careful note of the enemy's strength and disposition, then moved back to where his radioman as waiting. He sent his findings to Polgar, who would then pass them on to the ARVN commanders. Polgar agreed with Granier's assessment and acknowledge that the communist juggernaut seemed unstoppable, its momentum fueled by years of sacrifice and revolutionary zeal. The CIA would do its best to keep the ARVN informed even if it was a desperate cause. One never knew how the tide of war could suddenly shift even when all seemed lost.

The ARVN commander at Xuan Loc was Brigadier General Le Minh Dao. He had twelve thousand soldiers defending Xuan Loc and another eighteen thousand defending the outlying area. The communists had captured a large number of artillery pieces with plenty of ammunition at Ban Me Thuot and Da Nang. They would now use those guns against his forces. He knew that his forces would be outnumbered two to one at the very least. Normally, those would not be bad odds since he was defending and his enemy was attacking. But unlike other field commanders, Dao had no intention of keeping his troops within their trenches and letting the communist forces surround them. He believed that aggression would send the overconfident NVA and VC reeling. His fellow generals had made things far too easy for the communists. He would attack first chance he got. First, he needed to the enemy to reveal their battle plan and position of their forces. He would not have the resources for a second strike. He would put everything into one mighty blow. Timing and momentum would be key.

Dao had done everything he could to boost the morale of his men. Although he lacked veterans, in some ways he was lucky. Many of his men were local reserves and had not seen combat. They had not been beaten by the communists and felt they were up to the task of defending their city. It was a chance for a young man to prove himself and even become a hero. Dao constantly reminded them that they were true patriots, and he was confident they would be victorious. They believed in their commander.

Captain Nguyen Van Phuoc of the ARVN 43rd Infantry Regiment crouched low in his foxhole, his eyes scanning the dense foliage ahead. The air was thick with tension, the soldiers around him fidgeting nervously as they awaited the inevitable communist assault. Phuoc had seen action before, had fought the North Vietnamese in the jungles and rice paddies of his homeland. But this was different. This was Xuan Loc, the last major defensive line before Saigon. If they failed here, the capital would surely fall.

The stillness of the morning was shattered by the sudden roar of artillery fire. Phuoc instinctively ducked as shells whistled overhead, exploding in massive fireballs that shook the earth. He knew what this meant - the communist offensive had begun.

Reports began to filter in over the radio, each more dire than the last. The communists had struck hard along Highways 1 and 20, their tanks and infantry overrunning ARVN outposts and towns. At Dinh Quan and the La Nga bridge, the fighting was especially fierce, with the NVA 209th Infantry Regiment leading the charge.

Phuoc's own battalion, the 3rd of the 43rd Regiment, was stationed northwest of Hoai Duc. As the morning wore on, they found themselves engaged in heavy fighting with NVA forces. Phuoc led his men with skill and courage, directing their fire and calling in artillery support. They took casualties, but they held their ground, determined not to yield another inch of their homeland.

But the true test was yet to come. At Ong Don, just one of the many outposts surrounding Xuan Loc, the NVA and VC launched a massive assault. Artillery shells rained down on the ARVN positions, followed closely by waves of infantry. The defenders, an RF company supported by an artillery platoon, fought back with everything they had. Phuoc could hear the distant rattle of machine gun fire, the booming of the howitzers. It was a scene straight out of Hell.

Reinforcements were dispatched to Ong Don, but they ran into fierce resistance along Highway 1. The communists had planned their offensive well, targeting key bridges and culverts to isolate and fragment the ARVN forces. Phuoc knew that if they couldn't break through, Ong Don would be on its own.

As the day wore on, the scale of the communist offensive became clear. The NVA had committed two full divisions to the battle, the 6th and the 7th. They outnumbered the ARVN defenders significantly, and they had the captured artillery from Ban Me Thuot and Da Nang to back them up. It was a daunting prospect, even for a seasoned soldier like Phuoc.

But despite the odds, Phuoc and his men refused to give in. They had General Dao, a commander who believed in taking the fight to the enemy. They had the morale boost of defending their own homes and families. And they had each other, a bond of brotherhood forged in the crucible of war.

As night fell on the first day of the battle, Phuoc hunched in his foxhole, his rifle cradled in his arms. The fighting had lulled, but he knew it was only a temporary reprieve. The communists would be back, probing for weaknesses, looking for the chance to break through.

But Phuoc and his comrades would be ready for them. They were the soldiers of the ARVN, the defenders of South Vietnam. They would fight to their last breath, would spill their last drop of blood, to keep the red tide at bay. In the darkness, Phuoc whispered a prayer for strength, for courage, for victory. And then he steeled himself for the long night ahead, ready to face whatever the enemy might bring.

As night fell over Xuan Loc, an eerie silence descended upon the battlefield. Phuoc and his men were on high alert, knowing that the Viet Cong often used the cover of darkness to launch their attacks. They had fortified their positions as best they could, digging trenches and setting up barbed wire entanglements. But the jungle was vast, and the enemy was cunning.

Phuoc was making his rounds, checking on his men and offering words of encouragement, when the first shots rang out. It was a probing attack, a small group of VC sappers trying to find a weak point in their defenses. Phuoc's men responded instantly, their rifles cracking in the darkness.

But the sappers were just the beginning. As the

night wore on, the attacks grew in intensity. The VC had infiltrated the jungle around their positions, using the dense foliage to conceal their movements. They would strike suddenly and then melt away, leaving Phuoc's men firing blindly into the shadows.

The fighting was close and brutal, the kind of combat that tested a soldier's mettle to the breaking point. Phuoc moved among his men, directing their fire and calling out targets. He knew that if the VC broke through, it could spell disaster for the entire defensive line.

At one point, a group of VC managed to breach the perimeter, their sappers cutting through the barbed wire and hurling grenades into the ARVN trenches. Phuoc rallied his men and led a counterattack, driving the enemy back with a hail of gunfire and hand-to-hand combat.

It was a long and brutal night, with neither side giving quarter. The VC were determined to break through, to shatter the ARVN's will to fight. But Phuoc and his men were just as determined to hold the line, to defend their positions to the last man.

As dawn approached, the VC finally withdrew, melting back into the jungle as silently as they had come. Phuoc's men were exhausted, their uniforms stained with sweat and blood. But they had held the line, had repulsed the enemy's attack.

Phuoc knew that it was only a temporary respite. The VC would be back, probing for weaknesses, looking for another chance to strike. The VC were a tenacious and skilled enemy, with a seemingly endless supply of men and materiel. To defeat them would require more than just bravery and determination - it would require strategy, cunning, and perhaps even a bit of luck. But for now, Phuoc and his men had earned a moment to catch their breath, to tend to their wounded and regroup.

As dawn broke over the embattled city of Xuan Loc, Phuoc and his men were already in motion. General Dao had issued his orders: they were to take the fight to the enemy, to strike hard and fast before the communists could consolidate their gains. It was a bold strategy, but one that Phuoc believed in. He had seen the ARVN on the defensive too many times, had watched as they were slowly ground down by the relentless PAVN assaults. This time, things would be different.

Phuoc's battalion had been tasked with retaking a key hill overlooking Highway 20. If they could secure this position, they could disrupt the NVA's supply lines and give the other ARVN units some much-needed breathing room. But the hill was well-defended, bristling with communist troops and heavy weapons.

As they advanced through the dense jungle, Phuoc could feel the eyes of his men upon him. They were looking to him for leadership, for courage in the face of the enemy.

The attack began with a barrage of artillery fire, the ARVN gunners targeting the NVA positions with ruthless precision. Phuoc and his men moved forward under the cover of the bombardment, their rifles at the ready.

They met fierce resistance as they neared the hill, the communists pouring fire down upon them from well-concealed bunkers and trenches. Men fell all around Phuoc, some crying out in pain, others simply crumpling to the ground like marionettes with their strings cut.

But Phuoc urged his men forward, his voice rising above the din of battle. They surged up the hill, throwing grenades and firing their rifles. The fighting was brutal and bloody, a close-quarters melee of bayonets and rifle butts.

In the end, it was the courage and tenacity of the ARVN soldiers that won the day. They overran the communist positions, taking the hill and planting the South Vietnamese flag atop its crest. It was a small victory in the grand scheme of things, but it was a victory nonetheless.

News of their success spread quickly, bolstering the morale of the other ARVN units. General Dao seized upon the momentum, ordering further attacks along the communist lines. Phuoc and his men were in the thick of it, fighting with a ferocity that surprised even the battle-hardened NVA and VC troops.

But the communists were not so easily defeated. They counterattacked with fury, throwing wave after wave of infantry against the ARVN positions. The fighting raged for days, each side struggling to gain the upper hand.

Phuoc lost count of the number of times he cheated death, of the close calls and narrow escapes. He saw friends fall, men he had trained and fought beside, their lives snuffed out in an instant. But still, he fought on, driven by a sense of duty and a fierce love for his country.

In the end, despite their valiant efforts, Phuoc and his men could not hold the hill they had captured. Their losses were too great and the communist forces were too powerful and seemingly endless. On Dao's orders, Phuoc and his men were forced to pull back to their defensive lines at Xuan Loc.

As Phuoc and his men fought their way back to the city, he couldn't help but feel a sense of bitter disappointment. They had given everything they had, had fought with a bravery that would be remembered for generations. But it hadn't been enough.

Yet even in defeat, Phuoc found a measure of solace. They had made the communists pay dearly for every inch of ground, had shown the world that the ARVN was not a force to be underestimated. And they had bought precious time for the people of South Vietnam to find some measure of safety.

Granier lay prone on a hilltop overlooking the NVA positions surrounding Xuan Loc. He peered through the scope of his M40 sniper rifle, watching as the enemy soldiers moved about their trenches and bunkers. The M40 was a modified version of the Remington 700 rifle, fitted with a heavy barrel, a scope, and a suppressor for silent, long-range shooting.

Granier had spent the past three days observing the NVA's movements, mapping out their positions and studying their patterns. He had marked the location of the command post, a well-camouflaged bunker dug into the side of a hill. That was where he would find his target: the NVA commander.

Granier knew that taking out the commander would be a strategic blow to the enemy. Without clear leadership, the NVA assault on Xuan Loc would falter, buying precious time for the ARVN defenders. But getting to the command post would be no easy task. The area was heavily guarded, with sentries posted at regular intervals and patrols roaming the perimeter.

As he watched, Granier formulated his plan. He

would wait until nightfall, using the darkness to cover his approach. He would move silently through the jungle, avoiding the patrols and sentries. Once he was in position, he would take the shot, then exfiltrate back to friendly lines before the enemy could react.

Granier checked his equipment one last time. His M40 was zeroed and loaded with match-grade ammunition, each round hand-selected for accuracy. He carried a suppressed M1911 pistol as a backup weapon, along with a combat knife for close-quarters work. He had also packed a set of night vision goggles, essential for navigating the dark jungle.

As the sun began to set, Granier slipped away from his observation post and began his approach. He moved like a panther through the undergrowth, his footsteps barely making a sound. He had learned the art of stealth from the best, the US Marine Corps Scout Sniper School. They had taught him how to become one with the jungle, to use the terrain and the shadows to his advantage.

As he neared the NVA perimeter, Granier slowed his pace. He could hear the voices of the sentries, the crackle of their radios. He knew that one wrong move could give away his position, could bring the entire enemy force down upon him.

Inch by inch, he crept forward, his senses on high alert. He paused behind a fallen tree, watching as a patrol passed by just meters away. He controlled his breathing, waiting until they had moved on before continuing his approach.

Finally, he reached his chosen firing position, a small rise overlooking the command bunker. He settled into a prone stance, resting his M40 on a small sandbag for stability. He peered through the scope, scanning the area for his target.

There. A figure emerged from the bunker, flanked by two bodyguards. Granier recognized the insignia on his uniform: a colonel, likely the regimental commander. He centered the crosshairs on the colonel's chest, his finger hovering over the trigger.

But just as he was about to take the shot, one of the bodyguards turned, his eyes scanning the darkness. Granier froze, hardly daring to breathe. Had he been spotted? The bodyguard stared in his direction for a long moment, then turned away, apparently satisfied.

Granier let out a slow breath, then refocused on his target. The colonel was moving now, heading towards a waiting jeep. It was now or never. Granier took a deep breath and let half of it out, then gently squeezed the trigger.

The M40 bucked against his shoulder, the suppressor muffling the sound of the shot. Through the scope, Granier saw the colonel stagger, then collapse, a dark stain spreading across his chest. The bodyguards rushed to his side, shouting for help.

Granier didn't wait to see the aftermath. He was already moving, slipping away into the night like a wraith. He knew that the enemy would soon be swarming the area, searching for the sniper who had taken out their commander.

But Granier was too skilled, too experienced to be caught. He melted into the jungle, leaving no trace of his passing. Granier took no pleasure in killing another human being, but he didn't regret it either. He did what had to be done. The colonel's death would slow the enemy and give the ARVN at Xuan Loc a fighting chance.

ARVN Headquarters in Xuan Loc

News of the NVA Colonel's assassination was well received at ARVN Headquarters. He had only been a small piece of the puzzle, but a critical one and everyone was sure the NVA would feel the loss.

General Le Minh Dao stood over a large map of the region. Around him, his senior officers waited tensely for his orders. The sound of distant artillery fire echoed through the command bunker, a constant reminder of the PAVN forces closing in on the city.

Colonel Nguyen Van Phuc, the chief of Long Khanh Province, pointed to a spot on the map. "Our intelligence reports that the NVA 4th Army Corps is massing here, to the north and northwest of the city. They're preparing for a full-frontal assault."

Dao nodded grimly. "And what of our own forces?"

Phuc traced his finger along the map. "The 48th Regiment has returned to the city, along with two of its battalions. They've sent their 2nd Battalion to secure Ham Tan District and the port. We've also received about 500 troops from the remnants of the 2nd Division, refugees from I Corps. Once they're re-equipped, they can help secure Ham Tan."

Dao turned to another officer. "What's the status of the 52nd and 43rd Regiments?"

The officer consulted his notes. "The 52nd is pushing forward on Route 20, south of Dinh Quan. They reported heavy fighting yesterday, estimated over 50 NVA and VC casualties. The 43rd is engaged along Highway 1, near the city. They're in contact with a major enemy force."

Dao traced his hand over the map, his mind racing. He knew that the coming battle would be the toughest test yet for his men. The NVA and VC had them outnumbered and outgunned, and they had the momentum of their recent victories behind them.

But Dao was determined not to let Xuan Loc fall. He had made a promise, to his men and to the people of South Vietnam, that he would stand and fight. And he intended to keep that promise.

He turned to his officers, his voice firm with resolve. "Gentlemen, we have a difficult task ahead of us. The enemy is at our gates, and they will stop at nothing to take this city. But we will not let them. We will fight them with everything we have, on every street and in every building. We will make them pay for every inch of ground they try to take."

He pointed to the map, his finger tracing the defensive lines. "I want the 48th Regiment to reinforce our positions in the north and northwest. The 52nd and 43rd will continue to press the enemy along Routes 20 and 1. We must keep them off balance, disrupt their plans. And when they come for the city, we will be ready."

The officers nodded. They knew the odds were against them, but they also knew that they had a leader who would fight to the last. And that gave them the courage to face whatever was to come.

As the meeting broke up, Dao turned to Colonel Phuc. "I meant what I said earlier, to the foreign press. I don't care how many divisions the communists send against us. We will smash them all. The world will see the strength and skill of the Army of the Republic of Vietnam."

Phuc nodded solemnly. "And we will be right beside you, General. To the end."

Dao clasped the man's shoulder, a gesture of

solidarity and respect. Then he turned back to the map, his mind already racing ahead to the battles to come. Outside, the sound of gunfire and explosions grew louder, a symphony of war that would soon engulf the city. But in that moment, Dao felt a sense of calm, a clarity of purpose. He knew his duty, and he would see it through, no matter the price. For his men, for his country, and for the ideal of freedom that he had sworn to defend.

Frontlines – Xuan Loc, South Vietnam

As dawn broke over Xuan Loc, the stillness of the morning was shattered by the thunderous roar of artillery. The NVA 4th Army Corps had opened up with a massive bombardment, raining down over four thousand shells on the ARVN positions with a ferocity that seemed to shake the very earth. It was the largest artillery bombardment of the war, evidence that the communists were committed to take Xuan Loc and destroy the ARVN defending it.

Private Nguyen Van Minh huddled in his foxhole, his hands clasped over his ears as the barrage slammed into his position. He had never experienced anything like this before, the sheer volume of fire was overwhelming. Around him, his fellow soldiers of the 52nd Task Force, their expressions a mix of fear and determination. It was the type of violence that unhinged a man or steeled his fortitude. It just depended on the man.

Across the lines, Sergeant Tran Duc Huy of the NVA 341st Infantry Division was leading his men forward, taking advantage of the artillery barrage to close in on the ARVN communications center. Huy was a veteran of many battles, his face scarred and weathered by years of combat. He urged his men on with shouts and gestures, his AK-47 held ready.

As the communist soldiers neared their objective, the ARVN defenders opened up with a hail of gunfire. Huy dove for cover, bullets whizzing past his head. He could see his comrades falling around him, cut down by the accurate fire of the entrenched ARVN troops.

For over an hour, the two sides fought bitterly, the ARVN defenders holding their ground. But finally, under the relentless pressure of the enemy assault, they were forced to fall back. Huy and his men surged forward, capturing the communications center and the nearby police station.

To the east, the NVA 7th Infantry Division was having a tougher time. They had advanced without tank support, and the ARVN soldiers were exacting a heavy toll. Private Le Thi Hoa, a young nurse attached to the 7th Division, worked frantically to treat the wounded, her hands slick with blood. She had seen so much death in this war, but it never got any easier.

The arrival of NVA tanks seemed to turn the tide, but the ARVN soldiers at Bao Chanh A were ready for them. Using anti-tank weapons and sheer courage, they managed to destroy three of the armored behemoths, buying precious time for their comrades.

At the 18th Division headquarters, the fighting was intense. The ARVN 43rd and 48th Infantry Regiments were putting up a fierce defense, but the NVA 209th and 270th Infantry Regiments were relentless. Corporal Tran Van Sau of the 43rd Regiment fired his

M79 grenade launcher until his ammunition was exhausted, then switched to his M16 rifle. Beside him, his friend and fellow soldier Private Nguyen Huu Chau fell, his chest torn open by a burst of gunfire. Sau kept fighting, determined to hold the line.

But it was a losing battle. By midday, the communists had captured both the 18th Division headquarters and the Governor's Residence, leaving a trail of destroyed ARVN tanks in their wake.

In the south, the NVA 6th Infantry Division was pushing hard along Highway 1, their tanks and infantry working in deadly tandem. The ARVN 322nd Armored Brigade was fighting back hard, but they were outmatched and outgunned. Eleven of their tanks were destroyed, the burnt-out hulks littering the highway.

Throughout the long, bloody day, the ARVN 18th Division fought desperately to slow the communist advance. They launched counterattacks on the flanks, trying to disrupt the enemy's momentum. Men on both sides fought and died in the sweltering heat, the air thick with smoke and the stench of cordite.

For the soldiers on the ground, it was a hellish experience. The noise was deafening, the chaos total. Men watched their friends die before their eyes, powerless to help. They fought on instinct and adrenaline, their world narrowed down to the next moment, the next shot, the next desperate struggle to survive.

And through it all, the battle raged on, the fate of Xuan Loc hanging in the balance. Both sides knew that this was a crucial moment, that the outcome here could decide the future of the entire war. And so they fought, with a savagery and a resolve that defied description, each man driven by his own sense of duty, of loyalty, of the desperate need to prevail.

It was a day that would live in infamy, a day of blood and fire and unimaginable courage. And for those who survived it, it would forever be seared into their memories, a testament to the human spirit in all its terrible glory.

As the battle for Xuan Loc entered its final, brutal days, the tide of the conflict shifted irreversibly in favor of the North Vietnamese forces. On April 15, the NVA artillery abruptly ceased its bombardment of Xuan Loc itself, turning its sights instead on the vital Bien Hoa Air Base. The impact was immediate and devastating. Within a single day, the relentless shelling forced the RVNAF 3rd Air Force Division to suspend all operations at Bien Hoa. In a desperate attempt to maintain air support for the beleaguered troops at Xuan Loc, the RVNAF scrambled to mobilize the 4th Air Force Division from Binh Thuy Air Base.

On the ground, the situation was rapidly deteriorating. A massive artillery barrage, numbering some 1,000 rounds, rained down on the headquarters of the 52nd Regiment, its 3rd Battalion, an artillery battalion, and elements of the 5th Armored Cavalry Squadron. The results were catastrophic - four 155mm howitzers and eight 105mm howitzers were destroyed, their crews killed or wounded. West of Xuan Loc, the NVA 6th Infantry Division and 95B Infantry Regiment steamrolled a combined ARVN force, including the 52nd Task Force and 13th Armored Squadron.

The following days brought no respite for the ARVN. On April 16 and 17, the PAVN 6th Infantry

Division and 95B Infantry Regiment dealt a series of crushing blows to the ARVN 8th Task Force and 3rd Armored Brigade, as they desperately tried to recapture the military zone of Dau Giay. In and around Xuan Loc itself, the ARVN 43rd and 48th Infantry Regiments, along with the elite 1st Airborne Brigade, found themselves beset on all sides by NVA and VC infantry. They fought bravely, but the casualties were staggering.

The armored task forces along Route 1, their strength cut in half by the relentless communist assaults, were forced to fall back. The 1st Airborne Brigade, their attempt to reach Xuan Loc thwarted, had no choice but to withdraw through the dense plantations and jungles towards Ba Ria in Phuoc Tuy Province.

With the fall of Dau Giay and the severing of the main roads, Xuan Loc was now completely isolated. The 18th Division, once the proud defenders of the city, found themselves cut off and surrounded by the NVA 4th Army Corps. Reinforcement or resupply was impossible. The end, it seemed, was inevitable.

Faced with this grim reality, the Joint General Staff made the painful decision to order the evacuation of Xuan Loc. On April 19, General Le Minh Dao was instructed to pull out the 18th Division and other supporting units, to fall back to a new defensive line at Trang Bom, east of Bien Hoa. It was a bitter pill to swallow, a tacit admission of defeat, but there was no alternative.

The withdrawal began on April 20, under the cover of heavy monsoon rains. A convoy of some 200 military vehicles, packed with soldiers and civilians alike, began the perilous journey out of Xuan Loc. It was a scene of chaos and desperation, the once-proud ARVN reduced to a fleeing mass.

The 1st Airborne Brigade, true to their reputation as the ARVN's most tenacious fighters, were the last to leave. But even for these elite soldiers, the NVA's fury proved too much. In the early hours of April 21, at the hamlet of Suoi Ca, the Brigade's 3rd Battalion was annihilated in a final, tragic stand.

By the end of that fateful day, Xuan Loc, the scene of such heroic resistance, such sacrifice and valor, was firmly in the hands of the North Vietnamese. The gateway to Saigon, the capital and heart of South Vietnam, now lay open. The battle of Xuan Loc, the last great stand of the ARVN, was over.

For the soldiers who had fought and died in the jungles and rice paddies around the city, it was a bitter and heartbreaking defeat. They had given everything, had fought with a courage that would be remembered for generations. But in the end, against the relentless tide of the communist advance, it had not been enough.

And so, as the North Vietnamese tanks rolled through the shattered streets of Xuan Loc, as the red flag with its gold star was raised over the citadel, there was a sense not just of loss, but also of a certain tragic nobility. The ARVN had fought the good fight, had held the line for as long as humanly possible. In the end, that would be their legacy - not the final outcome, but the courage and sacrifice with which they had faced the ultimate test. It was a legacy that would endure, even as the country itself fell into shadow.

The Battle of Xuan Loc marked a turning point in the Vietnam War, a decisive moment that effectively sealed the fate of South Vietnam. In the wake of their hard-fought victory, the North Vietnamese forces found themselves in control of a staggering two-thirds of South Vietnam's territory. It was a remarkable achievement, a testament to the tenacity and strategic brilliance of the communist commanders.

For the South Vietnamese, the loss of Xuan Loc was a devastating blow. The ARVN had committed nearly every unit from its general reserve to the defense of the city, and the casualties they suffered were catastrophic. Entire divisions were decimated, their fighting strength reduced to a mere shadow of what it had been.

The impact of this defeat on South Vietnamese morale was overwhelming. On April 18, just days after the fall of Xuan Loc, III Corps commander General Toan delivered a grim assessment to President Thieu. The South Vietnamese forces, he reported, had been beaten, and could only hold out for a few more days in the face of such overwhelming losses.

With the fall of Xuan Loc, the communists had effectively removed the last major obstacle standing between them and Saigon. The South Vietnamese capital, once thought to be an impregnable bastion, now lay open and vulnerable.

The sound of distant artillery and the chatter of small arms fire echoed through the jungle as the remnants of the 18th Division trudged along the muddy road. They were exhausted, their uniforms torn and stained with blood and sweat. Many were wounded, limping or being carried on makeshift stretchers by their comrades.

At the rear of the column, Rene Granier and his team of snipers kept a watchful eye on the jungle behind them. They knew the North Vietnamese forces were in hot pursuit, eager to finish off the battered ARVN soldiers.

Granier signaled to his men to take up positions on either side of the road. They melted into the foliage, their camouflaged ghillie suits blending seamlessly with the vegetation. Each man carried a scoped M40 rifle, a weapon designed for long-range precision shooting.

As the last of the 18th Division's soldiers passed by, Granier heard the telltale sound of movement in the jungle behind them. He peered through his rifle's scope, scanning the treeline for any sign of the enemy.

Suddenly, a group of North Vietnamese soldiers emerged from the jungle, their AK-47s at the ready. They began to advance cautiously down the road, searching for any stragglers from the retreating ARVN force.

Granier held up his hand, signaling his men to hold their fire. He wanted the enemy to get closer, to give his snipers a better shot.

The North Vietnamese soldiers continued to advance, unaware of the danger that lurked in the jungle around them. They were just a hundred meters away when Granier gave the signal.

The crack of sniper rifles split the air, the sound echoing through the jungle. Four North Vietnamese soldiers fell, their bodies crumbling to the ground. The rest of the enemy force immediately sought cover, diving into the undergrowth on either side of the road.

Granier and his men continued to fire, picking off the enemy soldiers one by one. Each shot was carefully aimed, each bullet finding its mark with deadly precision.

The North Vietnamese returned fire, their AK-47s chattering as they sprayed the jungle with bullets. But the snipers were well-concealed, and the enemy fire was largely ineffective.

For several minutes, the firefight raged, the sound of gunfire and the cries of the wounded filling the air. But gradually, the North Vietnamese fire began to slacken, as more and more of their men fell to the sniper's bullets.

Finally, the enemy force began to retreat, pulling back into the jungle from whence they had come. Granier and his men continued to fire until the last of the North Vietnamese had disappeared from view.

As silence returned to the jungle, Granier stood up, his rifle cradled in his arms. He surveyed the scene before him, taking in the bodies of the enemy soldiers scattered along the road.

It was a small victory, but a vital one. By forcing the North Vietnamese to pull back, Granier and his snipers had bought precious time for the 18th Division to continue their retreat. They had given their comrades a chance to escape, to fight another day.

Granier signaled to his men to move out, to follow the retreating ARVN column. They would continue to provide rear-guard protection, to keep the enemy at bay for as long as possible.

Saigon, South Vietnam

Coyle stood on the rooftop of the apartment building, his eyes scanning the horizon. In the distance, he could see the telltale signs of the advancing communist forces - plumes of smoke rising from the outer cities, the distant thunder of artillery growing ever closer. He knew that it was only a matter of time before Saigon itself fell, before the streets erupted into chaos and bloodshed.

Behind him, he heard the sound of footsteps, and turned to see Nguyet emerging from the stairwell. Her face was drawn and worried, her eyes shadowed with fear.

"Coyle," she said softly, coming to stand beside him. "What are we going to do?"

Coyle took a deep breath, steeling himself for the conversation he knew they had to have. "Nguyet," he said gently, "we need to leave. Saigon is going to fall, and when it does, it won't be safe for you or Tuyet."

Nguyet shook her head, her eyes filling with tears. "This is our home, Coyle. My family is here. I can't just leave. Where would we go? How would we survive?"

Coyle reached out, taking her hand in his. "I know it's hard," he said. "But we don't have a choice. The communists are coming, and they won't show mercy to anyone they see as an enemy."

Nguyet's face paled, her grip tightening on Coyle's hand. "But we're not their enemies," she whispered. "We're just trying to live our lives."

Coyle sighed. "Nguyet, there's something you need to know about Tuyet. About her father."

Nguyet's eyes widened, her body going still. "What do you mean?"

"Tuyet's father was James McGovern, the American war hero. You knew him as McGoon. What you didn't know was that he was famous, a symbol of the resistance against the communists. And because of that, because of who Tuyet is, she's in danger. If they find out who her father was, the communists may see her as a threat, as someone to be eliminated."

Nguyet's face crumpled, a sob tearing from her throat. "No," she whispered. "Not Tuyet. She's just a little girl. She wouldn't hurt anyone."

"I know, but they may not see it that way. The communists fear symbols that can move the people against them. They will see Tuyet as a symbol."

"No. They can't hurt my baby."

Coyle pulled her into his arms, holding her close as she wept. "I won't let that happen," he said fiercely. "I'll do whatever it takes to keep her safe, to keep both of you safe. But we need to leave, Nguyet. We need to get out of Vietnam before it's too late."

For a long moment, Nguyet clung to him, her body shaking with grief and fear. But then, slowly, she pulled back, her eyes red-rimmed but determined.

"Alright," she said softly. "For Tuyet. We'll go."

Coyle nodded, relief and gratitude washing over him. "Thank you," he said. "I promise, I'll take care of you both. I won't let anything happen to you."

But even as he spoke the words, Coyle knew that getting out of Vietnam would be no easy task. The streets were already filled with people desperate to escape, with crowds clamoring at the gates of the American embassy. He would need to find a way to cut through the throng, to get Nguyet and Tuyet to safety before the city fell.

As he looked out over the rooftops of Saigon, Coyle's mind raced. He had contacts, resources, favors he could call in. He would use every last one of them, move Heaven and earth if he had to, to get Nguyet and Tuyet out.

Because he had made a promise, not just to them, but to McGoon. And no matter what it took, no matter what sacrifices he had to make, Coyle intended to keep that promise.

He turned back to Nguyet, his face set with

determination. "Come on," he said. "We have work to do."

Together, they descended from the rooftop.

Mayhem

Bien Hoa Air Base, South Vietnam

Granier moved with the battered remnants of the 18th Division, a grim procession of wounded men and haggard faces. The fighting at Xuan Loc had been fierce, a brutal last stand against the relentless advance of the communist forces. But in the end, even the courage and sacrifice of the ARVN soldiers had not been enough. The city of Xuan Loc had fallen, and with it, the last hope of stemming the tide of the North Vietnamese offensive.

As they made their way towards Bien Hoa Air Base, Granier couldn't shake the sense of impending doom that hung over the column of soldiers like a shroud. The men around him were exhausted, their spirits broken by the unending battles and the knowledge that their country was slipping away from them with each passing day.

As they approached the air base, the sound of shelling grew louder, the deep boom of artillery mixing with the distant crackle of small arms fire. Granier's heart sank as he saw the plumes of smoke rising from the runway, the twisted wreckage of aircraft littering the tarmac.

The communists had been pounding Bien Hoa for days, their artillery wreaking havoc on the vital lifeline of the ARVN forces. The runways were cratered and pitted, useless for the stream of planes that had once ferried supplies and reinforcements to the front lines.

Granier and his team were directed to a makeshift command post, where a haggard-looking officer briefed them on the situation. The 18th Division was to continue its retreat to Tan Son Nhut Air Base, to the DAO compound that had become the last bastion of American power in South Vietnam.

As they made their way through the chaotic streets of Bien Hoa, Granier couldn't help but feel a sense of surreal detachment. The city he had once known, the vibrant heart of the South, was now a ghost town, its streets deserted save for the occasional band of frightened civilians or the ominous presence of ARVN patrols.

Saigon, South Vietnam

For days, Coyle had been trying to get through to the U.S. Embassy, desperate to speak with Polgar. The phone lines were constantly jammed, the signal interrupted by the chaos engulfing the city. Coyle had lost count of the hours he'd spent dialing and redialing, each unanswered ring adding to his growing sense of frustration and despair.

When the call finally connected, Coyle almost couldn't believe it. The voice on the other end was harried and tense, but unmistakably Polgar's. "Chief, it's Coyle. Thank God I got through."

"Coyle?" Polgar's tone was a mix of surprise and exhaustion. "What's going on? I don't have much time."

Coyle could hear the sound of voices in the background, the clatter of telephones and the urgent shouting of orders. He knew Polgar must be in the middle of the evacuation efforts, trying to get as many people out as possible before the city fell.

"I need your help, Chief. It's Nguyet and her daughter, Tuyet. I need to get them out of the country."

There was a pause on the line, and for a moment, Coyle feared the connection had been lost. But then Polgar's voice came through again, strained but clear.

"Coyle, I'm doing everything I can to get our people out. But the situation is a mess. The airport is barely functioning, and we're running out of time."

Coyle closed his eyes, his grip tightening on the phone. "I know. But I can't leave them behind, Chief. I made a promise."

Another pause, longer this time. When Polgar spoke again, his voice was low and serious. "The girl, Tuyet. Who's her father?"

Coyle's heart skipped a beat. He knew what Polgar was asking, knew the implications of his answer. But he also knew that he couldn't hesitate, couldn't risk losing this chance. "I am," he said firmly. "Tuyet is my daughter."

The lie tasted bitter on his tongue, but Coyle pushed down his guilt. He would do whatever it took to keep Nguyet and Tuyet safe, even if it meant bending the truth.

Polgar sighed, the sound heavy with weariness. "Alright, Coyle. I'll do what I can. But you need to get them to the embassy as soon as possible. We're processing visas and paperwork around the clock, but we are understaffed and time is running out."

Coyle felt a surge of relief, tinged with a new sense of urgency. "I understand. We'll be there as soon as we can."

"Good." Polgar's voice was brisk now, the momentary softness gone. "I've got to go, Coyle. Things are falling apart here. Just get to the embassy, and we'll do our best to get you and your family out."

"Thank you, Chief. I won't forget this."

As the line went dead, Coyle stared at the phone in his hand. He knew that getting to the embassy would be a risk, that the streets of Saigon were a war zone now. But he also knew that it was their only chance.

Coyle took a deep breath, steeling himself for what was to come. Then he went to find Nguyet and Tuyet, to tell them that they were leaving, that a new life awaited them beyond the chaos and the fear.

US Embassy – Saigon, South Vietnam

The streets of Saigon were a scene of utter chaos. Thousands of people, desperate to escape the advancing North Vietnamese forces, had converged on the American Embassy, the last beacon of hope in a city teetering on the brink of collapse. Coyle, Nguyet, and Tuyet found themselves caught in the middle of the frenzied crowd, struggling to make their way to the embassy front gates.

As they neared the embassy, Coyle could see the line of U.S. Marines, a mere eighteen men, trying to hold back the surging crowd. They were vastly outnumbered, their faces tense with the strain of maintaining order. Some Marines were perched atop the walls, pushing back people who tried to climb over. Others stood at the gates, a human barricade against the tide of desperate humanity.

The sound of shouting and screaming was overwhelming. People were pressing against the gates, their hands reaching through the bars, pleading for entry. Coyle saw a Marine push a woman back from the top of the wall, only to have two more take her place. It was a losing battle, but the Marines held their ground, their discipline and training the only thing standing between the embassy and utter chaos.

As Coyle and his family approached the gate, he caught the eye of one of the Marines. The young man's face was streaked with sweat, his eyes wide with the stress of the situation. "CIA," said Coyle showing his passport and ID.

"You can come through," said the Marine.

"With my family."

When the Marine saw Nguyet and Tuyet trailing behind Coyle, a flicker of understanding passed over his features.

"Let them through!" he shouted to his comrades.

The Marines at the gate parted, just wide enough for Coyle to push through with Nguyet and Tuyet. But as they stepped forward, the crowd surged, trying to force their way in behind them. Coyle heard the Marines shouting, saw them pushing back against the tide of bodies.

More Marines rushed to help, their arms straining as they fought to close the gate behind Coyle and his family. But the pressure was too great, and the crowd began to spill through the gaps, flooding into the embassy compound.

Coyle pulled Nguyet and Tuyet close, shielding them with his body as he looked around desperately for a way out of the chaos. He could see Marines running in all directions, trying to contain the crowd and prevent a full-scale breach of the embassy.

Some Marines were forced to abandon their posts at the walls to help secure the gate, leaving gaps in the perimeter. People were scaling the walls unchallenged now, dropping into the compound on the other side. The situation was deteriorating rapidly, and Coyle knew they had to move fast.

He spotted a Marine gesturing frantically towards a side door of the embassy building. Coyle understood immediately - it was their best chance at getting inside to safety.

With Nguyet and Tuyet in tow, Coyle ran for the door, dodging through the chaotic press of bodies. Behind him, he could hear the Marines shouting, the sound of scuffles and cries of pain as they struggled to maintain control.

As they reached the door, another Marine ushered them inside, slamming it shut behind them. Inside, the relative quiet was jarring after the chaos of the compound. But Coyle knew it was only a temporary respite.

He could only imagine the scene outside, the eighteen Marines now completely overwhelmed, the embassy compound in danger of being overrun entirely. He said a silent prayer for the young men out there, putting their lives on the line to protect people like him and his family.

Coyle knew that reinforcements were on the way,

that another forty-six Marines were being flown in by helicopter to help secure the embassy. But would they arrive in time? And even if they did, would it be enough to hold back the tide of desperation and fear that had engulfed the city?

As he held Nguyet and Tuyet close while climbing the stairs, Coyle could only hope that they had made it inside in time, that the Marines could hold out long enough for help to arrive. For now, all they could do was wait and pray, their fate resting in the hands of those brave few who stood between them and the chaos outside. He heard the three-bullet burst of an M16. He hoped it was just over the heads of the mob.

When he reached the top of the stairs, Coyle saw an impossibly long line of refugees waiting to submit their paperwork and talk with one of the embassy staff. He found a corner for Nguyet and Tuyet to sit and wait. "Keep an eye on me and don't live the building. I will signal you when it looks like I am getting close. Then you join me in line. Okay?"

Nguyet nodded that she understood. Coyle took their paperwork and got in line. It was all he could do... wait like the others.

Nguyet's Apartment

It had been three days since he had submitted Nguyet and Tuyet's paperwork for their visas. Coyle paced the small apartment, his nerves frayed. He had been hoping against hope that the call would come, that the paperwork for Nguyet and Tuyet would be approved. Every moment that passed felt like an eternity, the walls of the city closing in around them as the communist forces drew ever closer. He didn't dare leave the apartment for fear of missing a critical phone call.

When the phone finally rang, Coyle lunged for it. "Hello?" he said, his voice tight with anxiety.

"Coyle, it's Polgar. I have good news. The visas and paperwork for Nguyet and Tuyet are ready. You can come to the embassy to pick them up."

For a moment, Coyle couldn't speak, his relief so overwhelming that it stole his breath. He closed his eyes, silently thanking whatever gods might be listening for this small miracle.

"Thank you, Chief," he said finally, his voice rough with emotion. "You have no idea what this means to me, to all of us."

"I think I have some idea," Polgar said, his tone gentle. "But you need to hurry, Coyle. The situation is getting worse by the hour. The ambassador is going to be forced to evacuate the embassy at some point. No telling when, but we're running out of time."

Coyle nodded, even though Polgar couldn't see him. "I understand. I'll be there as soon as I can."

As he hung up the phone, Coyle turned to see Nguyet and Tuyet watching him anxiously from the doorway. He smiled at them, trying to project a confidence he didn't entirely feel.

"Good news," he said. "Your visas are ready. We'll be able to leave soon."

Nguyet's face lit up with relief, tears springing to her eyes. She rushed forward, throwing her arms around Coyle in a fierce hug. "Thank you," she whispered. "Thank you for everything."

After a long moment, he pulled back gently, looking down at Nguyet with serious eyes. "I need to go to the embassy to pick up the paperwork," he said. "I think it's best if I go alone. The streets are getting more dangerous, and I don't want to risk anything happening to you or Tuyet."

Nguyet's face clouded with worry, but she nodded slowly. "Alright," she said. "But please, be careful. Come back to us safely. I don't know what we would do without you, Coyle."

Coyle cupped her cheek, his thumb brushing away a stray tear. "I will," he promised. "And when I do, we'll be ready to leave. To start a new life, together."

He turned to Tuyet, kneeling down to look her in the eye. "I need you to be brave, little one," he said softly. "Can you help your mother pack your things? We'll be going on a big adventure soon."

Tuyet nodded. Coyle smiled, ruffling her hair affectionately. "That's my girl," he said.

He gave Nguyet and Tuyet one last reassuring smile, then slipped out the door.

Coyle stepped out into the streets of Saigon, the chaos and desperation hitting him like a physical blow. The city was in a state of utter pandemonium, with thousands of people desperately trying to reach the embassy, to secure the paperwork that would be their ticket to freedom.

The situation had deteriorated rapidly in the last few days, the communist forces advancing with a speed and ferocity that had caught everyone off guard. The streets were filled with soldiers and civilians alike, all of them with the same haunted, desperate look in their eyes.

Coyle fought his way through the throng, his elbows and shoulders bumping against the press of bodies. The air was thick with the stench of sweat and fear, the sound of shouting and crying rising above the din of the city.

US Embassy – Saigon, South Vietnam

As he neared the embassy, Coyle's heart sank. The building was surrounded by a sea of people, all of them clamoring for the chance to get inside. Soldiers and police formed a cordon around the entrance, their faces grim as they tried to hold back the tide of humanity.

Coyle took a deep breath, steeling himself for what was to come. He pushed his way to the front of the crowd, ignoring the angry shouts and curses that followed in his wake. When he reached the soldiers, he held up his hands, shouting to be heard above the noise.

"I'm here to pick up visas!" he yelled. "I have paperwork inside, I need to get it!"

The soldier shook his head, his face impassive. "No one gets in without authorization," he said. "Embassy's closed to the public."

Coyle felt a surge of anger, of desperation. He couldn't let this happen, couldn't let some bureaucratic red tape keep him from getting to Nguyet and Tuyet's documents.

He leaned in close to the soldier, his voice low and urgent. "Listen to me," he said. "I have a woman and a child depending on me. If I don't get those visas, they'll be trapped here when the city falls. I'm begging you, let me through."

For a moment, the soldier hesitated, his eyes searching Coyle's face. Then, with a curt nod, he stepped aside, gesturing for Coyle to pass.

Coyle didn't wait for a second invitation. He pushed

through the crowd, fighting his way up the gate and into the embassy. Inside, the scene was just as chaotic as the streets outside, with people crowding every available space.

Coyle scanned the room, looking for a familiar face. Finally, he spotted Polgar passing by, his face drawn and haggard.

"Chief!" Coyle shouted, pushing his way through the crowd. "I need those visas, now!"

Polgar turned, his eyes widening as he saw Coyle. "Jesus, Coyle," he said. "I didn't think you'd make it. It's a madhouse out there."

"I know," Coyle said, his voice tight. "But I need those documents. Nguyet and Tuyet are counting on me."

Polgar nodded, gesturing for Coyle to follow him. They pushed their way through the crowd, fighting for every step. Finally, they reached a small office, where a harried-looking clerk was sorting through piles of paperwork.

"Here," Polgar said, grabbing a stack of documents from the clerk's desk. "These are the visas and passports for Nguyet and Tuyet. They won't get past the guards at the gate without their paperwork, so make sure they keep it on their persons. But Coyle, listen to me. The airport... we don't know how much longer it's going to stay open. Bien Hoa Air Base is already shutdown, so it's Tan Son Nhut Air Base or nothing. The NVA is advancing faster than anyone expected. If you don't get out soon..."

He trailed off, his face grim. Coyle felt a chill run down his spine, a sense of urgency that bordered on panic.

"I understand," he said, taking the documents from

Polgar's hand. "I'll get them out, whatever it takes."

Polgar nodded, clasping Coyle's shoulder. "Good luck," he said. "And Coyle... be careful out there. It's going to get worse when the NVA breech the city's perimeter."

Coyle swallowed hard, he knew that the journey to the airport would be a gauntlet, a desperate race against time and the tide of history.

With a final nod of thanks to Polgar, Coyle said, "Are you gonna be okay, Chief?"

"Are you kidding? Marines are guarding the ambassador. I'm just gonna stick to his coat tails," said Polgar with a grin.

"Good plan. Next time I see ya, drinks are on me," said Coyle.

"That's a mistake. I'm a top shelf man."

"Fair enough," said Coyle as he turned and pushed his way back through the crowd, the precious documents clutched tightly to his chest.

On his way back to the apartment, Coyle got the attention of a taxi driver by holding out a wad of American dollars. In a city on the brink of collapse, American dollars were like gold. The driver wanted five times the normal fare to drive to the airport. Coyle agreed and paid him half, promising to pay the final half when they arrived at the airport.

Riding through the jammed streets, Coyle could hear the communist artillery pounding the ARVN defensive positions on the outskirts of Saigon. Coyle knew the ARVN were outgunned and outmanned. It was just a matter of time before the NVA and VC broke through their lines. And when that happened, the end of Saigon and South Vietnam was nigh.

Nguyet's Apartment

An hour later, Coyle, Nguyet, and Tuyet pushed their way through the frantic crowds in front of the apartment building and climbed into the taxi. The taxi inching forward through the chaotic streets of Saigon with thousands of people desperately trying to reach the airport, to escape before the communist forces closed in.

Suddenly, the taxi jolted to a stop, the driver cursing in Vietnamese. Coyle leaned forward, trying to see what was happening, but before he could react, the doors were wrenched open and a mob of people surged into the vehicle pulling the passengers and the driver out onto the street.

Coyle tried to fight them off, to protect Nguyet and Tuyet, but there were too many, their desperation fueling a strength born of pure fear. He felt a sharp blow to the back of his head, and then everything went black.

Escape

Saigon, South Vietnam

Coyle's head throbbed with pain as he slowly regained consciousness, the sounds of chaos and panic filling his ears. He blinked, trying to focus his vision, and saw Nguyet crouched beside him, her face streaked with tears.

"Nguyet," he croaked, struggling to sit up. "What happened?"

"The people… they attacked us," Nguyet sobbed, her voice breaking. "They took our bags, the passports... and Tuyet. Oh God, Coyle, they took Tuyet."

Coyle's heart stopped, a cold terror gripping his chest. He staggered to his feet, ignoring the pain in his head as he scanned the crowd desperately. "What do you mean, they took her? Where is she?"

Nguyet shook her head, her body trembling. "I don't know. The mob, they swept her away. I tried to hold on to her, but there were too many of them. I couldn't... I couldn't..."

She broke down, her sobs echoing in the chaotic streets. Coyle pulled her close, his mind reeling with the implications of what had happened. Not only were their passports and visas gone, stolen in the attack, but now Tuyet was missing, lost in the frantic, desperate crowds that filled the city.

"We have to find her," Coyle said, his voice low and urgent. "We won't leave without her. I promise."

Nguyet nodded, wiping her tears with a shaking hand. "But how? The city is in chaos, Coyle. She could be anywhere."

"I don't think she could have gone far. She's probably just scared and hiding. You and I have to stay together. There's no time. We have to hurry."

He took Nguyet's hand, leading her through the crowds as he scanned the faces around them, looking for any sign of Tuyet. Yelling her name above the din of the mob. They pushed their way past families and soldiers, past old men and crying children, the desperation and fear palpable in the air.

For hours, they searched, Coyle using every skill he had honed in his years as a soldier and a spy. He bribed street children for information, cajoled shopkeepers and taxi drivers, his eyes always moving, always searching for that one small face in the sea of humanity.

As the day wore on and the sun began to set, Coyle's heart grew heavy with despair. The city was falling apart around them, the communist forces drawing ever closer. On the horizon flashes of light from NVA artillery. If they didn't find Tuyet soon, if they didn't find a way out...

Suddenly, a shout rang out above the ruckus of the crowd. Coyle spun around, his heart leaping as he saw a figure running towards them, her face streaked with tears but alive, blessedly alive.

"Tuyet!" Nguyet cried, rushing forward to gather her daughter in her arms. "Oh my baby, my baby."

Coyle felt a wave of relief wash over him, so powerful that it almost brought him to his knees. He wrapped his arms around them both, holding them close as he whispered a silent prayer of thanks.

But even as they clung to each other, Coyle knew that their ordeal was far from over. They still had to find a way out of the city, had to get to safety before it was too late. And without their paperwork, without the visas that had been so hard-won, it would be a daunting task indeed. The guards at the airport would never let them board a plane without paperwork for Nguyet and Tuyet.

Coyle surveyed the chaotic streets of Saigon. The once-bustling thoroughfares were now choked with abandoned vehicles, the desperate citizens having fled on foot when the roads became impassable. He knew that driving out of the city in a car would be impossible, and time was running out. To make matters worse, all his money was gone, along with his flight pistol. He scanned the area for a solution.

At the end of the block, Coyle saw a motorcycle policeman pull to a stop, hop off his bike, and attempt to break up a fight between two men slugging it out. Coyle knew it was wrong, but he was desperate – with the policeman distracted, he jumped on the bike, and drove down the street to Nguyet and Tuyet. "Hop on!"

Tuyet climbed on in front of Coyle and Nguyet climbed on back. A gunshot from the policeman's pistol zipped over Coyle's head. Coyle sped off rounding the corner at the end of the block and out of sight of the policeman.

As he drove through the city, Coyle weaved through the abandoned vehicles and discarded belongings using the sidewalk and shoulder when necessary. He avoided groups of fleeing citizens believing they might try to steal the motorcycle. Anything to get through the tangle.

Nguyet gasped as Coyle narrowly avoided a group of looters smashing the windows of a nearby shop. Tuyet buried her face in her hands, her body trembling with fear.

"It's okay," Coyle reassured them, his voice calm despite the chaos around them. "Hang on tight. I'll get us through this."

As they made their way through the city, Coyle couldn't help but feel a sense of surreal detachment. The streets he had once known so well were now almost unrecognizable, transformed into a nightmarish landscape of a society torn asunder.

After several hours, Coyle and his family made it to the edge of the city. Coyle maneuvered the stolen police motorcycle through the dense crowd, a sea of desperate faces. Nguyet clung to his back, her arms wrapped tightly around his waist, while Tuyet sat in front of him, her body nestled against his chest.

As they approached the ARVN defensive perimeter, Coyle saw the roadblock looming ahead, a barricade of sandbags and barbed wire manned by South Vietnamese soldiers. The crowd around the checkpoint was a seething mass of humanity, civilians desperate to escape the city and the advancing enemy.

Coyle wove his way through the throng, his eyes scanning for a path through. He knew that time was running out, that every second counted if they were going to make it out before the communists overran the ARVN.

Finally, he reached the front of the crowd, the motorcycle's engine sputtering as he brought it to a stop. The officer in charge of the roadblock, a haggard-looking man with a weathered face, stepped forward, his hand resting on the butt of his pistol.

Coyle met the man's gaze, his voice steady and calm despite the chaos around them. "I'm CIA," he said, his words carrying a weight of authority. "Let us through."

The officer's eyes narrowed, his expression skeptical. "To where?" he asked, his voice thick with exhaustion and resignation. "The airport is closed from enemy shelling. There are no more flights out."

"I'll find a way out," he said, his voice filled with a quiet intensity. "Let us through."

"Take your family back to the city where they will be safe. We will protect you."

"I wish I could believe that. But we both know that's not true. It's not your fault. Now, let us through."

The officer shook his head, his eyes filled with a weary sadness. "You will all die," he said, his words heavy with the weight of inevitability.

Coyle met the man's gaze, his own eyes blazing with a fierce resolve. "So be it," he said, his voice unwavering. "Let us through."

For a long moment, the two men stared at each other, a silent battle of wills playing out amidst the chaos and desperation of the crowd. And then, with a sigh, the officer nodded to his men, his voice carrying over the din. "Let them through," he said, his words heavy with the knowledge of what he was condemning them to.

As they passed through the roadblock, Coyle could feel the eyes of the soldiers on them, could sense the pity and the sorrow in their gazes. They knew, just as he did, that the road ahead was a gauntlet of danger and uncertainty, that the chances of survival were slim to none.

With a roar of the engine and a surge of adrenaline, Coyle guided the motorcycle forward, his eyes fixed on the horizon and the airport with columns of smoke rising into the sky above.

Behind them, the roadblock faded into the distance, the last remnant of order amidst the madness of a city consumed by war. Ahead, the road stretched out like a ribbon of fate, a path that would lead them to either salvation or oblivion.

As Coyle approached the airport, the scene before him was one of utter devastation. The once-bustling airbase was now a smoldering ruin, the front gate abandoned and the guards nowhere to be seen. Plumes of black smoke rose from burning buildings and aircraft, the acrid stench of fuel and charred metal hanging heavy in the air.

Coyle guided the motorcycle through the gates, his heart sinking as he took in the extent of the damage. The runway was a cratered moonscape, pitted with deep holes that made it impossible for any aircraft to take off or land. Ammunition from the destroyed ammo dump cooked off in sporadic explosions, the sound echoing across the desolate tarmac.

For a moment, despair threatened to overwhelm him. They were too late, the airport a shattered husk of its former self. But even as the realization hit him, Coyle refused to give up. He had come too far, fought too hard, to let this be the end of the line.

With a critical eye, he scanned the apron in front of the hangars used to taxi planes. It was damaged in places, the surface cracked and uneven. But there were stretches that remained unscathed, sections that might just be long enough for a small STOL plane to take off.

Coyle's heart raced as he searched the area, his eyes desperately seeking any sign of a suitable aircraft. But the small planes and fighter jets were gone, the helicopters reduced to twisted metal and ash. The larger aircraft, once the pride of the South Vietnamese Air Force, were now just burning husks, their wings and fuselages blackened and torn.

And then, like a beacon of hope amidst the chaos, Coyle spotted a maintenance hangar that seemed miraculously untouched by the destruction. He steered the motorcycle towards it, his determination renewed by the sight of that lonely building standing amidst the ruins.

Inside, the hangar was cool and dark, the air heavy with the scent of oil and metal. Coyle's eyes adjusted to the gloom, and he felt a surge of relief as he spotted a Cessna O-1 Birddog STOL airplane parked in the center of the space.

But his elation was short-lived as he drew closer to the aircraft. The engine cowling was open, and he could see that the engine itself had been disassembled, its parts scattered across a nearby workbench. It was clear that someone had been in the process of rebuilding it when the airport had fallen.

For a moment, Coyle felt the weight of despair pressing down on him once more. But he shook it off. He had come too far to let a disassembled engine stop him now.

With Nguyet and Tuyet by his side, Coyle set to work, his hands moving with a sense of urgency as he began to reassemble the engine. The manual on the workbench was handwritten in Vietnamese, but it did have assembly diagrams and charts for torque wrench settings. He had spent enough time around aircraft to have a basic understanding of how they worked. Although it looked like all the pieces of the engine were on the work bench, he had no way of knowing for sure until the engine was finished. One missing piece and the engine wouldn't run.

As he labored over the engine, Coyle could feel the seconds ticking by, each moment bringing the enemy closer to the airport. The sound of explosions and gunfire grew louder, the battle drawing ever nearer to their temporary sanctuary. After few seconds, he would glance at the open hangar door for signs of the enemy he knew was coming.

He focused on the engine, his hands moving with a sureness and a skill that belied the tension that coiled within him. Piece by piece, he fitted the parts back together, his mind racing as he tried to remember the correct order and placement of each component.

Nguyet and Tuyet watched in silence, their faces etched with a mixture of hope and fear. They knew that their lives depended on Coyle's success, that this fragile aircraft represented their only chance at escape and survival.

US Embassy – Saigon, South Vietnam

The situation at the U.S. Embassy in Saigon was becoming increasingly dire as the North Vietnamese forces closed in on the city. With the last airport closed because shelling, the paths to escape Saigon were narrowing. Ambassador Graham Martin, who had been reluctant to leave his post, was now faced with the grim reality that the time had come to evacuate.

In the early hours of April 30, 1975, Martin received a direct order from President Gerald Ford and Secretary of State Henry Kissinger to begin evacuating only Americans from the embassy. The decision was made due to the imminent fall of Saigon and the administration's desire to announce the completion of the American evacuation.

With a heavy heart, Martin made the announcement to his staff. Many of them had worked tirelessly to assist South Vietnamese allies and their families, and the order to leave them behind was a bitter pill to swallow.

As the evacuation proceeded, chaos ensued outside the embassy walls. Thousands of desperate South Vietnamese civilians gathered, hoping for a chance to escape the advancing communist forces. The scene was one of desperation driven by terror, with people clinging to the embassy gates and pleading for help. The US Marines exhausted and frustrated, but professionals through and through as they dealt with a terrible situation.

Inside the compound, the embassy staff worked frantically to destroy sensitive documents and equipment. The sound of shredders and incinerators filled the air as they raced against time to ensure that nothing of value fell into enemy hands. American dollars unloaded from safes in the embassy's basement were shoveled into burn barrels on the back lawn, dowsed with gasoline, and set aflame. Millions of US dollars turned into ash and smoke.

As the night wore on, the evacuation flights continued, with American helicopters landing and taking off from the embassy's front lawn and parking lot, ferrying personnel and refugees to safety. Ambassador Martin, however, remained stubborn in his resolve to stay until the last possible moment.

Unbeknownst to Martin, President Ford had issued a direct order for him to board a specific helicopter, call sign "Lady Ace 09," piloted by Gerry Berry. The orders were so crucial that Berry had them written on his kneepads in grease-pencil.

As "Lady Ace 09" landed on the embassy rooftop, Martin reluctantly boarded the helicopter. The gravity of the situation weighed heavily on him, knowing that he was leaving behind many South Vietnamese who had trusted in American support.

In a poignant moment, it was discovered that Martin's wife, Dorothy, had left behind her suitcase to make room for a South Vietnamese woman to escape. The small act of kindness underscored the human toll of the evacuation and the bonds that had been forged between the Americans and their Vietnamese allies.

As the helicopter lifted off at 04:58, the Marines tasked with securing the embassy prepared to follow at dawn. Unbeknownst to the evacuees, the North Vietnamese had been tracking the helicopter flights but refrained from firing on them. The Hanoi leadership, calculating that allowing the Americans to leave would reduce the risk of intervention, had instructed their forces to hold their fire.

The final group of Marines departed the embassy at 07:53, leaving behind a crowd of 420 Vietnamese and South Koreans inside the embassy who had been unable to escape. The desperate pleas of those left behind echoed in the minds of the evacuees as they flew towards safety.

In the end, the American evacuation managed to fly out 978 Americans and approximately 1,100 Vietnamese. It was a bittersweet victory, knowing that so many had been left to face an uncertain fate.

As the helicopters disappeared into the horizon, the reality of the situation began to sink in. The Vietnam War, which had consumed American foreign policy for over a decade, was coming to a close. The scars it left behind would take generations to heal, both for the Americans who had fought and for the Vietnamese who had endured unspeakable hardships.

For Ambassador Martin and his staff, the evacuation marked the end of an era. They had done their best to uphold American interests and support their South Vietnamese allies, but in the end, the tide of history had proven too strong to resist.

As they flew towards an uncertain future, the evacuees could only reflect on the sacrifices that had been made and the lives that had been forever changed by the conflict. The Vietnam War may have ended, but its legacy would endure, shaping the course of history for generations to come.

Presidential Palace - Saigon, South Vietnam

The situation in Saigon was dire. The city, once a bustling metropolis and the heart of South Vietnam, was now a shadow of its former self. The streets were empty, save for the occasional group of refugees fleeing the advancing communist forces. The sound of distant explosions and gunfire echoed through the abandoned buildings, a constant reminder of the war that had consumed the country for so long.

In the presidential palace, General Duong Van Minh sat at his desk, his face overshadowed with fatigue. He had only recently taken over as president, following the resignation of his predecessor, Tran Van Huong. Minh had hoped that his longstanding ties with the communists would allow him to negotiate a ceasefire, to bring an end to the bloodshed that had ravaged his country for so many years.

But it was not to be. The North Vietnamese forces, emboldened by their victories in the northern provinces, were in no mood to negotiate. They had fought their way into the outskirts of Saigon, seizing key bridges and infrastructure. The South Vietnamese military, once a formidable fighting force, was in a state of utter collapse, its leadership resigned to defeat.

As Minh contemplated his options, his advisors entered the room, their faces grim.

"Mr. President, the American ambassador has left the country by helicopter." one of them said.

"We have received reports that the communists have dropped bombs on Tan Son Nhut Air Base," said another advisor. "Our air force attempted to intercept them, but they were unable to do so. The runway is destroyed, and the airport is shutdown."

Minh sighed heavily. "And what of our forces in the city?" he asked, dreading the answer.

"They are fighting bravely," still another advisor replied, "but they are outnumbered and outgunned. The communists are closing in on the city center. It is only a matter of time before they break through our defenses."

Minh closed his eyes, his heart heavy with the knowledge of what he must do. He had always been a man of peace, a believer in the power of diplomacy and negotiation. But he knew that there could be no negotiation with the communists, not anymore. They had come too far, had sacrificed too much to turn back now.

"Gentlemen," he said, his voice heavy with emotion, "I have made a decision. We cannot continue this fight any longer. Too many lives have been lost, too much suffering endured. It is time for us to accept the inevitable, to surrender to the communists and hope for the best."

The room was silent for a long moment, the weight of Minh's words hanging in the air like a physical presence. Finally, one of the advisors spoke, his voice trembling with emotion.

"But Mr. President," he said, "what will become of us? Of our people? The communists will show no mercy to those who have opposed them."

Minh nodded, his eyes filled with a deep sadness. "I know," he said softly. "But we have no choice. We cannot win this war, and to continue fighting would only lead to more death and destruction. We must do what is best for our people, even if it means sacrificing ourselves."

He stood from his desk, his shoulders squared with resolve. "I will confront the communists myself," he said. "I will offer our surrender and plead for mercy on behalf of our people. It is the only way."

The advisors bowed their heads. They knew that their president was right, that there was no other path forward. And so, with heavy hearts and a sense of inevitable defeat, they prepared to face the fall of their nation that they had fought so long and so hard to defend.

As Minh stepped out onto the rooftop of the Presidential Palace, the sound of gunfire and explosions growing ever closer. He knew that he had done what he believed was right, that he had put the needs of his people above his own. And in that knowledge, he found a measure of peace, even in the face of the darkness that lay ahead. There was nothing left to do but wait…

22 Gia Long Street - Saigon, South Vietnam

The Huey's rotors whipped the air into a frenzy as Scott Dickson maneuvered the helicopter over the chaotic streets of Saigon. Smoke billowed from burning buildings, mixing with the haze of exhaust fumes and dust. Artillery rounds and rockets streaked through the sky, a stark reminder of the desperate battle raging below.

Scott's co-pilot, Mike, scanned the rooftops below, his eyes straining to pick out the designated landing spot. "There!" he shouted, pointing to a small, flat area amidst the jumble of antennas and air conditioning units. "That's our LZ!"

Scott nodded. He had made countless runs like this over the past few days, ferrying people out of the doomed city as the North Vietnamese forces closed in. But each mission was a gamble, a roll of the dice with death and destruction waiting at every turn.

As he brought the Huey in low over the rooftop, Scott could see the desperate faces of the people below, their arms waving frantically in the air. He could hear their shouts and cries even over the roar of the rotors, a chorus of fear and hope that tore at his heart.

"We're going to have to make this quick!" he yelled

to Mike, his voice barely audible over the din. "We're sitting ducks out here!"

Mike nodded, his hand already on the door handle. As soon as the skids touched the rooftop, he leaped out, his rifle at the ready as he scanned for any sign of trouble.

The refugees surged forward, their desperation overriding any sense of order or caution. They clambered into the back of the Huey, their hands clutching at anything they could find to steady themselves.

One of the CIA officers, a grizzled veteran named Joe, helped to pull them inside, his face grim with the knowledge of what they were leaving behind. "That's it!" he shouted, his voice hoarse with emotion. "We're at capacity!"

Scott looked back, his eyes taking in the scene. There were still so many people on the rooftop, so many faces pleading for salvation. But he knew that they couldn't take any more, that the Huey was already dangerously overloaded.

With a heavy heart, he lifted the chopper off the rooftop, the rotors straining against the weight of its human cargo.

In the back of the chopper, CIA officers and Vietnamese refugees huddled together, their faces fixed with fear and exhaustion. They had been waiting for hours on the rooftop of the apartment building at 22 Gia Long Street, praying for a miracle that would take them to safety.

The Huey's rotors thumped rhythmically as Scott guided the aircraft over the war-torn cityscape of Saigon.

Suddenly, a burst of gunfire erupted from a rooftop,

the muzzle flashes stark against the darkened buildings. Scott instinctively banked the helicopter hard to the left, his eyes widening as he realized the true nature of the threat.

"VC, VC!" he shouted over the intercom.

The passengers cried out in fear as the Huey shuddered. Scott's hands flew over the controls as he tried to evade the incoming fire.

A CIA officer in the back let out a grunt of pain, his hand clutching at a crimson stain spreading rapidly across his shoulder. "I'm hit!" he yelled, his voice tight with agony.

Before Scott could respond, a new threat emerged from the streets below. An RPG streaked towards the helicopter, its smoky trail a deadly arrow pointing straight at the vulnerable tail boom.

"Incoming!" Scott screamed, wrenching the cyclic handle with all his might to gain altitude.

The Huey lurched sickeningly, the nose pitching down as the RPG passed just beneath the tail, the heat of its exhaust singeing the paint. The passengers braced themselves against the sudden maneuver as they gripped anything they could find.

Scott pushed the helicopter to its limits, the airframe vibrating with the strain of the evasive action. More bullets punched through the thin skin of the fuselage, the sound of tearing metal filling the cramped interior.

Several more passengers cried out in pain, their bodies jerking as the high-velocity rounds found their mark. Scott's mind consumed with the singular focus of getting his human cargo to safety.

With a final, desperate push, Scott urged the battered Huey over the outskirts of the city, the pockmarked rice paddies, and shattered tree lines of the countryside rushing up to meet them. The Viet Cong fire began to slacken, the distance and the Huey's speed finally putting them out of range.

As the helicopter limped towards the sea on the horizon, Scott allowed himself a brief moment of relief, his breath coming in ragged gasps. They had made it, but only just. The Huey was riddled with bullet holes, and the moans of the wounded filled the cabin with a somber chorus.

But they were alive, and they were free. Scott looked back at Joe, saw the haunted look in the man's eyes. "We did it," Scott said softly, his voice barely audible over the roar of the rotors. "We got them out."

Joe nodded, "But how many more are still down there?" he asked. "How many did we leave behind?"

"We do what we can, Joe. We do what we can," said Scott, knowing his words held little consolation. He knew that they had risked everything to save as many lives as possible. But in the end, it would never be enough, not in the face of the suffering and devastation that had engulfed the city.

As the Huey flew on, over the war-torn landscape of Vietnam, Scott could only pray that someday, somehow, the wounds of this conflict would heal, that the people of this shattered nation would find a way to rebuild and move forward.

Saigon, South Vietnam

The sound of battle was deafening with explosions, gunfire, and the screams of the wounded. The ARVN soldiers manning the perimeter of Saigon were locked in a desperate struggle against the relentless onslaught of the NVA and Viet Cong forces.

Overhead, South Vietnamese Air Force planes roared through the smoke-filled skies, their bombs and rockets raining down on the advancing enemy columns. But for every tank destroyed, every squad scattered, it seemed that two more would take their place, an endless tide of communist forces surging towards the city.

On the ground, ARVN tanks and artillery units fought back, their guns blazing as they sought to stem the tide. The earth shook with the impact of shells and rockets, the air thick with the stench of smoke and burning metal.

In the trenches and bunkers that ringed the city, ARVN soldiers fought with a desperate fury, their rifles and machine guns chattering as they cut down wave after wave of attacking infantry. They knew that they were the last line of defense, the only thing standing between the people of Saigon and the horrors of communist rule.

Despite their bravery and their sacrifice, the ARVN lines were being pushed back, the weight of the enemy assault proving too much to bear. The NVA and Viet Cong forces seemed to have an endless supply of men and materiel, fueled by years of hardship and a fanatic belief in their cause.

As the ARVN perimeter began to crumble, the order came down to fall back, to retreat into the city and make a stand in the streets and alleyways of Saigon itself. The South Vietnamese soldiers obeyed, fighting a rearguard action as they pulled back, their blood staining the pavement and their courage holding firm.

In the heart of the city, the battle took on a new level of savagery, the fighting devolving into a brutal, house-to-house slog. The communist forces, their ranks swelled by infiltrators who had slipped into the city in the chaos, seemed to be everywhere, their fire coming from windows and rooftops, from sewers and side streets.

The ARVN fought back with everything they had, their commanders directing the battle from hastily-established command posts in government buildings and police stations. Tanks rumbled through the narrow streets, their guns roaring as they engaged the enemy at point-blank range. Infantry squads moved from building to building, clearing rooms with grenades and flamethrowers, their faces blackened with soot.

But for all their valor, for all their skill and sacrifice, the ARVN could not hold back the NVA and VC tide. The communist forces were too many, their resolve too strong. Block by block, street by street, the NVA and Viet Cong pushed deeper into the city, their red and blue flags fluttering from the shattered ruins of once-grand buildings.

The remnants of the ARVN fell back to their final defensive positions, the presidential palace and a handful of key government ministries. They knew that the end was near, that the dream of a free and independent South Vietnam was slipping away with each passing moment.

But still, these final few fought on, their courage and their devotion to duty undiminished by the hopelessness of their cause. They would not surrender, would not lay down their arms while breath still remained in their bodies.

And so, as the flames of war consumed the city, the battle for Saigon raged on. It was a tragic end to a long and bitter struggle, but one that would be remembered for generations to come, a shining example of the heights of bravery and sacrifice to which the human spirit could soar, even in the darkest of times.

South China Sea

As Scott's Huey touched down on the deck of the aircraft carrier, the roar of the rotors was drowned out by the shouts and cries of the refugees and CIA officers as they clambered out of the chopper. Scott sat back in his seat, his hands trembling slightly as the adrenaline began to wear off.

As he climbed out of the cockpit, a CIA handler rushed up to him,. "Scott, we've got a problem," he said, his voice tense with urgency. "One of our informants, a high-level asset, was supposed to be on that rooftop with his family. But they never made it out."

Scott knew what it meant to be left behind in a city about to fall, knew the trepidation that must be gripping the informant and his loved ones. "What happened?"

"I don't know. His pregnant wife was having health problems. That could be it."

"Where are they?" he asked, his voice rough with emotion. "Do we have a location?"

The handler nodded, his eyes scanning the chaotic deck of the carrier. "Last we heard, they were holed up in a safe house near the old French Quarter. But with the NVA closing in, there's no telling how long they'll be able to stay hidden."

Scott closed his eyes for a moment. He knew that with the NVA overrunning the city, going back deep into Saigon and the chances of making it out alive were slim to none.

"Scott, this informant risked everything to help us when we needed it most. He's worth saving. We owe it to him," said the handler.

Scott opened his eyes, "Alright. I'm going back," he said, his voice brooking no argument. "I'll bring them out."

"I'll go with you. I know where the safe house is located," said the handler.

"Alright. That'll help."

As they climbed back into the Huey, Scott could feel the eyes of the refugees and CIA officers on him, their gazes filled with a mixture of hope and fear. They knew the risks they were taking, knew that they were putting their lives on the line for people they had never even met.

But that was the job, the burden of being a CIA operative in a war zone. You did what had to be done, no matter the cost.

As the Huey lifted off from the deck of the carrier, Joe raised his fist to signal defiance. Scott grinned and raised his own fist before banking the aircraft and heading back to Saigon.

The flight back to Saigon was a blur, a mad dash through enemy fire and falling rockets. The city was in chaos, the streets clogged with desperate civilians and panicked ARVN soldiers.

The CIA handler directed Scott to the safe house. "There," he said pointing to a nondescript building tucked away in a narrow side street, its windows boarded up and its doors heavily barricaded.

Scott brought the Huey down in a nearby courtyard, the rotors kicking up a blinding cloud of dust and debris. As the handler leaped from the cockpit, he could hear the sound of gunfire in the distance, the unmistakable boom of artillery growing closer with every passing moment. He sprinted to the safe house door and pounded on the heavy wood with the butt of his pistol. "Open up!" he shouted, his voice hoarse with tension. "CIA, we're here to extract you!"

For a moment, there was nothing but silence, a stillness that seemed to stretch on forever. And then, slowly, the door creaked open, revealing a pale, frightened face peering out from the darkness.

"Thank God," the man whispered, his voice trembling with relief. "You came."

"The CIA doesn't forget its friends."

"My wife… she's in labor."

"Lovely. Let's go," said the handler as he ushered the family out of the safe house, his eyes darting back and forth as he scanned for any sign of danger. There were four of them - the informant, his pregnant wife, and two young children, their faces streaked with tears and grime.

He led them back to the Huey, as he heard the sound of tanks and heavy artillery growing ever closer. They were cutting it close, too close for comfort.

The Huey lifted off just as the first NVA troops rounded the corner, their rifles blazing as they tried to shoot down the fleeing aircraft. But Scott was too quick, too skilled, and they were soon soaring over the rooftops of Saigon, the city falling away beneath them like a distant memory.

As they flew out over the countryside, the informant's wife began to sob, her body shaking with the force of her relief and gratitude. "Thank you," she whispered, her voice barely audible over the roar of the rotors. "Thank you for saving us."

Scott nodded, his throat tight with emotion. He knew that he those that flew with him had given this family a chance at a new life, a future free from the horrors of war and oppression. They had made a difference in the face of overwhelming odds.

Newport Bridge, Saigon, South Vietnam

The sound of gunfire and explosions echoed through the streets of Saigon as the communist forces advanced towards the heart of the city. The ARVN troops, though battered and weary, were determined that they would not go down without a fight.

At the Newport Bridge, a group of ARVN Airborne soldiers manned their positions. They had repulsed an earlier attempt by VC sappers to seize the bridge, but they knew that the real attack was yet to come.

As the day wore on, the sound of engines filled the air, growing louder with each passing moment. Then, out of the haze of smoke and dust, a column of NVA tanks emerged, their metal treads clanking against the pavement.

"Here they come!" shouted one of the Airborne soldiers, "Get ready!"

The lead T-54 tank rumbled forward, its gun turret swiveling to take aim at the ARVN positions. But before it could fire, a shot rang out from an ARVN tank, the shell slamming into the T-54's armor with a deafening clang.

"Got him!" yelled the ARVN tank commander, his face split in a triumphant grin.

The T-54 lurched to a halt, smoke pouring from its shattered hull. The NVA Battalion commander, who had been riding in the tank, was killed instantly, his body slumping over the controls.

But the communist forces were not to be deterred. They surged forward, their infantry moving up to engage the ARVN in fierce house-to-house fighting. The sound of small arms fire filled the air, punctuated by the blast of grenades and the screams of the wounded.

Tan Son Nhut Air Base, South Vietnam

At Tan Son Nhut Air Base, the situation was equally desperate. The base was under constant attack, with NVA rockets and artillery raining down on the sprawling complex. The ARVN 3rd Task Force, 81st Ranger Group, commanded by Major Pham Chau Tai, had taken up defensive positions around the perimeter, determined to hold the line against the communist onslaught.

As the communist forces pressed their assault on Tan Son Nhut Air Base, Granier and his team found themselves in the midst of a desperate battle. The NVA tanks had reached the Bay Hien intersection, just a short distance from the base's main gate. Granier and his team of snipers had taken up positions to defend the critical crossroads, but their rifles were useless against the heavily armored vehicles.

Granier watched in awe as the lead T-54 tank was hit by an M67 recoilless rifle manned by one of the rangers, the explosion ripping through its thick hide. A second tank was struck by a shell from an M48, the ARVN's own armored behemoth. But even as the tanks burned, the communist infantry surged forward, engaging the ARVN defenders in fierce hand-to-hand fighting.

As the battle raged around him, Granier realized that his position was becoming untenable. The enemy was too strong, their numbers too great. He ordered his team to fall back deeper into the base, to take up new positions and continue the fight. But even as his men retreated, Granier knew that he could not abandon his position.

And so he stayed, his rifle hot in his hands, his eyes scanning the smoke-filled streets for any sign of the enemy. It was then that he saw the battalion commander, perched atop the lead tank, directing the attack with cold precision. Granier knew that if he could take out the commander, he might be able to disrupt the NVA assault, to buy his comrades precious time to regroup and counterattack.

He raised his rifle, his finger tightening on the trigger. But before he could fire, the tank's machine gun chattered to life, a hail of bullets ripping through the air around him. Granier dove for cover, his heart pounding in his chest as he realized the full extent of his peril.

The tank's main gun swung around, its muzzle pointing directly at Granier's position. He knew that he had only seconds to act, to find some way to stop the armored behemoth before it could unleash its deadly payload.

In a moment of desperate inspiration, Granier raised his rifle once more, aiming not at the tank itself, but at the yawning barrel of its main gun. He knew that it was a long shot, that the odds of hitting the shell inside were vanishingly small. But he had no other choice.

He fired, the rifle bucking in his hands as he sent round after round into the tank's barrel. The bullets spiraled around the thick metal, lodging themselves between the shell and the barrel like tiny wedges. Granier held his breath, praying that his gambit would work.

And then, in a moment of blinding fury, the tank fired. But instead of the devastating explosion Granier had feared, there was only a dull thud, followed by a gout of flame and smoke from the tank's interior. The shell, slowed by the jammed bullets, had detonated prematurely, the backpressure blowing open the breech and killing the gunner instantly.

Granier watched in stunned disbelief as the tank began to burn, its ammunition cooking off in a series of deafening explosions. The battalion commander, caught in the inferno, was incinerated in seconds, his body consumed by the flames.

For a long moment, Granier could only stare at the burning wreckage, his mind struggling to process what had just happened. He had done the impossible, had single-handedly destroyed a communist tank with nothing more than his sniper rifle and his wits.

But there was no respite, no time to celebrate. The communist forces were still pressing their attack, their determination undiminished by the loss of their commander. Granier could hear the sound of more tanks approaching, the roar of their engines mixing with the crackle of small arms fire.

Granier took a deep breath, steeling himself for the fight to come. He knew that the odds were still stacked against him, that the communists would not rest until Tan Son Nhut had fallen. But he also knew that he would not give up, that he would fight to the last bullet and the last breath to defend the base and his fellow soldiers. And so, with a grim smile on his face, Rene

Granier raised his rifle once more, ready to face the enemy.

Saigon, South Vietnam

The streets of Saigon were in chaos as the communist forces pushed their way towards the heart of the city. The sound of gunfire and explosions filled the air, mingling with the shouts of soldiers and the cries of frightened civilians.

At the forefront of the advance were the tanks of the NVA 203rd Tank Brigade, their engines roaring as they rumbled through the narrow streets. The tank commanders, each eager to be the first to reach the presidential palace and claim victory for North Vietnam, urged their crews forward with shouts of encouragement.

As they approached the palace gates, the tension between the rival tank crews reached a boiling point. Tank 843, a Soviet T-54, surged ahead, its commander determined to be the first to breach the compound. But Tank 390, a Chinese Type 59, was hot on its heels, its crew equally determined to claim the honor for themselves.

With a deafening crash, Tank 843 smashed through the side gate of the palace, its metal treads churning up the manicured lawn. But Tank 390 was not to be outdone, and moments later, it too burst through the main gate, its engine roaring in triumph.

As the tanks rolled to a stop in the palace courtyard, their crews leaped from the hatches, each claiming to have been the first to enter the compound. Angry shouts and accusations filled the air as the rival crews confronted each other, their weapons raised in a tense standoff.

"We were the first ones through the gate!" shouted the commander of Tank 843, his face flushed with anger. "The victory belongs to us!"

"Nonsense!" retorted the commander of Tank 390. "We breached the main gate while you were still struggling with the side entrance. The honor is ours!"

As the argument escalated, Lieutenant Colonel Bui Van Tung arrived on the scene, his presence bringing a measure of order to the chaos. He quickly took control of the situation, ordering the tank crews to stand down and secure the palace.

Inside, President Duong Van Minh and his cabinet sat waiting, their faces filled with resignation and defeat. As Tung entered the room, Minh stood to greet him, his voice heavy with emotion.

"We are waiting to hand over the cabinet," Minh said, his eyes downcast.

Tung replied immediately, his voice firm and unyielding. "You have nothing to hand over but your unconditional surrender to us."

With those words, the fate of South Vietnam was sealed. Tung quickly wrote out a speech announcing the surrender and dissolution of the South Vietnamese government, then escorted Minh to the Radio Saigon studio to read it over the air.

At 2:30 PM, Minh's voice crackled over the airwaves, his words heavy with the weight of history, "I, General Duong Van Minh, president of the Saigon administration, appeal to the armed forces of the Republic of Vietnam to lay down their arms and surrender unconditionally to the forces of the Liberation Army of South Vietnam. Furthermore, I declare that the Saigon government is completely dissolved at all levels. From the central government to the local governments must be handed over to the Provisional Revolutionary Government of the Republic of South Vietnam."

As Minh's words faded away, Lieutenant Colonel Tung took the microphone, his voice ringing with triumph and determination, "We, the representatives for the forces of the Liberation Army of South Vietnam, solemnly declare that the City of Saigon was completely liberated. We accepted the unconditional surrender of General Duong Van Minh, the president of the Saigon administration."

With those words, the Vietnam War came to an end, the long struggle for independence and unification finally achieved. And though the road ahead would be difficult, the people of Vietnam could now look forward to a future free from the shadow of foreign domination and the suffering of war.

Tan Son Nhut Air Base, South Vietnam

As the smoke from the burning tank began to clear, Granier heard the crackle of his radio, the voice of the base commander cutting through the chaos of the battle. At first, he couldn't believe what he was hearing, the words seeming to come from a great distance, as if in a dream.

"Attention all units," the commander said, his voice heavy with resignation. "President Minh has surrendered to the communists in Saigon. We have been ordered to lay down our weapons and prepare to surrender to the communist forces. I repeat, lay down your weapons and prepare to surrender."

Granier felt a wave of shock and disbelief wash over him, his mind reeling at the implications of the commander's words. After everything they had been through, all the sacrifices they had made, all the blood they had shed, how could it end like this? How could they be expected to simply lay down their arms and submit to the enemy?

He looked around at the men beside him, saw the same mixture of anger and despair in their faces. These were soldiers, warriors who had sworn to defend their country to the last. The thought of surrendering, of giving up without a fight, was a denunciation of everything they believed in.

For a long moment, Granier struggled with himself, his loyalty to his commanders warring with his own sense of honor and duty. He had always been a good soldier, had always followed orders without question. But this... this was different. This was a betrayal of everything he had fought for, everything he held dear.

In the end, the decision was easy. Granier knew that he could not surrender, that he would rather die fighting than live as a prisoner of the communists. And so, with a heavy heart, he made his choice.

And with that, he clicked off the radio, his decision made. He would not surrender, would not give up the fight. He would pull back deeper into the air base, taking his sniper rifle with him.

As he moved through the shattered buildings and debris-strewn streets of the base, Granier couldn't help but feel a sense of detachment. Everything he had known, everything he had fought for, was crumbling around him. The country he fought for was falling to the enemy, and there was nothing he could do to stop it.

In the end, if he fell in battle, then so be it. He would die with honor, with the knowledge that he had done his duty to the last. For in a world gone mad, in a war that had consumed everything he held dear, that was all he had left to cling to.

Maintenance Hangar

Finished rebuilding the engine and running out of time before the communists arrived, Coyle pushed open the hangar doors and climbed into the cockpit of the birddog, his hands moving with practiced precision as he worked to start the engine. He checked the fuel levels in the wings. The starboard wing was completely empty, but the port wing was half full. It had to be enough. There was no time to find a fuel tanker. Fortunately, the 7th Fleet was not far off the coast and Coyle was confident that they could make it. Nguyet and Tuyet watched anxiously from their passenger seat, behind Coyle.

Despite his best efforts, the engine refused to start. Coyle felt a surge of frustration, but he pushed it aside, focusing instead on the task at hand. He tried different techniques, adjusting the fuel mixture and checking the ignition, his mind racing through the possibilities.

As he worked, movement outside the hangar caught his eye. Coyle glanced up, and his heart nearly stopped. There, walking past the front of the building, was a familiar figure. It was Granier, his friend and fellow soldier.

Without hesitation, Coyle leaped from the cockpit, calling out to Granier. Hearing a familiar voice, Granier turned to see Coyle. The two men embraced, their faces breaking into grins of relief and joy. For a moment, the chaos of the world around them seemed to fade away.

Coyle quickly explained his plan to fly out to sea and land on an aircraft carrier. "Come with us," he urged Granier. "We can make it out together."

But to Coyle's surprise, Granier shook his head. "I can't," he said softly. "Vietnam is my home, Coyle. I've lived here for thirty years - longer than the US and France combined. This is where I belong."

Coyle stared at his friend, confusion and disbelief written across his face. He tried to argue, to convince Granier to change his mind. But Granier was resolute, his eyes filled with a calm certainty.

"This is my path, Coyle," Granier said. "I have to see it through, no matter where it leads."

Coyle felt a lump forming in his throat, a sense of sadness and loss washing over him. He knew that Granier had made up his mind, that nothing he could say would sway him.

"Where will you go?" Coyle asked, his voice thick with emotion.

Granier smiled sadly. "It's probably better that you don't know," he said. "Just remember me as I was, as your friend and brother-in-arms."

The two men embraced one last time, their eyes glistening with unshed tears. They had been through so much together, had faced death and overcome impossible odds. But now, their paths were diverging, each following his own destiny.

As Granier walked away down the apron in front of the hangars, Coyle watched him go, a sense of finality settling over him. He knew that he might never see his friend again, that the world they had known was crumbling around them.

But there was no time for grief, no time for regrets. The sound of gunfire and explosions was growing closer, a reminder of the urgency of their situation.

Coyle climbed back into the cockpit, his hands moving with renewed determination. He had to get the engine started, had to get Nguyet and Tuyet to safety.

And then, miraculously, the engine roared to life. Coyle felt a surge of relief and exhilaration as he guided the plane onto the apron, the small craft bouncing and shuddering as it gathered speed.

Behind them, the NVA soldiers were closing in, running in a desperate attempt to stop the fleeing aircraft.

The small Birddog aircraft shuddered as Coyle pushed the throttle to its limit, the engine straining against the weight of its precious cargo. In the passenger seats behind him, Nguyet and Tuyet clung to each other, their faces pale with fear.

As Coyle had lifted off from the runway, an NVA soldier had emerged from the shadows next to a hangar, his AK-47 raised to fire. Bullets had ripped through the birddog's fuselage, the sound of metal popping filling the cockpit.

Coyle didn't feel the impact of the rounds, but had seen the telltale spray of fuel on the port side wing. But it wasn't until he heard Nguyet's cry of pain that he realized the true extent of the damage.

"Nguyet!" he shouted. "Are you hit?"

He turned to see Nguyet slumped in her seat, her face contorted in agony. Tuyet was beside her, tears streaming down her cheeks as she tried to stem the flow of blood from her mother's back.

While continuing to fly the aircraft, Coyle tried to assess the situation. He knew that Nguyet needed medical attention, and fast. But he also knew that they were still far from safety, the vast expanse of the South China Sea stretching out before them.

He scanned the horizon, desperate for any sign of the American fleet. He had heard rumors that the ships were stationed offshore, ready to receive the last of the evacuees. But in the chaos of their departure, he had been unable to get a clear fix on their location.

As the minutes ticked by, Coyle grew increasingly desperate. He could feel the plane starting to shudder beneath him, the damaged wing struggling to maintain lift. And then, with a sinking feeling in his gut, he saw the needle on the fuel gauge begin to drop.

At first, he tried to convince himself that it was just a malfunction, a glitch in the system. But as the needle continued to fall, the reality of their situation began to sink in. The port side fuel tank had been hit, and they were losing fuel fast.

Coyle's mind raced as he tried to calculate their remaining range. The starboard tank was already empty. With only one functioning tank, they had limited options.

He looked back at Nguyet and Tuyet, saw the fear and pain in their eyes. He knew that he had to do something, had to find a way to get them to safety. But with each passing moment, their chances grew slimmer.

And then, through the haze of smoke and sea spray, he saw it. The unmistakable outline of an American destroyer. He knew the aircraft carrier would be close. He scanned the horizon and spotted the aircraft carrier, its deck crowded with helicopters and personnel. Coyle reached for the radio.

"US aircraft carrier off the coast of Vung Tau.

Mayday, mayday," he called, his voice tense with urgency. "This is Birddog 2-1, requesting emergency landing on your deck. We have wounded on board and are losing fuel rapidly."

There was a crackle of static, and then a voice came through the speakers. "Birddog 2-1, this is USS Hancock. Your request is denied. Our deck is at capacity with evacuees. We cannot accept any more aircraft at this time."

Coyle felt a wave of despair wash over him. They were so close, so tantalizingly close to safety. But with the carrier unable to accept them, they had nowhere else to go.

He looked back at Nguyet and Tuyet, saw the fear and desperation in their eyes. And in that moment, he made a decision.

"Nguyet, Tuyet," he called, his voice calm and steady. "I need you to listen to me very carefully. We're going to have to ditch the plane in the water. I'm going to try to get us as close to the carrier as I can, but it's going to be rough."

He reached behind him, grabbing two life preservers from the storage compartment. "Put these on, but not until we're out of the plane. When I give the signal, I need you to brace yourselves and then get out as fast as you can. Swim towards the carrier, and don't look back."

"I can't swim," cried Tuyet.

"Well, there is always a first time for everything. 'Sides, you'll never learn any younger. Just hang on to the life preserver once you climb out the doorway. It'll keep you afloat until I can reach you. Okay?"

Tuyet, unsure, nodded, then said, "What about Mom?"

"I'll take care of your mom. You just get out that door when the plane stops moving."

Coyle turned back to the controls, his hands gripping the yoke. He could feel the plane starting to sputter beneath him, the engine coughing and choking as it struggled to find fuel.

He tipped the wings back and forth, trying to coax every last drop of gas into the fuel line within the wing tank. But it was a losing battle, and he knew it. The carrier was looming larger in the windshield now, its deck tantalizingly close.

Coyle took a deep breath, steeling himself for what was to come. He had faced death before, had stared into the abyss and come out the other side. But this was different. This time, he had more than just his own life in his hands.

He reached for the radio one last time, his voice steady and clear. "USS Hancock, this is Birddog 2-1. We are ditching the plane. I repeat, we are ditching the plane. We have two passengers on board, one wounded. Request immediate rescue assistance."

There was a moment of silence, and then the voice came back, tense with urgency. "Roger that, Birddog 2-1. We have a rescue team standing by. Ditch as close to the carrier as you can, and we'll be there to pick you up."

"Roger that, Aircraft Carrier."

Coyle looked back at Nguyet and Tuyet, saw the trust and faith in their eyes. And in that moment, he knew that he would do whatever it took to get them to safety, to give them the chance at a new life that they so desperately deserved.

The plane was shaking violently now, the engine sputtering and coughing as it finally ran out of fuel.

Coyle gripped the yoke with all his strength, fighting to keep the aircraft level as it began to lose altitude.

Coyle could see the rescue team standing by in their raft, their bright orange suits a beacon in the chaos.

He looked back at Nguyet and Tuyet one last time, his eyes locking with theirs in a moment of silent understanding. And then, with a final, desperate prayer, he pushed the nose of the plane down towards the water, bracing himself for the impact that he knew was coming. At the last moment, he pulled the yoke back lifting the plane's nose for a brief moment.

The world seemed to slow down, the roar of the wind and the sea filling his ears. And as the plane hit the water, the impact was jarring, the fuselage shuddering and groaning under the strain. Icy spray washed over the cockpit and the fuselage began to break apart, Coyle knew that he had done all he could, had given everything he had to give.

Now, it was up to fate to decide their destiny, to determine whether they would live to see another day, or whether their journey would end here, in the unforgiving waters of the South China Sea.

As the plane hit the water, Coyle felt the icy water rushing in, flooding the cockpit and passenger compartment. He knew they had only moments to act.

With a desperate cry, he kicked open the door, the metal twisting and yielding under the force of his blow. "Hold on to this, Tuyet," he shouted, his voice raw with emotion. "Don't let go, no matter what happens."

Tuyet's eyes were wide with fear, but she nodded, her small hands gripping the preserver with all her strength. He pushed her out the doorway and into the churning sea.

He watched as she struggled against the waves, her

head bobbing up and down as she fought to keep herself afloat. He knew she wouldn't last long without him. The plane was sinking fast, the water rising higher with each passing second.

Coyle turned back to Nguyet. She was slumped in her seat, her face pale and her breathing shallow. The water was already up to her waist, the blood from her wound mixing with the icy sea.

He reached for her, trying to pull her towards the door. But she was pinned down, her leg trapped under the mangled pilot's seat. Coyle strained with all his might, his muscles screaming in protest as he tried to lift the seat. But it was no use.

He looked back at Tuyet, saw her form struggling in the waves. He knew he had to make a choice, had to decide who to save. But how could he possibly choose?

As the water rose higher, Nguyet's eyes fluttered open. She looked at Coyle, her gaze filled with pain and understanding. The plane was sinking, the cockpit already submerged, only the pocket of air left in the cabin endured.

"Save Tuyet," she whispered, her voice barely audible over the roar of the sea. "Promise me, Coyle. Promise me you'll keep her safe."

Coyle felt his heart break, felt the weight of the impossible choice crushing down on him. He knew he couldn't save them both, knew that he had to let one of them go.

With a final, anguished cry, he let go of Nguyet's hand. He watched as the water closed over her face, as her body went limp and still. And then he turned, pushing himself towards the surface with all his strength.

He broke through the waves, gasping for air. Tuyet

was nearby, clinging to the life preserver with desperate strength. Coyle swam to her, wrapping his arms around her and holding her head above the waves.

Together, they fought against the churning sea, the wake of the aircraft carrier tossing them like rag dolls. But Coyle refused to let go, refused to give in to the exhaustion and the despair from losing Nguyet that threatened to overwhelm him.

And then, through the spray and the chaos, he saw the rescue team, moving towards them in the raft. Putting his head underwater, Coyle looked down into the depths of the sea. The sinking plane was but a distant apparition disappearing in the abyss. Nguyet was gone. A promise broken.

Coyle felt relief as the rescuers pulled Tuyet, then him from the water. Inside the raft, the rescue team wrapped them in blankets and carried them to the safety of the carrier. But even as he held Tuyet close, even as he whispered words of comfort and reassurance, he felt a hollowness in his chest, a void that could never be filled.

Later, as they sat in the ship's infirmary, Tuyet looked up at Coyle with tears in her eyes. "Where's Mommy?" she asked, her voice small and frightened.

Coyle felt his throat tighten, felt the weight of the truth pressing down on him. He took a deep breath, willing himself to be strong for her sake.

"Your mommy loved you very much, Tuyet," he said softly, his voice cracking with emotion. "She wanted you to be safe, to have a chance at a better life. She gave her life so that you could live."

Tuyet's eyes filled with tears, her body shaking with sobs. Coyle gathered her in his arms, holding her close as she cried.

"Where will I live? Who will take care of me?" she cried.

"I will. You are going to live with me in America. And I promise you, Tuyet," he whispered, his own eyes stinging with tears. "I promise you that I will always be there for you, that I will protect you and keep you safe. Your mommy may be gone, but you will never be alone. I will love you and care for you, for as long as I live."

And as he held her, as he felt the warmth of her body against his own, Coyle knew that he would keep that promise. She had survived the war, had escaped the chaos and the violence that had consumed her homeland. But the scars would remain, the memories of all she had lost forever etched into her heart.

And yet, as Coyle looked down at Tuyet's tear-stained face, he felt a flicker of hope, a sense that perhaps, in time, they could find a way to heal, to build a new life together. They had each other, and in the end, that was all that mattered. For in the midst of the darkness and the pain, they had found a bond that could never be broken, a love that would endure forever.

The Journey North

Saigon, South Vietnam

The narrow alley reeked of garbage and desperation, the perfect hiding place for those who trafficked in secrets and lies. Granier moved through the shadows like a ghost, his eyes scanning for any sign of danger. North Vietnamese patrols were everywhere in Saigon and hadn't been easy slipping past them. He found the door he was looking for, a battered piece of wood with peeling paint and a rusted number hanging askew.

He knocked three times, paused, then twice more. The sound of multiple locks being undone echoed in the cramped space, and the door creaked open to reveal a thin Chinese man with darting eyes.

"Granier, what are you doing here?" the man hissed, his voice barely above a whisper. "I'm closed… for good."

"Congratulations. You just reopened," said Granier pushing his way past the man and into the forger's workshop.

"No. I barely have time to leave before the communist figure out who I am. I'm not the type that can survive a re-education camp."

"I need papers - French passport, communist travel documents. The works."

The forger's eyes narrowed, a calculating gleam in their depths. "That's dangerous work, my friend. Very dangerous. It will cost you."

Granier reached into his pocket and pulled out a roll of cash bound with a rubberband, American dollars that would be worth their weight in gold in the chaos to come. "Will this cover it?"

The forger's hand shot out, snatching the money with a speed that belied his scrawny frame. He counted it quickly, his lips moving silently. "It's a start," he said finally. "But for work this delicate, this dangerous... I'll need more."

Granier's hand moved to the small of his back, where his suppressed pistol was tucked away. "How about your life?" he said softly, his eyes cold and hard. "Is that enough?"

The forger's face went pale, his Adam's apple bobbing as he swallowed hard. "No need for threats, my friend," he said, his voice trembling slightly. "I'm sure we can come to an arrangement."

For the next eight hours, Granier watched as the forger worked his magic. The man's hands moved with a practiced skill, creating documents that looked authentic even to Granier's trained eye.

"What name do you want on the passport?" the forger asked, his pen poised over the blank document.

Granier thought for a moment. " Henri Bouchard," he said finally. "Born in Lyon, 1925."

The forger nodded, his pen scratching across the paper. "Occupation?"

"Plantation owner," Granier replied. "Rubber."

"Bourgeoisie is dangerous. The communists don't like capitalists."

"That's why I chose it. It can't be too simple or they'll see through it. They won't hurt a Frenchman, even if he owns a plantation. Their war with the French ended long ago and they are not anxious to start a new one."

"Alright. It's your skin."

As the forger went back to work, Granier paced the small room, his mind racing with the details of his plan. He knew that these documents were his lifeline, the only thing that stood between him and certain death if he was caught.

Finally, the forger looked up, a sheen of sweat on his brow. "They're done," he said, holding out the passport and a sheaf of travel papers. "As good as I can make them."

Granier took the documents, examining them carefully. The passport felt right in his hands, the weight and texture identical to the real thing. The travel papers bore all the correct stamps and seals, a masterwork of deception.

"Not bad," Granier said, nodding approvingly. He pulled out a sheet of wax paper from his pocket and carefully wrapped the documents, sealing them against the moisture and tucked them in his jacket pocket.

The forger watched him with curious eyes. "Planning a swim?" he asked, a nervous laugh in his voice.

"Planning for every contingency." Granier turned and fixed the forger with a cold stare. "You know me and you know I don't die easy."

The forger nodded.

"If these papers don't hold up, if I'm caught because of your work... I'll find you wherever you're hiding. And you don't want that, understand?"

The forger's face went pale, and he nodded frantically. "They'll hold up," he said, his voice barely above a whisper. "I swear it."

Granier gave him one last, hard look, then slipped out into the alley, melting back into the shadows of a city on the brink of chaos.

The basement was dimly lit, the air thick with the smell of gun oil and cigarette smoke. Granier stood before a scarred wooden table, his pistol and suppressor laid out before him. Across from him, a heavyset man examined the weapons with an expert eye.

"Nice piece," the dealer grunted, hefting the pistol. "American made. M1911A1, if I'm not mistaken. And the suppressor... custom job?"

Granier nodded, his face impassive. "Built it myself. Tested in the field. It works."

The dealer raised an eyebrow, impressed despite himself. He attached the suppressor to the pistol, aiming it at an imaginary target. "Balance is good. How much?"

"Six hundred," Granier said flatly.

The dealer barked out a laugh. "In this market? I'll give you three hundred."

Granier shook his head. "Five hundred. And I'm not interested in piasters."

The dealer's eyes narrowed. "What then? Dollars? Gold?"

"French francs," Granier said. "New ones. Not the

old colonial currency."

The dealer stared at him for a long moment, then shook his head. "You're a strange one. Planning a trip in the middle of all this?"

Granier didn't respond, his eyes cold and hard, unwilling to disclose any information on what he might be doing and why.

The dealer sighed. "Fine. Four hundred. In French francs. But it'll take me a day to get them."

"You have two hours," Granier said. "I'll be back then. If you don't have the francs, I'll find another buyer."

The dealer scowled, but nodded. "Two hours. But don't expect me to—"

He was cut off by the sound of gunfire in the distance. Both men tensed, listening intently.

"Sounds like the VC are getting antsy," the dealer muttered. "You sure you want to stick around, my friend?"

Granier's face remained impassive. "Two hours," he repeated. "I'll be back."

Without another word, he turned and climbed the stairs out of the basement, leaving the dealer staring after him with a mixture of admiration and disbelief.

As Granier emerged onto the street, he took a deep breath. The pistol had been a comforting weight at his side for so long, but he knew it was a liability now. The francs would be more useful where he was going, would help smooth his path north.

He glanced at his watch. Two hours. Time enough to make final preparations, to say goodbye to the city that had been his home and battlefield for so long.

With a last look at the basement door, Granier melted into the crowded street, just another soul in a city on the brink of chaos. In two hours, he would return. And then, with or without the francs, he would begin his journey north.

The streets of Saigon were a hive of nervous energy, the air thick with tension and the acrid smell of fear. Granier moved through the crowds with practiced ease, his eyes constantly scanning for danger. He had ditched his military fatigues for simple civilian clothes, blending in as best he could with the local population.

His first stop was a small general store tucked away in a side alley. As he entered, the elderly shopkeeper looked up, his eyes widening in surprise at the sight of a foreigner.

"Monsieur," the old man said in halting French, "it is not safe for you here. The Americans, they have all gone."

Granier smiled disarmingly, replying in fluent French. "I am not American, my friend. Just a traveler caught in unfortunate circumstances."

The shopkeeper's surprise deepened, but he nodded cautiously. "Hurry then. What do you need?"

"Supplies for a journey," Granier said, his eyes roaming over the shelves. "Rice, dried fish, matches, a slingshot, and a pair of good boots if you have 'em."

As the shopkeeper gathered the items, Granier kept one eye on the street outside. He could see a patrol of Viet Cong moving down the main road, their AK-47s slung casually over their shoulders.

"You should be very careful, monsieur," the shopkeeper said, following Granier's gaze. "They are everywhere now, and they do not like foreigners."

Granier nodded, quickly paying for his supplies and stuffing them into his rucksack. As he turned to leave, the old man caught his arm. "The city... it is not what it was. Trust no one. Many will betray to save themselves."

With a nod of thanks, Granier slipped out of the store and back into the crowded street. He needed more supplies, but he'd have to be careful.

He made his way to a small market, weaving through the stalls with purposeful strides. He picked up a few more essentials - water purification tablets, an extra pair of shoelaces for his boots, a sewing kit.

As he was examining some dried fruit at one stall, he heard the unmistakable sound of marching feet. A VC patrol was coming down the street, their eyes scanning the crowds.

Without missing a beat, Granier ducked behind a nearby stall selling fabric. He grabbed a length of cloth and draped it over his head and shoulders, mimicking the posture of an old woman examining the wares.

The patrol passed by, their eyes sliding over him without a second glance. Once they were gone, Granier straightened up, nodding thanks to the bewildered stall owner.

His final stop was a small pharmacy. The young woman behind the counter eyed him suspiciously as he entered. "Medicines," he said quietly. "For a journey."

She hesitated for a moment, then nodded, gathering antibiotics, painkillers, and bandages. As she wrapped them, she leaned in close.

"You're not the only one trying to leave," she whispered. "Be careful on the northern roads. They're watching those most closely."

Granier thanked her, slipping the medicines into his pack. As he stepped back out onto the street, he took a deep breath. He had what he needed now. It was time to leave Saigon behind.

With one last look at the city he had called home for so long, Granier melted into the crowds, just another shadow in a city full of ghosts.

Jungle

As the first light of dawn crept over the horizon, Rene Granier made his final preparations for his journey north. He had already donned his disguise as a French plantation owner and replaced his US Army rucksack with a French hiking rucksack.

But there was one last task to complete before he could set out. Granier pulled out his sniper rifle, the weapon that had been his constant companion through countless battles and missions. He would need it.

With practiced hands, he began to disassemble the rifle, carefully separating each component and laying them out on a piece of tattered cloth. He worked quickly and efficiently, his movements precise and deliberate.

Granier surveyed the dense jungle around him, his eyes scanning for the perfect materials to conceal the pieces of his M403A sniper rifle. He knew that every component had to be hidden with meticulous care, each piece disguised to avoid detection by the militia patrols guarding the path north.

For the barrel and receiver, Granier selected a thick branch of acacia wood, prizing it for its density and strength. With his combat knife, he carefully cut the branch to size from a nearby tree, his movements precise and controlled to maintain the natural appearance of the wood. Using the same knife, he stripped the bark and smoothed the surface, fashioning it into a convincing walking stick.

To hollow out the stick, Granier cut off the top of the stick and created a bow drill to carve out the interior. He found a flexible branch for the bow and a harder wood for the drill itself. He used the extra pair of shoelaces he had purchased for the bow's string. With patience and skill, he used this primitive tool to bore a hole through the length of the acacia branch. Several times the drill created so much friction the wood caught fire which Granier quickly blew out. He working tirelessly until the walking stick was hollow.

With the hollow core created, he cut the top fourteen inches off creating two sections to the stick. He bore three spaces for wooden dowels between the two sections so they would attach snuggly.

Granier carefully inserted his rifle's barrel, receiver, and a narrow cleaning rod into the bottom section of the stick. To prevent any telltale rattling, he filled the empty spaces with fine sand, ensuring a snug fit. Next, he wrapped a small pile of gauze cleaning pads in wax paper as a cushion. Lastly, he placed the rifle's scope wrapped in wax paper in the stick's handle on top and secured the two halves with wooden dowels. He wrapped a long strip of leather to create a handle near the top of the stick and to disguise the seam between the two sections.

The result was a seemingly ordinary walking stick that concealed the heart of his rifle. The only problem was that it was very heavy. If it was inspected closely, the stick's weight could be a problem. He would do his best to explain it away. Afterall, he was a large man that required a strong walking stick made from dense wood.

The bolt mechanism presented a unique challenge, but Granier was up to the task. He separated the bolt into its individual parts and disguised them as components of a simple water filtration system. The bolt handle became a small hand pump.

Next, he sewed two small hidden compartments in the bottom of a cloth bag with a drawstring. In the bottom compartment, he placed a handful of river stones so that the bottom of the bag felt like it was filled with stones. Then, he placed the trigger guard with internal magazine filled with five rounds of ammunition in the next hidden compartment above the bottom compartment. Finally, he filled the bag with smooth river stones for a slingshot he carried with him for hunting. The illusion was complete. The bag felt and looked like it was only filled with stones for the slingshot.

As for the rifle stock, Granier made the difficult decision to discard it, knowing that although it would be difficult, he could fashion a new one upon reaching his destination. He broke it down into small pieces, scattering them across a wide area to prevent any chance of discovery. He also abandoned the rifles accessory plate and bipod legs burying them in the ground.

He had the major components of his rifle and that was all he dared take with him. To anyone who might search his belongings, the rifle components would be undetectable, scattered and hidden amongst the mundane items of a traveler's possessions.

With the rifle safely concealed, Granier turned his attention to the final item that tied him to his past. He reached into his pocket and pulled out a small, blue booklet - his American passport.

For a long moment, he stared at the document, his eyes tracing the embossed eagle on the cover. This passport had been his lifeline, his connection to the country he had served for so long. It had brought him to Vietnam, had given him a purpose and a mission.

But now, as he prepared to embark on a new journey, Granier knew that he had to leave that life behind. He could not risk being identified as an American, not where he was going.

With a heavy heart, Granier walked to the edge of the small clearing where he had made his preparations. He knelt beside a small fire, the flames casting flickering shadows across his face.

Slowly, almost reverently, he held the passport over the fire. He watched as the flames licked at the edges of the pages, the heat singeing his fingertips. Then, with a final, decisive motion, he released the booklet, letting it fall into the heart of the fire.

As the passport burned, Granier felt a sense of profound loss. He was cutting his ties to his past, to the country and the people he had fought for. But he also knew that it was a necessary sacrifice, a price he had to pay for the mission that lay ahead.

He watched as the flames consumed the passport, the blue cover curling and blackening as it turned to ash. And with it, he felt a piece of himself burn away as well - the part of him that had been Rene Granier, American soldier and CIA operative.

When the last of the passport had been reduced to embers, Granier stood, his eyes fixed on the rising sun. He shouldered his rucksack and grabbed his walking stick.

And then, without a backward glance, he set out into the jungle, his footsteps carrying him ever northward.

As he walked, Granier kept to the side of the road, his eyes constantly scanning the surrounding jungle and road ahead and behind for any sign of danger.

He moved with the easy grace of a man who had spent his life in the wilderness, his footsteps nearly silent on the packed dirt. When a patrol vehicle approached, he would melt into the undergrowth, becoming one with the foliage until the danger had passed.

The days blurred together as Granier pushed deeper into northern territory. He subsisted on what he could forage from the jungle, supplemented by the meager rations he carried in his rucksack. At night, he slept in the branches of trees, his senses attuned to the slightest sound or movement.

He knew that he was the deadliest man in the country, a weapon forged in the flames of war and tempered by the unrelenting brutality of the jungle. He was up to the task. And he would not rest until he had fulfilled the purpose that drove him ever northward.

The sun beat down mercilessly on the narrow, dusty road as Granier made his way through the countryside. His French businessman disguise, once crisp and clean, was now stained with sweat and grime, evidence of the long miles he had traveled.

As he rounded a bend in the road, he caught sight of a group of armed men blocking the path ahead. They wore the mismatched uniforms and red armbands of a local militia, their weapons held at the ready.

Granier felt a flicker of unease, but he kept his expression neutral, his pace steady. He had come too far to be turned back now, and he knew that he would have to rely on his wits and his cover story to see him through.

As he approached the checkpoint, the militia

commander stepped forward, his eyes narrowing as he took in Granier's appearance. "Halt!" he barked, his voice sharp with suspicion. "State your business."

Granier came to a stop, his hands held out to his sides in a gesture of non-threat. He summoned his most disarming smile, his accent flawless as he spoke in French.

"Good day, Commander," he said, his tone friendly and respectful. "I am Henri Bouchard, a French national. I am traveling to my rubber factory just outside of Hanoi."

The commander's gaze raked over Granier's rough clothing and worn rucksack. "A Frenchman, you say? And what brings you to this part of the country, so far from the city?"

Granier shrugged, his smile never wavering. "The factory has been idle for too long, with all the chaos of the war. I have come to oversee its reopening, to bring prosperity back to the region."

The commander's expression seemed doubtful, his suspicion still evident. "And your papers? Let me see your identification."

Granier reached slowly into his pocket, his fingers brushing against the wax paper that protected his forged passport. He handed it over to the commander. He watched the man examine the document.

For a long moment, the commander studied the passport, his eyes flicking back and forth between the photograph and Granier's face. Granier fought the urge to hold his breath, to betray any sign of nervousness.

Finally, the commander handed the passport back, his expression still guarded. "Everything seems to be in order, Monsieur Bouchard. But tell me, why are you traveling alone? Surely a man of your importance would have an escort, no?"

Granier laughed, the sound easy and relaxed. "Ah, Commander, you flatter me. I am but a simple businessman, not a dignitary. My factory is small. And in times like these, it is better to travel light and fast, to avoid drawing unnecessary attention from the rabble."

The commander nodded slowly, his gaze still searching Granier's face for any sign of deception. But Granier held his ground, his expression open and guileless.

The commander turned to his men and said, "Search his belongings."

Two militia soldiers approached, roughly grabbing Granier's rucksack and walking stick. Granier's pulse quickened as one soldier hefted the acacia wood stick, frowning at its weight.

"This is quite heavy for a walking stick, monsieur," the soldier remarked.

Granier shrugged nonchalantly. "I'm a large man and my legs no longer work as when I was young. I require a sturdy support."

The soldier examined the stick closely, running his hands along its length. Granier held his breath as the man's fingers traced the leather-wrapped seam, but the soldier moved on, apparently satisfied.

Meanwhile, the other soldier dumped the contents of Granier's rucksack onto the ground. He poked through the clothing and supplies, then picked up the water filtration system.

"What's this?" he demanded.

"For purifying water," Granier explained smoothly. "One can't be too careful with one's health in the jungle."

The soldier disassembled the filtration system, examining each piece. Granier's heart skipped a beat as the man turned the disguised bolt handle over in his hands, but after a moment, he tossed it aside.

Finally, the soldier picked up the cloth bag of stones. He loosened the drawstring and peered inside.

"Just stones?" he asked, puzzled.

Granier nodded. "For my slingshot. A useful hunting tool."

The soldier shook the bag, listening to the stones rattle. Satisfied, he dropped it back onto the pile.

After what felt like an eternity, the commander stepped back, waving his men aside. "Very well, Monsieur Bouchard. You may pass. But be warned - the roads ahead are treacherous, and not all those you meet will be as understanding as we are."

Granier bowed his head in thanks, his relief carefully hidden. "I understand, Commander. And I thank you for your kindness and your vigilance. It is men like you who will rebuild our country, now that the fighting is done."

With a final nod, Granier gathered his things and stepped past the checkpoint, his pace steady and unhurried. He could feel the eyes of the militiamen on his back, could sense their lingering suspicion.

But he did not look back, did not betray any sign of the tension that coiled within him. He had passed the test, had convinced the commander of his false identity. And now, the road north lay open before him, a path that would lead him ever closer to his true objective.

With the sun beating down upon him and the road stretching out before him, Rene Granier walked on, his steps carrying him ever northward, towards a destiny that only he could foresee.

The sun was beginning to dip towards the horizon as Granier crested a small hill, his legs aching from the long hours of walking. He had been following the road north for days now, his disguise and forged documents serving him well as he passed through villages and checkpoints.

But now, as he reached the top of the rise, he saw something that gave him pause. Ahead, the road split in two, a weathered wooden sign marking the diverging paths.

Granier approached the sign as he read the faded lettering. The arrow pointing to the right indicated that Hanoi lay to the northeast, the city's name spelled out in both Vietnamese and French.

For a moment, Granier hesitated, his gaze lingering on the sign. He turned his gaze to the left, to the road that led west. It was narrower than the main highway, its surface rutted and uneven. There were no signs indicating where it led, no markings to guide the way.

Granier took a deep breath, his hand tightening on the strap of his rucksack. With a final glance at the sign, Granier stepped off the main road, his boots crunching on the gravel of the western path.

As he walked, the sun dipping lower in the sky behind him, Granier felt a sense of peace, a calm certainty that he was exactly where he was meant to be.

Granier walked on, his steps carrying him ever closer to a fate that would be forever entwined with the land he had once called his enemy.

The storm raged through the jungle, the wind howling like a wounded beast as the rain lashed down in sheets.

Granier stumbled through the underbrush, his clothes soaked through and his mind numb with exhaustion.

He had been walking for hours, his body pushed to the brink of collapse. The road had long since disappeared, swallowed up by the dense foliage and the relentless downpour.

Suddenly, a deafening crack split the air, and Granier looked up to see a massive tree toppling towards him, its roots torn from the earth by the force of the storm. He tried to dodge, but the ground was slick beneath his feet, and he lost his balance, falling hard on his back.

The tree crashed down on top of him, pinning his legs beneath its massive trunk. Granier cried out in pain, his voice lost in the roar of the wind and the rain.

He tried to free himself, his hands scrabbling at the rough bark of the tree. But it was no use. He was trapped, his body crushed beneath the weight of the fallen giant. He laughed to himself. This was the end... after all he had been through, he was squashed by a tree?

As he lay there, his mind growing fuzzy with pain and despair, Granier heard a sound that cut through the chaos of the storm. It was the sound of footsteps, of someone approaching through the underbrush.

He turned his head, his eyes widening as he saw an old man emerge from the trees, a machete clutched in his weathered hand. The man's face was lined with age, but his eyes were sharp and clear.

Without a word, the old man set to work, his machete flashing in the dim light as he hacked at the branches that held Granier pinned. The minutes stretched out like hours, but finally, with a groan of splintering wood, the tree shifted, and Granier was able to drag himself free.

The old man helped him to his feet, his strong hands gripping Granier's shoulders as he steadied him. He spoke in a language that Granier didn't understand, but his gestures made his meaning clear.

Together, they stumbled through the jungle, the old man leading the way with sure steps. After what felt like an eternity, they emerged into a small clearing, where a cluster of simple huts stood sheltered beneath the trees.

The old man led Granier into one of the huts, where a group of villagers looked up in surprise at the sight of the stranger in their midst. The old man spoke to them in rapid-fire bursts of their native tongue, and soon Granier found himself seated by a fire, a bowl of steaming broth pressed into his hands and two women tending the cuts and scraps on his legs.

He reached into his pocket, pulling out a handful of coins. "For the food," he said, his voice hoarse with exhaustion. "And the medicine, for my legs."

But the villagers shook their heads, their smiles kind and gentle. They pushed the coins back into his hand, their gestures making it clear that they would not accept payment for their aid. It was not their tradition.

Granier felt a lump rise in his throat, a wave of emotion that threatened to overwhelm him. He had been alone for so long, fighting a war that had taken everything from him. But here, in this simple village, he had found something that he had thought was lost forever.

Kindness. Compassion. A reminder that even in the darkest of times, there was still goodness in the world, still those who would extend a helping hand to a stranger in need.

As he sipped the broth, feeling its warmth spread through his battered body, Granier knew that he would never forget the simple generosity of these people who had taken him in without question.

And as he drifted off to sleep, his wounds tended and his belly full, he knew that he had found something precious.

The sun was high in the sky, its rays filtering through the dense canopy of the jungle as Granier made his way deeper into the wilderness. He had been traveling for days, following the winding path of the river as it cut through the rugged terrain.

He stopped by the edge of the river and pulled out his compass and map. Granier was an experienced pathfinder and knew immediately where he was at. He was getting close to his final objective. It wouldn't be long now.

Suddenly, a sound caught his attention, a rustling in the underbrush that seemed out of place in the stillness of the jungle. Granier froze, his senses on high alert as he scanned the foliage for any sign of movement.

And then he saw it, a massive shape emerging from the trees, its form speckled with sunlight and shadow. It was an Asian elephant, its tusks gleaming in the dappled light, its eyes fixed on Granier with a primal intensity.

For a moment, the two stood frozen, the man and the beast, each sizing up the other with wary anticipation. And then, with a trumpeting cry that shook the very earth, the elephant charged.

Granier leaped aside, his reflexes honed by years of combat. He rolled to his feet, his hand reaching instinctively for the pistol that was no longer there.

The elephant wheeled, its massive head swinging from side to side as it searched for its prey. Granier backed away slowly. He drew his slingshot from his rucksack along with the bag of river stones. He knew the primitive weapon would do little to stop the beast, but just having a weapon in hand made him feel less helpless.

Moving behind a thick tree, Granier loaded a stone in the cradle of the slingshot and took aim at the approaching elephant. "You don't want to mess with me," he told the elephant. "I'm a mean son of bitch. I can't kill you, but I can take one of your eyes."

The elephant stopped, almost as if he understood what Granier was saying. He bellowed. Granier stood his ground and held his fire. He didn't want to anger the beast any more than needed. "Truce?" he said.

The elephant's trunk swung from side to side kicking up dirt into the air as he kept his eyes on Granier. Then, the beast turned and vanished into the jungle. Granier was surprised. The elephant could have easily killed him. But he didn't and Granier had no idea why.

And so, with a final glance in the direction of the vanished beast, Granier turned and resumed his journey in the dappled light of the jungle.

The jungle had begun to thin, the dense foliage giving way to scattered patches of open ground and rocky outcroppings. As Granier made his way through the changing landscape, he knew that he had been here before, that the contours of the land were familiar to him.

He moved carefully, his senses on high alert as he scanned the surrounding terrain for any sign of danger.

His beard, once a carefully maintained disguise, had grown long and shaggy after the weeks he had spent in the wilderness.

As he crested a small rise, he caught sight of a village nestled in the valley below. The huts were simple structures of bamboo and thatch, their walls weathered by the elements. Smoke curled from the cooking fires, carrying with it the scent of rice, roots, and spices.

Granier dropped to a crouch as he watched the villagers below… searching. He opened the top of the walking stick and pulled out his rifle's scope.

Raising the scope, his eye pressed against the eyepiece as he scanned the village below. He could see the villagers going about their daily lives, their faces lined with the cares and concerns of a people who had known too much of war and hardship.

And then, as he panned the scope across the village square, he saw her. A woman, her hair streaked with gray, her face lined with the passage of time. She was bent over a cooking fire, stirring a pot of rice with a weathered hand.

Granier's breath caught in his throat, his heart pounding in his chest as he stared at the woman through the scope. It was Spitting Woman, the fierce and beautiful guerrilla fighter he had fallen in love with so many years ago, when he had been a young OSS operative fighting alongside the Viet Minh against the Japanese. It had been thirty years since they first met on a battlefield, but he never forgot her.

Memories flooded back to him, memories of stolen moments in the jungle, of whispered words of love and devotion. He had carried the memory of her with him through all the long years of war and conflict.

But now, seeing her again after so many decades,

Granier felt a sudden rush of doubt, a fear that the years had changed them both too much, that the love they had once shared had faded like a dream in the harsh light of day.

He lowered the scope, his hand trembling slightly as he reached up to touch his beard. The rough hairs felt strange against his fingertips, so different from the young idealist who had first fallen in love with Spitting Woman.

With a sudden, decisive motion, Granier reached for his knife, his fingers wrapping around the hilt with a sense of purpose. He moved to the edge of a stream that ran along the base of the hill, the water clear and cold as it bubbled over the rocks.

Kneeling beside the stream, Granier dipped his hand into the water, cupping it to his face as he began to shave, the sharp edge of the knife scraping against his skin with each careful stroke. The beard fell away in clumps, revealing the face beneath, a face that had been hidden for so long behind a mask of hair and grime.

As he worked, Granier's mind raced with thoughts of the woman below. He didn't know what he would say to her, didn't know if she would even remember him after all this time.

But he knew that he had to try, that he had to take this one last chance at happiness, no matter how slim the odds might be. For in the end, that was all any of them could do, all any of them could hope for in this strange and savage land.

And so, with a final stroke of the knife, Granier rose to his feet, his face clean-shaven with only a few small cuts and his eyes bright and hopeful.

As he climbed down the hill and approached the

village, his heart raced with a mixture of anticipation and trepidation. He had dreamed of this moment for so long, had imagined a thousand different scenarios in his mind. But now that he was here, now that Spitting Woman was here, he found himself almost paralyzed with fear and doubt.

He entered the village square, his footsteps echoing on the hard-packed earth. The villagers looked up at him with curious eyes, their gazes taking in his foreign, clean-shaven face.

But Granier had eyes only for Spitting Woman, for the woman who had haunted his dreams for so many long years. She was squatting by the cooking fire, her back turned to him as she stirred the pot of rice.

And then, as if feeling a presence, she turned and saw him. Her expression was one of sheer shock like she couldn't believe her eyes.

Granier wanted to say something, anything, but the words wouldn't come. He just stood and stared. As tears welled up in his eyes, he smiled. A small thing full of meaning.

And then, she smiled back…

Epilogue

The aftermath of the Vietnam War was a period of significant upheaval and change for the people of Vietnam, the United States, and the international community. The war, which had lasted for nearly two decades, had a profound impact on all parties involved.

After the fall of Saigon on April 30, 1975, the communists renamed the city Ho Chi Minh City, although many residents continued to use the name Saigon. The Communist Party of Vietnam sought to reduce the population of the city, which had become overcrowded during the war. Within two years of the capture of Saigon, one million people had left the city, either voluntarily or through government pressure.

One of the most controversial aspects of the war's aftermath was the treatment of former South Vietnamese soldiers and officials. According to official and non-official estimates, between 200,000 and 300,000 South Vietnamese were sent to re-education camps, where many endured torture, starvation, and disease while being forced to do hard labor.

The war had a lasting impact on the United States as well. Over 58,000 American soldiers died in the conflict, and many more were wounded or suffered from post-traumatic stress disorder (PTSD). The war also had a significant impact on American politics and culture, with protests against the war becoming a defining feature of the 1960s and early 1970s.

In Vietnam, the war's aftermath was marked by a period of economic hardship and international isolation. The United States imposed an embargo on Vietnam that lasted until 1994, and Vietnam was not allowed to join the United Nations until 1977. However, in the decades following the war, Vietnam underwent significant economic and social changes, with the government adopting market-oriented reforms and seeking to improve relations with the West.

Today, April 30 is celebrated as a public holiday in Vietnam, known as Reunification Day. Among overseas Vietnamese, however, the week of April 30 is referred to as "Black April" and is commemorated as a time of lamentation for the fall of Saigon and South Vietnam.

Post-Traumatic Stress Disorder (PTSD) is another significant issue that has impacted many veterans of the Vietnam War. Here are some key statistics and information about PTSD among Vietnam veterans:

PTSD is a mental health condition that can develop after a person experiences or witnesses a traumatic event, such as combat, sexual assault, or a natural disaster. Symptoms of PTSD can include flashbacks, nightmares, severe anxiety, and uncontrollable thoughts about the event.

According to the National Vietnam Veterans Readjustment Study (NVVRS) conducted in the 1980s, an estimated 30.9% of Vietnam veterans had experienced PTSD at some point in their lives, and 15.2% were still experiencing PTSD at the time of the study. This prevalence rate was significantly higher than that of the general population and veterans of other wars.

A more recent study published in JAMA Psychiatry in 2015 found that 271,000 Vietnam veterans still had full PTSD or sub-threshold PTSD symptoms forty years after the war, indicating the long-term impact of combat exposure on mental health.

PTSD can have a profound impact on veterans' lives, affecting their relationships, employment, and overall well-being. Vietnam veterans with PTSD have been found to have higher rates of unemployment, homelessness, and substance abuse compared to veterans without PTSD.

The Department of Veterans Affairs (VA) has taken steps to address the mental health needs of Vietnam veterans, including establishing specialized PTSD treatment programs and increasing access to mental health services. As of 2020, the VA reported that:

- More than 1.7 million veterans received mental health treatment from the VA, including treatment for PTSD.
- The VA operates more than 200 specialized PTSD treatment programs across the country, including inpatient and outpatient programs.
- The VA has also established a National Center for PTSD, which conducts research and provides education and training on PTSD treatment.

Despite these efforts, many Vietnam veterans

continue to struggle with PTSD and other mental health issues related to their military service. Stigma, access to care, and the complexity of the VA benefits system can be barriers to seeking treatment for some veterans.

The impact of PTSD on Vietnam veterans highlights the long-term mental health consequences of combat exposure and the importance of providing ongoing support and treatment to veterans and their families. It also underscores the need for continued research and advocacy to improve our understanding of PTSD and develop more effective treatments for this complex and debilitating condition.

Agent Orange was a herbicide and defoliant used by the U.S. military during the Vietnam War to clear dense jungle areas and destroy crops that could aid the enemy. The U.S. sprayed an estimated twenty million gallons of Agent Orange and other herbicides over Vietnam, Laos, and Cambodia between 1961 and 1971.

The herbicide contained dioxin, a highly toxic substance that has been linked to a range of health problems, including cancer, birth defects, and other chronic illnesses. The Vietnamese government estimates that up to three million people in Vietnam have suffered health problems due to exposure to Agent Orange, including 150,000 children born with birth defects.

American veterans exposed to Agent Orange have also suffered from a range of health problems. The Department of Veterans Affairs recognizes certain cancers and other health problems as presumptive diseases associated with exposure to Agent Orange and other herbicides during military service. These include:

- Chronic B-cell leukemias
- Hodgkin's Disease
- Multiple Myeloma
- Non-Hodgkin's Lymphoma
- Parkinson's Disease
- Ischemic Heart Disease
- Prostate Cancer
- Respiratory Cancers (including lung cancer)
- Soft Tissue Sarcomas (other than osteosarcoma, chondrosarcoma, Kaposi's sarcoma, or mesothelioma)

According to the Department of Veterans Affairs, as of 2020:

- More than 22,000 veterans have received disability compensation for health problems associated with Agent Orange exposure.
- More than 350,000 veterans have undergone health examinations through the Agent Orange Registry program.
- The Department of Veterans Affairs has paid out more than $24 billion in disability compensation to Vietnam veterans and their survivors for health problems associated with Agent Orange exposure.

In addition to the health impact, the use of Agent Orange has had significant environmental consequences in Vietnam. Large areas of forest and agricultural land were destroyed, and dioxin contamination has persisted in the soil and water in some areas for decades.

The legacy of Agent Orange is a painful reminder of the long-term consequences of war and the importance of understanding the full impact of military actions on both combatants and civilians. It also underscores the ongoing need to support veterans and their families who continue to deal with the health effects of exposure to Agent Orange and other toxins during their military service.

In terms of statistics, the Vietnam War had a staggering impact on all parties involved. Some key figures include:

- 58,220 U.S. military personnel died in the war, with an additional 153,303 wounded.
- Estimates of Vietnamese military and civilian deaths vary widely, but most sources suggest that between 1.5 and 3.6 million Vietnamese died in the conflict.
- The United States spent over $168 billion on the war (equivalent to over $1 trillion in 2021 dollars).
- Over three million tons of ordnance was dropped on Vietnam, Laos, and Cambodia during the war, making it the most heavily bombed area in history.
- Over 3,000 fixed wing aircraft, 5,600 helicopters, and 10,000 armored vehicles were destroyed or lost by the United States during the war.
- By 1975, the U.S. had provided over $4 billion in military aid to South Vietnam, but this was not enough to prevent the country's collapse.

These statistics provide a glimpse into the immense scale and impact of the Vietnam War, which continues to be felt by those who lived through it and the generations that have followed.

The Four Operations

Operation Babylift
White House – Washington DC, USA

The Oval Office was quiet, the only sound the soft ticking of the antique clock on the mantel. President Gerald Ford sat behind his desk, his face lined with worry as he listened to the briefing from his advisors.

"Mr. President," said Secretary of State Henry Kissinger, his voice grave, "we have a situation in Saigon that requires your immediate attention."

Ford nodded, his eyes fixed on the papers in front of him. "Go on, Henry."

Kissinger cleared his throat. "As you know, sir, many of our servicemen stationed in Vietnam have fathered children with Vietnamese women. With the fall of Saigon imminent, we have to decide what to do about these children."

Ford looked up, his blue eyes sharp. "How many

are we talking about, Henry?"

"Hundreds, possibly thousands," Kissinger replied. "Many of these children are living in orphanages or with their mothers, but they face an uncertain future if the North Vietnamese take control."

Ford sighed, leaning back in his chair. "We have a moral obligation to these children," he said, his voice firm. "They are the sons and daughters of American soldiers, and we cannot abandon them. They are Americans and must be protected."

The room was silent for a moment, the weight of the decision hanging heavy in the air. Finally, Ford spoke again.

"I want a plan in place to evacuate these children," he said, his tone leaving no room for argument. "We'll bring them to the United States, with the help of our allies if necessary. They deserve a chance at a better life, away from the chaos and danger of Vietnam."

Kissinger nodded, making a note on his pad. "Yes, Mr. President. We'll start making arrangements right away."

Ford stood, his tall frame silhouetted against the windows behind his desk. "These children are innocent victims of this war," he said, his voice filled with emotion. "They didn't ask to be born into this conflict, and they shouldn't have to suffer because of it."

He turned to face his advisors. "We'll call it Operation Babylift," he said, the name coming to him in a moment of inspiration. "We'll bring these children to safety and give them the opportunity to grow up in a world of peace and stability."

As the meeting adjourned, Ford remained in the Oval Office, his thoughts turning to the enormous task ahead. He knew that the decision to evacuate the

American-Vietnamese children would be controversial, that there would be those who opposed it on political or logistical grounds.

But in his heart, he knew it was the right thing to do. These children were the legacy of American involvement in Vietnam, and they deserved a chance at a better future. And as president, it was his duty to ensure that they received it, no matter the cost.

Ford picked up the phone and began making calls, setting in motion a chain of events that would change the lives of countless children forever. It was a decision that would define his presidency, and one that he would never regret. For in that moment, he knew that he was not just acting as a political leader, but as a father, a protector, and a champion of the innocent.

Saigon, South Vietnam

The distant thunder of artillery fire echoed through the crowded orphanage in Saigon, a reminder of the war that raged just beyond the city's borders. The children, a mix of infants, toddlers, and teenagers, huddled together in small groups, their faces etched with fear and uncertainty. The caregivers, a dedicated team of Vietnamese nuns and American volunteers, moved among them, offering comfort and reassurance in the face of the growing chaos outside.

Sister Mary, a young Vietnamese nun with a kind face and gentle demeanor, cradled a crying baby in her arms, rocking the child softly as she hummed a traditional lullaby. She looked up as Sara, an American volunteer with the organization Childhelp, approached her, a worried expression on her face.

"Sister," Sara said. "we just received word from the

U.S. government. They're going to start airlifting the children out of Saigon, to safety."

Sister Mary's eyes widened, a mix of hope and apprehension flickering across her face. "When will this happen?" she asked, shifting the baby to her other arm.

"The first flight is scheduled for this evening," Sara replied, glancing around the room at the sea of young faces. "We need to start preparing the children for evacuation, as quickly as possible."

Sister Mary nodded, her gaze drifting over the children in her care. "It won't be easy," she said softly. "Many of these little ones have never been outside the orphanage before. They'll be frightened and confused."

Sara laid a comforting hand on the nun's shoulder, feeling the weight of the responsibility they shared. "I know," she said, her voice filled with empathy. "But we have to do what's best for them. The fighting is getting closer every day, and we can't guarantee their safety here anymore."

As the two women began to discuss the logistics of the evacuation, a young boy named Quy approached them, his dark eyes serious beneath a mop of black hair. He clutched a small backpack in his hands, his knuckles white with determination.

"I want to help," he said, his voice barely above a whisper. "I can take care of the younger children on the plane, make sure they're not scared."

Sara smiled at him, touched by his compassion. "Thank you, Quy," she said, kneeling down to meet his gaze. "We're going to need all the help we can get."

Over the next few hours, the orphanage was a flurry of activity as the caregivers worked to prepare the children for the journey ahead. They packed small bags with clothes, blankets, and a few precious toys, trying to reassure the little ones that everything would be alright, that they were going on an adventure.

As the sun began to set over the city, Sara stepped outside for a moment, her heart heavy with the weight of the task before them. She looked out over the rooftops of Saigon, watching as the last rays of light painted the sky in shades of orange and red. In the distance, she could hear the sound of gunfire and explosions, a stark reminder of the danger that lurked just beyond the orphanage walls.

Suddenly, a loud blast shook the ground beneath her feet, and the sky lit up with the flash of anti-aircraft fire. Sara's heart raced as she hurried back inside, where the children were huddled together, their eyes wide with fear.

"It's time to go," she said, her voice calm and reassuring despite the urgency of the situation.

The children were quickly loaded onto buses, their small faces pressed against the windows as they watched the only home they had ever known disappear behind them. At the airport, the scene was one of controlled chaos as military personnel worked to load the youngsters onto the waiting planes, the roar of the engines drowning out the sound of crying babies and shouted orders.

As Sara helped the other children onto the plane, she felt a deep ache in her heart. She knew that her place was here, in Vietnam, helping the countless other children who still needed her. With a heavy heart, she hugged each child goodbye, whispering words of encouragement and love as they boarded the aircraft.

Inside the plane, the usual rows of seats had been replaced with a makeshift nursery. Many of the seats had portable bassinets strapped in with seatbelts, each one holding a tiny, precious cargo. The babies, some just a few weeks old, lay swaddled in blankets, their eyes wide and curious as they took in their unfamiliar surroundings.

The older children sat in the few remaining seats, clutching small bags filled with their meager possessions. Some cried softly, while others sat in silence, their faces filled with fear and wonder.

At the front of the plane, a team of nurses and caregivers waited, ready to attend to the babies' needs. They moved through the cabin with practiced efficiency, checking on each child, offering bottles and changing diapers. In the back a team of stewardesses offered words of comfort to the older children along with puzzles and coloring books with crayons.

Once the last child was safely on board, Sara stepped back, watching as the plane's engines roared to life. The wind from the propellers whipped through her hair, and tears stung her eyes as she watched the aircraft taxi down the runway.

As the plane lifted off into the night sky, Sara stood alone on the tarmac, her gaze fixed on the receding lights. She whispered a silent prayer for the children who were leaving their homeland behind, hoping that they would find happiness and peace in their new lives.

In that moment, as the plane disappeared into the clouds, Sara felt a mix of emotions wash over her. She was heartbroken to see the children go, but she knew that they would be safe, far from the violence and destruction of the war.

Sara took a deep breath, squaring her shoulders as she turned back towards the orphanage. There was still so much work to be done, so many more children who needed her help.

As she walked through the quiet streets of Saigon, Sara knew that the children on that plane would always hold a special place in her heart, and that their journeys were just beginning.

Operation Eagle Pull
Phnom Penh, Cambodia

The once vibrant city of Phnom Penh had become a shadow of its former self. The streets, once bustling with life and commerce, were now eerily quiet, the only sounds the distant echo of artillery and the occasional whine of an aircraft overhead. The Khmer Rouge, the brutal communist insurgency that had been waging war against the US-backed Khmer Republic for years, had finally succeeded in cutting off the last remaining supply line from the Mekong Delta. The city was now surrounded, its inhabitants trapped and facing an uncertain future.

For months, the Khmer Rouge had been slowly tightening their grip on the country, seizing control of key towns and outposts along the Mekong River. The river, once a lifeline for the capital, had become a deadly gauntlet, with Khmer Rouge forces laying mines and ambushing any ships that dared to make the perilous journey from the South Vietnamese border. By February, the Khmer Republic had been forced to abandon any attempts to reopen the river route, knowing that the cost in ships and lives would be too high.

With the Mekong closed, Phnom Penh's only link to the outside world was Pochentong Airport. The United States, recognizing the dire situation, had quickly mobilized an airlift of food, fuel, and ammunition into the city. But even this lifeline was tenuous, as Khmer Rouge artillery batteries shelled the airport and rockets struck supply planes on the tarmac. The US embassy, in a desperate bid to keep the city alive, increased the number of flights and aircraft, even as the security situation deteriorated by the day.

On the ground, the mood was one of despair and resignation. The FANK troops, once a formidable fighting force, were now a shadow of their former selves, demoralized and depleted by years of constant warfare. Many had deserted, melting away into the countryside to avoid the inevitable fall of the city. Those who remained were exhausted and poorly supplied, forced to make do with dwindling stocks of ammunition and food.

In the streets, the people of Phnom Penh tried to go about their daily lives as best they could, even as the sound of gunfire and explosions drew ever closer. Many had fled the city, taking what possessions they could carry and heading for the relative safety of the countryside. Those who remained huddled in their homes, praying for a miracle that seemed increasingly unlikely to come.

At the US embassy, Ambassador John Gunther Dean and his staff worked tirelessly to manage the crisis. They knew that the fall of Phnom Penh was inevitable, but they were determined to do everything in their power to protect American citizens and their Cambodian allies. In secret meetings and hushed conversations, they began to plan for the worst, drawing up lists of those who would need to be evacuated and making arrangements for their safe passage out of the country.

As April dawned, the situation in Phnom Penh had become critical. The Khmer Rouge had overrun the last remaining FANK positions on the Mekong and were now free to concentrate all their forces on the capital. The city was in a state of panic, with thousands of people desperately trying to find a way out before the final assault began.

It was against this backdrop that the United States launched Operation Eagle Pull. The plan was simple but daring: to evacuate all American personnel and as many Cambodian allies as possible before the city fell. It was a race against time, with the Khmer Rouge closing in and the clock ticking down to the final collapse of the Khmer Republic.

For those involved, the operation was a nerve-wracking blur of activity and danger. Military aircraft, flying low to avoid Khmer Rouge fire, ferried evacuees to safety amid chaotic scenes at the airport. Embassy staff worked around the clock to process visas and travel documents, trying to ensure that no one was left behind. And all the while, the sound of battle grew closer, a constant reminder of the urgency of their mission.

In the end, Operation Eagle Pull succeeded in evacuating over a thousand people from Phnom Penh, including the ambassador and his staff, US citizens, and their Cambodian allies. It was a bittersweet victory, however, as they knew that many more had been left behind, doomed to face the brutal reality of life under the Khmer Rouge.

As the last helicopter lifted off from the embassy roof, those on board could only watch in silence as the city receded into the distance. They had done all they could, but they knew that the tragedy of Cambodia was only just beginning. For the people of Phnom Penh, and for the country as a whole, the future was a dark and uncertain one, with little hope of escape from the nightmare that had engulfed them. But even in the darkest corners of their imaginations, the Cambodians had no idea of the horrors that were about to happen…

Operation New Life
White House – Washington DC, USA

As the North Vietnamese forces closed in on Saigon, the United States government scrambled to evacuate not only American personnel but also thousands of Vietnamese who had worked closely with the U.S. during the war. The task of processing and resettling these refugees fell to the newly created Interagency Task Force (IATF) for Indochina, headed by L. Dean Brown of the State Department.

In a meeting at the White House, President Gerald Ford addressed the assembled officials. "We have a moral obligation to these people," he said, his voice grave. "They put their trust in us, they helped us when we needed them, and we cannot abandon them now."

Brown nodded, "It won't be easy, Mr. President. We're talking about tens of thousands of people, and we need to find a place to process them before we can bring them to the United States."

"Make it happen, Dean."

Guam, USA

That place, it turned out, would be Guam. Governor Ricardo Bordallo had agreed to grant the Vietnamese

391

temporary asylum on the island, despite the reluctance of other Southeast Asian countries to accept the refugees.

On April 23, Rear Admiral George Stephen Morrison received his orders. "You are to accept, shelter, process, and care for refugees as they are removed from South Vietnam," his commanding officer told him.

Morrison nodded, his mind already racing with the logistics of the operation. "We'll need to set up temporary housing, medical facilities, and processing centers," he said. "It's going to be a massive undertaking."

As the first ships and planes began to arrive on Guam, the scale of the operation became clear. Over 130,000 Vietnamese had been evacuated in the final days of April, and the vast majority of them would pass through Guam on their way to the United States.

Julia V. Taft, who had taken over from Brown as head of Operation New Life, toured the rapidly growing refugee camps on the island. "We have to make sure they have everything they need," she told her staff. "Food, water, medical care, and most importantly, a sense of safety and security."

But even as the refugees poured in, questions arose about how they would be integrated into American society. In a meeting with President Ford, Secretary of State Henry Kissinger expressed his concerns, "We need to be careful about how we handle this," he said. "There could be a backlash if it looks like we're giving these refugees special treatment."

Ford shook his head. "We have a responsibility to these people," he said firmly. "They've been through hell, and they deserve a chance at a new life."

As the weeks passed, the refugees on Guam began to process through the system, undergoing medical examinations, security checks, and interviews with immigration officials. Many were traumatized by their experiences, and the staff worked hard to provide them with counseling and support.

One young woman, who had worked as a translator for the U.S. military, spoke tearfully of her gratitude for the operation. "I never thought I would make it out. I thought I was dead for sure," she said. "But here I am, safe and alive."

Finally, after months of hard work, the last of the refugees were cleared to leave Guam and begin their new lives in the United States. As they boarded planes bound for their new homes, many wept with a mix of joy and sorrow.

Taft watched them go, a sense of pride and accomplishment washing over her. "We did it," she said to her staff.

And as the planes lifted off, carrying the refugees to a new land and a new beginning, the staff of Operation New Life knew that they had been a part of something truly extraordinary. They had shown the world the best of what America could be, a beacon of hope and compassion in a time of great darkness.

Operation Frequent Wind
Saigon, South Vietnam

As the North Vietnamese Army and Viet Cong forces closed in on Saigon, the capital of South Vietnam, the United States government initiated a massive evacuation operation. Codenamed "Frequent Wind," the plan was to remove all remaining American personnel, as well as tens of thousands of South Vietnamese civilians who had worked with the U.S. during the war.

On April 29, 1975, President Gerald Ford gave the order to commence the evacuation. In the Oval Office, he turned to his advisors, his face grave. "We have to get our people out," he said. "And we have to do it now."

The American Embassy in Saigon became the center of a frenzied effort to process visas and organize transportation for the thousands of people desperate to escape the city before it fell to the communists.

The scene at the embassy was one of chaos and desperation. Crowds of Vietnamese civilians gathered outside the gates, pleading for a chance to leave the country. Many had been loyal allies of the Americans, working as translators, intelligence assets, or in other support roles. They knew that they would face retribution from the communists if they were left behind.

"Please, you have to help us!" one woman cried, clutching her baby to her chest. "We have nowhere else to go!"

Inside the embassy compound, American diplomats and military personnel worked around the clock to process the massive backlog of visa applications. They had to make hard choices about who would be allowed to leave and who would be left to face an uncertain fate.

"We can't take everyone," one harried official said, wiping sweat from his brow. "We have to prioritize American citizens and those with direct ties to the U.S. government."

As the evacuation got underway, American

helicopters began ferrying people from the embassy to U.S. Navy ships waiting off the coast. The helicopters, many of them flown by brave South Vietnamese pilots, made countless trips back and forth, their rotors churning the humid air as they carried their human cargo to safety.

"We're going to get you out of here," one pilot reassured his passengers. "Just hold on a little longer."

The evacuation was not without its risks. The North Vietnamese forces, sensing that the end was near, began shelling Tan Son Nhut Air Base, the main airport serving Saigon. The attacks made it increasingly difficult for the helicopters to operate, and forced the evacuation to shift to the embassy compound itself.

In a desperate bid to keep the evacuation going, American Marines landed on the embassy roof and began to secure the perimeter. They set up defensive positions and worked to keep the crowds at bay, even as the sound of gunfire and explosions grew ever closer.

"Hold the line!" a Marine sergeant shouted, as his men took up positions around the embassy. "We've got to buy them more time!"

As the hours ticked by, the situation grew increasingly tense. The North Vietnamese were closing in, and it was clear that time was running out. The American Ambassador, Graham Martin, had been reluctant to leave, hoping to maintain a diplomatic presence in the city for as long as possible. But finally, with the enemy just blocks away, he gave the order to evacuate the embassy.

"It's time to go," he said to his staff, his voice heavy with emotion. "We've done all we can here."

In a scene that would become iconic, American

helicopters landed on the roof of the embassy, their rotors kicking up clouds of dust and debris. Marines helped the last remaining evacuees aboard, then climbed in themselves. As the helicopters lifted off, the Marines pushed desperate civilians back, some of them clinging to the skids in a last-ditch effort to escape.

"Let go!" a Marine shouted, prying a man's fingers loose. "You'll get yourself killed!"

From the air, the city of Saigon was a scene of chaos and destruction. Smoke billowed from burning buildings, and the streets were choked with abandoned vehicles and fleeing civilians. It was a heartbreaking sight, a stark reminder of the human cost of the long and brutal war.

In the end, Operation Frequent Wind managed to evacuate over 7,000 people in less than twenty-four hours. It was a remarkable feat, a testament to the bravery and dedication of the American servicemen and their South Vietnamese allies.

But for the millions of Vietnamese civilians left behind, the future was uncertain. Many would face persecution, imprisonment, or worse at the hands of the communist regime. The war had taken a terrible toll on the country and its people, leaving deep scars that would take generations to heal.

As the last American helicopter lifted off from the embassy roof, it marked the end of an era. The United States had invested so much in the war, had sacrificed so many lives and so much treasure, only to see it all come to a bitter and ignominious end.

"It's over," a soldier said, watching the Saigon disappear into the distance. "We did what we could."

But for those who had been saved by Operation Frequent Wind, it was a chance at a new beginning, a opportunity to build a life free from the shadow of war and oppression. And though the road ahead would be long and difficult, they knew that they had been given a precious gift, a chance to start anew in a land of freedom and opportunity.

"We made it," a tearful woman said, hugging her children close as the Navy ship carried them to safety. "We're going to be okay."

And as the evacuation wound down and the last Americans left Vietnam, those words echoed like a prayer, a hope for a better future rising from the ashes of a long and terrible war.

Letter to Reader

Dear Reader:

I hope you enjoyed *The Beast Cometh and the Airmen Series*. It has been my honor to write the full story of the Vietnam War in way readers will both enjoy and, I hope, remember.

There will be more books in the Airmen Series, special subjects that I have wanted to write but had no time and room in the core series. Make sure you subscribe to my newsletter so I can let you know each time I publish a new book in the Airmen Series. Here is the link to sign up and I will even give you a free book:

Newsletter Sign Up

In the meantime, if you haven't read "A Life Stolen," please give it a chance. I think it is some of my best work and is the start of a new series that I will be writing as I continue to write the Airmen Series.

Sharing my work with your friends and reviews are always welcome. Thank you for supporting The Airmen Series.

Regards,

David Lee Corley, Author

DAVID LEE CORLEY
A LIFE STOLEN
A NOVEL
THE CULPER RING SERIES

Author's Biography

Born in 1958, David grew up on a horse ranch in Northern California, breeding and training appaloosas. He has had all his toes broken at least once and survived numerous falls and kicks from ornery colts and fillies. David started writing professionally as a copywriter in his early 20's. At thirty-two, he packed up his family and moved to Malibu, California, to live his dream of writing and directing motion pictures. He has four motion picture screenwriting credits and two directing credits. His movies have been viewed by over fifty million movie-goers worldwide and won a multitude of awards, including the Malibu, Palm Springs, and San Jose Film Festivals. In addition to his twenty-four screenplays, he has written twenty-five novels. He developed his simplistic writing style after rereading his two favorite books, Ernest Hemingway's *The Old Man and the Sea* and Cormac McCarthy's *No Country For Old Men*. An avid student of world culture, David lived as an expat in both Thailand and Mexico. At fifty-six, he sold all his possessions and became a nomad for four years. He circumnavigated the globe three times and visited fifty-six countries. Known for his detailed descriptions, his stories often include actual experiences and characters from his journeys.